WOUNDED

WOUNDED

The Second Book of the Little Goddess Series

Amy Lane

iUniverse, Inc.
New York Lincoln Shanghai

WOUNDED
The Second Book of the Little Goddess Series

Copyright © 2005 by Shannon T. R. McClellan

iUniverse books may be ordered through booksellers or by contacting:

iUniverse
2021 Pine Lake Road, Suite 100
Lincoln, NE 68512
www.iuniverse.com
1-800-Authors (1-800-288-4677)

ISBN-13: 978-0-595-37914-9 (pbk)
ISBN-13: 978-0-595-82288-1 (ebk)
ISBN-10: 0-595-37914-1 (pbk)
ISBN-10: 0-595-82288-6 (ebk)

Printed in the United States of America

For the usual suspects—Mate, Big T, Chicken Boo and Funky Man, because you can never have too many names.

For Wendy although she probably doesn't deserve it, but she did try…

For Daddy & Janis and for Mom (who read the first one twice!) and Aunt Monica who cried!

For everybody who read the first one and loved it enough for me to keep plugging away…(You'll see a lot of their names on Amazon.com—they wrote my reviews!)

And for Ella, my biggest fan, but not in a creepy "Buddy/Syndrome" stalker chic way…

You guys keep baking me praise cookies, and I'll keep drinking the milk of creativity.

Who will staunch
This river of blood,
This river of blood
This river of blood
Who will staunch
This river of blood
That pours from my heart to my soul?

Because if someone won't stop it
This river of blood,
The breach in the dam will just grow.

So who can heal
This tear in my heart
This tear in my heart
This tear in my heart?
Who will heal
This tear in my heart
From whence my life and pain spill?

My bonny bright lover
Dreaming immortal dreams
Can heal me,
If only he will.

Contents

▼

GREEN

Healing

The boy was young and plain, with sandy hair and a smattering of freckles that hadn't disappeared although he was more than twenty-one. But in the sunlight of the bedroom, he was beautiful. With reverence he reached out a hand to the inhumanly lovely sidhe next to him, looking as he did so at the over-wide set eyes the color of new emeralds in shadows, the clean lined, narrow nose, the strong jaw and sensual mouth. After touching Green with his eyes, the boy used his hand to touch him languorously, his hand on Green's elongated stomach, his semi-hard manhood, his flank, smooth as marble, and then back again.

Green thought fondly that Owen didn't really need this anymore—he was seeking Green's comfort more from habit than from need. But that was okay, Green realized fretfully, because his power as a sidhe was in healing, and so it comforted him to be Owen's habit. And he didn't want to look at Cory's empty room one more time.

"Where are you?" The boy asked, and Green was truthful.

"I miss her." He said, and there was no translation needed.

"It's only one weekend, Green." And in spite of Green's immortality, Owen was the one who sounded like the exasperated parent.

"It's more than one weekend." Green said after a moment, turning on his side and starting a slow, lazy, skilled stroke of his own. "She's been gone as long as Adrian has…except she comes home. She comes here, she crawls into our bed and shivers, and shivers, and begs me to make her warm."

"But you do." Owen said, quietly, arching his back, his breathing beginning to quicken. They had lain in the big, light oak-framed bed for a long time, silently. It was a good-bye, Green recognized now. Owen was saying good-bye to this part of them—Owen didn't need him anymore, not like this. "You…do…" The boy hissed, and Green moved down, taking his shaft into his mouth. It was a tight fit, a pleasurable chore, a skill Green had always enjoyed.

"Come." He whispered, his breath tickling the head of Owen's cock, wanting to see Owen's face this last time, before he let his fledgling out into the world, healed, happy, ready to love on his own.

"Say it first." Owen insisted, fisting his hand into Green's hair, pulling it back to expose the pointed ears, the faint green cast to the delicate flesh behind his ears. It was a demand, a surprising one, from a lover who'd been so scarred by sadism, by drugs, by a corruption of the act itself to know how to ask such a thing without causing or receiving pain. He took his own body from Green's control, stroked it in his fist, running his thumb over the glistening end. Green felt a hunger for the boy then, and enjoyed that.

"Say it." Owen said again. "Tell me that you make her warm, that she needs you like you need her…say…it…" He was close. Agonizingly close, and Green almost wept with the wanting of the purple-head in his mouth, and the taste, and with the boy's touching refusal to believe that there was a wound that Green couldn't heal.

"She needs me." He murmured, praying it was true. "She needs me so badly, she doesn't know how to ask…" And Owen pressed the back of Green's head, and Green devoured the boy, his prick, his kindness, his seed, because Owen had asked, and Green could only do his best to make his people happy.

Later that night, after meeting and greeting his people, taking bread with them in the vast, hand-carved downstairs dining hall, and letting his leaders and captains report to himself, Arturo the second most powerful sidhe at his hill and his second in command, and Grace, acting head of the vampires now that Adrian was gone, Green reflected on Cory, and Owen's assumption that Cory would let him heal her.

She was more than wounded, he realized, she was bleeding and numb. He had assumed when she had gone off to college that some distance, some space between herself and the preternatural community that had caused her such joy and such heartbreak would do her good—it would give her time to grieve, and time to come to terms with her new role in the world. Because her life *had* changed. She had gone from being a gas station clerk with hopes of college to the head vampire's lover, and his elfin lover's lover, and to being perhaps the most powerful mortal sorceress Green had ever encountered. And then Adrian, the one who had set the whole thing into motion had gone and gotten himself killed, marking her with a third vampire mark, and leaving her the queen of the Foresthill undead as well.

It was a lot to take in Green had thought at the time, when, after a month, Cory didn't seem to be any less lost than she had been the morning after Adrian's blood had covered them both like summer rain. Maybe she needed to be normal. Maybe she needed to be free. So he had packed her into a brand new BMW and shipped her off to the college of her choice, held to him only with the solemn promise to visit whenever she could.

She came back every weekend, and it was all Green could do to pull her out of bed when she was there. Not in a good, can-we-make-love-all-afternoon way, either, but in a frantic, stay-here-and-be-inside-of-me-so-I-won't-feel-empty kind of way. Green's worry for her sanity was not quite eclipsed by his certainty that the decision to let her leave was terribly, terribly wrong.

Her decision to stay in San Francisco for a party was actually a relief—he longed to see her again, but he also longed for her to feel happy, complete and confident again. That confidence was a part of her, and he missed it. It was a good sign, the desire to meet other people. He almost hoped she'd take a lover that night—he'd asked her if she would want to. He could not afford to be monogamous—too much of his preternatural power lay in being worshipped in bed, and too many of the people who fed that power depended on him for safety—and he had no right to ask the same for her. But Cory had begun to cry when he'd mentioned it, saying that he was never unfaithful to her or Adrian in spirit, which was true, and that she didn't think her heart could bear another lover after Adrian, which, unfortunately, was also true. So he could hope she spent her night sweating, demanding, getting fucked beyond her wildest dreams so that when she came to him it was for companionship as well as for a mate, but mostly he could hope that she had a good time.

At 2:39 a.m. she cried out for his help, and he was one hundred and fifty miles away.

Green was out the door and down the long, mazed hall before the cry in his head had faded. He crashed into Arturo's room to find his second—and Grace, his other second—naked and sweaty, and both facing the door.

"Holy fuck..." Grace choked, separating from Arturo and covering her lanky, broad-hipped form with a blanket. The red-haired vampire and Green had made love before, it was true, but until she died she'd had only one lover, and that had been her husband. She was not quite as casual as Arturo, who sat back on his heels, panting, looking at his large erection in frustration, then glowering at Green. He cleared his throat in the shocked moment of silence, but Green stepped into it first.

"Cory's hurt...worse..." He said, closing his eyes, thinking about her. "Something preternatural..." He opened his eyes and looked frantically at them, not seeing their nakedness or their shock, only seeing his lieutenants, whom he needed. "I'm leaving in ten minutes."

"Take the Suburban." Grace choked out as she tumbled to the floor in bundle of plaid sheets. "I'll come with you and put Phillip and Marcus in charge." Phillip had been a stockbroker when he was alive—he'd love to be in charge. Marcus had been a school teacher—he'd hate it. Between the two of them they'd be both fair enough not to stir up trouble and autocratic enough to keep any of the vampires—already lost and puzzled from the loss of Adrian, their leader—from going on a blood rampage. Adrian had been the only vampire in his kiss old enough and powerful enough to turn a living human into a walking receptacle for the Goddess, and without him the others couldn't channel enough power or sheer stinking will to bring the dead back to life. Of course with Adrian gone and Cory carrying three of his psychic marks on her neck, Cory should have led the vampires. But she'd been Adrian's girl for less then two months before he'd died, and as powerful as their love had been her connection to his world had been tenuous. The vampires loved her. They were dying to follow her. But many of them had been dead for decades, and they could wait, patiently, for their beloved living Queen.

"I'll wake Bracken." Arturo said decisively. "He'll want to go too." He looked at Green calmly. "Don't worry, leader, we'll all be here when you get back. We always are."

"I'm always grateful." Green said before he turned to walk out the door. Without bothering to get dressed, Arturo followed him, moving down the hall and up the stairs to wake Cory's self appointed big brother, her other favorite elf.

Grace may have been 5'10" of mama vampire, but Bracken was 6'8" inches of freaked out elf. As they shouldered their way through the late night hum of the city hospital, both looking grim in sunglasses (at night!) and trench coats, it was no wonder that patients, nurses, and doctors dodged out of their way. Green, emanating a glow of calm and forgetfulness to counter the terror the other two were instilling, trailed after like the reigning monarch he was. The admitting nurse would have protested the invasion, but Grace removed her glasses and rolled the little girl's mind. In less than two minutes they were through the waiting room and in the elevator, headed for the trauma ward. Oddly enough, no one wanted to board the elevator behind them.

They continued to sweep through the scored taupe corridors, Grace following the directions unerringly as she saw them through the nurse's memories; anybody who thought to stop them simply forgot that they were there. Green would have told Bracken to tamp down the glamour, if he hadn't been responsible for at least half of it himself. And a left, and a right, and around a cart of linens and past a darkened room shadowed with sobbing, and another right into another room, and abruptly there she was.

She looked small, Green thought. All people looked small on hospital beds—they were wide and white, and rumpled because the sheets were thick and had no elastic to keep them in place. But Cory was 5'2" on a good day—and this wasn't a good day. She'd lost more weight, too. She had been plump once—that night Green had first seen her, hosing off her parking lot to cover for the death of one of his people, she'd been plump, and substantial. Experience, stress, had honed her, and by the time of Adrian's death she was still substantial, but leaner, more muscular—powerful. Now she was tiny—delicate. The bones of her face stood out, and her chin pointed, where it hadn't pointed before. Her nose was not small, but now it looked knife edged, and her cheekbones—peasant low, but charmingly placed, made her face look stretched, pinched, unhappy even when lax with drugs. Green closed his eyes against her there in the hospital bed, trying to summon an image of Cory, vital, vibrant, strong, and sexual to fight the tearing sensation in his chest. With his eyes closed, things were worse.

Brack saw it too, and made a murmuring sound in his throat, and Green could not stand in the doorway anymore. He *moved,* so quickly the curtain around the vacant bed in the front of the room blew back, spewing little metal clips that hit the floor long after Green had taken her in his arms.

Grief poured from him. Grief, and love, and his own particular magic of sex and healing and need, that stirred a spark on her skin, moved the blood quicker in her veins, and had her back arching and her thighs clenching, even under the murkiness of morphine. Within the circle of his arms she convulsed, gently, murmured, rawly, and went limp against him. When her breathing recovered it wasn't the shallow breathing of the drugged sleeper, but the deeper, more animated breathing of the waking lover. Her bruises faded, the pinched look between her eyes eased, and her body, which had been taped and bandaged, relaxed against the sheets. Some wounds are easier to heal than others.

She took one look at Green, her moss green eyes moving over his face, and her own face broke out into a smile, weak, but full of sunshine.

"I knew you'd come." She murmured, and Bracken and Grace, because they were awake and had sat in the Suburban with him during the fraught trip to the city, could smell remorse that rolled through the room like sweet perfume.

CORY

Wounded

"I should have been here." Green murmured to me, some time after the three of them burst into my hospital room like angels of vengeance. Grace was holed up in the windowless shower of the hospital room, and Bracken was sprawled on the vacant bed in the next cubicle. Green had just spent a good hour pulling tape and gauze off of my body, now that I didn't need it anymore. The sun had barely risen, and it beamed a weak, fuzzy grey light through the bay area fog.

"Bullshit." I murmured against his chest. I breathed in again, lightly, smelling him. He smelled like earth, and mustard flowers, and long dry grasses and oak trees and lime trees and roses. He smelled like home, and I could taste my yearning for home like I could taste the blood that had exploded in my mouth when that fucker Nicky had hit me. My first lover was a vampire—the taste of blood was sweet, life-affirming, and noxious all at the same time. My homesickness was a swelling, aching balloon of misery in the pit of my stomach.

"You're right." Green agreed, burrowing underneath my hospital gown to touch me more. Green healed with his touch, and I craved it now, maybe more than ever, but I wondered if there was enough touch in him to cure us both. "You're right." He said again, after passing his hands along my stomach and my breasts and my thighs. "I shouldn't have been here—you should have been home, with me, where you belong."

I couldn't argue with him. Oh Goddess, I wanted to—I wanted to tell him that I was strong enough, and smart enough and that I should be able to exist in the big bad city on my own without a baby sitter, but I couldn't. All I could do was burrow my face against his flesh, and let the salt tears make a soggy, sting-y mess of his shirt.

"Yes." I whimpered against him, shaking with the effort not to sob. "Take me home…please, Green…take me home…"

"Oh yes…" He murmured into my hair, and I was suddenly happy, as I had not been happy since that one giddy night when Adrian had taken me on a ride on the back of his motorcycle into the Placer County night, or that one, heart stopping night when…when…when what?…

"Green…" Don't panic. Cory, don't panic. I got socked in the face and thrown into a concrete pole and anything was possible…

"What, luv?"

How could I ask this? "Green, is there something missing in me?"

"Explain." He said flatly, as though he were not entirely surprised.

"There's something I can't…think…its like, you know when you're really tired, and driving somewhere, and suddenly you're home, but you can't remember because you drive there all the time, and two weeks or a month later you realize they put a stop light in when you weren't paying attention and you couldn't tell for sure if you'd been braking, looking both ways, and just blowing off the light because that time was just gone…" I was babbling. I was *panicking*…there was a hole in my mind somewhere…a big, important hole and I couldn't even place where the hole was because it had been stolen so seamlessly from the fabric of my mind….

"Hush…" Green murmured, and to my horror, as I reached for him and that well of sweetness that he'd given to me so often with his touch, he cringed, just for a second, from my touch…oh, Goddess, had I sucked so terribly at him, these last months, in my mortal grief that he would need to brace himself against me? My own body started to thrum, in stress and panic and pain, and he murmured "hush," this time with authority, and cocooned me again with his flesh, blanketing me with his skin, and his spirit, and I forgot my resolve not to suck him like some emotional vampire and gave a baby's whimper of contentment. Green *could* heal me. Together, we *would* be well…

"We saw it." Brack murmured from the next bed, and I flushed uncomfortably, heating Green's skin and my own with embarrassment. I had thought he was asleep—I didn't even mind that he had heard us moving our flesh together—I'd had a concussion, bruised ribs, a bruised kidney, and a split lip, but even that crippled coupling had relieved me of those major pains. My first sight of Bracken had been buck naked, and, yes indeed, he had a fabulous ass, among other things.

But he was an elf—he'd been around for Goddess knows how many years—God didn't pay attention. So it was not the sex that was embarrassing, but he had seen me *cry,* whimper like an infant, when I had made such pains to be brave for Bracken, and all his kin. I had told them that I could live with what I had done to protect them…to protect *us,* all of us, and I couldn't let that knowledge destroy me now.

Green nodded, his chin rubbing in my hair. It was a mess, a curly red-brown disaster that went below my ears. Green's fairy sprites had trimmed it in June—I needed their services again. "I had no idea what it could be." Green murmured, then he tilted my chin up to him, and gazed kindly into my eyes. It was that kindness that sent me spiraling into his eyes from the beginning, putting me into the odd and erotic position of being truly in love with two men, who also loved each other. The kindness was no less powerful now, when I was huddled in his arms on a hospital bed, than it had been in June when I was comfortable and sated by Adrian. Adrian's eyes had not been kind—but they had been beautiful, silver spangled blue—they had pulled me in from the very beginning, but I hadn't really fallen into them until…when? I was getting lost, I realized dreamily. Lost in Green's eyes, drawn back to that brief moment in time when the three of us snuck off at odd hours in the night like horny teenagers. Well, I *was* barely twenty, but Green was only a hundred years or so short of the memory of Christ, and Adrian had come over the oceans during the California Gold Rush.

It should have made them patient, slow, and even bored with love, but we had been urgent, and giddy, and drunk on what our bodies and magic could do. And what could we not do? A garden flashed before my eyes, with oak and lime trees and thorn-less rose bushes contorted into lovely, sinuous, sensual bodies, bodies I had been in midst of…bodies I had been…but I couldn't remember when…had it been me? Had I been the model for those trees? I could see Green in the lime trees, could remember the stroke of his body, on other occasions, but I couldn't remember *that* moment…And Adrian—I could remember Adrian in my bed—I could remember him in my body…but not this moment in time…not when the three of us had done that…

I whimpered a little, thrashed against the pull of those eyes, and saw Green nod a little, as though I had done well.

"Well enough, luv," He murmured, but there was something choked in his voice, as though he were holding back tears, "Are you well enough to tell us how you got here, yes?"

Now *that* should have been easy enough. "Kestrel." I said, thinking harder than I should have. "His name was Nicky Kestrel—he was in my…" think,

think, think…"European History 42—the Victorians…no…no…after that class…" Green's eyebrows rose. He hadn't known I'd been taking the Victorian History. That was Adrian's time. The thought of Adrian made Kestrel stronger in my head—the contrast between the two of them had been so great…especially since Nicky had been trying unsuccessfully all semester to fill Adrian's shoes. But Nicky was small, 5' 6" or so, where Adrian had been over 6' and Nicky was pretty. Not that Adrian wasn't beautiful—Adrian had all those planes and angles in his face that made every woman for a five-mile radius sniff the wind if he so much as blinked in their direction. Nicky, on the other hand was an average, everyday, sort of delicate pretty, and…

"He wasn't human." I said, "But he didn't know I knew that. He'd been hitting on me, all semester, and I was curious enough about…you know if he was one of us…and I let him take me to…" Where? "To eat?" We'd eaten…why *was* this so hard to remember? "But there were other people there…" A thought, "It felt like Green's hall." I said abruptly still looking into Green's eyes. "People were there, and they were happy and laughing and they all knew each other…and there was someone…" Who? I'd met him. He'd bent and kissed my hand, and sent a look to Nicky but his face was all in shadows, and only his eyes glinted tawny and orange in the dim light of the room…"He was dark—not like a black man, but like…like black wood, or feathers, or a lacquered car was…" And he was like Green, for all Green was tall and pale and gold and lovely…"Leader…and…he was a leader." But…But Nicky hadn't wanted to follow him, because he had looked sad when we left. Sorrow. Regret. I knew those two emotions so well I could practically smell them on another person, like a familiar cologne. "I know we were down in the parking lot, and he looked at me like he was sad…like he was sorry for something…and he tried to kiss me…"

Green smiled then, happy, I guess, because he'd been asking me to take a lover if I could. I couldn't. It would be like trying to bandage a severed limb with sandpaper—but Nicky had been charming, and although I still didn't know what he was, I had thought there would be nothing wrong with letting him steal one little kiss. I could see, and I let Green see, Nicky's delicate features, the slight hook to the nose, the pointed chin, little, childlike ears, and the spiky, downy, rust colored hair that jutted out from a cowlick at the back, swirling a little to the side. But there was a pain to his features, as he lowered his head, a regret that he let me see. Then I felt it. I'd had my eyes opened, a pleasant smile on my face, a willingness to kiss and walk away, but something pulled at me—in a bad way. As though all my memories of all my kisses ever, were pulled to the surface of my lips, rushing to my face like blood. I fought against it, hard, and Nicky had looked at me then, surprised, angry, as I put my hands on his shoulders and fought to keep my memories to myself. He had used force then, and I knew that until Green healed me, I had still had his fingerprints on my shoulders, where he had bent his fingers like talons and pulled me against him, his body hard as a weapon when he mashed his mouth against mine. And that was when I'd felt my mad coming on.

I'd opened my mouth then, and let the lethal sunshine that sex, anger, or any strong emotion could conjure up inside of me spin him back into the car behind him. He'd broken the window and dented the door, then rushed at me again. I opened my mouth again, to scream, to punish, and sunshine had poured out. But it was a clumsy weapon—great for devastating small armies or terra-forming, lousy for taking out one stupid asshole who had betrayed my trust and was trying to mindfuck me. I almost stamped my foot when he ducked as my power came pouring out—and the car behind him melted instantly into goo on the blackened, scorched concrete. Nicky took advantage of my bad aim, and stepped to the side before he backhanded me physically, with a little bit of supernatural strength in the blow. I'd gone flying back into the wall of the garage and bounced forward into the concrete pole a little to my right and all was darkness. When I came to, I'd been on a gurney, having my clothes cut off and my ribs taped. My next memory after that had been of Green.

And there he was now, gazing into my eyes. I blinked, and then he blinked, and I saw silent tears slipping down his face. How had I missed them? I was drained, sweating, feeling as though I'd been wrung out like a wet towel, and snapped against a wall. "Wha…" I tried to speak, but he shhd me again, and I felt his hands on me, stripping me out of my sopping hospital gown and sponging me off from a basin that smelled of herbs and clean water. Bracken must have brought it, I thought fuzzily, but not for long because suddenly I was in clean sweats—too big and a T-shirt, with Brack's favorite Sacramento King's sweatshirt over the whole thing.

"Where we goin'?" I asked groggily. How long had I been lost in Green's eyes, I wondered? How long had I been back?

"To the apartment." Green said briefly. "I called Renny—she's ready for us."

"What about Grace?" Hadn't she been asleep in the shower? I remembered that—I'd made Bracken put an aura—and a sign—in front of it to make people go find the one down the hall.

"I'm right here, sweetie." She said beside me, and I looked out the window. Wherever I had been, pulled into Green's eyes and into my own green pool of memories, it had taken me the day. It was full winter dark in the pink lit fog out-side.

"We can't leave." I said, trying hard to be here, in the moment. "What will the cops say?"

Green chuckled weakly, and looked at Grace. "I'm done in, luvie—would you do the honors here?"

Grace took my face in her hands, and kissed my forehead, and suddenly I was six again, and my mother was giving me medicine for a fever, and I was safe and warm even though her hands were as cold as November, and I was asleep.

GREEN

Gathering

Nothing in San Francisco was very far away from anything else, and it didn't take them long to get from the hospital on Mission to the apartment building on Bay and Larkin. It was a tannish, nondescript building from the outside, and not in the best of neighborhoods, because the sidhe leader in the area was very careful not to let other elves take up residence near good earth—elves got strength from walking the earth, and Mist wanted his enemies weak with the city. So the Twin Peaks were out, and the lovely homes with yards on Portola were out, and anything near Golden Gate park was strictly forbidden. But Mist hadn't counted on Green's canniness—and he thought it was beneath him to journey to the poorer parts of the city—so he was unaware of the odd little space of grass and eucalyptus trees across from Green's building, and since none of the sidhe in his sphere knew about it, nobody else had enlightened him, and Green kept it that way.

And the outside may have been nondescript stucco, but the interior was pure Green. Light paneled wood on the floors and walls, ceilings as high as the building's design would allow, and a large kitchen/dining room that opened into a vast living room/conversation pit made the space open and inviting. Green had bought four apartments and converted them to one large space, so the bedrooms, connected by a narrow hallway, were vast, and each one had it's own bathroom and small sitting room space. There was a bedroom sized darkling in the center of the space, hidden by a broom-closet at the end of a deceptively small hall bathroom for vampire guests, and Adrian had stayed their often, when Green had come to visit.

The living room/conversation pit had a decorative wooden railing and a brief set of stairs between the raised kitchen and the lowered living room. It was spacious and cozy at the same time, and he'd always found the San Francisco apartment restful, as far as living on the road went. But Renny and Cory had spruced up the place, Green thought as he sat at the kitchen table with his head in his hands. He had it done in blonde wood and white brocade, with dark green accents, but the girls had done better. There was a rainbow of throw pillows over the couch, and pretty drapes in front of the four bedrooms, and a big cardboard trailer poster of Shrek II as a backdrop of the living room. That made Green smile, and the effort made his face ache. Christ and Finn, what a day.

Grace slid a plate of food in front of him, then put her arms around his shoulders and pressed her face against his neck. He felt his shoulders start to tremble, and his whole body relaxed—ah, comfort. Bracken came around the table and wrapped his arms around them both, and Renny twined around their legs in cat from and they stayed there for a moment, giving strength, receiving it from the simple act of touch. Then, almost in tandem, they straightened, and Grace finished putting food in front of the others, seating herself at the only empty place at the table. Since her conversion to vampire, Grace had no use for any food but blood; however, she'd been a housewife for fifteen years before her cancer had awakened the yearning in her to become part of the night. Feeding her family was a habit that never died.

As though to prove it, she gave a tsk-tut sound and glared at Renny, who morphed seamlessly from 100 lb. fuzzy, tawny-brown cat to 100 lb. naked young woman with fuzzy, tawny-brown hair. Bracken reached behind him and found the extra T-shirt hanging from his chair and passed it to her without comment, and she wiggled into it and sat down. They ate in silence then, and again as Grace refilled their plates, and finally they pushed the plates back and sighed as a whole. Brack broke the spell, by looking at Green and saying "Well?"

Green shook his head. "A shapeshifter of some sort—but he wasn't acting on his own—he was under orders…"

Brack frowned. "That's all? A shapeshifter? She should have been able to handle that easily—hell, she should have kicked his ass…"

"That's not all he was…or all he was given to use…" Green frowned back. "He mindfucked her—in a big way…and it would have been worse, too, but I don't think he knew what she was…"

"Mindfucked?" Grace interrupted. Part of her power as a vampire was the ability to roll someone's mind—put a person to sleep, hypnotize someone, insert a false memory—these were a vampire's stock and trade.

"Mind raped—took from her mind something she didn't want to give...and..." He looked away. He could feel her wound, now, even when she was asleep. It was huge, and gaping, and the more she came to, the more she would miss what had been stolen.

"What did he take?" Bracken asked sharply, suddenly more concerned with what Green wasn't saying than with what he was.

"Her firsts." Green said simply. "Her first kisses, her first sex." His throat tried to close with anger and grief.

"Like...like stealing a computer file?" Brack asked eyes wide and horrified, and Green nodded.

"She didn't have that many firsts to steal." Grace said, in shock and pity.

"And all her firsts were..." Bracken trailed off, and the full import hit everyone at the table.

"Adrian." Green finished for Bracken. He smiled bitterly.

"And you." Grace told him gently.

"And me." He agreed, touched. "But her first kiss, her first sex—Adrian."

"Wait a minute." Bracken looked at him, aghast. "She doesn't remember creating the Goddess Grove? The crown of the faerie hill—all of that...gone?"

"And her first kiss, Bracken—that's not small!" Grace's voice was like a smack on the back of the head, but Green held up a hand.

"No, Grace—he's right. The loss of any memory of Adrian is devastating of course—partly because there were so few of them for her to have. But the fact that she can't remember summoning the power of the Goddess grove—that's dangerous. That's dangerous to all of us. If she doesn't remember that she can do that, she might do it again, and there might not be a faerie hill there to terra-form when she does."

Grace nodded, agreeing. "I hear you." She said, "But...Jesus, Green, does she know? Has she realized yet what she's lost?"

Green shook his head. "No—that's partly what took so long today—she fought, him, and fought well." He smiled grimly, then, at her memory of hurling the 'little fucker' as she thought of him, into a parked car.

"But?" Grace asked.

"But her mind was rolled by a professional. He didn't want to do it—I think this Nicky Kestrel was under orders from his leader, but he was smooth. Took her to dinner, introduced her to the family, then Papa Bird decided she wasn't good enough for the family, and little Nicky did what he was told. Looked at her sadly, gave her time to accept the kiss, and then, as every memory of first kisses and first sex came rolling back to her, he stole them from her lips as she gave them breath. I think, if she hadn't fought back, he would have stolen it all—every moment with Adrian, every moment with me, gone."

They looked at each other then, cold and angry, when suddenly Renny burst into sobs, and Green almost smacked himself on the head with his hand—he should have sent her for ice cream, or Chinese food, or to make a phone call or catch a mouse or something, anything, but to hear the details of the one thing worse than losing your lover to a bloody, violent fate. Renny, who had been so lost without her Mitch that Green had sent her here to the city with Cory in hopes that the two women who had suffered such loss would heal each other. Green opened his arms and she rushed into them, choking on sobs and ranting with the rusty voice of someone who rarely spoke. They all listened, in the silent kitchen, to make sense of what she was saying, and all they could make out, in the end, was "I'll kill him, I'll kill him, I'll fucking kill him...."

Green clutched her to him and made eye contact with Grace and Brack, who looked grimly back. "You'll have to get in line, luvie." He said at last, and was relieved to hear her sobs shudder to a still last hiccup as she calmed down. She looked at Green then, through reddened eyes, and smiled a feral little smile that made Green realize how far away the honors student who had fallen for Mitchell Hammond had become.

"We knew him." Renny said into the silence. "We had classes together, saw movies, he came visiting—he smelled like a shapechanger, and I thought...you know...he was one of us...It never occurred to me...I never even suspected..." For a moment they thought she was going to start crying again, but she didn't. She just shook her head and leaned weakly against Green's chest, like an infant.

"It's not your fault." Green said, angry. "It's not—it should have been safe." He rubbed his faced with his hand. "Goddess—I made treaties, I forged alliances, I gave up a fucking gas station in Vacaville to keep you two safe here while you went to school. I met with high elves, shape changers, and a freaking scary vampire that made Crispin look sane and Adrian look like a kitten, and not a one of them mentioned the Papa Bird I saw in Cory's head."

"Then who is he?" Bracken asked after a moment.

"Someone new." Green decided. "Someone who needs to be kept secret. Nicky had two goals when he rolled Cory—the first was to hide Papa Bird from view, but Nicky didn't get that done—he was too busy going for his second goal, which was, I suspect, to feed on her memories. Some fey species can feed on emotion like that, yes? It's usually the bad shit, but not this one—he took the choicest stuff, the best things she had to offer. The stuff she'd miss the most."

"Not the best stuff, Green." Cory said from the doorway, and they all startled guiltily to see her there as they talked about her. Even Renny startled, then slithered in a silent rush of skin to fur, leaving her T-shirt puddled behind her as she jumped into Grace's arms instead. Cory moved into the room on unsteady legs, Bracken's XX-tra large King's sweatshirt brushing her knees as she took Renny's place in Green's lap. "Not all the best stuff. Not you. If he'd taken you, then I'd be lost."

"Pretty words, luvie." Green murmured, gathering her to him, holding her with strong hands and a quiet reserve to his muscles. Don't drop her, don't break her kind of holding, and Cory moved restlessly against him, demanding more. Grace, Brack and Renny were all suddenly somewhere else, leaving them in a quiet kitchen with a plate of food in front of Cory.

"He didn't take our first." She whispered against his chest. "All Adrian, because I was grieving for Adrian, and it was all on top and ready to be taken, but not you. I kept you close inside, and I remember…I remember our first kiss, the time you watched me and Adrian together, our first time, just you and me…" She started to weep then, helpless, tired weeping, and he forgot that she was made out of glass and held her to him like she would shatter if he didn't. "Adrian's destined to be stolen from me Green." She sobbed. "I was so afraid he'd fade from my memory even before this, and now…just big holes where he should be. I'll die before they take you too…"

Green's blood ran cold because he knew that she was speaking the truth. He'd been so happy this summer, when he realized that she was not entirely mortal, that the power that built up in her with her mortal emotions of anger and lust altered the world in amazing ways. But humans could withstand heartbreak. Humans could have their spirit broken again and again, and still live, and still love, and still find small amounts of happiness. Cory, it seemed, had lost just enough of her humanity to make her fragile to the disease of heartbreak that could kill the fey and sidhe quicker and less cleanly than any knife or bullet. She was straddling some sort of metaphysical fence, he discovered, and whichever side she was pulled down into, he wasn't sure she could survive the fall.

But he didn't have experience as a mortal, he thought, somewhat panicked. How did you heal a mortal of an immortal wound? All he knew was his calling—touch, blood, song: sex. It was all he could do—it was how he bound his people to him, and how they returned the energy. It was all he could offer her now. And still he was afraid, because although her cuts and bruises and even her concussion had been cured by their brief time in the hospital, she looked so thin now, he was almost afraid that her mortality would crack and shatter, and the small immortal part of her would be too small to save her. But, as she so often did, she saved him instead. Her body stopped heaving, and she gave one last snuffle on his shirt, and then gave another, more predatory sniff.

"Did Grace cook?" She asked, sniffing some more. Then she gave a shiver that was almost sexual in its ecstasy. "Grace *cooked!*" She sat up in Green's lap then, and twisted towards the table. "What did Grace cook? Hm…Roast Beef, garlic mashed potatoes and broccoli with cheese." She turned a smile to Green that almost blinded him with its brilliance. "Can I, Green?" And suddenly the world, and her predicament, seemed so much less dire.

"All yours, Cory luv." He told her, even as she fell upon the plate in front of her with a hunger he hadn't been sure she still possessed. He wrapped his arms around her middle and watched her eat, teasing her as he did so about the diets of starving students. She answered in kind, mostly with her mouth full, and by the time she was done with the first plate, the others had ventured back in the kitchen in time for Grace to dish her up a second plate. Renny had returned to human form and took another plate from Grace, who, in addition to the roast beef (which she had made especially for the girls since elves are vegetarian by nature) she also dished out a ration of shit for their poor eating habits.

"Do you have any idea how hard it is to explain wearing sunglasses at night in a grocery store? And that Safeway was microscopic—I've seen Walgreen's with more food. You had nothing but Top Ramen and Ritz crackers—there's no rule that says you have to live on that, you know?"

"Yeah," Cory said, "But who has the time?"

"You're not working full time now." Bracken told her, getting a couple of sodas from the fridge and giving one to her and one to Renny. "What are you doing with your time?"

"Well, for one thing, I'm taking 24 units." Cory said through a mouthful of food, and Green almost dropped her in surprise.

"What on earth possessed you to do that?" He asked, baffled and exasperated. "I thought that fifteen was a full load."

Cory shifted, uncomfortably, but not unpleasantly, then turned and gave Green a weak grin. He grinned back, and felt his heart turn over. She had clung to his first she said, and something he had not known was broken in his heart fixed itself. He had never minded being second to Adrian, but Goddess, it was good to know he had a place other than as solace and healer.

"I wanted to keep busy." She said evasively, and Green gave his knee a little jiggle, so she shrugged and talked into her roast beef. "And I wanted to justify your faith and your money." She said, making eye contact with nobody. Green jiggled her again and dug his chin into her shoulder and she humphed and chewed through another piece of succulent roast beef, knowing the idea nauseated Green as much as tasting garlic on her breath had nauseated Adrian, then sighed and mumbled, "And I knew that the quicker I got my degree the quicker I could come back and live with you."

"I *knew* it." Green said savagely. "I *knew* it was that…" He fought with some choice swearwords, and settled for, "I was *dying* for you to come home, you lackwit—how come you didn't ask?"

"Green…" she whined, putting her fork down and wiping her mouth, "Do we have to talk about this now?"

"Please?" Renny echoed. "But first, what did you just call her?"

"Fuckwit." Bracken supplied.

"No," Cory corrected, with a ghost of a smile. "He calls *me* lackwit. Adrian was fuckwit."

And before the table could make an awkward pause out of that, Green scooped her up in his arms and said "We're all fuckwits, keeping you up like this when you still need to heal."

"I needed to eat." She murmured lazily, and they could look at her and see that she was falling asleep in his arms.

"Well, can I pack while you sleep?" Renny asked from the table, looking hopeful. She had gone to keep Cory company, and to escape her own pain from losing Mitch, but she missed wide fields to hunt, and the solace of the place where she grew up.

"NO!" Green and Cory said in tandem, and both sighed in sympathy when Renny's face fell.

They all looked at Cory for explanation. "I want it back." She said simply. "If he could take it, he can give it back." Her pointed chin hardened, and her eyes became flat. "I'll kill him before I let him keep any more of Adrian." Her voice lowered. "There wasn't enough of him as it was."

Green kissed her hair, tenderly, and nodded. "We need to find who did this." He agreed. "We want to find Nicky Kestrel, figure out who he was working for, and teach him that my people will be *safe.*"

CORY

Little tiny pieces

Green brought me back to my bed and tucked me in, then shucked to his skin and slid in next to me. This was the part I'd been waiting for since I'd awakened and heard them, hushed and awful, in the kitchen. They'd needed me, I thought. They needed me to be better, strong and okay. And so I had been. But now I was exhausted, and saddened to the bottom of my toes.

"When do I get to see it, Cory luv." Green murmured in my ear as his arms, strong and solid, wrapped around me from behind.

"See what?" But I knew. I'd known I couldn't fool Green.

"See past that bullshit you were trying to feed us tonight?" he murmured, and I would have fallen asleep but he touched me in a nurturing way, and I felt myself feeding off of him in a way I hadn't been able to do when I'd gone back home for those frantic weekend visits. It's like, now, I could *allow* myself to feed from him, I could *allow* myself to seek comfort from him, because I'd been obviously wounded. When I woke up I'd find myself wondering how long I'd been selling myself the idea that I had to suck it up and heal without Green's help. And then I'd find myself wondering if I hadn't been draining Green dry because I hadn't let him help me at all. But right now I would just let him keep touching me like there was nothing in the touch but wonder, and pleasure.

"You've seen it, Green." I murmured, cuddling into his hand around my stomach as he pulled me back against the hard line of his body. "It's sad, and wounded, and needy and right now it's screaming in anger and pain."

His hand tightened around my hip. "Then why aren't you screaming?" He asked. "Why aren't you yelling or stamping your foot or swearing or vowing to hunt down Nicky and threatening death?"

"I can always kill Nicky." I said, a breath away from sleep, "But I can't always be touched by you."

I woke slowly, disoriented, because it was still dark outside and I couldn't figure out whether it was Sunday morning or Sunday night. I had been assaulted on the last day of November, I thought muzzily, so, what day was this?

"I can hear the gears turning." Green said softly from behind me, "But I can't see where you're headed." Goddess, he was there, I thought. I had awakened at various times during my sleep to reach for him, and every time I touched his smoothly skinned body a little part of me thawed and warmed.

"Small gears." I mumbled. "I can't even figure out what time it is."

He folded me into him again. "Sunday morning." He said, "Sleep."

I turned, and spread my hands over his chest. He had muscles everywhere, I thought happily. Smooth, peach colored skin, little body hair, and lots and lots of lean, long boned muscles. If I had to share my lover, I was lucky that he was more than man enough to share. "Sunday morning." I returned, licking a hard nipple, nursing from him until his body trembled. "Make love."

"No." He told me firmly, if breathlessly. "Make love Sunday night, sleep Sunday morning; plan Sunday afternoon."

"No." I returned, moving down his stomach and breathing on his lovely male sex organ before licking the head, "Make love Sunday morning, sleep Sunday day, make plans Sunday night." I punctuated each plan with a lick, or a nip, or a deep throated suck to him before I spoke. All these months of trying so hard not to take what Green had to offer, and bleeding him dry, suddenly I wanted to give him comfort and pleasure more than anything in the world.

"Good plan…" He breathed as I took him deep into my mouth again. Before I could even clench his buttocks and bring him to me, he had rolled over and moved me up his body, sheathing himself inside me and making me moan. "I'll try to remember it when I'm fucking you blind."

Later—much later—he asked me why on Heaven's earth and under the Goddess's sky, I couldn't have accepted his healing in the long and dreadful months between July and December.

"I didn't want to hurt you." I mumbled against his chest. Elves have longer torsos, as a rule, and longer legs than humans. It makes their tummies nice and concave, and their fifteen ribs very well muscled. It was a very good chest for cuddling into and asking for protection.

"You didn't want to what?" He asked, incredulous. And very hurt. Goddess did I feel stupid.

"Everything inside me was weeping, Green." Reaching up I caressed the sensitive curve of his pointed ear. I don't know what it did for him, but I never got tired of playing with that inhuman line of his body. "Everything. I didn't think there was a force in the world that could swallow that much grief. But then…yesterday, I reached for you and you…" I choked here, because it still hurt, "You *cringed*…like I'd been bleeding you dry."

"Touching you hurt me." He said, unhappy at the admission. "I'm a healing elf, Cory—you wouldn't let me do my job…"

"I know…" I said, and couldn't take his own misery any longer, "Shhh…sh…I know…I hurt you, and you couldn't heal me because I hurt you and then I saw that you were hurting so I pulled back more…and I never gave you a chance to grieve for him because you were…"

"Grieving for you." He finished simply.

"I know." I felt so awful. I had been selfish, trying to keep this big aching pain to myself, and not letting Green help. He loved me. I knew he loved me. I was so stupid sometimes. "I wanted to comfort you this morning." I tried to explain. "I wanted to please you. And in pleasing you…"

"You let me in to heal you." He finished, laughing wryly, but looking tired, from my angle on his chest. He turned his face into the hand at his ear, and I stroked his cheek instead. So tired. When would we be able to grieve for the third lover in our bed without grieving for each other? "You know, Cory, luv, mortal's live far too short a time to complicate their lives with that much bullshit." He murmured, but he was falling asleep when he said it, and so was I so I couldn't have argued if I'd tried.

We really did sleep a lot of Sunday day. Between that and making love and talking quietly, we weren't ready to emerge from my bedroom until around two o'clock in the afternoon, and by then we were starving. Renny and Bracken had anticipated us, though, and there were two extra large pizzas from Cirro's one with full meat, and one with veggies only. We were sitting in white-painted hardwood kitchen, stuffing our faces, when the bell rang. Green was buck naked, Bracken was wearing a pair of my old sweats—which fit him like a second skin—and Renny was wearing cat fur. I was wearing a pair of Sponge Bob pajama pants and Bracken's King's T-shirt. I didn't have a bra on, but that was okay, I guess, because I'd lost quite a bit of weight and my boobs had just up and disappeared. I mean, in July I'd had cleavage—handfuls of cleavage, and both Green and Adrian had assured me that handfuls of cleavage were a good thing. But when I emerged from the bedroom, Bracken informed me that my chest looked like cherries tacked to a plywood wall and that if I didn't eat something even they'd fall off. I'd looked accusingly at Green, and he'd shrugged and said that at least they were ripe cherries. At the time it meant I could smack him over the head with a pillow, but now, a quarter of the way through a very good pizza, it meant that I was the only one presentable enough to answer the door.

Dark hair, hawk-like nose, slightly crossed blue eyes—damn! Maxwell Johnson was the last person I'd expected to see, and from the look of surprise on his face, the feeling was mutual.

"You're okay!" And he sounded like it was a good thing.

"And you're in San Francisco!" I shot backed, a little bowled over. But deep down I was touched. Yes he'd dismissed me as white trash, and maybe yes, he'd judged me as a whore, and then he'd been at a loss as to what I was, but he knew he wanted me to himself like a big Neanderthal baby wanted a club made of candy. But he seemed genuinely happy to see me up and about.

"But Arturo said you'd been..."

I nodded, and gestured him in. "I was." I said, and turned back the table and the food.

Green was still naked when we turned to the dining room table, although I knew he could have done that blurry thing he does and been dressed if he wanted to. But it was Officer Max, and there was that male thing in Green that said "Mine *is* bigger than yours, see?"

"Nice place." Max said grudgingly, and I warmed to his presence. "Now what the hell happened to you? Arturo sent me to the hospital, and then, when I got there, they looked at me blankly, so he gave me directions here."

I sighed, and padded back to the kitchen. "Pizza?" I offered him with my mouth full, and to my surprise he accepted. He sat down at the table and sent Green an unfriendly, then uncomfortable look over his pizza, but he was appropriately grateful for the food. I moved to sit on Green's lap, and what would have otherwise been a very comfortable and welcome intimacy suddenly became embarrassing. What can I say? A year ago, I'd been working in a gas station, determined to avoid men like a supermodel avoids fried cheese, and now, even through the awfulness of Adrian's death, I needed Green's skin against mine like I needed my next breath. But Max was here, and he was being nice to me, and I didn't want to offend him by being that thing he disapproved of so badly when he'd apparently just driven through the rain to see if I was okay. The look I sent Green was both apologetic and pleading, and he stood fluidly then and kissed me on the forehead. Our bodies were close—we were lovers, how could we stand together and not be close?—but he kept enough distance to not do more than suggest what we had spent our morning doing.

"I'll go shower, Cory luv. I'll be back in a few, and you can catch Max-the-cop up on current events."

I watched him pad down the hall, his bottom long and lean and muscular, and his hips narrow. His shoulders swayed in time to some music that had been forgotten before my ancestors came to America, and his long, straight yellow hair swayed in counterpoint and I couldn't believe the Goddess had given him to me. Max made a disgusted snarky noise next to me and my attention was drawn back to my all too mortal companion.

"I was attacked." I said abruptly, plopping down on Green's empty seat and savoring his warmth on the chair cushion. I was blunt partly to keep Max from saying anything rude about Green being naked in the kitchen, and partly because he was starting to look mad about driving down to the city and I couldn't blame him.

"By what, pigeon shit?" He asked sourly.

I met his eyes sympathetically. "The birds nailed the Mustang, didn't they?" There wasn't a car for miles that hadn't been practically smothered in pigeon shit. It was weird, actually. "Yeah—they've been really bad this year. Renny's been a walking target."

His face softened a little, and he grinned back, and suddenly we were both reminded of the big "if only." If only Max hadn't judged me from the very beginning, then Adrian might not have been a shoo-in. Except my life would have been very colorless, if I had never allowed myself to love Adrian, and hence, had never met Green.

"But it wasn't a pigeon." I said into that softened silence. "The thing that attacked me, it wasn't a pigeon. It was a…well he wasn't human…" Max blinked in surprise, so I continued on into the silence. "I had a concussion, some bruised ribs, and a bruised kidney." I could barely remember the doctor telling me this as I lay there, wanting Green so badly it was all I could do not to whimper his name. The doctor had asked if there was anyone he could call, and I had murmured "He's coming" under my breath until the drugs kicked in. Yup—them's good times.

Max was a little stunned. "You look fine." He said in defense.

I nodded. "Green." I said simply. Green had healed me before—I had a scar on my leg and one on my shoulder from wounds that should have ended my life but didn't. Max had seen them both—he should know this.

"He healed all that with a little…fucking?"

I shivered. When Green said that word it had all sorts of good things attached to it. Max only carried contempt. Suddenly Bracken was up by my side, touching my shoulder and glaring at Max.

"He heals with love." Bracken spat, and I covered his hand with my own to calm him down. He had never liked Max, and I hadn't realized until this moment how very worried he'd been for me. Big brother, Bracken—so gruff and so kind at once. "And even Green couldn't heal everything." Brack finished. Damn. I looked away then, embarrassed suddenly that he would mention the entire 'hole in the memory' thing. These wounds were personal, humiliating in a way my body's hurts had not been. That little fucker had been *inside* me…where I had never invited him, and it hurt that I couldn't have stopped him.

Max saw my look—embarrassed and ashamed—and he leaned forward in sympathy. I felt a breath of something then, something static and tight, that I should have paid attention to, but I thought that the tightness in my chest was due to my anger, my mortification, and not to anything else.

"What happened?" He asked gently, so obviously concerned that I had to answer him, but I couldn't. He moved to cover my hand with his own across the table and I moved restlessly away. Bracken wrapped his arms around my shoulders and answered for me, which I wouldn't have let him do if I were feeling whole and myself.

"He mind-raped her." He murmured, and I shivered in his arms.

"What does that mean?" Max wouldn't understand, I thought miserably. He couldn't. But I had underestimated Brack's anger and his willingness to defend me.

"It means he thrust himself into her mind and took what she didn't want to give." he barked out succinctly.

"I don't…what did he take?" Max asked, and I felt my face crumple. I had been so brave the night before, but here, trying to explain to someone who wouldn't understand, I hadn't known how much admitting this would hurt. I felt stupid and violated, and as though nothing I could say would make anybody understand. Mind rape. Body rape. There were a million victims out there that could identify with what I felt, but at the moment I felt like I was the only one.

"He took her firsts." Bracken told him softly, rocking me against his arms, where I could feel safe and protected. "Her memories of firsts. First kisses. First time with a lover. Firsts."

"But…" Max said in confusion, and what he said next warmed me, because I knew that for a time he had thought the worst of me. "But there couldn't have been that many."

"Two." I choked brokenly into Brack's skin. "There were two—and he took one."

"Oh God." Max was stricken. "Let me guess. Adrian." He murmured, with Bracken as an echo, and then his hand actually reached mine in sympathy. And then all hell broke loose.

There was a spark at first, as his hand covered mine, warm and rough and mortal. Then the spark grew, and traveled through me, and bounced off Bracken, gaining power and momentum, whirling through me again, hitting Max with enough force to make him clench his hand around mine and again through me, fuelling itself through both my body then through my power. And it built, and grew, like water thundering into a valley towards a dam—it heaved, pushing my will and my inhibitions and everything I knew about what my power could do out of my way. Goddess, I thought, Goddess, I couldn't breathe…I couldn't…

With a surge of strength that knocked both men to the floor on their asses I came to my feet and heaved myself to the sink where I trembled over the plumbing for that one awful minute you have before you know you're going to be sick. Then my body convulsed and it came vomiting through me, out my mouth, and into the drain, pouring, spattering, cleansing through the pipes and onward and onward into wherever the water went. The small part of me left for humor hoped it wasn't the bay, and as the power finally waned and trickled into a little hiccup of sunshine, a vision of thousands of fish belly up in the brass monkey cold waters of the bay added a little extra giggle to my weeping when I collapsed on the floor, spent and exhausted and sobbing my heart out onto the pretty wood.

GREEN

Blood dance

God, Goddess and other, what in the blue *fuck* just happened?

Green raced out of his room with wet tangled hair and a pair of faded jeans that had fit him just fine in June but were coming off of his hips now. When he got to the kitchen, Cory was whimpering on the floor by the sink, Renny was hissing and growling in front of her, and Bracken was, by turns, swearing viciously at Max and trying to calm Renny down enough to get to Cory. He had a deep scratch the length of his arm, dripping precious elfin blood on the floor. Jesus, how had that girl gone so far from human in such a short time? And why would she want to protect Cory from Bracken?

"Renny, *down.*" Green ordered, and hoped she would. Adrian would have been able to calm her down in a second—the were-creatures had been his specialty—but with the exceptions of Adrian and Mitch, Renny had always pretty much only listened to the noises of her own heart. This time, her heart must have been on his side because she retreated a bit from Cory and he was able to move in and scoop her into his arms. Renny sat, panting, a soft growling sound emitting non stop from the back of her throat, and Green straightened, glaring furiously at the other two alpha males in the room, sniffing the air as he did so.

"Power." He said, speculatively, smelling the yeast and ozone smell of it. Risking a glance into the sink he found himself blinking at warped silverware and plastic glasses melting into the drain like a Salvador Dali painting of the trivial. "Power down the sink?" He looked at Cory, truly at a loss.

"Green…" she said plaintively, "I think I killed all the fish in the bay. Isn't that where pipes go? In the bay?"

"No, luvie," He said carefully, nuzzling the top of her head. "There's a water treatment plant, I'm pretty sure…at most what you did was save the city a couple hundred thousand in processing expenses…feel better?"

She nodded, and sighed like a sleepy child. "I'm so tired, Green." She murmured. "I'd forgotten what that could do to me…it didn't used to be so queasy…" And like that she fell asleep.

"Right." Green murmured, shaking his head, then he looked back up at the others. "I'm going to put her to bed. Renny's going to change back if I have to turn into a vampire and take her blood to make her, I'm going to heal that obscene gash on Brack's arm, and you people are going to tell me why I can't leave the fucking kitchen without something hellacious happening to the woman I love."

He padded into Cory's room and put her down, only to have her wake up suddenly. "Don't let me sleep until morning." She murmured. "If I go to class I can catch Nicky."

"We'll catch him later." He murmured, smiling. She had a preternatural sense of vengeance, he thought—much like his own kind, in some respects. It promised well for the years to come.

"But I need to drop off my papers." She told him, obviously fighting for coherence. "Finals are next week."

"I'll think about it." He murmured. "Now enough. Sleep. I'll wake you for dinner, we'll discuss it then." Grace awoke in two hours, dinner would be ready by seven—that was four hours of sleep he thought, hoping it would be enough. But Cory seemed satisfied, because she had already fallen asleep as he left the room. He stopped by the room he had stayed in before the girls moved in and snagged two extra-large T-shirts, one of which was over his head before he made it back to the kitchen, and the other of which he threw at Renny as he padded in. It was a good thing too, because Max was straining his neck in an effort not to look at the naked young woman who was spitting anger from the middle of the kitchen.

"Wha'you do?" She growled, mostly at Max, but partly at Bracken as well, who was saying patiently, "It was an accident, Renny…he touched her hand, that was all…we wouldn't hurt Cory—you know that." Renny took the T-shirt as Green threw it, and then hissed at them all, in a very non-human way, and sat down abruptly on the floor, her knees drawn up on either side of her, while she sucked the webbing between her thumb and forefinger. Green sighed at her, then turned towards Bracken and gestured towards his hand.

"Give us your wound, mate, I'll do for it."

"Thanks, brother." Bracken said wearily, and held out his arm. He was dripping blood steadily. Elves healed very quickly, and could sustain massive injuries before their bodies stopped their self-sustaining regeneration, but Bracken was a red-cap, and his very power pulled blood from bodies as easily as breath moved in and out of them. Broken bones, fractures, road rash would all heal in a few moments; a deep bleeding scratch like this one might bleed for days before it closed.

Green slid his hands up the other elf's arm, and took a deep breath, pulling from that place where his healing came from—his heart, his sex, his loins—and he touched his tongue delicately to the crook at the inside of Bracken's elbow, savoring the other man's shiver of reaction. Slowly—delighting in the contact, as was his nature, he ran his tongue along the wound, up the inside of the sidhe's elongated arm, ending where the cut got wide, where he sucked at his palm. Bracken, in his turn, tilted his head back, sighed, and shivered in the tiny completion that healing brought. Green shivered in his turn, and the men shared a small smile. Sex, healing, love: Green's brand of elf.

Max made a snort of disgust, and they turned to him wearily. "What?" Green asked with a taunting kiss at the crook of Bracken's arm, knowing the officer's uptightness wouldn't even let him speak without this prompting.

"You said you loved her." Max said disgustedly. "You said you loved her, and you've probably boned every woman and half the men in Northern California, and here you are, and she's hurt in the other room, and you're...you're..."

Green shook his head wearily, sad that Max had risen to the bait so easily. He let go of Bracken's arm and ran his hands through his tangled hair.

"I'm healing my brother." He said succinctly, and Bracken held out his whole hand and wiggled his fingers. "And, mortal, your understanding of us is not the issue here. What's at issue is what happened, and you're obviously ignorant, so I'm going to ask the only coherent being in the room."

"It was the damnedest thing." Bracken said, glad for his moment to talk. "She was telling uptight bumfuck here about her attack..." He looked away, unhappy. "It was hard. It was hard for her. It was hard for me to watch. I wrapped my arms around her to comfort her and...I felt a sort of static thing...like a cloud gathering lightning. Then..." Bracken's mouth which held a fell and grim line just as a matter of his own warrior's character took on an even leaner twist. "Well, even cop-fuck here can have a moment of compassion. He touched her hand while I was holding her…and…"

"What was it?" Max asked abruptly, and Renny hissed at him, even in her human form. "And what in the hell is wrong with *her?*"

"She's grieving." Green told him shortly. "Just like Cory, except Renny didn't have another lover to step in and take up some of that pain, now did she?" With that he turned to Bracken again, and was met with a shrug.

"I've seen her do it before." He said, not meeting Green's eyes. "Except then she was touching you and Adrian."

"Ah…" Green said, and then the full impact hit him, and he fought against the slugged feeling in his solar plexus. It had worked with Green and Adrian because they had wanted her and loved her and their emotions buzzed through her like power—power she couldn't contain. They all knew Max felt an unwilling attraction for their little sorceress, but in order for her to overfill like that, it would have to mean…well hell. There was only one thing it could mean. Taking a deep breath, and feeling bitter and kind at once, he asked "Even so, Bracken Brine Granite op Crocken?"

Bracken looked away, then back at his leader defiantly. "Even so, leader."

Green nodded. "As it will." He conceded. He'd been wishing that she would take another lover—even when Adrian was alive. But Green had thought, in the back of his mind, that she would choose someone unsubstantial. Someone he could ignore, or overlook, secure in the knowledge that she *would* be monogamous if only Green himself *could* be. But Bracken was not such a man. Bracken would be a real lover, if she would take him, someone who would vie for her attention, and she would receive his full concentration in return. Green tried to tell himself that it was all in the nature of the Goddess. *She* was known for coming to earth in several guises, taking lovers in each guise. Cory was one of the Goddess's creatures—a sorceress of more power, and more *female* power than Green had seen since the middle ages. It only followed that she would need more than one lover to match the different parts of her—Green for her kindness and her protectiveness, Bracken for her fierceness and loyalty. It fit. And if he could not relinquish his position as leader to be all to his little mortal goddess, then she would need others to fill what he could not. So, he was a leader, and a healer. Bracken was a warrior, and they could work together to keep her safe.

"I don't understand what you two just agreed on." Max was saying, "But I think you're full of total and complete horseshit."

"Bully for you." Bracken said with a decidedly unfriendly tilt to his head. "But until you can learn to keep your disrespect to yourself, you need to keep your distance from her."

"I wish we could do that." Green said, after a moment, "But I think we're going to need him."

"Not until the two of you tell me what just happened in here." Max interrupted, irritated at being talked about like a child.

"Power." Green said after a moment. "Cory channels power—the kind generated by emotions. You've had psych classes in that job of yours. What are your three major emotions?"

Max thought for a minute. "Love, fear, and anger."

"There you go." Green shrugged.

"No—there you don't go." Max stood up angrily, knocking his chair over. "That still doesn't explain what just happened...it's not like I...it's not like he..."

"It's not like I what?" Bracken demanded, suddenly nose to nose with the man. Max was a tall man at 6' 1" or so, but he wasn't an elf. Bracken stared down at him from an extra six inches of height, his once knee length black hair hanging over his shoulders like a shroud. He was wearing a pair of Cory's sweats that hugged his hips like bike shorts with nothing else and the breadth of his chest alone was massy enough to make the smaller man choke off the air in his lungs.

"It's not like she's anything to you." Max said, trying hard to look away from Bracken and not finding anywhere to look that wasn't filled with the warrior's presence.

"I love that mortal girl child." Bracken said clearly. "Whatever kind of love she'll give me, that's what I'll return."

"She's a gas station clerk!" Max spat out, "Not Madonna!"

And like that, Brack's hand was around Max's throat, not to choke, but to pin. Max tried to swallow, and found that he couldn't. Bracken snarled at him, an ugly, warrior's grimace. "I'm a red-cap, cop." He hissed into Max's frightened eyes. "That means I can make blood dance. You've seen me do it. Can you hear your blood dance in your ears, little human? Can you hear it thundering past your ear drums, through your throat, down into your heart? I can. I can hear it...I can hear your heart pump, and the sound of sweet, sweet blood whooshing through your veins, whooshing through your capillaries..." Brack stopped, smiled that warrior's grin again, and it wasn't pretty. "Ah ah ahhhh...one's weak...right there—right by your temple...a little dance, cop man, and it would break...it would break and bleed into your brain, and the only one who could save you would be Green, but he'd have to fuck you, and we all know you'd die before that ever happened."

The tension in the room massed, and hardly even quivered when Green asked, in a voice so dangerously soft that it barely stirred the air, "So, Officer Max, I guess what will save your skin here, is an honest answer. You drove two hundred miles in the rain for someone who hasn't worked in a gas station for more than six months. We love her. We'll kill or die for her—as she will do for us. So, sir, what is she to you?"

Max swallowed, looked up at Bracken, then past his shoulder to Green, and the denial in his eyes was painful to see. "She's a regret." He whispered at last. "I had my chance, I missed it, and she ended up with you people and your sexual menagerie. My fault. She's my fault."

"She's nobody's fault." Bracken murmured in protest. "She's glorious."

"And you're lying." Green said pointedly to Max. "You're lying to yourself, and you're lying to us, and your lies are tailor made to make Cory feel inferior and lowly to your high and mighty cop bullshit power trip. Now you can tell yourself fairy stories until you think you're the King of fucking Annuvin, but if your lies hurt Cory, undermine her confidence, make her feel bad about the things she has to do, they could get us all killed. Because whether you choose to acknowledge it or not, she wields a truckload of fucking power, and you just denied that you're a part of it. So since you're here, we'll keep you. We'll use you even. But until you learn to tell the truth, you don't get to touch her. You don't get to talk to her alone. You don't get to break bread at my table. You don't get to sleep under my roof. So you can walk out of here and find yourself a cheap hotel and wait for our call like a despised prom date, or you can tell us one little tiny truth that will make me think that you're worth treating like an ally."

There was a silence so complete that even Renny stopped growling. "I want her." Max said brokenly. "I want her, and I hate myself for that."

The storm feeling in the room eased up, and Max started to breathe again. Green sighed, resisting the temptation to tell Bracken to kill him, just to satisfy his own contempt. But Green had never killed lightly—especially not mortals, who were so very very easy to kill. "And that, Max," He said after a taut moment, "Is why she vomited power into the sink. She just had one asshole fucking with her head, and there she is, being comforted by two men who want her. Except one of them—the one she's the most afraid of—colors the whole thing with self-loathing. You do the math. You tainted her power, you tainted the feeling it gave her. You did the next best thing to mind-fucking her. You made her do it herself with her own power. Congratulations, Officer Max. You're the bad guy."

Max flinched, and then went pale. "I didn't mean to hurt her." He said rawly.

"Another lie." Green said lightly, although his face remained grim. "Nevertheless, you told a truth, and that's all I asked for. You can sleep on the couch, unless you want to sleep in the darkling with Grace," No living person ever did. "Fair enough, cop?"

Max nodded, weakly.

"Good" Green agreed. "Now, if we can sit down like sentient creatures, we need to discuss other things besides your shortcomings."

The men backed away from each other, and between them they managed to straighten up the kitchen. Green looked over at Renny, curled up in human form, and sighed.

"Renny, luv, you need to remember who you are." Green said gently. Renny eyed him doubtfully. "Please, luvie. We need your help for this, and you're no good to us when you're more kitty than girl."

"I control the bird population." She said on a growl.

"I imagine so," He replied smiling tenderly, "But I know you take classes and do homework and all those human things during the week, and I need that part of you with us now." He opened his arms and gestured with his arms. "Come sit on my lap, yes?"

She practically leapt there, curling up like a child—or a kitten, and Green rocked her softly for just a moment, and whispered in her ear. "What's your name, luvie."

"Renny." She growled softly.

"All of it," He insisted.

"Erin?" As though she weren't sure.

"All of it." He said again, persistently.

"Erin...Erin Alexis Joyce..." Her voice caught, quivered, and he held her tighter.

"You're not done yet." He reminded her, compassion radiating from every line in his body.

"Erin Alexis Joyce *Hammond.*" She said at last, her voice quivering, but still strong on the last word.

"Right, Erin Alexis Joyce Hammond." He affirmed, "You are a human girl, who can change her shape at will. Who's will?"

"Mine." She said, firmly this time.

"Very good." He finished. "Never forget that again." He looked up at the other two men who had sat patiently through the conversation. Even Max, he noted, looked softly at the slender child in his arms. "Okay." Green said on a starting over breath, "Here's the deal. Cory wants to go to school tomorrow, because she thinks she can catch this Nicky Kestrel. I want more than anything in the world to go with her."

"You can't." Bracken said immediately. "Green, you need to find out what happened in this city. There is something very hinky going on here. Besides the fact that pigeons are shitting *everywhere*, I could swear I saw a flock of starlings take out a housecat when I went out for the paper this morning."

Green shuddered. "Ouch! And you're right—thanks mate—that's exactly where I was going with this. I need the two of you on campus with the girls—for one thing, Cory's not as healed as she thinks she is. If channeling power wipes her out like it did tonight she has no defenses against this little fucker. Or anyone, for that matter."

Bracken grinned wolfishly. "Haul her to her classes and feed her cheeseburgers…haven't I done this already?"

Green grinned back. "You'd think we have these crises during finals week to just give her an extra challenge, wouldn't you? But you're right. Haul her to her classes, keep her healthy, keep her fed, and be ready to capture our precious little Nicky." He turned to Max. "Are you understanding what we need, cop?"

"Hang with Cory." Max affirmed.

"No, my friend, you hang with Renny."

Renny started to hiss, but Green jiggled her on his lap much as he'd jiggled Cory, and she cleared her throat and used her words. "Why me, Green? I'd just as soon rip out his soft, tender stomach and nibble on his liver." She said succinctly.

Max laughed shortly, then caught the feral gleam in her eyes and realized that, with her double nature, she might not be kidding. "What'd I ever do to you?" He asked, alarmed.

Renny didn't answer, but looked to Green instead.

"Yes." Green said in a tone that brooked no argument. "Yes—the two of you need to work together. Yes, I know you have a reason to hate him, but I need Bracken with Cory because he can actually carry her around the school and I don't want you alone, Renny. Bracken is right—there is something very odd going on here. This is an old city for this part of the country and the preternatural community is fairly well established. And not a soul has contacted me to warn me off or threaten me or even to greet me. I need to do the royalty thing and find out who this 'Papa Bird' is that I saw in Cory's mind, and I need to see why he hasn't introduced himself in a friendlier way."

"I have no idea what you just said." Max said, at a loss. "Walking into your home at any given time is like walking into Oz."

"Well, cop," Green said after a bemused moment, "Why don't you ask some respectful questions as you follow the yellow brick road, and you'll feel better about being the cowardly lion, yes?"

"Ain't it the truth." Brack murmured under his breath, and for a moment, there was an uneasy peace around Green's table.

CORY
Beguiled

I love the campus at CSUSF. It smells like eucalyptus, rain, and ocean, and there's more trees than you could imagine, especially back by the main tiered parking structure. True, the trees represent a safety hazard—anything could be hiding back there in the fog to jump out and grab you, even though there are those nice lamps with the round glass covers marking the way to the dorm structure. But less than five percent of the campus lived in the dorms, and everybody else who had to walk to the parking structure at night had had a night shiver at least once, wondering what hid in the trees and the fog. Or at least every woman.

Of course, on this particular day, Bracken's body heat kept me warm in the chilly drizzle, and today there was something a little extra hot running under his skin, but I'll be damned if I could figure out what it was.

It started even before he scooped me out of the car after driving us to the campus. He didn't know the city very well, and the drive had been filled with terse, explosive questions—*Are you sure this isn't a one way street? Why in the fuck can't I turn left at nine o'clock in the goddamned morning?* And my personal favorite, *What do you mean 19th street is really Highway One? Why don't they just call it Highway One and not put a fucking school next to it?* (To which I'd replied *Because, sweetie, the students are so busy fucking themselves that the campus doesn't get any action.* He'd laughed then, looking at me sideways from his exotic dark eyes, and his foul monologue subsided.) Usually Renny and I caught the Muni about a block away from Green's apartment building, and that took us straight down through Golden Gate park to the school, but that opened us up to all sorts of problems—and way too many contacts with strangers, so the giant blue Chevy Suburban that Green had brought down with him was what we drove. In the apartment parking garage I had a nice little BMW SUV that Green had bought just for Renny and I, but Bracken's legs were way too long to fit. Max and Renny had slid into the middle back seat of the Suburban without a word, and eyed each other warily during the entire ride. When Bracken pulled to a stop, Max got out and opened up my door for me. And that's when things got really strange because Brack had…well…

"What the hell was that sound out of your throat?" I asked, secure with my legs looped over one arm and the other arm around my back. My own arms were up around his neck, and I was conscious of glimpses of skin beneath my hands. For the barest of moments I wanted to raise my hands to *Bracken's* pointed, curved ears, the way I did with Green's, and it took a moment for me to remind myself that this was a very different person before the urge died.

"It was a sound." He replied implacably. "Left, right, straight?" Besides carrying me in his arms, he had my backpack on his back as well, and it was a good thing he was an elf because I think he was planning on traveling like this the whole freaking day.

"Straight—towards that ugly two story building you can see from Nineteenth. Seriously—did you just *growl* at Officer Max? Isn't he trying to, like, help us?"

"He will not touch you again." Brack stated, so autocratically that I almost let go of him and dumped myself ass-down on the ground.

"Jesus, Bracken, who died and made you my father? Cause I could swear the man's alive and well in Loomis, and wishing I'd visit more often."

He stopped short on the path, and people had to move around him. He pulled me up so that our noses were almost touching, and said very seriously, "I'm not your father. I'm not your goddamned big brother. And I'm not going to let that asshole touch you again if I can help it."

And then, as though that made any sense at all, he kept walking. Speaking of assholes!

"I should have kicked your balls harder when we met." I said conversationally, and was rewarded by a slight twist of his lips. So he remembered that—good. I may be exhausted and sore and weak, but he could still fear me. Swell. I sighed, and decided to treat the whole thing lightly. "He's Max," I said dismissively. "I'm not going to break Green's heart for Officer Max."

"It's not Green's heart I'm worried about." He replied cryptically. Almost casually, he looked behind him to make sure Max and Renny had sheered off to take Renny to the science building where she held her eight a.m. class. Their body language was both angry and intimate, to the extent that they looked like estranged family members and I was beginning to know the feeling.

"Oh, good, we're being an enigmatic asshole today. Because the day isn't going to be stressful or anything, you need to just dick with my head."

"I live for dicking with your head—what's changed?" He asked, bitterly.

Good question. "A lot—but it happened last summer, and I thought we were over that whole 'Why am I wasting my time with this skanky human' thing." I said, disgusted with the both of us.

Bracken stopped abruptly again and almost did dump me on my ass, but what he did instead was loop the arm that was under my knees around my waist, so that I slid down and against his body, clenched like a lover, except my feet didn't touch the ground. We were face to face, and for a moment I thought he was going to be really pissed, but he looked kindly and old for a moment, and once again I was reminded that he was nearly the same species as Green.

"I never thought you were a 'skanky human'." He said softly. "I thought you were Adrian's girl."

I swallowed, hard, and wondered how many people walking by in the fog could hear my heart. "Now I'm Green's girl." I meant to say gently, but it came out as a question.

He nodded, seriously. "You will always be Green's girl." He agreed. "When Green chooses a mate, he's there until the end."

"Even when I'm old and wrinkly?" I asked, trying to lighten the moment, but it stayed securely leaden.

Brack shook his head. "Power does strange things." He said after a moment. "Try not to get to attached to the idea of being old and wrinkly."

My eyes got really wide, then, because Green told me that immortality didn't come automatically with power, and we had never mentioned it again. But Bracken was still holding me too close, almost intimately, and suddenly I had a giant light bulb moment.

"No." I said abruptly, and struggled to break free of him. He was strong and big, and I'd had the shit kicked out of me both physically and metaphysically this weekend, so I ended up cradled in his arms like a baby again, with the harsh admonition that if I didn't sit still he was going to sling me over his back like a sack of flour.

"No." I said again, when I was finally situated.

"No what?" He asked, trying to look all innocent, but obviously amused. Asshole.

"You will not read anything into what happened yesterday." I snapped. "It was a power anomaly. It was a fluke. I was upset, and there were two different creatures touching me…it was a simple metaphysical battery thing…it was…"

"Exactly what happened with Green and Adrian, smartass." Bracken finished smugly, and he sounded so much like himself that I relaxed enough to make a face at him.

"I was going to say that it was queasy." I told him truthfully, because it had been, and I was now legitimately afraid of releasing my power at all. An image came to me, apocalyptic and terrifying, of over a hundred people in the bowl of a slag heap, looking surprised as a sudden burst of sunshine violence burnt them into ashes. Maybe I should be afraid of using my power at will, I thought feeling a little ill. But Bracken hadn't seen the memory cross my face.

"Blame that on cop-fuck Max." He was saying, and now he was pissed off again. Huzzah.

"He didn't know it would happen." I told him defending Max on principle— the man had driven all the way out here to make sure I was okay, after all. Why shouldn't I defend him?

"He taints the air you breathe." Bracken hissed, and then we were at my humanities building, which was just as well because I had no words with which to answer that.

I took some kidding from my classmates about having my very own stud taxi, enough to make me take a good look at Bracken to see what glamour he employed to pass as human, and the answer was "not much". Pretty much the only thing missing today were the pointy ears and unusual, pond-rip-pling-in-shadow eyes, which made me glare at him through much of the class. I'd seen him when he went with humans up in Placer County, and he was 100% gen-u-wine redneck. He was good at it—he even had a mullet. Of course, it was a shorter mullet, since I melted the lovely dark length of his hair up to his shoulder blades this summer, but it was an honest-to-pete Joe Dirt mullet, and he often put on deep, saturnine creases at his mouth and his eyes, to make him look pre-maturely bitter, like so many of the once young men up in the foothills. But not today.

I wasn't prepared for the envious, speculative looks that my classmates gave him, both male and female, and I felt oddly protective. It was irrational to see Bracken as country elf in the big city, but what can I say? I wasn't used to seeing any of my guys out of our home place. It seemed wrong, somehow. Almost as wrong, I thought miserably, watching a sweet-voiced queen named Bryan flirting with Bracken for all he was worth, as I felt here, in this lovely, old, deadly city. I was so tired by the end of class that I almost didn't notice my professor signaling for my attention as everybody else left. I moved to talk to him, and realized that Brack moved with me. I shot him an irritated look and he gazed back unrepentantly. Asshole, I thought, but suddenly the word seemed affectionate.

"Are you feeling alright this morning?" My Industrial Revolution professor wanted to know. He's a short, stout man, with a broad, homely face, and a bemused, puzzled air about him.

"I'm fine, Professor Cruikshank." I lied. "I got hit by a little something hinky, that's all—I'll rest when I go back home." Now *that* was the truth.

"Glad to hear it." He mumbled. Prof Cruikshank was one of the nicer professors I'd encountered—not a great teacher, because he tended to get lost really easily—but he always gave you the benefit of the doubt with late papers, and he knew all of our names by the second day of class. Now he was looking a little embarrassed, and a little guilty, and a little frightened, and a little…little. In fact, he was looking decidedly shorter, and grayer, and he kept shrinking and turning colors before my eyes.

I blinked, and Bracken said "Hell—I can't believe you're this surprised, Einstein." But I was, and now that I looked at Professor Cruikshank with power in my eyes I saw that he was, in fact, a red-cap/sidhe mix, much like Brack's father, only where Brack's father's body was a misshapen pile of rock-colored slabs, the prof's body was simply, well, stout.

"Well I am surprised." I said unhappily. "Jesus, I'm surprised I'm still alive, if I can be stupid enough to sit in this room all semester and not even see."

But Professor Cruikshank was looking at me kindly, his squat, smooth face the color of eucalyptus bark and his suit crumpling in weird places around his shortened body. "I wouldn't be too hard on myself, Cory." He murmured. "After all, I had the cloak of respect on my side—never underestimate how much natural glamour comes with being an authority figure. Very hard to shake, that aura. But I had to ask you truly, if you were going to be all right. Your leader has been raising holy hell this morning about one of his people being assailed, but it wasn't until you were carried in here, glowing with power, that I realized that my favorite student had been in danger."

I winced. "Jesus, Bracken—why didn't you tell me to tamp it down!" I demanded. Satisfyingly enough, Brack looked surprised, and the professor looked at us both assessingly, tsking as he did so.

"You are both too innocent to be let out of the faerie ring." He said after a moment, and I had the pleasure of seeing Bracken flush and look uncomfortable.

Since Cruikshank wasn't looking at me, I risked making a face at Bracken over my shoulder, and was rewarded with a sour look in return.

"What Bracken is not telling you, my dear, is that he is feeding you power as he taxies you around, and I have the feeling he's not telling you because that means something in particular to the both of you. But, as important as it is that you tone that down, it's not nearly as important as what I broke my cover to tell you."

We both looked at him in surprise, and I know that I, for one, was pleased as bleedin' Jesus to not have to deal with all of the implications of being some sort of supernatural sex beacon when held in Brack's arms.

"If you are here on campus looking for Nicky Kestrel, he's here—I believe the two of you have class in less than ten minutes, am I right Ms. Kirkpatrick?"

I nodded, my mouth dry, and reached a hand blindly for the table I'd been standing by. I was so undone that I didn't protest when I felt Bracken's arm under my fingers, nor when he'd hoisted me back into the traditional stud-taxi position. "Renny will be there too." I said from my place safe in Brack's arms.

"That lost little were-creature?" The sympathy on his face made him instantly my friend for life.

"She's out for his blood." I said.

"And you, dear?" He asked.

"I just want my memories back." I said, but I wasn't so sure I was telling the truth. I was too emotionally exhausted from the events of the past year to go on a vendetta, I'd decided this morning. I'd be content with what little of Adrian I'd started with in the first place. However, that entire rational decision thing didn't stop me from dreaming of beating the living shit out of Nicky.

Cruikshank was shaking his head. "I can't get involved here." He said regretfully. "In fact, I was told by my own leader, to tell you and your friends here, that you are on your own."

I gaped. "But...but Green has *treaties* here—isn't that important? Sacramento is a bedroom community to your people—it's surrounded by running water on both sides—it's impossible access unless you're welcome there—why would you risk that? Why..." Water was a big furry deal to the fey. Their power didn't travel well over water, and if a sidhe—what Green and Bracken were, the most powerful of the elves, who were the most powerful of the fey—managed to cross water and sustain his magical/physical power base, he pretty much had run of the land. Sacramento sat in a delta—the American and the Sacramento rivers made a vee, and Green had managed to not only cross the whole Atlantic Ocean, and then down and around the Isthmus of Panama, and into the San Francisco Bay and *then* over those two rivers. In an unguarded moment, he once told me it had taken him a hundred years to hoard the power to keep him alive during this trip, and he had anchored it in forty lime trees, which he'd shipped with him. And all of that power, he had planted up in Foresthill, in his hill, and he used it to keep his people as safe as he could.

"Why could your leaders cut your people off from half the state when all they have to do is help us?" I asked, exhausted, puzzled, unable to fathom how I was going to get to my next class, much less the weird politics of the fey.

Regretfully, Cruikshank held up his hand. "I'm sorry Cory, I know my own leader would like to change things, but until he talks to Green, my hands are tied. We're at war here. If we'd known what was going to sail into our harbor this September, we would never have guaranteed safe passage for your people. Clorklish—my leader—would like to make a stand, but until he gets some back up, right now, with this particular enemy soldier, we can't step out of our glamour or our shadows to help you."

I stopped talking, my mouth open in surprise at the turn of this entire conversation, and rested my head on Brack's conveniently strong chest. I had been tired when class had ended. I was exhausted now, and I had four more classes to attend today. And apparently, one were-creatire to apprehend. Cruikshank saw my desolation, and his expression softened. He reached out, and regardless of Bracken, pinched my cheek gently. There was no flare up of power, no electric shock of anything, just a bone deep comfort that took the edge off the weariness and made me feel as though things weren't so hopeless after all.

"Don't worry, little sorceress." He said gently. "I may not be able to march to your rescue as a red-cap, but as a professor, you have the comfort of knowing you can always come to my office for tea, and," he laid a finger aside his nose, just like Santa, to seal our conspiracy, "Don't worry about that final, dear one. Consider it taken and aced." And with that, he grew again in stature, form, and pinkness, before my very eyes. When he was back to his full glamour as a sweet faced, dumpy-but-human History professor, he turned to leave.

"Wait!" I said, a sudden question in my mind. He turned. "You were alive, then, in the industrial revolution?" I asked. He nodded, looking kind. It made sense—it explained why he couldn't give a lecture without muddling through a haze of nostalgia. "You didn't happen to know...a vampire named Adrian, did you?"

"No, my little sorceress, I didn't." He replied. "I'm sorry. But you will not always be as heart sore as you are now." And the compassion on his face was devastating. I buried my face into Brack's chest then, and wished with all my heart for the day to be over. Bracken, wisely, simply turned and started towards the library where my next class was to be held. He was quiet all the way there.

When we entered the library, I wanted to giggle helplessly. When you enter on the ground floor at the west entrance, there's a large room of tables and a bank of couches, filled with mostly sleeping students. I couldn't imagine anything sweeter than sleeping on those couches at this very moment, but I told Bracken to keep walking, past the couches and down towards the East Wing, where the small classrooms and research computer rooms were.

Renny and Max were already there, and they looked marginally more comfortable with each other than they did earlier in the morning. On a usual day, Nicky, Renny and I all parked ourselves in the back set of the computer cubicles. That was how I first got to know Nicky—and why Renny felt just as betrayed as I did when he attacked. We had been fellow students and strangers in a new city, since Nicky claimed to have grown up in the Midwest. We had eaten at the student union, seen movies together, and signed up to use the lab at the same time. We had been friends.

"Nicky's here." I murmured to Renny as Bracken sat me down, gently as a toothpick sculpture without glue. "And you wouldn't *believe* what happened in history class this morning!" *I* didn't believe what happened during history class this morning, I was pretty sure it would blow Renny's mind. Max looked at me and rolled his eyes, and I could feel his dismissal from three feet away. Bracken turned and glared at him so horribly that he looked down at his shoes and shifted farther away. And the four of us were so involved in this odd byplay, that none of us noticed Nicky until the arrogant son of a bitch came to the back as usual, and without even looking around slid casually into the seat between Renny and I.

He did an honest to God double take—I thought those were just for cartoon characters, and I almost laughed as Max and Bracken flanked Renny and I from the back wall and I could see him trying to decide whether to bolt or to smooth it out.

"Cory!" He said greenly in a sick attempt at pleasant surprise. "Did you get your paper done, because mine sucks."

"My paper was done last week, Nicky." I said calmly, the fury burning my throat. "You should remember that. I remember ***everything*** from last week, don't you?"

"Yeah." He said, nodding. "Yes. I remember everything." His pretenses dropped then, just like Professor Cruikshan's glamour. "I didn't want to…give you anything bad to remember." He said, finally meeting me in my eyes. "I…you were just supposed to wake up in the morning and forget the whole thing."

"Forget the whole thing?" My voice rose to a squeak. "Does that include my boyfriend? I was just supposed to wake up and pretend he never existed?"

Nicky shook his head, confused. "Nobody ever notices." He said, almost to himself. "I know you're different—but that one first...I mean—it's such a small thing—how is it you know it's gone?"

I felt Brack's body burning behind me with the effort not to backhand the slightly built man next to me, but he needn't have worried. My mad was coming on—and unlike the queasy power that Max had sent through me and Bracken, this was a clean, true fury.

"Not a big thing? That one first? You *stole* him from me." And even I could see wisps of sunshine leaking from my breath as you spoke. "We had a handful of days—barely two months together, and you *stole* Adrian from me, you ***dirty rotten fucking thief!***"

Nicky bobbed to the side, and looked horrified as the computer in front of him melted cleanly into a puddle of plastic and glass, so evenly heated that even the vapors were consumed by the combustion of my anger.

"Cory, calm down." And if Nicky had said it, I might have killed him then and there, but it was Renny, and as she had been for the last few months, she was the one odd element in my life that could balance all of the mad emotions that seemed to rule my destiny these days.

"I didn't realize." Nicky said in a small voice. "You and Renny—you're both so closed mouthed about everything—you never told me your lover had died."

"Would it have made a difference?" I asked bitterly, and Nicky's look back was surprisingly sincere.

"Of course it would have." He said earnestly. "I never would asked you out—I never would have risked that Goshawk would have asked me to borrow from you—I like you, Cory. I wouldn't steal something that important to you, not if there wasn't any way to replace it!"

"But you've stolen this thing from other women?" I asked, calm enough now to realize how totally naïve Nicky had been all along. He nodded, looking somewhat abashed. "Most of them...well, it's something they'd rather forget. I just help them out—and the power we get from it...I mean, we've doubled in people, just from the boost Goshawk can give them, feeding off the memories alone."

I shook my head in disgust. "You are so fucking stupid, Nicky, I can hardly believe you've lived this long. You have no idea what you've done—not just to me, but to everybody else you've touched. You need to give them back."

"I...I can't..." He murmured, and at that point something in his melted computer caught fire and the alarm went off, and the class practically ran the professor over going out the door. Renny and I stayed towards the back, and Max and Bracken flanked Nicky as we exited. The professor was hollering something about putting our papers in his boxes as we entered the quad, which was just as well, I thought, because I didn't think I could make another class today. I was already regretting giving Brack up as my stud taxi, and I was certainly regretting melting Nicky's computer with my mad. I had been tired this semester, and sad, and lethargic, but this was the first time I realized how weak I had made myself in my mindless, selfish grieving. Last year I would have come back from this attack much more quickly, I thought disgustedly.

When we got outside, we separated ourselves from the milling crowd, all of whom were turned, almost herd-like, towards the library to see if it was going to spontaneously conflagrate or anything nifty like that, now that the alarm had gone off.

Now that nobody was watching us, Bracken could unleash some of the fury that had been quivering through his body like a plucked bow string. "What do you mean you can't give her back her memory?" He ground out, catching Nicky's throat in his hand and pushing him against the nearest tree.

"Goshawk's got them!" Nicky squeaked. "He says we can't spare any of them if we're going to be strong as a people."

"Wait a minute." I murmured. "You keep talking about all this power for your people—do you have any idea what this power is going to be used for?" Because Nicky was talking like a religious zealot—one of those types who doesn't believe that his life savings is going to the preacher's stretch limousine and special 'companions'.

"To make us strong. Give us unity." Nicky said earnestly. Goddess, he needed to be slapped.

"To go to war?' I asked pleasantly, and was rewarded by his big-eyed blink.

"Why would Goshawk want to go to war?" He asked blankly.

"I don't know." I replied sweetly. "Why don't you ask the other preternatural communities in San Francisco and find out why they think there's a war on—and why you're at it, why don't you come talk to our leader, and explain to him why you're assaulting his people and you can't even make an *attempt* at *mangeldt*, recompense, even a freaking apology? Okay? How about that?"

"What other communities." Nicky looked blank again. "Goshawk told us that he was the only leader in this city. We were all birds—we thought that gave us some sort of special pass, because of Goshawk."

"Well my boyfriend gave a gas station in Vacaville to *someone* he thought could give Renny and I safe passage here." I snapped at him. "And it sure as shits-afire is not your precious fucking Papa Bird."

"I thought your boyfriend died?" Nicky asked, and it was actually a good question, and I was so mad that I wasn't even embarrassed to answer him.

"We were three." I choked out. "I had a night lover and a day lover." I said, and it felt like poetry, just to say it there in public in the middle of the quad, under the foggy sun. "And they loved each other like night loves the day. And then the night lover died, and the day lover and I were naked in the sunshine, with only ourselves for cover." And Jesus, it was poetry. "And you," I snarled, snapping out of it. "You stole two nights out of a handful, and you stole them to buy blood...Goddess, Nicky—Goshawk is using you to fund a coup."

Bracken had dropped his hand from Nicky's throat in order to wrap his arms around me in comfort, and the confusion on Nicky's face was terrible to see.

"Oh no." He said sincerely. "You're wrong. Goshawk wouldn't lead us into war. He's our leader—he just wants to keep us powerful, and safe." Suddenly his face lit up, and I did not like the frightening hope that I saw in it. "You'll see." He said definitively. "You'll see—once he knows you have a protector, he'll give you back his memory—wait—I'll get it for you. Don't worry, Cory," He smiled, and it looked like the Nicky that Renny and I had taken to the movies and poured coffee into when papers were due and I was suddenly sick at the duplicity that had lied to that sweetness, which had twisted all of that good intention into the awfulness that he'd inflicted on me. "Don't worry." He said again. "I'll make it right again."

And like that, with a flash of feathers and a panicked whoosh of strong wings, he was gone, up into the tree, through the branches, and into the murky San Francisco sky. In another flash of bare skin and fur, Renny was a big tabby cat again, leaving her wool sack of a dress in a puddle on the sidewalk as she went frolicking across the campus after him.

"Fuck." I murmured into Brack's chest, more grateful than words that he had offered it to me, and too wrung out to question the wisdom that had chosen to comfort me instead of keeping Nicky by the throat. "Bracken, you'll have to get her." I said, and sank wearily onto the handy bench that sat next to the tree. "She loses her goddamned mind in that form—the last time she did that, she called me naked from Stern Grove about two hours later."

Bracken swore and threw Max a truly evil look over his shoulder, and then did that *moving* thing that Green could do, but I'd never seen Brack do. No one noticed him, because no one but me apparently could see him.

"Where'd he go?" Max asked, to confirm that this was something magical and elvish and I was reassured.

"To get Renny." I said, and rested my chin on my hands. "She's got her cell phone around her neck—that's a good thing." I said tiredly. The first time she'd lost total control and gone tearing out into the world we'd decided that wearing her cell like an ipod made a great deal of sense. Now, all she had to do was change quickly in the shadows, make the call, and stay put until I got there to pick her up.

"Shouldn't she just think before she changes?" Max asked, making too much sense for Renny.

"I think Renny is more suited to be a giant tabby cat than any person on earth that I've ever known." I said after a moment. "And her emotions are so changeable..." I shrugged. "When anything stresses her out right now, her first line of defense is cat." And I couldn't think of anything more to say about that, because even words were exhausting. I sank my face into my hands. "After they get back, I think I'll put my papers in my professor's boxes and get back to the apartment."

Max looked at me, not without sympathy, and actually took note of my appearance for the first time of the day. "You look awful." He said after a moment. "I think that's a good idea." His hand made an abortive move to pat me on the back, then returned to his lap. Good move, I thought sourly. If Bracken didn't kill him for that touch, something in me might go out of control and do it for him.

"What was that you were saying about a war?" He asked suddenly, and I gave him the abbreviated version of what Professor Cruikshank had told us. I was secretly validated by how stunned he was.

"God—these people—this world—it's much bigger than I ever imagine..." He looked at me again, and this time his eyes were sober. "Did I ever tell you how sorry I was about Adrian?"

I smiled a little, because he was sincere, and said "No—but thank you. You know, if you ever want to tell Renny the same thing about Mitch, she might stop fantasizing about shredding your skin off your body." And then, in a moment of perfect sympathy, I pat his knee.

I am such a goddess-forsaken buggering fuckhead dork.

I was unprepared for the sudden surge of human sex and longing that pounded through me, via the stoic Officer Max. I knew—I had always known—that he wanted me, but I never knew that once I'd chosen Adrian, once I'd mourned him like a woman, that Max's want had changed, grown, and was now the choking monster of yearning and self-loathing that poured through me now.

I was too tired for this shit, I thought disgustedly, and I allowed my head to tilt back, and I yawned, and my final burst of sunshine for the day poured into the sky. As I yawned, I felt myself smile, because the sunshine made the winter sky bright, and the pigeons up there happy, and suddenly the pigeons and wrens that had been huddling miserably on the rooftops and in the trees started flying like Spring. Really like Spring, I mused, beyond exhaustion and logic as I watched them frolic up in the sky. The damn birds were boinking each other silly in the flood of sunshine over the rooftops of the college. Go to it, you horny little bastards, I urged them in a weary sort of silent cheer.

But the yawn eventually stilled, leaving the birds to continue their fornication without my help, and I snatched my hand from Max's knee like a child touching a hot stove. Bracken, who had seen the whole thing as he approached holding a giant wriggling tabby cat in his arms swore at me gently, then plopped Renny on Max's lap, and told him gruffly to get her dressed. Max dragged Renny off by the scruff of the neck to comply, and Bracken bent over me, murmuring lovely things like "fuckwit moron" in a voice that warmed me in spite of his irritation.

"I knew you liked me." I said after a moment, and he replied "Bite me, dumb shit."

It was the last thing I heard before I fell asleep on his chest.

GREEN
Betrayed

Green looked at the human form of the werewolf sitting across from him and fought the urge to blast the man with the suppressed force in his preternatural veins. The woman sitting next to the werewolf had an equally closed expression on her face, but then, Morana had never thought highly of Green, even when she'd come begging to his bed. Compared to the irritation he felt towards to the two larger guests sitting on his couch, the tiny surge of irritation he felt towards the gnome who represented the lesser elves and fey was almost affectionate. Goddess, he swore to himself, how did they manage to make smug isolation an art form? He sighed, and tried again.

"So now I'm asking all of you," He said patiently, "Why would you not tell me that you're under attack?"

"Why would you care?" Morana wanted to know. "It's not like we deal closely with anything but financial matters, Lord of Leaves and Shadows."

"Because I could have helped?" Green returned exasperated. "Because when this Goshawk person has kicked your collective asses, he'll be on my doorstep with all of the people he's kept from his victories with you?" Because of common fucking courtesy? He restrained himself from finishing with. But there was no talking to the high sidhe about courtesy. He knew elves like Morana—the hierarchical, elitist people that had forced him to flee his native country and to find a home in this dry, hard land that was alien to everything he had known for fifteen centuries. They may have enjoyed things like cars and running water, but they hadn't changed one little bit to fit the times.

Orson, the werewolf, was a lawyer in his regular life, and seemed to realize that Morana had come dangerously close to pissing Green off beyond courtesy. "You've got to understand," He said in that smooth, conciliatory way that lawyers have, "We didn't realize that we were under siege for a couple of months. It felt like a run of bad luck in our business ventures, a series of mishaps in our physical surroundings—seagulls getting stuck in our ventilation, starlings swarming over our mercantile ventures, that sort of thing. We haven't really had any fatalities—although many of our people have turned up injured, and car accidents because of the birds have been continuing in frequency. If Goshawk hadn't come to each of us and announced his intention of taking over, we wouldn't even realize we were at war."

"And when was that?" Green asked, trying not to grind his teeth.

"Last month." The gnome said, looking at Orson like he had a bad taste in his mouth. "And he didn't come to us in person—he sent a flunky—a real sadistic bastard named Eyeass." The look on the gnome's face was outwardly hostile. "Let's just say it's untrue to say that we haven't had any fatalities."

The werewolf looked uncomfortable, and the high sidhe looked unfazed.

"Oh come on," Morana said impatiently, tapping her foot. "It's not as though you could have done anything about it—look at you—you're barely a power."

Green eyed Morana levelly. "I have five times your numbers under my hill, luvie."

"But not true sidhe." Morana returned with a disdainful laugh. "We differ on our idea of 'people'"

"You didn't consider Goshawk's people 'people'." Green snapped. "And they can kill you just as dead as I can. If I were you, I'd start thinking a little broader, Morana. Part of the reason we're here is that you didn't consider Goshawk a threat because he wasn't your sort of 'people'."

"Don't get too worked up about it." Harrumphed Clorklish, the gnome. "She doesn't rate too many of us as people."

At that moment, Bracken burst through the door holding Cory in his arms and all conversation stilled. She looked spent, all but asleep in Bracken's arms, and Bracken's expression was unrelievedly grim. At Green's nod, he stepped into the living room and came directly to Green, who tenderly touched Cory's chin and felt the now familiar jolt of power, flavored with Bracken's unique colors, and, terrifyingly, very very weak.

"My my my," He murmured, "What *have* you two been doing?" And before Bracken could answer, Green leaned forward and touched his forehead to Brack's, while still cupping Cory's face in his hand. When this had first happened with Adrian it had surprised him—it had stunned him—but through those lovely, frantic, amazing few weeks that the three of them had shared, he had learned to control the power that Cory could channel, and now he used it to heal both of his children from some of their exhaustion. He needed Cory for this meeting, as much as it broke his heart to rouse her from the sleep she truly needed.

"I melted a computer." Cory said gruffly, still speaking from Bracken's chest.

"Don't forget the birds." Brack urged wryly.

"I have no idea what I did to the birds." Cory returned, a corner of her mouth turning up, "But they seemed very happy when we left."

"I hate to interrupt this reunion…" Morana began sardonically, only to be interrupted by Green.

"Then don't." Green snapped, and ignored her for just one more moment. "I'd love to let you both go sleep." He told his two dear ones, "But I need you here for this."

"Is Grace cooking steak tonight?" Cory asked.

"Count on it." Green murmured back, smiling in admiration and gratitude. "Where're Max and Renny?"

"They're taking Muni back." Bracken told him. "Cory couldn't make it through the rest of her classes—they're putting her papers in professor's boxes, and if Renny can make it for a half an hour without going kitty on Max, she might make it to all of her own classes."

Green looked pained. "I'm going to have to solve that problem very soon." He said, "But not right now."

With that, he turned to the sidhe, the werewolf and the gnome and made introductions. Cory nodded her head to each, as regally as she could still cradled in Bracken's arms, and when Clorklish was introduced as the leader of the lesser fey, she gave him a genuine smile.

"Professor Cruikshank spoke to me today." She told him. "Is he one of yours?"

Clorklish looked pleasantly surprised. "Yes—I wasn't sure if you'd put that together. He's spoken very highly of you, little sorceress. He says you're brilliant and kind."

Cory flushed. "He's the one being kind. I'm very pleased to meet you, Master Gnome."

"Wait a minute." Morana interrupted. "Cruickshank broke his cover to a mortal?" She gave Clorklish a disgusted look. "What the hell are your people thinking?"

"Maybe they were thinking about protecting our own." Clorklish said bitterly. "Since our higher-ups don't seem to think it's a priority."

"You're on our 'to do' list." Morana retorted nastily, and Green found himself shaking his head. Not even when his elves were at their arrogant worst had the spoken to the vampires in his enclave the way Morana had just spoken to another fey.

"He wanted to warn us." Cory defended. "Nic…" She stopped suddenly, oddly protective of Nicky's identity in front of this unpleasant woman. "My attacker was on campus. He wanted to tell me to be ready."

"And did you meet him? Where is he?" Green's eyes took on a predatory gleam.

Cory shook her head. "Nicky's drunk the magic kool-aid, Green—he didn't understand…We couldn't…" She looked at Bracken, hoping for back up.

"He's a pawn." Bracken said, shaking his head in disgust and pity. "He changed form, right in the middle of campus, saying he was going to go to Goshawk and get Cory's memories back. We couldn't…even Cory couldn't hurt him, Green. The delusion on his face was just painful."

"That's important." Cory said, looking out at the other leaders. "Not all of this Goshawk guy's people know what Goshawk is trying to do. I don't think his numbers would be quite so large if we could actually talk to them, try to make them see reason."

"Or we could just kill them." Orson said, surprised at her offer of mercy.

"Or we could try to save the lives of your people by not going into battle with theirs." Green interjected. "We could try to join forces and communicate and possibly not destroy any more of the Goddesses children than destroyed habitat necessitates."

"Our people will give their lives to this fight." Morana said arrogantly.

"You mean *my* people will give their lives in this fight!" Clorklish overrode.

"But why should anyone have to give their lives at all!" Cory broke in, both angry and distraught. "When was the last time your people lost someone to battle?" She looked at all of them, and noticed that both Morana and Orson looked uncomfortable. "Ten years? Twenty?"

"We lost two last month." Clorklish replied, looking angrily at the two larger leaders.

"Then you *know.*" Cory cried. "You know…one person is too many."

"Oh, please." Morana dismissed Cory with a wave of the hand. "Don't be melodramatic. You're a child—what would you know about it?"

"She lost her childhood this summer." Green stated, his face hard. "When she defended my people to the death and beyond."

"This summer was a fluke." Morana sneered. "You were getting above yourself and that little half-breed was too stupid to do what we..." She trailed off, realizing that her arrogance had revealed much more than she had intended.

"To do what you....what?" Green asked, his voice deceptively mild.

Morana licked her lips, and her eyes moved sideways, as though looking for escape. She made as though to move, and Green moved his hand, just a little, and the love that moved him to heal was suddenly powering him to do so very much more. "What are you doing, Green?" She demanded, trying to color her sudden fear with outrage.

"Have the courtesy to finish your sentence." Green responded, his voice still sweet and courteous, but his usually kindly gaze suddenly sucked all of the heat out of the room, as he zeroed it in on Morana. "What was that last word that you didn't quite get to."

"Let me go!" She howled.

"FINISH YOUR FUCKING SENTENCE!" Green exploded, and Morana's face threatened to buckle to tears. "Sezan didn't do what he was...*WHAT?*" And Green's power expanded, surrounding her body, pushing in at it, and then the tall, elegant sidhe began to weep.

"Expected to do." She whispered. "He didn't do what we thought he was going to do."

The temperature in the room dropped even further, and Green turned to catch Bracken and Cory's gaze. "Did you hear that, my loves?" He asked, his voice crooked with anger and pain. "Sezan, the killer of our beloved, didn't do what Morana and her leader **EXPECTED** him to do." Bracken's expression was stunned, angry, and upset. Cory, still exhausted, was confused.

"Now, Green..." Morana made a sudden, belated attempt at a conciliatory smile, which was hard to do, since she was still weeping in fear.

"You knew." Green swallowed, hard, still stunned at the careless duplicity of his own people. "You **knew**. He came into Crispin's land, and set up shop, and did horrible, poisonous things to Crispin's mind, and Crispin's people, and he **plotted** to destroy Adrian and you **knew he was there?**" And like that, Green felt what Cory called her "mad"—the berserkers rage, the surge of adrenaline and power that was his birthright—and it hit his bloodstream like a freight train, charging both Cory and Bracken by their proximity to him, and cloaking him with the sort of massive power that so very few people of any descent had ever seen. Green seemed to grow in stature, his sunshine hair streaming behind him like a crackling chaperone, built up by the power of righteous anger that fueled him.

"Mitchell. Ratso. Jon. Janine. Gary." He said simply, naming the shape shifters who had been killed by Sezan, the man who had killed his beloved. His voice took on a thunder and a lightning that filled the living room with electricity and fear. "**ADRIAN.** You ugly, arrogant, icy bitch—he could have lived. They *all* could have lived. One lousy fucking phone call…" He looked back at Cory, and saw the mute rage in her eyes, the helpless pain, the useless regret, and his mad took on a whole new dimension.

"Do you *see* that child there?" He demanded. "She has lived barely twenty mortal years, and she wore her first lover's blood like a sheen of sweat because of your callousness. Her rage overwhelmed her…do you know what happened to Crispin's people?" He asked, and was not surprised when Orson and Morana both looked bewildered. Clorklish, older, compassionate and human in a way that even the human born Orson was not, looked at Cory with the weight of the world in his eyes.

"We assumed they joined yours." Orson said numbly.

"They would have." Cory told him, her small voice empty and shell shocked. She looked at Morana, bitter and lost. "If I hadn't killed them all, down to a man."

Morana gave a short bark of laughter, suspended in motion as she was, but it died in her throat as the two sidhe and the girl in front of her stared back with bleak, angry faces. Cory's hand reached out from her position in Bracken's lap, and she pulled out a lock of his hair, that now reached only down to his shoulder blades. She held it out to Morana, like an angry talisman.

"It fell down to his knees like a dark waterfall." She whispered, looking at Bracken in anguish, and then she turned to Morana, anger burning in her voice. "I almost killed him." She choked out. "Adrian died—he flew to my rescue and *died,* and I killed a hundred men, and Brack and Arturo barely made it out with their lives and…" She looked helplessly at Green. "Why wouldn't someone warn us?" She asked, bewildered. "Why would someone send that madness up and not even tell us we were at war? All of that pain…"

And the pain in her eyes was Green's undoing. With a fearful gesture, and a sweep of green lighting, he swept Morana from her place standing before the couch and into the closed front door. "You are forbidden from my home. If you ever venture here again even *accidentally*, you will pay with your own life." A shaft of light passed through her, and her eyes bulged out in surprise. "You feel my power, you know that it's true."

"You are not this strong..." Morana protested, but another surge of power passed through her, and her silence was shocked and frightened. With a final and mighty surge of anger, Green smashed the Elvin woman's body through the door and into the hall outside. There was a startled yelp from Renny and Max who had just come up the stairs, and a sudden happy growl from Renny, followed by an exasperated, "For Christ's sake, not again!" from Max. The last the people in the living room heard of Morana for that day was her startled shriek as she turned tail and inelegantly raced down the hallway, pursued by a very familiar giant tabby cat.

Cory giggled, once, weakly, and Bracken repeated the sound, helplessly, into her hair. Green chuckled, for a moment, and then the three of them stilled. Green's aura of power abruptly faded, but the face he turned towards Orson and Corklish was grim.

"I think discussions are over for this day." He said quietly, and his lips only twisted a little at the understatement. "But before you go, I need you to answer one thing that Morana refused to. Where are the vampires?"

Orson looked back at Green, and all but rolled on his back and grinned like submissive retriever. "I don't know." He whined. "We all have contacts, here. Their leader, Andres, keeps one were on retainer for each vampire, so that his people always have food. After you called, I contacted my people—none of us have had a call from a vampire in over three days." He swallowed, looked away. "Tasha is a friend—she has a number of steady donors, so I don't get to be food that often, but I...I hope that she's okay."

Green nodded. "Grace told me this morning that she hasn't met any of Andres' people. No one's answering messages—not Andres, not Robert—there's forty vampires in this city, and not a one of them available to talk. She'll be going out tonight on a true hunt. She will need one of your people for sustenance, and as many as you can spare to help."

"They'll be here tonight." Orson agreed eagerly, trying to make up for his earlier obstructionism. "Eleven O'clock."

"Then you have things to do." Green told him, and Orson backed out, and down the hall, running into a surprised Max on the way.

The face Green turned to Clorklish was not the face he had turned towards Morana, or even Orson. "I'm grateful for all you've given us so far." He said, and nodded towards Cory, who was lying with her head on Bracken's shoulder, looking empty and lost. "I'm especially grateful for the help you've given to my beloved. Please, all I ask of your folk is that you keep us apprised of any other overtures Goshawk makes towards you." He paused, and his look turned conspiratorial, and grim. "And be sure to make it known that I have sided with you—and so have my people. By all means spread the fact that Folsom has no more vampires—but try to keep Cory's name out of it, agreed?"

Clorklish bowed, truly respectful. His wizened little face then took on a moment of concentration, and he used a thick fingernail to open a small red line on his brown, wrinkled arm "It would be my honor to ally with you, Green of shadows, Green of streams, Green of quiet, Green of floods and droughts." He sang, tasting his own blood as he did so. Then, with surprising dignity, he offered his wrist to Green, who bowed to the offering and touched the little gnome's wrist to his lips. "By touch, blood and song, my sidhe." Clorklish said formally, "Mine are bound to you."

"I thank you, Master Clorklish." Green said, moved beyond words. "Completing the binding could make you formidable enemies—are you sure?"

Clorklish smiled in earnest then, and his wrinkled face suddenly appeared wicked and puckish. Green could see, in that wicked grin, how the images of the nasty little goblins had spread throughout Christendom like wildfire, back in the dark ages of Europe. "I've prayed to the Goddess for a chance to align with you, Lord Green." He said gleefully. "Your call this morning was like hearing Her voice in Matins bells."

Green bowed again, and much as Clorklish had, ran his nail along his wrist so that a small red line against his cloud white flesh followed, and he offered it to Clorklish, humming under his breath. A sudden flash of green and blue light colored the room like a disco ball and Clorklish crowed with triumph. And with that sound, and a deep bow, the little man practically skipped out of Green's living room. He looked behind him for a moment, and turned to flash a quick grin at his now acknowledged leader. "I'll send some brownies up here to fix your door, sir." And with a bare acknowledgement of Green's surprised thanks, the little gnome was gone from the room.

"Green…" Bracken's voice, empty and lost, called Green back to the two on the couch. "Green…I think she's in shock."

"As are we all." Green agreed, looking musingly after the little gnome who had now brought more than a thousand tiny, but devoted lives under Green's aegis with one surprising move. He came back to Bracken abruptly, and to the new pain added to the fragile skin barely grown over the old one.

"Come here, my loves." He murmured, and helped Bracken up, with his arms full of Cory. With infinite gentleness he guided them into Cory's room, and took her from Bracken, and they were all so stunned and exhausted, there was not even a hiccup of power from the three-way touch.

"I don't understand." She whispered, and he murmured nothings against her face, pointed now, almost pixie-like in its plain prettiness.

"Sleep." He said at last. "We'll be here when you wake." Her eyes closed without a flutter, and he pulled the comforter back and laid her down on the sheets, removing her shoes and tucking her in carefully.

"I don't understand." Bracken said behind him, a hint of irony in his voice, and Green reached out and took Bracken's hands in his own. Bracken had been a lover, early in his adulthood, when elves experiment. Until Cory, who had changed everything for all of them, Bracken and Adrian had been especially close. When they hadn't been lovers, they had been best friends, brothers of the spirit, and friendly competition for the same women. Green believed truly that all that had kept Bracken alive when Adrian died was the fact that Green and Cory survived.

He pressed his face against Bracken's, putting his hands on the other elf's shoulders and kissing him on the forehead. "It means, my brother," He murmured, "That you and Arturo are the best of our people, and that you must hold onto that greatness, or we will never survive."

Bracken nodded, weeping still tears. "As are you, leader." He said at last. Green kissed the side of his temple, then, and murmured "Sleep, my brother." And then caught Brack's body in his arms as he fell. He laid him next to Cory and pulled off both his shoes, tucking the dark green coverlet under their chins. As he did so, he thought with bitterness and bemusement that he may want to get used to that idea.

Feeling a little lost, he wandered back into the living room, noting dryly that the brownies were there already, and that Max was leading Renny past them by the scruff of the neck. Renny had a scrap of material hanging from her teeth that looked suspiciously like Morana's once impeccable white jumpsuit, and Green summoned up enough energy to grin wickedly.

"Come here, lovely." He said to Renny, and obligingly she hopped into his lap with a thump. She was tiny as a girl, but a hundred lb. girl still made a hundred lb. housecat. She purred, kneading slightly on his blue jeans, and rubbing her cheek against his face. "We all love you, right?" He whispered in Renny's ear, and was rewarded by the steady rumbling sound from her chest. "Good. I'll tell you what, then, 'kay luv?" She licked his face, and he laughed a little, stroking her gently behind the pointed tabby ears. "You promise to stay girl for a whole day, then, and I promise to let you chase that snotty rat from here to home as a pussy cat, yes?" Renny gave him what amounted to a kitty cat chuckle, and she jumped smoothly off his lap to curl up on a violet throw pillow and fall instantly asleep.

Green cocked his head at Max, saying, "Obviously she'll think about that." And then he scrubbed his face with his hands with a sigh.

Max flopped down onto the couch next to Green with a similar sigh. "Nice door." He said, gesturing loosely to where the brownies, apparently *extremely* grateful for Green's offer of protection, were building a lovely piece of art featuring light oak, brass work and glass. He didn't hardly blink as the tiny, brown creatures swarmed over the handiwork, pulling materials from what appeared to be thin air.

Green watched them for a moment, and gave an actual laugh. "They're a marvel, aren't they?" He asked, sincerely. "Morana thinks marvels like that are her due."

"How?" Asked Max, watching the show just like Green. Green could tell by his widened eyes that the stalwart officer was trying to hide his delight.

"Court was already established here when Adrian and I got off the boat in San Francisco." Green said, seemingly out of nowhere. "Mist and Morana weren't in charge then, but it didn't matter—they were on the ship right behind me, trying to reign me in. But I wasn't good enough to be free at court, so I didn't want their grace or their tribute, and Adrian didn't give a fuck about them anyway and we just wanted to be left the hell alone. We moved up to the hills, where no one gave a damn, and I promised A' that after nineteen years of having the shit kicked out of him and the spirit buggered out the other end, that nothing would ever hurt him again." He turned to Max, then, as though he remembered who he was talking to. "It's a powerful thing, a promise like that."

"I don't understand." Max said honestly, and Green almost laughed again, because there was a lot of that going around. Instead he shrugged.

"People—our kind of people—came to know that Adrian was safe because I would keep him safe. And then the weres started coming to Adrian because he's a vampire, and the Goddess made them sort of a team—unlimited blood supply from the were-creatures, unlimited muscle from the vampires—and A'...well, the only good thing Adrian had ever known came with that promise of safety, right?"

Max nodded. He was a sheriff, and still young and idealistic enough to know what that promise could mean.

"So..." Green trailed off.

"You keep your promises, right?" Adrian's face was absolutely guileless with faith in the lamplight.

"I do my best!" Green had protested, rolling over from his stomach and looking at his beloved laying beside him in the newly carved bed. He was remembering, less than a year before, when he'd had to push a make-shift coffin into soft earth with main strength, to avoid the approach of a quick dawn. Neither of them had been prepared for the bright brutality of the summers in the Sierra foothills.

Adrian leaned back to meet Green's eyes. He'd just finished feeding from the back of Green's thigh, and the dinner and the lovemaking had left both of them bright and ruddy. For a moment, Green could almost imagine Adrian was still the living, breathing young man he'd rescued two years before, but there was wisdom in Adrian's eyes now that Green hadn't seen then, and his beloved hadn't needed to breathe for a thousand thousand heartbeats. "Your best has worked so far." Adrian said optimistically, and, when Green would have protested, he'd been silenced with a kiss that grew and became passionate before he could even gather his thoughts. Goddess, Adrian had always been able to scramble every rational thought Green had ever had. But, still, when the kiss had ended, he tried to put his misgivings into words.

"Shhhh." Adrian said, his body weight pressing Green face down into the soft mattress of down and straw. Adrian's chest was cool, and hard and rippled against Green's back, and his manhood was also cool and hard and rippled against Green's taut bottom, and it was hard to pull himself from the sensuality of his beloved and into the worry for them both, but he managed. Adrian licked the curve of Green's ear, his breathy laughter spilling him into the moment. "You try, I try...the were's will try—that's the best we can do, right?"

"Right..." Green murmured shakily. "Right. Fine. Just...just..." And Adrian just did, and for a night, a moment, Green believed their best would do.

"So Adrian gave that promise freely." Green said, yanking himself back into the present with a wrench that was almost physical. "He started looking for others to give it to, in fact. And then other fey started coming to me, hating the whole court thing as much as I had, and...I promised to protect them, to the best of my ability. And when that failed, I gave them whatever I could to ease the pain."

"Your body?" Max asked, and for once his voice wasn't full of censure, just the struggle to understand something that was outside his ken.

"My love." Green corrected simply. "Love is a simple thing, I've always believed. Emotionally, love is safety. Physically, love is pleasure. Love is simple to us—it doesn't come with rules and boxes. Sex is never loveless to the fey," His face tightened for a moment, "To *my* fey anyway," He amended, "So it's never a moral problem. Not as long as the respect is there." There was a silence, and Max nodded, as though he could almost grasp what Green was trying to say.

"But the problem with love," Green continued, trying to make the matter clear to himself as well, "Is that it tends to grow." He looked at the door then being quickly built, tiny board by tiny nail, and shook his head in exasperation. "Adrian and I...we managed to build more than five times the numbers of the fey in this part of the state. Do you know why?"

Max shrugged. "Love?" He asked, too lost to be sardonic.

"Close." Green's mouth tried not to twist. "Elitism. You know—that force that meant that I wasn't good enough to be a part of the court of San Francisco as an equal? Well, it wouldn't have taken in the people that Adrian and I bound to us by love."

Max's lips formed the same twist. "So...you basically told them all to fuck off, you'd live your own life..."

"And then they envied the life I lived." Green finished. "And they couldn't stand that."

Green stood abruptly, and looked sadly at Max. "I've been betrayed by my own people, Officer Max. They knew Sezan was here in the states. They told him where Adrian lived. They *must* have sent him to Crispin. It's my bet that they hoped that by destroying Adrian, they'd break me. And as a result, they left us all—Cory, Bracken, Renny, myself—even Arturo and Grace, desolate and empty and hurting. And now I'm here to save their asses." And with that, Green couldn't bear to sit in his embassy of a living room any longer. With an abrupt movement, he left the apartment, careful not to slam the lovely new door.

It would have been wonderful if he could have simply blurred to Mist's faerie hill. But Green's apartment was in the city proper, in spite of the scant little park across the street, and the city—however cosmopolitan—was not good enough for the high sidhe; they had to make their home with land, lots of it. An elf lost his life energy when his feet went for too long without touching earth.

However, a century or so earlier, land had been in plenty on the peninsula, and although the more populated the state became, the more dear the land cost, those who had lived there for a hundred and fifty hears had at their disposal a good twenty-acre estate, tucked back west of the 280 interchange, somewhere east of Seal Rock and hidden in the hills. Green could find it—it was a good forty-five minutes of commute from the heart of the city, but Green's anger hadn't dimmed in the drive.

Because it was winter, the hills approaching the estate were green, but the sea wind was bitterly cold. Green had left the apartment down the stairs and through the parking garage, and was wearing only the Aran sweater and jeans he'd been wearing inside. Shoes—a human convention that most of the fey avoided when they could—had been left in the hallway as he'd stormed out.

It didn't matter. Green opened the wrought iron gates (built by humans, since only spells and upholstery could protect the fey from even the metal frame of the cars they rode in) with a wave of his hand and continued down the drive in the sturdy automobile that he'd bought and spelled to protect Cory and Renny from their own mortality. Obviously, he thought with some bitterness, this had been an empty precaution, since his own people had conspired to destroy his family. That anger stormed through him again, enough to give him the power to stride through the wood and glass doors at the entrance without opening them, and to blow through the house as a wind of fury, finding with unerring accuracy the large living area where Morana's lover was holding court.

Mist was the true leader of the coastal cities from San Francisco to Monterey, and the more central parts of California as well. Green took no small amount of satisfaction in the fact that in terms of area, his domination of the northern part of the state took in more than three times Mist's amount of territory, and that the sheer number of supernatural beings that looked to him for protection at the very least, and livelihood should it be needed, tallied more than five times what Mist's numbers were. More than that now, Green thought grimly, since over half of Mist's court now claimed allegiance to Green through Clorklish. Of course Mist didn't count many of Green's people *as* people, but Green didn't care. He'd made a promise of safety, and he'd kept it, and good things had followed, and Mist could never, not in a hundred years, not in a thousand, claim the same thing.

When Green held court, he held it at banquet, with his seconds sitting near by, and though there was usually a pecking order in who brought concerns to Green's table, anyone in his hall was allowed to approach him, with either a concern or conversation. It was often noisy, and occasionally rude, but never disrespectful, and Green and Arturo and Adrian used to accomplish more in one banquet than governors of small states did in one session of congress. Now that Grace had taken over—temporarily, she insisted—as Adrian's successor, the same still applied, and Green hadn't thought of changing his system of rule since it had started, informally, when the people under his aegis could all fit under the roof of his hill.

When Mist held court, he sat in a high backed satin chair, surrounded by his sprites to illuminate him, with Morana seated at his side, and a bevy of high sidhe seated on various colored cushions surrounding him. The long-bodied, elegant, and beautiful sidhe were a useful chorus. They laughed when Mist laughed, mocked those who met with Mist's disapproval, and applauded his every decision.

Today, as Green strode through the room, regardless of decorum and blazing with a frightening brilliance of power and anger, they could only stare in shock.

"Green!" Mist was so rarely taken unaware that Green might have savored the surprise on his face.

"Fucking bloodless traitor." Green responded viciously, and felt even more satisfaction when he watched Mist—and his entire group of elegant courtiers—recoil.

"I'm sorry…" When it was obviously that not only was Mist not sorry at all, but that he was about to get nasty, which was fine with Green too.

"You've never been sorry about anything." Green cut off, and for a moment, he could hear his own voice, nearly three-hundred years before.

"What do you mean I can't leave? This isn't what I came here for, Mist. You said if I didn't like it, I could leave." Green's voice echoed in a tapestry-strewn room with no door and no window. Until this moment he hadn't known the room was a beautiful prison.

Mist had smiled then, but it hadn't been the kind smile Green was used to. "I'm sorry little Green." *He'd said.* "But your talents are too…enjoyable to let you go…"

"Not true." Mist replied, breaking into that unwelcome vision of the past. "I was sorry when you left Oberon's."

"Only because Oberon was so pissed he kicked you out." Green returned evenly. "And then you arrived here, and you got to stay in this place of mist and shadows and we didn't give a shit about each other…until now…why, Mist? All the fucking pain and turmoil—why?"

Mist blinked. His appearance fit his name, actually—he was all about grays and beiges, right down to his hair, which hung in a thin, colorless queue down his back. Green, who had known him for nearly three-hundred years, knew that blink. Mist was preparing to evade the question. Elves were physically unable to lie—it was one of the God's limitations on their forms, since he seemed to feel that the Goddess' get had been given so many other gifts that humans were not. Lying came with nausea, headaches, and physical body pains until the truth was either told, or made to come true. But as with humans, some elves learned to live past the discomfort. Mist couldn't out and out lie—but he could make promises he didn't intend to keep, and he could equivocate with the most practiced of the human lawyers. Mist and Orson had always gotten along well, Green mused, but there was no room for evasion today.

"Causing pain was not our intention." Mist answered carefully, and Green knew that to be true.

"Only because you could give a shit about how you make others feel. Don't fuck with me, today, Lord Mist."

Mist smiled faintly, caught the eyes of his hangers-on with a superiority that used to make Green quail, until he'd lived in this free land long enough for complete confidence. "Since I haven't 'fucked' with you for quite some time, I could hardly expect to have that pleasure today, now could I?"

Green smiled grimly, knew what would hurt, and said it, just to make himself feel better. "Since it hasn't been a 'pleasure' in more than two-hundred years, I wouldn't expect it anytime soon."

Mist flinched as though struck. "So we've learned to lie, have we, little Green?"

"Say it." Mist had never been cruel, before they'd come to court, Green thought wretchedly. He'd lived for fifteen hundred years, and never known his own kind were capable of this depth of callousness.

"If you need me to." Green had answered proudly, but he knew his own bravado from his own capabilities.

"Oh, I'm not the one who needs to be able to say it, little Green." Mist sneered.

"Very well then." Green swallowed. "I feel nothing but contempt for you now, Mist." And this had been true. "You're cruel and wanton and ugly in places I didn't know existed." And this had also been true. "In fact, I never gave a cockroach's cock about you." Nausea had rolled over him then, but he'd held his bile. Anything, to avoid the humiliation of having his lover see how thoroughly he'd been beguiled.

"Now Green..." Mist had been both kind and condescending, and his hand had been gentle on the side of Green's face.

"I've never cared about you." Green said again; his skin was clammy and his palms were slick with sweat.

"Not even when we were in the woods together? Just you and me and the wood nymphs and pixies?" And for a moment, Mist's confidence had wavered, a sadness passing across his sand and shadow colored face. "Not even when you allowed me to mark you with touch, blood, and song?"

"Not even then." Green finished weakly. And then he had run for his chamber pot, where he was violently ill as Mist laughed mockingly by his side.

"I've learned to see the truth for what it is." Green said now, pushing that memory away, replacing it with the look on Adrian's face, Adrian, his beloved, Adrian, his beloved's beloved, who had loved Green and trusted him as no one had. Adrian, whose quiet faith in Green had made all of Green's other accomplishments—including Cory's love for him—possible. Adrian—who had swooped in to defend Cory, and Bracken, and Green and who had died before their eyes, exploding in a sheen of blood and blowing his soul through Cory's like summer wind through a dandelion, scattering her strength and her joy to the winds. A rumble of heartache thundered through Green's chest. Eons ago, he had believed the best of the elf standing in front of him, and that mistake in judgment had cost him Adrian.

"Yes," Green continued, his voice taut with pain, "I know the truth, and the truth is, you have exactly the sort of cold soul to have done what I'm accusing you of."

"What is it I've done?" Mist asked, condescension dripping from his voice. But his gaze darted, just a little too quickly, to check on the appreciation of his court. Mist was afraid. And with that guess, Green could see through the glamour of insouciance that always cloaked him like his namesake, and could smell the fear, rolling off him like fog.

Green smiled. "You tell me, Mist—what could you have possibly done to me that would justify me laying hands on you in your own home?"

"I'm sure I don't..." And it was a lie. They both knew it. He said it anyway. "I'm sure I don't know." He kept his voice firm, and his eyes fixed desperately on Green as sweat popped out on his brow.

"Don't know what?" Green asked pleasantly.

Mist took a deep breath. "I don't know what could have justified your..." He stopped and took another breath.

"My what?" Green murmured, keeping Mist's eyes locked with his. "What is it I'm feeling right now?"

"Your grief!" Mist howled, with triumph, because, Green knew, Mist honestly couldn't understand grief. Grief was an honest emotion that had had never gripped Mist because he'd also never known love and never known loss.

"It's not grief that makes me want to rip your heart out with my bare hands, *Lord* Mist." Green ground from between his teeth. "Now tell me, why I hate you at this moment more than I've ever hated another being, with all of the formidable power at my command."

"We didn't know Goshawk would attack your girlfriend...I swear to Goddess I didn't know..." Mist cried out, and Green had to reign in his temper, because the truth was that Mist just hadn't cared, not that he hadn't known, but the other man was very good at splitting hairs, and Green just stood and looked, and waited, knowing intimately the nausea, the aching body pains, the thundering in the head, that was turning his old lover, his old tormenter, a sickly shade of grey.

But Mist had never been strong, and Green didn't have long to wait.

"It's not my *fault.*" He cried at last, tears running down his face from the sheer agony of holding a lie of that magnitude inside. "We gave the little bastard the silver net and told him to go out make your life miserable, but we didn't expect him to attack other elves with it, or kill sprites!" He fell to his knees then, arms wrapped around his middle, where, Green knew, the cramps would be subsiding enough for Mist to actually breathe. "Fuck it all, Green…I wanted you to come to me for *help*…I wanted you to come in and beg, and then I'd make you…we could have that…what we had at Oberon's…and I didn't give a fuck whether your piece of dead flesh were walking or prone and I'm *glad* he's dead, because now I have you in my city, and you *have* to deal with me and my court."

It was the detail about the silver net that added the final flash to Green's temper. Bending down he wrapped his hand around the silk shirt at Mist's chest and hauled him up face to face. "I will *never* deal with your court." He hissed. "And as Goddess is my witness, I will find a way to avenge my beloved."

"It didn't take you long to find a new one." Mist said cattily, too arrogant now that he was only inches away from Green's full fury.

"Do you seek death?" Green asked, incredulous. "You arrange for the death of my beloved, and my beloved's beloved, and you laugh at me? What do you think can come from this, Mist? I don't rely on your court for *anything*. And you rely on mine for things you don't even think of." He spared a glance around the room, confirming his first suspicions. "Everything in this room was bought from one of my merchants. Your food was grown in my orchards." He smiled then, because Mist didn't know this yet. "Your lower fey—they answer to me now." And he enjoyed watching Mist's surprise. "What do you expect to gain from making me angry enough to kill?"

Mist smiled then, as though he knew something Green didn't. "You can't kill me, little Green." He said gently. "You still wear my mark on your skin—or don't you remember?"

"What's this, Green?" Adrian asked, the second morning they had woken up together, happy in the cabin of the ship, before Adrian's rape and Sezan's death, when they'd believed that happy endings were easy. He was pointing to a small cloud, the size of a silver dollar, grey, indistinct, moving in an angry roil in its fixed position, tattooed on Green's hip. Green looked at it in disgust, and sent a course of will through his body. The little spot didn't even pain him as it disappeared.

Green laughed then, and laughed and laughed and laughed, dropping Mist to the ground where he tumbled gracelessly to his hands and knees. With a grim sneer, he looked around the room, to Mist's court, every sidhe hanging avidly on to the exchange between the two leaders. Every one in the room was more than a thousand years old, and Green was quite sure that none of them had seen a struggle of powers like this in their entire lives. Fuck them. Let them see.

With deft fingers he undid the buttons of his jeans and dropped them to his knees, then turned his back on Mist, looking at the other man over the long, elegant line of his shoulder.

"I haven't worn your mark in years, Mist." He said quietly. "Since I woke up in Adrian's arms." He smiled faintly, thought about what Cory would say at this moment, improvised. "You can kiss my skinny white ass and fear for your life, Lord Mist. The only thing keeping me from killing you is the idea that your own self-denial might hurt worse." With that, he swept his jeans up his hips and did the fly, and prepared to walk out of Mist's hall with his head held high. But Mist had one parting shot, Green thought bitterly, later. The other man had always been so much better at inflicting wounds than Green had been, probably because he took pride in it when Green took none.

"What kind of leader lets his second grab death with both hands, Lord Green?" Mist asked, as Green started walking. "I may have pointed Sezan in the right direction, but you're the one who let Adrian die. Remember that, Lord Green! You're the one who let him grab that silver net, not me!"

Mist's voice followed him out of the waiting area, and out of the house, and it was still ringing in Green's ears as he tore out of the driveway, ripping the BMW through the wrought iron gates using metaphysical power and momentum, and leaving them in a clanging pile behind him.

CORY

Bereft

I woke up surrounded by warm man, and assumed for a moment that it was Green. I gave a groan, and a snuggle, and my hands found their way under a T-shirt, and I dug my face into a strong chest and inhaled, just to smell the comfort of my beloved. But the smell was wrong. The chest felt lovely—smooth skinned, hairless, broad, hard little nipples that pointed under the spread of my palms, but the smell…

Green smells like sun warmed grass, or the foothills right after it rains, in the spring before the grasses turn brown, and sometimes, when he was aroused, or really happy, he smelled like a meadow full of mustard flowers and lupins. This man smelled like stone in the sun, or like trees growing over a freshwater pool

"Oh, shit." I murmured, and tried to move myself apologetically backwards. "Apologies, Bracken." I said formally. "My hands started moving before my brain woke up."

"By all means, stay asleep." Brack rumbled above me. There was amusement in his voice, but arousal too, and I knew that the familiar feeling that was nudging me in the stomach was all male, all hard, and all ready for action. I bolted up and was out of the bed before my next heartbeat.

"Green won't need to put us together again." I said stiffly, scrubbing at my face and trying to wake up. The gentleness on Bracken's face was enough to make me stumble and sit down abruptly. He moved around to sit next to me and cup my chin in his fingers.

"Hey," He murmured, "Don't worry." He smiled then, and used both hands to comb his fingers through my wild hair before taking my face in his hands and scenting the air lightly. "Can you smell that?" He asked. "That's you and Green, making love in this room. I know that smell. It permeates Green's hill—it's around corners, it lingers in front of your empty room, and at the oddest times, I smell it in the garden, with Adrian's smell mixed in. I love that smell. The scent of the two of you, intertwined, is home. I don't want that to go away." He leaned forward then and put his face in the crook of my neck, so he could smell the warmth rising from it. His nose touched my skin, just enough to make me shiver. When he spoke again, it was right next to my ear, and his voice was deep, and his breath moved the fine hairs on my ear, starting a vibration deep within my eardrum. "But that smell, right there," He murmured, "That smell is all you. I love that smell too. I want to wear that smell on my skin and roll around in it. I want to live in that smell alone. But I don't want the smell of home to go away."

His words stopped my throat, and his hands on my face were so warm and sure. Goddess, I thought, feeling weak and liquid, I needed to touch him. Not in a sexual way, not now, but I needed to touch him. With a sigh I lay my head against his shoulders, and felt my back muscles relax when he wrapped his arms around me.

"You used the magic word, big brother." I said softly. "You said 'home'."

"I've been gone for three days and I want to go back." He said wryly, stroking my hair from my face. "How can you stand it?"

"It's so stupid." I murmured, a weak tear trickling down my nose. "I'm old enough to go away to school. But I didn't leave my parents home when I came here, I left *Green's* home. I fell in love with Adrian there. I fell in love with Green. I mean…" I sighed, helplessly, and looked up at Bracken, and his expression was grim, as always, but compassionate too, and I tried to articulate what had spilled out so helplessly on Green. And even though it was Bracken, and I had tried to be so strong for him, I thought that maybe he'd understand. "I fell in love with *home*. And it's so stupid!" I repeated, this time with passion. "I love this city. I love the clubs with the music. I love the stupid fog. I love the theatre. My whole life I wanted to get out of the freaking foothills of California, but now all I can think of is going back, because I fell in love with Green's home, and Green's people, and now I want to be there again. I mean I'm what? A hundred and fifty miles from home?"

"Too far." Bracken murmured. "You're too far from home."

"It feels like a hundred and fifty mile hole in my heart." I told him, feeling that hole heal a little, just to say it. "Can you really fall in love with a life? With a…preternatural flop house for the fey and undead, just by falling in love with its leaders?"

"Have you?" Bracken asked, kissing my hair.

"I guess so." I answered, feeling a little humbled by his tenderness. Big brother, Bracken—not a bad guy for someone I'd had to knee in the balls upon a first meeting. "I wish I could just, 'appear' like the sprites, and that I didn't even have to drive."

He chuckled then. "Speaking of the sprites," He said, his laughter brushing against the top of my head, "They've been whining to Green since we got here. It seems that you and Renny don't give them enough to do."

Crap on toast, I thought, I hadn't known any sprites had come with us. But then I tried asking myself when the last time one of us had cleaned a toilet had been, and I came up with a big fat blank, so I said archly, "They could always cook."

"But then you'd stop feeding them pizza." Bracken said sincerely, and I found myself giggling helplessly into his chest. "Nicky." He said suddenly, and my giggles died a natural death.

"What about him?" I asked, feeling dumb. "We were friends all semester, Renny Nicky and I. We went to clubs, saw some shows, drank a shit load of coffee. He told me that his family was in town, and he wanted a date to make them comfortable about him being here and going to school…" I felt so dumb about this. At first I'd wondered if he wanted a cover date—I had suspicions that he might be gay, and being surrounded by the fey and undead, almost bisexual by lifespan, curiosity, and lack of censure, I'd thought I'd be a good bet for that sort of thing. And a good friend.

"He wanted more." Bracken said flatly. I wondered if he knew this, or the thing he wanted to happen between us was speaking, and not knowledge.

"I figured that when he tried to kiss me." I said dryly. "I was going to say no."

"I thought so." Bracken said arrogantly.

"You wanted me to take another lover." I told him irritably. He could be such an asshole.

His fingers cupped my chin again, more roughly this time, and my head tilted up to meet his gaze. "When Adrian was alive, an inconsequential lover would have made your life easier." He said bluntly.

I bit my lip and stated the obvious. "Adrian is gone." I whispered.

"And I will not be an inconsequential lover." He told me firmly, and of a sudden, I felt a tingle through my body, one of those breathless, loin-gushing, nipple hardening rushes that said *Yes, Goddess, yes, I want this man to touch me every-*

where. And I realized that he was right. Adrian gave his day to the Goddess. Green gave his life to his people. Bracken would give himself only to me.

"You scare me." I told him bluntly, breathlessly, and before I could explain why, there was a tremendous ruckuss in the front room, and even as we rushed out my room to see what it was, I could feel an almost physical hurt where Bracken wasn't holding me anymore.

What met our eyes when we reached the living room stunned us silent for a moment. Renny was in giant house-cat form, tawny brown hair raised at the neck and lip curled over her long carnivorous teeth. She was standing on her hind legs with her forepaws on one of the two huge book shelves that flanked the front room, batting at a giant brown predatory bird with rust-colored tips to his black wing feathers.

Well, she was batting at Nicky Kestrel I realized when my shock had cleared and I got a good look at the bird. He was a lot worse for the wear, and I felt bad for him. Poor bird had gone home to Papa, and gotten some feathers ripped out, if the blood on his wings meant anything. And Renny was about to make his situation worse.

"Renny." I called. "Renny—sweetie, don't hurt him—look he's been hurt enough." But the only response I got from Renny was the growling in her throat that usually meant she was about to crunch on some poor pigeon. "Shit. Where's Green?" I looked around the room, and Max was standing near the couch, looking as though he were through with trying to get Renny to do anything at all, Bracken was behind me, and Green was nowhere to be seen.

"He took off right after you guys went down for your little nap." Max said unhappily. "Renny and I were watching TV, Nicky came and knocked on the door, I answered it, and the next thing I know, he's a bird, and she's right there. Have any of you ever thought of just putting a leash on her and forgetting the whole 'girl' thing?"

"Fuck you." I shot back, and my anger made my next command far more authoritative. "Renny, goddammit, ***down.***" I barked, and to my surprise she sat, her tail swishing, and the growling in her throat mutinous. I gave a sigh of relief and went over to her and crouched on my knees to speak in her ear, burying my hand in the silky fur at her nape. "Remember Nicky? I know he hurt me, but it was a mistake. He's a friend, remember?" Bracken made a sound in his throat that was similar to Renny's and I shot him a quelling look. "Don't start, you." I snapped, and then turned my attention back to Renny. "C'mon, sweetie." I cajoled. "Let him change into a boy again—we need to hear what he has to say." The growling in her throat stilled as she lay flat on the floor, putting her chin on her forepaws. I scratched the top of her head, and made a few clucking sounds to Nicky. I guess that's how you call a falcon—like I would have a freaking clue.

Nicky knew, apparently, what it meant, because he swooped gracefully down off the bookshelf to land on my arm. Then, with a miserable shiver, because I could see that he was missing a *lot* of feathers, he was suddenly standing in front of me, fully clothed and I would wonder at that later, because when Renny changed, her clothing didn't go with her. (This was why she spent her days in public wearing things like the flowing, shapeless woolen dress that Max still had in his hands.) But there he was, and he was bleeding and sobbing, and then stumbling into my arms. Ah, Goddess, I sighed. Poor Nicky. I wondered what hurt worse—the giant ripping wounds on his arms and chest, or the disillusionment of knowing that you've hurt people, and you couldn't take it back. Without a second thought, I wrapped my arms around him in comfort, and to my surprise, enough of the girl remained in Renny for her to change form and comfort him too.

"Stupid fucker." She murmured in her slight voice, but there was compassion there and affection too, and I realized that my rage against Nicky had faded completely. As I rocked him back and forth, I met Bracken's eyes, and between us was the knowledge that among us foothills folk, a whole new rage was starting to form, with an entirely different target.

"Fix him." Bracken muttered gruffly. "There's first aid in the darkling bathroom. I'm going to get find out where the hell Green went." And with that he grabbed Officer Max and pulled him through the front door. Renny's dress came sailing through the air to punctuate the snick of the lock, and I realized they wanted to give us a chance to talk to Nicky when he wouldn't be intimidated. Of course this was a total laugh, because Brack hadn't reckoned on his own capacity to scare Nicky shitless.

"Shh…" I told Nicky a few minutes later when he hissed in pain. His upper torso had been entirely raked by what appeared to be bird talons of a huge size. He grimaced and apologized, but I waved him off. I was frequently known to turn my head and vomit when confronted with great pain—who was I to throw stones?

"So," I began when I started the next bandage, "Are you really a Kestrel falcon, because you look bigger?"

"I'm Avian." He said shortly, then shrugged. "We're really all one kind of bird—but we started taking bird last names, through the years, sort of an Avian pride thing."

"Ah…" I said, taking a delicate swipe at the tanned skin on his upper arm with a cotton ball and hydrogen peroxide. The tan fascinated me for a moment, because you don't get tan from the sidhe or the vampires, but then I saw how deep the scratch was, and had to ask. "What got you?"

"Eyeass." He murmured. "I always knew he had a mean streak, but he turned on me in a heartbeat."

"What happened?" Renny asked, and because it was Renny it didn't sound like prying.

"Goshawk…" Nicky murmured, and shook his head. His usually flawless rust colored hair was a spiky mess, and he looked damned forlorn. "I told him—I told him that I'd taken something from you that you didn't want to give…I asked to get it back. He got the weirdest expression on his face…" His own expression twisted, and he looked at me, searching for words. "It was like a junkie, remembering his best fix…he said that no…I couldn't give that particular memory back. Then he got all sharp faced and said that he couldn't give back any of them." Nicky shook his head again, denying, I think, his leader's duplicity. I didn't blame him. It would be like finding out that your own people didn't give you the information you needed to save your beloved. Or like being date-raped by a friend.

"I asked him why." Nicky continued. "I asked him that, if this was just to make our people strong, why couldn't we only take what wasn't needed…and I said 'It's not like we're fighting for our lives or anything.' Goshawk said we were. He said that the Goddess' children would never let the Avians live—that they were too jealous of our God…"

Renny and I both laughed then, the kind of snork you make when your tongue is glued to the roof of your mouth in concentration and then you spit air out through it and you're not ready. "Your *God*…" Renny snorked incredulously, but I shushed her, because Nicky was looking hostile.

"We were taught that all shape changers were the Goddess' get." I said gently. "That the Goddess came down, frolicked a bit, and, well, bore the weres and made the vampires…" my voice trailed off with that one, because the story was unbelievably sad, "And that her adventures with the other are what created the fey." I finished. "You're a were—a shape changer. We just assumed you were Goddess' get."

Nicky looked pained. "That's what I was always taught too." He admitted. "I was told that the Goddess came down as a male hawk, and lived out the bird's life with one mate, and that's why hawks mate for life and we carry through the male line."

I grimaced. "Then what was that crap you were just…"

Nicky grimaced too. "Goshawk. As soon as I came into the city, he was inviting me to his hall, feeding me, having deep discussions about how we'd been lied to, and how we'd been deprived the love of God by the lies of the Goddess…"

"That's bullshit…" Renny burst out. "There's nothing in the stories about God not loving…"

"I know." Nicky said tiredly. "I know. It was bullshit. But I was alone in a new place, and I didn't know any other Goddess' get here…"

"You knew us!" Renny returned. "You had to know—if you couldn't smell were-tabby on me a mile away, you shouldn't have lived this long."

"*You* I knew about." Nicky conceded, "But you were…you were hurt…you seemed lost, and Cory was your only anchor, and I never even guessed what she was, until she nearly cooked me in the parking garage."

"Not before you mind-raped me first." I pointed out grimly, giving a scratch on his back an unnecessarily rough scrub with the wash cloth.

Nicky looked away from me, not even reacting to the physical pain. "You'll never know my shame." He said formally, and I sighed.

"So what did you say when Goshawk told you about the war?" I asked.

Nicky shrugged. "I said that I couldn't fight that war, and that I'd do everything I could to repair the damage I've wrought on the women I've stolen from."

"And then?"

"And then Eyeass and Osprey turned bird right there in the room and kicked my ass. And then I turned and barely got away." He grinned then, "Kestrels do pretty good in cities as well as wide open spaces." He said proudly, liking the play on his name.

"Well I'm glad you survived." I said at last, meaning it.

"All that," he said, pulling away from me and slipping on the clean T-shirt that Renny had snagged him from Green's drawer, "And I'll be lucky if that 'day lover' of yours doesn't kill me in my sleep."

"But you haven't met Gree…Oh…" I figured out after a moment, "You mean Bracken—he's not my 'day lover'. That's Green—he'll be back in a moment."

"Oh." Nicky said, frowning, "I must be out of practice, but I could have sworn…"

"It wasn't your imagination." Renny said in disgust. "Bracken would have made his move this summer, but he and Adrian didn't share well."

"I didn't know they'd ever tried." I murmured, not surprised as I might have been.

Renny shook her head, bemused by the antics of the other Goddess' get. "They were close, you know? When they weren't competing for the same girl, they were each other's booty call."

Nicky looked appalled, but I wasn't surprised at that either. The first time I'd seen Bracken, from a distance, I had guessed. "It makes sense." I said mildly. "Adrian loved women—if his childhood hadn't been so completely fucked up, he would have been a ladies man completely. But as it was…" I tried to put it into words. "As it was, women were something wonderful that he loved, but…but he could only relate to men as human beings, you know?"

"Until you." Renny said gently, as though aware she might have hurt me by her earlier candor.

"Until me." I agreed. "But," I continued crisply, starting to clean gauze, tape, and hydrogen peroxide out of the spacious bathroom, "That didn't last long, now did it?"

"How did he die?" Nicky asked into the sudden quiet.

"Adrian had enemies he didn't know about." And the bitterness in my voice had even Renny looking up, but then, Renny didn't know. "And they started out preying upon the were folk."

"Mitch was the first to go." Renny muttered, and I was surprised because I didn't think she could even say it.

"And there were others." I finished for her. "They started coming after me, because I was Adrian's girl…but…"

"But you can cook people?" Nicky said as I tried to put that first awkward, terrifying, exhilarating use of power into words.

I nodded, painfully. "You don't know the half of it." I added dryly. "When they figured that out, they forced a confrontation by snatching Renny-puss here, and cop-fuck Max." It was my turn to look away. "Sezan worked with sound. He had this organ hooked up to a big silver net…"

"I tried to warn him…" Renny choked out forlornly. That guilt had weighed heavily on her, no matter how hard I tried to comfort her.

"I know, puss, I know." I soothed her, hugging her to me. She was wearing that shapeless wool thing, and underneath it her ribs were clearly defined. Neither of us had been eating much, this last semester. "So he flew into it and disintegrated." Nicky gasped, and I found that I was bright eyed, on the brink of falling apart, but I couldn't just leave the story there. "So Green—he and Adrian had been, like, *like*…" I was making vague gestures in the air with my hands because 'lovers' was such a tame word for what Green and Adrian had been. Protector to protected, parent to child, oldest child to youngest child, brothers in arms, best friends, best lovers…not a single human word covered the span of their relationship, the scope of Green's grief…"Anyway, they'd been together since the gold rush, and Green's heart felt like it was ripped out, so he let his grief rip out Sezan's heart and Crispin's heart literally. He held their beating hearts in his hands until they both barfed blood and died."

Nicky's face went little gray around his pouty lips. "And you?" He asked in a tight voice.

"You know, in Star Trek," I said musingly, "When you hear that phaser start charging, and you know that it either needs to be deactivated or it will explode.?"

"Yeah…"

"That was me. Green…well, he knew I was a weapon, so he grabbed my arms while I was charging, and I could still feel Adrian, like baby's breath in my face, and so it was the three of us again. We…I…" How to explain? "I do fearsome things, when I'm touching people who love me…" Understatement. And there was more to it, but it was on the fringes of that big black hole that Nicky himself had left. Unlike that memory, though, this one was mine, and it was clear, and, Goddess help me, it was with me forever because no one else would want to claim it. "I charged. And I charged. And Green screamed at his people to move, and they moved, and like a good weapon, I fired."

"What do you mean?"

I turned from Renny who was holding my hand to her cheek, and looked Nicky in the eye. "I mean you were lucky, Nicky. I melted two acres of slag rock into obsidian that night. And I turned a hundred vampires to vapor and dust." Then my voice choked on the few small details that always seemed to hurt the worst. "I almost killed Arturo because he was rescuing Renny at the time…and Bracken's hair…" It had been beautiful, like a black silk cloak. "Bracken too…" I forced out. My throat was so tight I could barely speak, and suddenly, I had to leave the room.

"I killed a hundred people that night." I said evenly from the doorway, clinging to the shreds of my composure. I looked back at Nicky, sitting forlornly on the top of the toilet, all of his wounds neatly bandaged. "You know, Nicky, I would have given you that memory for free."

I would have liked to have run into my room then and fallen apart, but Bracken was down the hall standing very still so we couldn't hear that he was back. We looked at each other levelly for a moment, until he realized that I wasn't going to cry on him any more that night, and then he spoke, his voice irritated.

"You make too much out of the hair." He said gruffly. "It will grow back."

"It's not your hair that hurts me, genius." I snapped, walking by him. I was tired of crying, because I was tired of remembering that no matter how hard I cried, there was always more hurt waiting for me when I was done. And if I touched Bracken I might fall completely apart. But it was oh, so tempting. Remembering my earlier skin hunger for him, the way my palms still tingled from his smooth chest, I thought that maybe I needed to clear my head and so I was very careful not to touch shoulders as we passed in the hallway. "It's that I almost killed you." Whew, I was past him, without feeling the pressure of his actual touch.

"You did worse than that." He said bleakly, reaching out to me and brushing my own wild hair with his fingertips. I didn't have an answer there. Knowing that he and Adrian had been lovers and rivals for lovers made our fate together seem almost more certain, but right then, he didn't sound very happy about it. "Green's in the front room." He sighed at last, when I didn't launch myself at him and go all soft in his arms. Then he went down the hallway, I assume to tell Renny and Nicky. I rounded the corner and sagged against the wall out of his vision. I wondered vaguely if I had ever known that love could hurt this much.

Green was in the kitchen with Grace, and I don't recall ever seeing him so very much in need of me as he was that moment. I rushed into his arms almost before he could put down his kitchen knife and carrots and did my very best to wrap myself around his body and give him everything my body had to take that strain and weariness off the clean, lovely lines of his face. He managed to put the vegetables down and he picked me up, with my legs wrapped around him and took what I was offering, giving his own warmth in return. We stayed like that for a moment, but eventually he had to slide me down against his body, and he leaned back against the counter, touching my chin with his fingers.

"Where'd you go?" I asked, worried. He looked so tired.

"To the leader of the elves in this city." He told me, then, wryly, "Except they live out by Seal Rock, and there was traffic."

I frowned at him. "You need to stop taking off on us like that." I admonished. This summer he had taken off in a panic once after I was attacked and stormed right into the enemy's lair. Adrian and I had laid into him for days after that, but 1800 years of living doesn't necessarily make your learning curve steep. "Have us flunkies go, delegate or something." I told him. Behind us I heard Grace make a harrumphing sound that meant she'd lectured him on this same thing, and I winced. Mothers lecture. Lovers accept.

"I'm sorry." I murmured, and buried my face into his neck.

"My lack of leadership must be showing." He returned, and his voice was subdued. What had they said to him? Suddenly I wanted to fry every elf in San Francisco almost more than I wanted to cook Goshawk and have Grace truss him up for dinner.

"What did they say to you?" I asked, and Green just shook his head.

"We have history, Mist and I." He evaded after a moment. "Mist knows where to hurt, that's all."

"I hate him." I whispered fiercely. "Whoever the fuck he is, don't let him make you feel like this." I ordered. "You are everything that is good about a leader, everything that we love. Don't let them use that old world 'we're so fucking superior' bullshit to make you doubt yourself. We need you to be you."

Green smiled at me, all that compassion in his eyes, and he cupped my face in his hands, as though it were delicate, and precious. "You must never leave me." He said solemnly. "You may take as many lovers as you want, but you must promise to always be here to make me feel like I can do all that needs to be done."

"Even till I'm old and wrinkly." I told him, both seriously and lightly. Goddess, I wanted to see him smile some more.

"You will never be old and wrinkly." He returned, smiling some more, and I grinned back until his mouth closed over mine. Our kiss deepened, lengthened, made me want and ache, and then Grace cleared her throat again and we separated, giggling a little. His expression grew serious again, but it was his usual, capable seriousness, and I was reassured. "So, luvie," He said after a moment, keeping the crinkles at the corners of his eyes, "Bracken tells me that little Nicky is back—how is he?"

I grimaced. "Sadly disillusioned and about a pint low." I told him, and he nodded, thinking.

"Well, there's not much I can do about the disillusion," He said truthfully. "But tell me—have you forgiven him truly?"

I sighed. "Yes." I said after a moment. "He was lost—truly lost—even from the faith that he knew he believed." I shrugged. Even in the depths of my grief, I had never been as lost as Nicky had been, a stranger in a strange city, without kin or kind. "Yes—I think Nicky has paid for what he did." I said, and like that, my anger against him evaporated. I had so many other people to want to make pay for those gaping holes in my memory that hurt whenever I felt for them.

"Well then," Green responded, breaking away from me and squaring his shoulders. "Let's see what I can do about him being a pint low."

"He's pretty homophobic." I called to him as he started down the hall. "Be delicate."

Green turned to me and smiled brilliantly. "We'll cure him of *that,* now, won't we?" He said wickedly, and then vanished down the hall.

There was silence in the kitchen then, for a moment, until Grace, ever practical, slapped the vegetable peeler and carrot that Green had left on the counter smack into my palm. "Dinner doesn't make itself." She said crisply, and I turned toward the sink. We worked in a comfortable silence for a few heartbeats, while I tried hard not to think about Bracken.

"So will you?" She asked after a moment.

"Will I what?" I asked, lulled by the whole 'food preparation' bit, and not prepared for conversation.

"Will you take another lover?" Her voice was nothing but curious, in that way that girlfriends are curious.

I looked at her, as she deftly chopped garlic to add to the mashed potatoes, and then moved to toss some pine nuts into the salad. She was tall, red headed, and lanky, wide-set cheekbones and skin that had been tanned and freckled when Adrian had brought her over as a vampire. I knew she'd been suffering from breast cancer, but thought her hair must have grown back since her conversion— only for vampires is that myth about hair and fingernails growing after death true. She had a kind, gruff, mother face, I thought. Adrian had told me that she had visited her daughters in their dreams for years after she had died, and I wondered how hard that had been, to choose to live, but to have to let your children keep going without you.

"I...well..." And I was having trouble answering her question.

"I'll take that as a 'I've got someone in mind but my insides are so muddled I can't give you a straight answer.'" She improvised dryly.

I shrugged, laughing a little. "I was planning to stay faithful to Green." I said after a moment.

"But..." She prodded.

I shrugged again.

"But..." She prodded again, and then finished the sentence herself. "But Green needs to lead his people, and most elves are a little fuzzy on this 'monogamy' thing."

"Boy howdy are they ever." I agreed emphatically.

"There's no law that says you have to take your lover's lovers." Grace replied, and there was sympathy on her face.

I thought about it. "If Adrian hadn't died," I thought after a moment, "It never would have occurred to me."

"I don't think it would have occurred to anyone." The woman next to me said gently. "That doesn't mean it's not right."

I squeezed my eyes shut tight for a moment. "You were mortal." I whispered. "Do you remember when any of this felt strange and right at the same time? Do you remember when you were supposed to have one lover, a husband, and live happily ever after because love could do all that?"

"Oh yes." She sighed. "I watched my family, after I died." She went on, trying to pretend her voice was not thick and choked. "And I kept expecting my husband to date again, find a girlfriend, find someone else to share his life with...I did. But I watched, and he kept bumbling about the house, and gruffly loving our daughters...Goddess, he was so tender to them, it made me weep blood...and I thought, "He's doing okay...he'll be okay..." And I thought I was good with that. I had been feeling all bad about my darkling lovers and I started enjoying taking men to my bed when I was taking my blood—it was wonderful and tremendous and free, after those clumsy human couplings that he and I clung to, you know?"

She turned to me, for understanding, and I nodded, but even as I nodded, I realized that I didn't know. My own two lovers had been preternatural, both of them, and they had been everything she was saying—wonderful, tremendous, and free. For a moment, as she was speaking, I wondered if I had ever been mortal at all, but then, this moment was not about me.

"And then one day," Grace was saying, "He was moving the entertainment center with one of the girls' husbands, so they could hook up a DVD player and this craft store receipt fell out."

I must have looked confused because she elaborated. "You know—yarn, fabric, whatever? It was my addiction, craft stores—still is." This I knew—in fact, Grace ran a store just like that called *A Yarning For Crafts*. She made quilts, beautiful, lovely quilts, filled with the colors of the night sky and moonlight on water and green meadows. She worked in hyper-time—the super accelerated speed that I noticed most of the Goddess' children could use when they needed to—or when they really concentrated on something and their nerve endings ran on magic instead of electricity.

"And that summer," She continued, "That summer I knew I was dying, I made a thousand things, for him and the girls. I didn't tell them about the cancer, you know. We had no health insurance—and it was pretty far advanced anyway—so I just made things for them, all summer, and tried to say goodbye. But I hid my receipts—it was stupid, really, because he..." And now she could really no longer pretend that her throat wasn't thick with unshed aching. "Because he never gave a shit, how much my craft things cost. It made me happy, and that was all he cared about. But I'd hidden that last receipt, the one I used to make all those last projects with, and it slipped out from behind the television."

She looked away, ignoring the spatter of briny blood that fell on the back of her hands. "And suddenly the man I thought had born everything so well, who would survive and prosper without me...suddenly he sank to the floor, sobbing these deep hulking sobs that just ripped out my heart. Ten years I'd been dead to him. Ten years I'd been watching them, secretly, missing them with all my heart but thinking, like everybody in Green's place that mortals are used to death, and that they could grieve and live, and then that man sank to his knees and died of grief as I watched from a corner in my daughter's mind."

Grace wiped her face on her shoulder, leaving a smear of red on her shirt and not really taking care of the mess on her cheeks. I turned towards her, not knowing what to do. She didn't look like she wanted a hug. She looked like she wanted me to go away and leave her with this horrible sadness pressing on her, because there wasn't anything anybody could do about it anyway. "So, sweetie," she said, facing stoically into the back wall, "When the elves look at you like they're afraid you'll die of grief, you need to know it can happen. And when Bracken looks at you like you are his absolute everything, and Green is willing to hold your hand and let you be just that, while holding his beating heart in your hands, you need to know how rare it is, and how frightening a thing it is for anyone to lose their everything, and how wonderful and precious it is, that *your* everything might not be tied up in the still beating of only one man's heart."

There was nothing to say to that. She didn't want me to say anything. I squeezed her shoulder tentatively, and she nodded and patted my hand. We continued to work then, in the aching silence of the kitchen until everybody else came in ready for food.

GREEN

Embittered

Green could smell the copper-brine of vampire tears as soon as he, Nicky, Renny and Max walked in to the kitchen. He stopped and looked from Grace to Cory, but Grace was tossing salad and staring stoically at the wall behind the sink. There was a silly print of cows tap-dancing there, but it could hardly have been as absorbing as Grace's fixed attention would have suggested. Cory was setting the table and looking determinedly as though she couldn't see Grace weeping. As soon as the group walked into the kitchen Grace turned, her face averted, and put the salad on the table, then slid by Green. Green moved towards her, but she waved him off, leaving Cory to finish putting the platter of steaks on the table. The others stopped talking abruptly and looked at Cory, who shrugged.

"It's funny." She said, her voice rough, "That no one thinks they're strong enough to live with pain, but we all have to, don't we?" She didn't expect an answer, and so she shook off their stunned silence. "Nevermind, everybody." She told them, and looked around. "Where's Bracken?"

Green shrugged in his turn, and took his cue to ignore what had been going on in the kitchen before he came in. "He said something about cleaning up before dinner. We can sit down, but I'd like to wait for him before we break bread, yes?"

Cory smiled. "Absolutely—Max, Renny, were you actually being civil to each other when you came in?"

Max shrugged uncomfortably, following Green's example and sitting down. "I apologized." He said gruffly.

"What'd you do now?" Cory asked, getting milk, soda, and juice out of the refrigerator and setting them on the table. Green noticed the giant cream pie in there, and Cory's semi-sweet smile when she saw it. He knew something of Grace's grief, and he thought maybe he could guess what they had been talking about.

"It's not what he did now." Renny spoke up, rolling her eyes as she pulled out her chair. "He just didn't remember what he did two years ago."

"What'd he do two years ago?" Nicky asked, taking his own seat while Cory reached around him and put the salad on the table. He'd been being healed when Renny and Max had started this conversation, and still looked completely infatuated with Green. He'd told Green, as the older elf had been delicately lapping at his wounds in a way that still made them both tingle all over, that no one had ever used power to heal him—he didn't realize that the Goddess' children could do that. Green had just smiled at him, and when the healing had rippled through them both, Nicky had been embarrassed, aroused, and star struck.

Renny grunted in disgust. "You tell them." She growled, and to everybody's surprise, Max looked ashamed.

"I didn't know." He said again, and then shook his head. "I rousted Renny and Mitch one night." He said. "I didn't remember until she came out of the bathroom just now—I mean..." His voice rose in pitch, "She's been cat more often than girl since I've known her..." He shrugged. "Anyway, I thought they were coming down from a high."

"Were-cats can't be drug addicts!" She said indignantly.

"I didn't know that!" Max burst out. "All I knew was that the two of you looked like you were coming down from a three day bender—of course I threw you in detox."

"It was the night before the full moon!" Renny spat, and it was obvious that the memory still hurt.

"Like I knew there was any such thing as giant shape-changing kitty cats!" Max expostulated, using his hands, and Green saw that he was not the only one hiding his smile behind his hand—Cory, also was looking suspiciously bright eyed as she put a bowl of pasta with mushroom sauce down on the table. "Anyway," Max was saying, "I said I was sorry." There was a quiet then, as the two of them glared at each other, and then Renny smiled, looking very feline.

"Don't worry, Officer Max." She said in a sensual, threatening way that only a young woman could manage, "I'll find a way to make it up to you."

Nicky looked at the two of them and raised his eyebrows. "You people are nice." He said after a thoughtful pause.

"We have our moments." Cory agreed.

"I mean…" Nicky looked at all of them. "You're nice to each other, the men and the women. There's respect here…" He shook his head. "It's hard to explain."

"It's hard won." Max said unexpectedly. He carefully avoided everybody's eyes. "I still don't understand why…why Green's people interact the way they do. But I'm learning to understand that there's a reason."

Green realized his mouth was open, and Cory's was as well.

Max looked at them both and shrugged irritably. "I'm not stupid." He said after a moment. "I'm just human."

"And on that note…" Green said, "I'm not sure if we should wait for Bra…"

Except Cory's eyes had moved to the hall, and what Green could only describe as a boo-boo face moved over her expressive features. He turned his head to see what she was looking at, and felt his own heart constrict. Cory came over to Green and put her hand on his shoulder and they exchanged looks of surprise. Green took her hand and pressed it, then gave her a little push towards Bracken, because he knew that's who she really wanted to go touch.

"Ouchie." Cory whispered, and Bracken stepped out of the shadows so Nicky, Max and Renny could see what had upset the other two so badly. His hair, which had fallen thick and straight past his shoulder-blades, was now short. Not military short, but cut straight and shaggy, parting in the middle and falling to the sides and over the slender, curved points of his ears, barely brushing the collar of his T-shirt. It wasn't a crew cut, but to the European sidhe, who usually grew their hair long past their hips, it might as well have been.

Cory walked up to him, distressed, and put her hands to the shorn ends of his hair, her finger brushing the sensitive ear-point. "Oh gees…why?"

"It's just hair." Bracken said gruffly, avoiding her touch. But Cory wouldn't be avoided. She placed one hand on his chest, and ran the other through his hair, her hands shaking.

"It's not just hair…it's…like your birthright, or something…Jesus Bracken, why?" She asked again, and he shrugged, avoiding everyone's eyes.

"You can't feel bad about it anymore." He said at last. "You can't carry it like a weight on your chest. I cut it, this time. Me. It's short, it'll grow, and you can let it go."

Cory ran a trembling hand over her face, and then thumped his shoulder hard. "You *asshole.*" She muttered, "You didn't have to do it like this—you didn't have to do this to hurt me. You were doing a good job of it already." She thumped him again, and Green saw a look of sorrow cross Bracken's face. He hadn't planned on this, Green thought. He had wanted to get her attention. He had wanted to erase the past, when he was just 'big brother Bracken'. He had wanted to be a different person than the one who'd been jealous of Cory's relationship with his friend, and then of his friend's intimacy with Cory. But Bracken had never been subtle, and, in spite of his usual sexual successes, he had never been particularly romantic. He had wanted to make Cory look at him differently, and had hurt her badly instead.

With a quick motion Bracken pulled her to him, and waited until the angry tension in her body melted against him. Green watched the silent apology with a happy, aching heart. It would never be easy between the two of him, he suspected, but there would be a two of them, and that would make his own relationship with Cory that much sweeter. Bracken bent his head to hers, and Green listened shamelessly to him saying gently, "I would never hurt you."

Cory shivered then, and drew back. "You just did." She replied. Then, as though becoming aware that she had an audience, she stepped back. "Come eat." She said quietly. Bracken made his way to the silent table, then, and sat down just as Grace was coming out of the hallway.

"Green, the sprites are awfully keyed up about something..." She was saying. "Holy shit, Bracken, what in the hell did you do to your hair?"

There was a low rumble of laughter at the table then, to break the tension, and Grace sat down in the one empty seat and they all looked at Green, sitting at the head of the other end of the table, who held out his hands. They all joined hands somewhat sheepishly, but then they relaxed, felt warmth, felt love. Green looked at all of them and smiled.

"Lovely Goddess, Merciful God," He began. "Please watch over us, lost as we are, holding our separate griefs, and far, so far from home. Let us be loyal to each other, and kind to each other, keep us safe from our enemies, and from the betrayals of those who should be our friends. Let us be strong, let us be safe, and let us show those who would hurt us that we are your children, and you will not forsake us. Blessed be."

"Amen." They all replied, and suddenly the awkwardness and the pain that had haunted the table for the last several moments disappeared. Max and Renny argued companionably over how often Renny should turn feline in the course of a day, Nicky got his two cents in about why it was easier to turn into birds (They stored their clothes in the oils that covered their pinfeathers—that's why he wasn't naked when he changed back.) Cory and Bracken cast each other dark, unreadable looks while they quietly bantered about when Cory got to cut *her* hair. Grace gave them all a ration of shit for arguing, and Green listened kindly to everybody's bickering, throwing out occasional input to one side or another. He watched them, when he wasn't speaking, with quiet satisfaction. He had wanted a formal dinner tonight—he had needed them, this impromptu household, to remember the feeling of home.

The peace was sweet, but it wasn't meant to last. Bracken, who had been Cory's stud taxi for part of the day was eating more salad and pasta, and Renny and Cory—always undernourished when they used power in any form—were on their second helping of *everything* when the buzzer by the call box rang. Green stood up to answer it, and wasn't surprised when a voice—oddly undistorted by the call box—called out "Mist, to see Green, Lord of Leaves and Shadows."

"We are breaking bread." Green replied, his voice congealing. "Would you prefer to wait in my hall or remain where you are." He noticed that the others were looking at him in surprise. It was unheard of for a guest in Green's home not to be invited to break bread at his table. Then Green saw Cory's eyes narrow with comprehension, and she glared fiercely at Green.

"The garage!" She mouthed urgently. Bracken looked from Cory to Green, then his eyes widened and he nodded as well, echoing her silent words.

Green smiled, shook his head, and listened to the rather stunned silence on the other side of the speaker.

"I suppose I'll come up and wait in your sitting room." Mist said at last, obviously stunned by the insult.

"Very well." Green told him crisply, and hit the buzzer next to the intercom. As he sat down then, in the charged silence, he watched Cory push her plate away, murmuring something about not being hungry anymore.

"Please eat, dearest." He said gently. Then he grinned. "In fact, feel free to eat that extra rare piece of cow still sitting on the trencher—but wait until Mist comes in to see you."

Cory grinned weakly back, and then Green saw her take in the confusion of the rest of the table. She looked to Green, reminding him gently, and he nodded.

"The elves here in San Francisco knew about Sezan." He said bluntly, feeling their stunned hurt all over again. "They knew he was a danger to Adrian—a danger to us—and they directed him to Folsom. They even," His mouth twisted, "Gave him the idea for the silver net."

Cory looked like she might vomit right there, and Green could have kicked himself. Well done, he thought grimly, and prepared for damage control. He needn't have bothered. Her face had turned nearly green, and she was staring glassily at the pile of food she'd been about to demolish when Bracken seized her arm and growled, "Don't you do it. You're too damn weak not to eat. You sit here and you let the blood run down your chin and you let this fucking arrogant sidhe know that you are someone to fear." Bracken looked across the table at Renny, then, and Green saw to his surprise that cop-fuck Max had it covered.

"You too, kitten." Max was saying grimly. "You let him know that you could rip out his liver if he ever goes belly up."

Renny and Cory both locked glances and pulled up their bootstraps mentally and pulled back their plates physically, and their faces flushed with anger and purpose. When Green heard the knock at the door they were both eating as though nothing had happened to disrupt their appetite, and Nicky and Max were making a concerted effort to maintain a conversation about fishing in North America, in order to cover up the fact that no one else was at the table was speaking.

Green opened the door Mist came in, meeting his gaze evenly. Standing, Mist was a good six inches shorter than Green, and Cory blinked in surprise and then looked at Bracken. "I didn't know you guys came in different sizes." Green heard her whisper.

"Yours are all sized extra-large." Bracken replied, so straight faced that Cory had to look twice at him to see if he meant what Green was sure he meant. A small smile tilted his features as he turned towards Mist, but when he saw the other elf's disdainful expression, his own features hardened.

"We'll be with you in our time." He said coolly, and was rewarded by watching an angry flush spread over Mist's features.

"I am not accustomed to waiting on...*carnivores*...little Green."Mist spat.

"I am accustomed to dining with my people." Green replied, feeling an immense satisfaction in the other elf's fury. With measured steps, he resumed his place at his own table, laying a hand on Cory's shoulder to encourage her to eat.

"Really, Green," She said, trying to sound natural, "I'm not that hungry."

"Cherry pits." Bracken sang, standing up and beginning to clear the table.

"Bite me." Cory snapped, shoving a chunk of steak in her mouth and chewing loudly. As Bracken had requested, she let the juice run down her chin—for about a second, anyway. She wiped her mouth after that, trying not to look sheepish.

"Ignore him, dearest." Green told her, his eyes twinkling. "They're apricots at the very least."

Grace snickered, although the jest hadn't been one of his best, because at least it helped break the tension. Nicky, Max and Renny followed, and finally Cory and Bracken, eyeing each other with grim amusement, joined in the laughter.

Bracken finished passing out pie slices and they finished dessert, murmuring quiet things, like how many more finals the three students had, and how few classes they could afford to attend between that day, Monday, and the next week. Renny and Nicky were in good shape, but Cory was looking so worn out by the end of the meal that Green made a mental note to call Professor Cruikshank and see what could be done to minimize her involvement in school for the next two weeks. It was just too hard that she should have to be defender of his people, and college student at the same time. But, at the moment, Cory's school was the least of his worries.

With a gesture meant for the others to follow him, Green stood and pushed back his chair, and the rest of the table followed suit. Cory took Green's arm, and like the Faerie Kings and Queens of old they descended into the sitting room as regally as any Prince and Princess of Storyland, in spite of the fact that they were both barefoot and wearing sweatshirts and jeans. The rest of the table fanned out behind them like court, and when Green and Cory sat down, with the exception of Bracken, who sat at Cory's feet, the others sat, evenly spaced on the throw cushions throughout the room. They looked like the courtiers in Mist's hall, except, Green thought, none of them looked afraid.

"So, Mist," Green said when all were settled, "What do you expect by showing up here?"

The other elf was still flushed with irritation, and his words were cruel and demeaning. "I expect an apology, little brother, for what happened to my emissary today. It's not bad enough you burst into my court without courtesy, but you sent a...a..."

"A were-cat." Renny murmured dryly.

"A *were-cat!*" Mist exploded. "You sent a *were-cat* after Morana, and she says it drew blood!"

"Like I'd actually want to taste that woman's tight ass!" Renny burst out, until Green shushed her with a look.

"You made me *wait* upon your dinner like a reigning monarch while I was forced to watch your current bedmates eat *cow...*"

"You were never invited here, Mist." Green said mildly, "And you are still not welcome. That I meet with you at all is courtesy—a repayment, of sorts, for smashing into your court this morning. But otherwise, I have no apologies to make. You and Morana not only welcomed a dangerous enemy to me and mine when he arrived here, you provided him with a weapon that he used to kill several of my people. You never declared war. You never claimed responsibility. What— did you think my people would fall apart and you could simply move in to the foothills like a new Oberon? What did you hope to gain with this? Did you think we'd just sit by and let you kill us off as you saw fit? I mean, I know the cost of housing is skyrocketing in the foothills, Lord Mist, but if this was a gambit for power it was poorly done."

As Green spoke, Mist sat, haughty and tense, his eyes occasionally darting to Cory. Cory was sitting upright, in spite of her weariness, her eyes flat, hard, and dangerous.

"My intentions are my business." Mist said when Green was done. "And to suggest that I would do it for your…'territory' is a little absurd. Even the humans disdain your little 'cow-town' as they call it. Morana and I sat at Oberon's court—we do have our standards."

Cory blinked. "Bracken." She murmured, "I think this guy just trashed our hometown."

Bracken smiled from his seat at Cory's feet, one long fingered hand wrapped casually around her bare ankle. "When San Francisco gets a basketball team he can talk." He replied in the same dangerously amused kind of way.

"Then why?" Green demanded, ignoring the byplay. "Did you expect us to sit back and take it, and you don't even have a reason why?"

Again Mist's eyes darted to Cory, and there was something in them—hatred, disdain…despair? That Green couldn't identify. "You remember politics from the old days, Green." Mist said smoothly, in spite of his preoccupation with Cory. "Things get…muddied. We have no interest in your little conclave up in the hills—you must be delusional to think otherwise. In fact, that's why I'm here. You blew into my home like a mad wind, you sent Morana running from your embassy when she did nothing but give you unwelcome news…the loss of your little blood toy seems to have made you unbalanced. I came to see if you were still fit to run your…teeming lot of…Goddess get."

Unexpectedly, it was Cory who broke the horrified silence of the foothills folk with laughter. "We can crush you as you sit." She said bluntly, when the others had joined in with her, and then subsided.

"I'm not speaking to you." Mist dismissed her, and turned again towards Green.

"You're speaking to me because you're not worthy of speaking to our leader." Cory retorted. "Your people kept information from us that hurt our people— that's betrayal, isn't it? I may be just a 'bedmate who eats cow' but I'm pretty sure I've got that down. My leader found out that his own people **betrayed** him—the only reason you're not dead is because he's a better person than I am, and so are the people who look to him."

"A vampire and his shape-changers." Mist said, as though that explained everything. "They're...get...that's all...Goddess' get. How can our actions against a bastard accident of fate qualify as betrayal..."

"My people." Green said quietly, before Grace, Renny, and Nicky could grow long teeth and danger right there in that moment.

"Not after the way you treated us..." Mist snorted.

"No, Mist," Green explained patiently, "Your people suck your toes and kiss your ass and I could care less about them—the vampire and his shape-changers were my people. They were under my protection. I tried to explain this to you this afternoon but you wouldn't listen long enough to hear. But you're in my embassy now, aren't you? You said you didn't plan to 'cause me any pain'—aren't those your exact words? Well cause pain is exactly what you did. You hurt every-one in this room, and we're not people you want to dick with. There's not a per-son here prepared to let you leave until you understand what it is you've done."

The elf cocked his head then, and eyed Green as though he had materialized there out of thin air. "What would they do about it?" He said, genuinely curious. Green felt Cory's hand, then, reaching for his own, and knew that Bracken was gripping her calf tightly from where he sat. Quickly, he caught her sweat-shirt covered wrist in his hand and raised a meaningful eyebrow at her. "Wait." He mouthed, and she nodded.

"Do they need to do anything?" Green asked, turning towards Mist. "You've effectively killed their dear ones—and yet they're here prepared to help you with a very tricky little problem—-don't you think you owe it to them to stay out of courtesy?" Odd thing, Green reflected that a charge of courtesy could discomfit his brethren far more quickly than a charge of murder.

"I thank them for their intent," Mist grudged, "But we don't need their help."

"That's funny," Grace snorted, "Because word on the street is, you're getting your collective ass kicked. Goshawk could have his birds shit on you until you drowned in it before you agreed that he's even a threat."

"And you're playing right into Goshawk's hands." Nicky said seriously from his position next to Bracken. "He told us that there was no leadership here—I think what he meant was that the leadership was too fractured to ward him off."

Mist went absolutely still. "You know Goshawk?" He asked intensely. Then, towards Green, "No wonder you're weak enough to attack—you let your ene-mies live!"

"Oh that can change in a hot second." Cory spat, and Green continued the struggle to keep her wrist still in his hand without hurting her. After a second's hesitation, he wrapped his long fingers around her bare wrist, and whispered in her ear, "Close your mouth, cup your hand, and use your will." She startled for a moment, then met his eyes. He could see from her expression that it was building within her, that between her desire for revenge and the sex and love that he and Bracken were pumping into her with their touch, her power was massing in her chest, making her skin prickle, threatening to blow the top off her head if she didn't use it. As he turned his attention back to his unwelcome guest he could feel her struggle as she gathered from himself and Bracken, and then, by force of battered will alone constrained the power building in her chest to her cupped hand.

"Nicky is not our enemy." Green said gently. "The captain who commanded him to battle against us is. Just like Sezan was not our only enemy—the force that gave him succor, strategy and aid is also our enemy. You comfort yourself with the idea that because the people he killed weren't your kind of Goddess' children that you have done no wrong—what you fail to realize is that you sent him to attack a stronghold of Goddess' children—and no matter how diverse we were, we reacted to this attack as one. And many elves nearly died in the backlash." His fury bubbled up inside him, fueling Cory, giving her impetus to do what she did next. "And five shape changers and one vampire did die. And we mourn them. And we hold you responsible."

"You can hold me accountable for nothing." Mist said derisively. "Sezan was at least part water sidhe—he had a better claim to vengeance than your plaything and his lunch."

"If you don't stop talking," Cory said in a strained voice, "You will die as you sit." And at last she had Mist's complete attention.

"That could be a formidable weapon." Mist gasped evenly, trying very hard not to be impressed by the brilliance of color and motion held in her cupped hand. "If you had the guts to use it against a full blooded sidhe."

"Didn't Morana tell you," Green replied sweetly, "the reason there are no more vampires in Folsom?" The magical nuclear ball in Cory's hand spun, so bright that just being in the same room with it left dark spots dancing across Green's eyes.

And at last, Mist believed. "I thought she was mad." He breathed, and his gaze flickered from Cory to Green. "She said *you* attacked her."

"I did." Green replied. "And I would have driven you from my home in the same way. But you didn't just kill my beloved. You killed my beloved's beloved as well. Cory deserves a show of force, don't you think?"

"This power is beyond you." Mist said stubbornly.

"Goddess you're dumb." Cory snorted, making her power dance, turn purple—Adrian's colors. Three purple spots were glowing on her neck, pulsing with her blood and her anger. "With you it's always the 'you can't' and 'I'm better than you'—don't you get it? We can. You're not better than us. We stay together because we love each other—not because we hate everybody else. That will make us stronger every blessed time."

And because Green could feel her drawing on him, he caught the minute flicker and instability in the whirling globe of light. "Close your fist, dearest." He murmured, and wasn't surprised when she turned towards him with a plea in her eyes.

"He all but killed them, Green." She begged.

"I know, luvie—but we want those memories back, right? They won't come if we kill the opposition and frighten Goshawk away. He still thinks we're weak."

Her eyes filled with tears then, and he wondered at the terrible conflict that must be tearing at her—revenge or recoup? But she did him proud.

"You'd better kiss our ass in public." She said to Mist, closing her hand as Green and then Bracken let go of her bare skin. "You'd better get up and offer obeisance and apology and give back that fucking gas station in Vacaville, plus a few, or I will come back here without Green and I will cook you in your sleep like a fucking egg."

"Make your pets mind." Mist snapped to Green, and was as shocked as Morana when a blast of fury from Green's outstretched hand sent him spinning back against the wall and pinned him there.

"You need a lesson in manners." Green said mildly, loving the contrast between his seething anger and his calm voice. Goddess, he'd needed to do this, he thought exultantly. He should have done it in Mist's own home, but he hadn't been angry enough, not then. But Mist had insulted Cory, insulted his *people,* and a dark lust to see his old lover brought low coursed through him. He felt Mist struggle against him—the elf was five-hundred years older than Green, and not weak. But Green was fueled by the love of his people, and had been exercising his own form of power in force to keep them healthy and safe, and he had more of them under his protection; as a result, his magic muscles were honed and massive and quick. But he was willing to share.

"Bracken, my red-capped darling," He murmured, "Would you mind giving our friend a reminder of his visit?"

"Anything special, leader?" Bracken asked formally, moving to where Mist was pinned and then using a long finger to rip Mist's coat and his fine silk shirt in two down the center of his back.

"Something creative—something that says "Green was here." Green asked with grim humor, and was not displeased when, after he had stopped Mist's mouth with a stray tendril of power, Bracken drew his finger along the pale, pulsing skin of his kinsman's back, drawing forth a welling of blood using his calling alone. A line, another, a flat bladed leaf, askant, then an oak leaf, point to point with the lime tree leaf, then (bloody artistry) a plain rose at the base. Bracken had seen the Goddess grove that Green, Cory, and Adrian had created—this was a token of the power and love that had wrought it. "Lovely." Green breathed upon its completion.

"Thank you." Cory murmured, her throat clogged. "That's really nice of you." She added, and Bracken made a formal bow to them both as his lord and lady.

Green took a deep breath, then, and continued with the penalty Mist would pay for insulting his dear ones in his own home. "Grace, my luv—keep that bleeding, will you? And mind you, don't drink him dry." And as Mist thrashed against the far wall, doing damage to the poster of Antonio Banderas that Renny had tacked up. Grace came forward and licked the line on his back, causing the ichor to run freely. She did this several times, and came away licking her lips. She even gave a little belch for show.

"Well done, lovely. Now Cory," Green murmured, looking at her, enjoying the blood-lust in her eyes, "I think he's bled enough, don't you? A bit of fire might help." And Cory didn't need Bracken or Green to summon just the tiniest laser line of power in her newly discovered fist. She didn't even flinch. Using her finger and thumb, as though holding a pencil, from across the room she traced along the silently screaming man's back. The scar stood out in perfect angry red relief to his fog pale, unblemished skin.

"That will stay, Mist." Green said firmly. "You may be sidhe, but we have all marked you, and you can not heal from your own treachery, do you understand? You will wear this mark forever, like we will wear what you've done on our hearts. And so you don't get bitter, you need to know we'd trade places with you in a moment, if you could turn back time."

Mist struggled, and his fury was obvious, but even as a grey glow of power encompassed him, the wound on his back grew no less red and no less raised. It was, Green knew, a shock and a defeat, for the great and mighty Mist to be humbled like this. Held captive by someone else's power and marked by a group of creatures he detested—Mist had become a formidable enemy on this night. Good. His humiliation wasn't over yet.

"Renny, dearest," Green concluded, "Make sure he doesn't stop running until he gets to Market Street—Max will pick you up by the Orpheum shortly, can we do that, Officer?"

"Yeah. No problem." Max breathed, and Green released Mist in the next heartbeat, keeping the man's furious mouth stuffed with power. Mist sagged to the floor, almost blue he was so pale, and sweating with pain. He looked at the collective of people who had marked him with pain and fear and surprise.

"So, Mist," Green continued conversationally, "You will show my people, *all* of my people, a little fucking respect. And so will your people, or soon all of you will wear my mark, and tithe to me, and lick my feet and kiss my ass—because we will vanquish this Goshawk because we have to, and then we'll take what we gain from that encounter, the one that you're too afraid to have, and we will come after you unless you make a whole lot of changes in a merciful hurry. Understood, precious?" And even saying it, Green knew he had to make plans immediately to back his words up. If he didn't make plans to defend his people now, Mist, for whatever reason, would always be a threat.

And with that he took the power from around Mist's mouth at about the time Renny bounded after him with a wild-cat snarl that the smaller elf would probably hear in his nightmares for months to come. Grace had thoughtfully moved towards the door and opened it, or Mist would have shattered the new one in all of its finely carved glory, as he fled from Green's home with Renny tight on his flank.

The people left standing in the room watched him go, surprised at themselves and at the stunning satisfaction that Mist's overthrow gave them, and at the darkness that they didn't know they had.

Cory summed it up when she said into the silence "Crispin and Sezan died too quickly."

"Amen to that." Grace agreed, flopping down on the couch she had vacated. Cory sat down abruptly next to Green, as though her strings had been cut. Green had known too, when he'd let her summon power, that she was pretty much at the end of her rope in that way. Too much, he thought bitterly, they asked too much from her.

Max was moving to the door when he stopped and said, "I have no idea how to get to the Orpheum theatre."

"I'll take you." Nicky volunteered, and the two grabbed their jackets from the peg by the door. Nicky stopped at the doorway and turned around. "Goshawk has no idea about you." He said after a moment. "If he knew who you were— how strong you are—he would have left Cory the hell alone."

"Pity poor Goshawk." Green said without mercy, and Nicky nodded.

"Amen to that too." He echoed, and followed Max out the door.

There was a silence in the room, then, broken by a nasal snoring sound and they all looked at Cory, who had fallen instantly asleep.

"We let her do too much." Bracken murmured his words so much an echo of Green's thoughts that Green almost laughed.

'You're right, brother." He said instead, "But I don't know how we could have stopped her."

"We should have." Bracken insisted, going over to where she lay and picking her up, much the way Green had spent his and Cory's first month together. She was much tinier now.

"You figure out how, and I'll back you up." Green said in quiet amusement— it would be like wind in autumn, watching the two of them. He almost looked forward to it. "Wait—" He said suddenly to Bracken, who halted in the hallway and turned back towards him. Green turned to his resident vampire, whose fangs were extended and whose chest was panting as though she were still human, she was so delighted with the elfin ichor that Mist had given her. "Grace, luvie, do you need accompaniment tonight? I don't know if I want to trust Orson's kind, all of a once, to keep you safe."

Grace nodded, licking her lips in thought of a hunt. "I'm with you there—I'll take Bracken. You need to be here to deal with any of Mist's people. There will be aftermath." She finished with satisfaction.

She was right, there would be aftermath. But Mist was a planner—sly, under-handed in a way that was the worst of their people. There would be retaliation, but it would come later, in ways that not even *he* could predict. But he didn't want to tell them that, Green thought sadly—they were riding a little victory high, and he wanted them to stay happy, so he would simply let it be. Instead of bringing Grace down, he grinned at her wolfishly and said "I'm looking forward to it."

"Amen." Bracken agreed, and turned back towards the hallway, Cory nestled in his arms.

CORY

Honesty, power, and time.

I woke up a little when Bracken was putting me to bed, and murmured Green's name as he pulled off my jeans and my shoes.

"No." Simply, "Not Green."

I struggled to get up then, but he put a larger than human, long-fingered hand on my chest and pushed me back down.

"Sleep." He said gruffly. "You are so exhausted—you'll make yourself sick if you keep using power like that."

"It was worth it." I murmured, my head on the pillow. I closed my eyes for a moment, and when I forced them open again, Bracken was sitting on the bed, putting his shoes on. All of the elves hated shoes—their feet were long and tough and capable, and hard to fit as it was. The shoes hit the floor in Green's house practically before the door closed, and only the most comfortable ones, with the most breathable materials made it on their feet in the first place. Bracken was putting on his favorite pair—sky blue Converse sneakers, size 17.

"Where're you going?" I muttered through the fog in my head. I was so close to sleep that I could feel myself, breath by breath, detaching from reality.

"Out to look for the vampires, with Grace." Bracken replied. He finished with the shoe and knelt by the bed, so we were face to face. His eyes, the color of a still pool in shade, were dark but not brown or black or blue or green, or at least any one of those colors alone. You could see that, even in the darkened room, I thought, feeling his breath against my face.

"Be careful." I told him soberly, "It's dangerous out there." We were vulnerable, alone in this city without the vampires, who were, I had gathered from Green, our only clear allies during regular, more peaceful times. And now the vampires were missing.

Bracken nodded. He was beautiful, like all of the sidhe. Even the ones like Professor Cruikshank had beauty in them, something from which you could not look away, and the high sidhe were inhumanly, heartbreakingly lovely as a matter of course. Their eyes were large—larger than human, and more widely spaced, with delicate, impossibly high cheekbones. Sometimes, I thought they were breathing anime characters, but only when I was feeling small, and unattractive, like I didn't belong to them or their world. Not tonight. Tonight, Bracken looked different, as though his high cheekbones and strong, pointed chin were *that* beautiful just for me.

"Will you worry?" He asked quietly, after we'd breathed in the dark, looking at each other for a few heartbeats.

"I always do." I told him, because I would, because he was my friend, and because I knew now how easy it was to lose people.

"Will you worry differently?" Goddess, I was too sleep-muddled to deal with this, I thought vaguely.

"I will worry about my Bracken," I said after a moment, "Who kicks my ass and yells at me and makes me feel better all in a minute. How could I not worry about you?"

A small smile played with his lips, then, and a fierceness gathered in his eyes, and suddenly his lips were on mine and they were *sweet,* and his tongue was in my mouth and his taste was wild and hard and he was pushing me back into the bed, tasting me, hands on my face, in my hair, running down my arms. He finally pulled away from me, leaving me languorous and breast-heavy, loin-aching, sleepy and terribly aroused and confused and too damn tired to sort it all out now. I made a sound, between a 'please come back to me' and a 'what in the hell are you doing' but words were not an option.

"Worry about that." He said with immense satisfaction, and then swept out of the room.

I fell instantly asleep after that, but it was an aroused sleep, a sexual sleep, filled with dreams of Green inside of me, on top of me, and of Adrian, kissing his way up my thigh, using his tongue, his fingers on me and inside of me, and then biting the tender flesh of my thigh right when I climaxed and making me scream with the force of what ripped through me. I must have been making sounds in my sleep because Green came to bed around midnight, slid next to me, his bare skin so cool and smooth that I couldn't sheathe him inside of my hot, slickness fast enough. He pounded into me then, slick and fast and hard through one climax, then another, and then his own. I slept immediately after, soundly and dreamlessly, so much so that I didn't notice he was gone until he slid in bed behind me once more.

This time, he was inside of me before I could even roll towards him, and I groaned, because I was still ready and still slick from our earlier coupling. But this time he stayed still, until I started to move restlessly against him, asking for more.

"Mmmm…in a moment, dearest." He murmured, "But first, you need to tell me what has you so stirred up…"

I was too sleepy and too desperate for him to be tactful. "Bracken kissed me." I told him plaintively. "He kissed me and he left…asshole." I finished under my breath.

"Ahh…" Green murmured, and then started to move inside me, and he was so big and so tight inside me that I almost wept with need, even now, even again. I groaned, but he was slow, this time. "So Bracken did this to you…how do you feel about that?"

"I could smack him." I panted, frustrated, needing more. But Green knew what he was doing—I wouldn't lie to him like this, sleepy and wanting and needing more than I wanted to please the man I loved. "Asshole." I groaned, meaning Bracken, meaning Green for not giving me what I needed, "I need some fucking *time…*" I gasped, because Green had rolled me under him, and was now behind me, moving a little harder and a little faster but not enough, not nearly enough.

"But it will happen, you think?" He asked gently—but breathlessly, and I was relieved to hear that, because it meant that he needed what I needed.

"Oh Goddess, *yes….*" I moaned, and that also meant two things. Green knew what both of them were, and suddenly he was moving, pounding, wanting me, driving me into the pillows, pouring himself into me while my world exploded, went white, came to itself again, leaving me limp against the sheets.

"I'm sorry." I whispered sometime later, when he had pulled the comforter around us and spooned me, our bodies damp and warm and chilling in the pre-dawn.

"Sorry for what, love?" He pulled the hair back from my face, a thing he had been doing since he'd come to pull me out of the hospital room. I liked it, I decided. Screw getting revenge on Bracken—I might let my hair grow longer just to feel Green's hands on my face.

"Bracken…I didn't want to…I was going to…oh, damn it Green…" I murmured, and to my complete horror I realized I was crying again. Goddess, I must be weak, I sniffled, but Green never minded tears, and he rubbed my arms and whispered little hushing noises in my ear until I quieted.

"You know," He said conversationally, when I was down to hiccups, "I always thought Arthur was the worst kind of schmuck."

"As in King?" I asked, so surprised I forgot my own muddle to focus on this one.

"Mmm, oh yes." Green affirmed. He sounded tired, I thought. What had he been doing tonight, between bouts of coming in and keeping me happy? Did Green ever sleep, when he wasn't next to me?

"King Arthur was a schmuck?" There's something they didn't tell you in the lit books, I thought.

"Yes—and Guinevere was spineless, and Lancelot was…well, he was perfidious, but if he'd been candid in the first place, the worst of the perfidy wouldn't have been necessary."

"Okay—you've got me—explain." I said, my voice growing lighter as his became weighted with sleep.

"Arthur was gone, all the bleedin' time…" Green's voice became more and more down-country British, when he was tired or angry—and pure Victorian cockney, when he spoke of Adrian. His speech to Mist tonight had been a mish-mash of California foothills colloquial and Lake County middle class. "And Guinevere—well, she wasn't as strong as you, love, but she was a good Queen, in her way. She needed help, moral more than administrative, right? But help all the same, and Arthur was gone. And Lancelot—he could have saved them all a lot of damned unhappiness if he would have just made one request of the man who loved him like a brother."

"Like 'can I bang your wife'?" I asked, a little disbelieving. It had always seemed like an easy solution, but humans rarely let anything like that be easy.

"Why not?" Green asked. "It was custom in those days, if a visiting dignitary arrived, to offer him your wife…if Arthur had made it public, and asked Guinevere if she consented, had offered her to Lancelot during his absences, the people would have agreed.

"But the whole 'Christian King' thing…" I muttered.

"Is the reason Camelot fell." Green said practically. "Arthur could never believe that the needs of a woman outweighed his own macho pride, or the dogma he was ramming down the peasant's throats…a woman of strength, of purpose—she's a mighty thing. And like you, my love, she is not meant to sit, languishing, waiting for her King to finish his business before she becomes the focus of his world."

"Women have been known to be faithful." I said stubbornly, with dignity.

"Yes they have. But you can't." Green returned, matter-of-factly. "The only women of the Goddess' get who have ever been monogamous have been women with limited form of power, of limited uses to their people…"

"Blissa…" I murmured, referring to Bracken's little pixie-sex-kitten of a mother. I liked Bracken's mother.

"Yes." Green agreed, pleased. He had folded his arm over mine, and our clasped hands rested below my chin. "Blissa and Crocken chose to bind themselves, and with the exception of Blissa's occasional attentions to her leader, they have been faithful to the point of nausea ever since. The weres can be monogamous—even unto death—most of them by choice, like Renny, and some by necessity, like the Avians."

"Nicky's people?" I replied, startled.

"Yes—you know the story, right?" Green was practically mumbling by now. "The Goddess came down as a male hawk, and found a female so brilliant that she sported with no one else until the female died, and the Goddess loved her so very much that from that moment on, hawks, and their like, have mated for life ever since. Pretty much from the point of orgasm on, whomever the Avian mates with, he bonds with."

"So when Nicky asked me out—asked me to Goshawk's for dinner…"

"He was thinking about marrying you, sweet." Green said. "And that's saying a lot."

"How would you feel?" I wanted to know, especially before Green fell asleep. "About Bracken I mean." Poor Nicky—he wasn't even on the map.

"It will be hard, my love." He told me candidly, his breath brushing my neck and his long arms tightening around my naked body as he did so. "It will be hard, because I'm selfish, and I've always needed my lovers to love me best. But you can't do this—be our Queen, be our sorceress, just do the things you need to do, without someone else to give you strength. In your case, literally. You need a man—a man you can love—to touch you to fuel your power." In the silence then I heard regret, and reconciliation. "I can't be that man for you all the time."

"Bracken will be…difficult." I said, understating things in the extreme.

"You already love him." Even asleep, I could hear the wry humor in his voice. "The rest will come."

"I am so unremarkable." I said to myself in the silent moment after, when I knew he was asleep and wouldn't argue. In that moment I forgot about weird sorcerous weapons and deadly, lust-fueled sunshine that erupted from my body periodically. In that moment I was the angry gas station clerk who didn't have chance at college. I was the plain, defensive virgin, who had lost oh-so-much time mak-ing Adrian prove he could love me. I was the desperate kid, about to flunk out of life. In that moment, I had lost the life I was living, the life I loved.

"I am such a plain little person." I asked myself. "How do I get to have two man-gods who worship me?" It was a question I didn't think I would ever answer, except to know that I'd give my life for either one of them. Was that all it took?

A few moments later the phone next to my bed rang, and I answered it quickly, hoping not to wake Green.

The connection was horrible, and dying as I picked up the receiver, broken into words like 'darkness', 'ambush', and 'dead were-wolfs', and the most awful phrase of all, 'get us before they wake up."

"Bracken…" I said desperately into the line, "Bracken, what street are you on?" But the line went dead then, and I was left shouting his name into the static void he'd left on the other end.

Whatever Green had been doing that night exhausted him, because he slept for the next two hours as I frantically dressed and woke the household. Max, Renny, and Nicky were, surprisingly enough, asleep in the living room, Nicky on the couch and Max and Renny on the pillows on the floor, almost like puppies. It looked like they had been watching television, and I had about a half a second to wonder at the friendships that form around us when we're not looking before I shook them awake at red alert. I wanted to come up with a plan before I woke Green from a sleep he needed and presented him with this next crisis.

And crisis it was, we decided, when we'd sorted out through the scattering of clear words I'd heard on the phone. "They wake up", he'd said—that had to mean the other vampires, and if he and Grace had found them and been trapped too, the odds were the vampires were starving. I shuddered—elf blood, especially the blood of a sidhe—that much power floating in their ichor—that was pretty potent stuff for a vampire. It would be like offering soft, sweet bread and pate' to a starving man. Except in this case, it was a lot of starving vampires, and the soft bread and pate' was Bracken, and the only thing between Bracken and an almost certain death—even for an immortal sidhe—was Grace, brave, protective Grace, who would die before Bracken did, trying to save his life.

Over coffee, soda, and mouthfuls of trail mix and Reese' Peanut Butter Cups cereal, we mapped out the city and made a plan. The idea was that we would split into groups, each group taking a third of the city, and on foot take a reading of every major crossroads in the city. Then Max remembered that before he'd left, Green had been telling him that Andres himself lived on Market and Diamond, but that he had darklings scattered throughout most of the Eastern half of the city—he especially liked the theatre district and North Beach, so odds were better to find a vampire in the North Eastern part of the city. I thought with despair that if we had enough people we'd search every alley way, parking lot or shadowed niche, but as it was, we only had three teams, and a lot of cramped city to cover.

Those with heightened senses—either preternatural or preternaturally olfactory—should be able to sense or smell Bracken's presence, at the very least. Nicky and Max made a big deal out of the walking—Nicky especially, wanted to fly— but Renny and I both remembered the last summer, when half of Green's people had canvassed every inch of Folsom by car. It wasn't until Green had touched the ground with his own feet that he had felt the evil that even the mortal residents had known. Driving wouldn't work and flying was out of the question, and walking it had to be.

Nicky and I would catch a bus to 19th Street below the school, and walk through Golden Gate Park through the Presidio, eventually cutting to the Embarcadero and continuing steadily East. Practically every North/South street in the city bottomed out at the Embarcadero, so we should be able to feel something at the crossroads. We would follow the curve along the bay, hitting the crossroads South of Market as well. Green, who could move twice as fast as a human being and still feel evidence of his own kind would start in the same place and walk Divisidero to Market and then cut down to Embarcadero. Between us, we'd turn the most likely parts of the city into a big slice of pie shaped earth, and Renny and Max would take Van Ness, doing some zigging and zagging to hit the streets that didn't run straight and cutting that piece of pie in awkwardly in half, to give Renny a chance to smell what she could.

So that was the plan. It was simple, it was hopeless, but it was better than nothing, and after two hours of logistics and stalling to give Green more sleep, by 8:30 we had packed a lunch, showered, donned comfortable shoes and were ready to roll.

It was not soon enough for me. Even though I had made the decision not to wake Green immediately, I found that after we'd drawn our search grid and discussed who would travel with whom, my hands were clammy and my breath shook in my chest with the effort not to bolt out the door, screaming Bracken's name.

Still, when I went to wake Green, I paused, watching the even fall of his chest, and then tracing the curve and point of his ears with my sight alone. His eyelashes glittered—I'd noticed that this summer, but when was the last time I'd looked at them, awed? I loved this man, this ancient non-human—he was the world to me. But he was, as always, right. I would die if I lost Green. But my world would darken and wither without Bracken.

His eyes opened then, brilliant green, and his hand, inhumanly long fingered, captured mine as I stroked his cheek.

"What's wrong?" He asked, immediately awake, although he stayed there, my hand in his, curled on his side in my bed.

"Bracken." I said, trying to keep my voice even. "He called at dawn—his cell phone was breaking up, but he and Grace are trapped in some sort of warehouse. He said "before they wake up" which means, I think…"

"That they've found the other vampires." He supplied, sounding weary and gentle. It almost undid me.

"And they're hungry." I finished, trying to sound grim. It didn't work. Green unfolded himself from the bed and wrapped his naked flesh around me, and I felt suddenly less vulnerable.

"We'll find them." He said, sounding sure, and with purpose. "We'll find them, and you can tell him all that's in your heart, and there will be time…don't worry, dearest." He murmured against my hair. "You are not meant to be abandoned at every turn."

I nodded, squared my shoulders, and felt my panic subside. "Fair enough." I said, just to say something, and he nodded into my hair.

"We have a plan, I assume?" He stated.

"Split the city up, walk the land, charge our cell phones and hope for the best." I said, knowing it was weak, but it was all we had. We had three maps, highlighted, with known fey, vampire or preternatural hang-outs circled in red, but really, it was the same plan every parent with a missing child had. Look everywhere, ask everyone, pray.

"Good enough." Green approved. "Who's with whom?"

"Me & Nicky, Renny& Max, you by yourself." My face twisted at this last one—I had fought, bitterly, to walk with Green, and the others had been kind but adamant that I walk with Nicky. Walking a third of the city would be exhausting and difficult by sunset at 6:00 pm. Walking half the city would be impossible, and Green was the only one of us strong enough, with enough power and clout, to walk alone. Max had put up a fight to be my walking partner, but Nicky told him dryly that every bird in the city was still mating feverishly, so that would be a bad idea. Renny had rubbed her shoulder against Max's arm and purred, "What's the matter, Officer Max, afraid of me?" This had silenced a confused Max and allowed me Nicky's restful company.

"Wise but painful." Green agreed, reading my mind. "Lunches packed?" He asked on a lighter note, so it was easier to respond.

"Trail mix, peanut butter and jelly, milk, water, sodas—in back packs and waiting at the door. We're just waiting for you to shower, change, and lead us into battle." I told him wryly, and I was finally feeling as though all my self restraint in not running screaming from the building in anxiety might have actually paid off.

"Good enough." He echoed. He bent down—far, I'm only 5'2", and he is, as most sidhe, well over 6'—and kissed me on the temple. "Thanks for letting me sleep in." And we were out the door five minutes later.

So we walked. And walked. And walked. At the beginning, Nicky and I passed the time by talking about our secret lives. Avians were largely monogamous, so Nicky's parents were still alive and well in Montana, and Nicky had had a glorious childhood. How many children could fly by the time their voices change? He spoke longingly of home, of big skies and fast game, and he talked hilariously about his first kill, a jack-rabbit so large for Nicky as a fledgling that he had to turn into a boy to carry it home, but by the time he'd walked the twelve miles home, his hawk self wouldn't touch the carcass. I laughed with him, but spoke little myself until he asked me how I met Adrian, and came to be.

"I was working in Green's gas station." I said briefly, "When Grace's lover, Arturo came in and touched my hand. And I spent the next two days clawing at my own skin because I was elf-struck. After Arturo touched me again, I started noticing…well, everybody." Now I knew that they were mostly the lower fey, the ones who hung out by that gas station, but then, as now, they held the same exciting awe and fascination of beings so obviously not human.

"So you noticed Adrian?" Nicky asked, when I was quiet for over half a block.

"Hard not to notice a 6' vampire with white blonde hair and a Harley Davidson glass pack." I told him wryly. It was now two o'clock; Nicky and I were foot sore and exhausted, sweating from exertion and cold from the fog chill that the city couldn't shake in the winter. We had stopped for lunch at a restaurant in Ghirradelli Square at noon, but when we finished, my hands were still shaking, and Nicky insisted on buying me a hot dog at the wharf. And then another one, until I told him we had no time for me to eat, and Nicky had simply held my hand as we walked. I could feel his desire for me then, and if I'd had any part of me left that was whole by all that had befallen in the last six months I would have mourned that I'd have to break his heart. As it was, all I could do was tell him thank you, shyly, graciously, and understand that his reply of "you're welcome" held all the sadness I seemed to hear.

"Goddess—I didn't have a chance with you, did I?" Nicky asked now, and all I could do was look away, embarrassed.

"You should have tried me last year at this time." I told him lightly. "But I wasn't nearly as interesting then."

Nicky breathed through his nose then, which, as winded as we were, was as close as he could come to laughing. "I doubt that." He said sincerely. "You just needed someone to see it."

"It would have been pretty hard to see." I told him honestly. "I hid it under hair gel and make-up and about a pound of jewelry—I didn't even see it." I blew out a breath. "Christ, I made Adrian pay for my blindness."

"What do you mean?" Nicky asked.

"I just gave him a hard time." I shrugged. I didn't know how to explain this to him. "I didn't know...I didn't know how he could be that sincere...he was beautiful!" I burst out awkwardly. "He was beautiful and exciting and desirable, and..." I shivered, "And he just smelled like sex and danger...and I was just...me. I didn't know about the whole "Goddess" power thing until..." I trailed off, then, because I scented something—something magical, floating with the tattered fog towards the water.

"Until what?" Nicky asked.

"Until he made me feel powerful." I responded, so preoccupied with the mental scent of sun-warmed granite in the air, the vibration of bedrock under my feet, that I could say honestly what otherwise would have made me blush to say out loud. "That's him." I said. "That's Bracken."

"What?" Nicky asked, alert.

"Can't you smell that?" I asked, trying not to be rude because I was so wound up. We had rounded the curve directly under 80, and beyond the Embarcadero, the neighborhood was a strange mix of warehouses, abandoned factories and booming and bust dot.com industries. This weekday morning we were unsure whether we'd round a corner and bump into a young man wearing business casual or a young-man-made-old wearing bum chic. I stood still on the sidewalk, clenching Nicky's hand and allowing all of the above to brush past us, and put my nose in the air. And there...beyond the smell of poorly washed humanity, beyond the smell of car exhaust and even safe from the smell of the ever-present ocean and the diesel of the freighters, was...

"It's sun on rain-soaked rock...it's the cool earth under it...it's the over-growth of brambles in the country...can't you smell him?" But he was far away—trapped in a hole and far way from me...I stopped, turned in a slow circle, let the fog-laden breeze blow him against my face...there were empty buildings between us, and a whole block of warehouses with broken windows in front of me...I ago-nized, and turned in that direction.

Nicky was fumbling for the cell phone in my pocket and dialing Green's num-ber. "Green—we've got him...where is he? I don't know—Cory, where is he?"

"Hush, I smell his need." I shushed, not mindful of the absurdity. Salt air, but not much...car exhaust, an endless wall of it, a hole in the city, where his scent could sneak through..."Follow me...down Brannan...I'm not sure how far..." I gasped. Nicky relayed my fractured directions to Green as I spoke.

"He's on his way..." Nicky called, but I was already off, running hell for leather down the Embarcadero with Nicky hard on my heels.

He caught me after a block and slowed me down to wait for Green, which meant his brain was working better than mine was, and we waited for him on the corner of Brannan and the Embarcadero, near a gnarly gas station that you couldn't pay me enough to use as a pit stop. I looked at it in disgust—it was a tiny old building, with wooden sides painted a peeling white, and trash gathered in the gutters. It was one of those places built pre-soda fountain and I wished des-perately that they had one—that they had anything. I was starving again, and when the cab pulled up to the curb, I almost fell into Green's lap when I put out my hand to pull him out—I was that dizzy with fatigue.

We huddled there for a few moments, until another cab pulled up and Max popped out as though he couldn't move fast enough, and Renny followed a bit more slowly, thoroughly enjoying herself. I realized that since she had chosen Max as her favorite play-thing, although her eyes would always be sad, that the lost, miserable look had left her face. Did Bracken do the same thing for me? I didn't have time to wonder, because, as Green outlined a new search grid, I real-ized that I could see the sun, which meant it was westering on the horizon and peeping out underneath the fog, it's light divoted by the skyline of the city itself. It was five in the afternoon, two weeks before the winter solstice. We had less than half an hour to go, and a lot of ground to cover.

Green finished the search grid—again, so easy. Nicky and I would take Bran-nan, Max and Renny would take Townsend, and Green would walk the perilous, exit ridden Bryant. The neighborhoods weren't great, but hey, Max was the least dangerous among us, and he was a cop.

"Right." I said tightly, "I've got a feeling of big hollow space—concentrate on the buildings or warehouses that are empty. What?" I asked, because they were all looking at me soberly.

"You look like shit, Cory." Renny said gently. I didn't want to think about how right she was. My hands were shaking, I was still sweating in spite of the chilly air, and my breath was coming in short pants. But all I could hear was Bracken's matter of fact voice, breaking up on the phone, and remember the kiss he'd given me as he'd left. Had it once occurred to me to tell him I loved him? Would it if I found him?

"Let's find them." I said, not answering her. "Can we all feel them now?" Renny and Green nodded.

"You're right about them being in something vast and empty." Green said. "I can feel that. Remember that the vampires have survived—look for places with basements and sealed windows."

Renny and Max nodded, and Green nodded them away, but they cast anxious glances at me over their shoulders. Nicky stood back then, giving me and Green some space, and he bent over me, holding my face in his hands. I felt healing wash over me, but gentle, and not enough. I looked at Green, at the weariness in his eyes and realized that not only had grief—mine and his—weakened him, but that he'd just spent a lot of himself chasing Mist and Morana out of our apartment, and, I imagined, spreading his power over the city to find Grace and Bracken.

I smiled at him, because I knew, sure as I was breathing, that Green would never let me down. Wearily I leaned in to kiss him, to reassure him, and the kiss flared, grew deeper, and as so often happens when you show someone faith, your faith is justified, and their strength grows. Green's healing washed over me for real, and I thought that maybe, just maybe, we'd both have the strength to save our people.

We pulled away from each other, touched hands to faces. "I love you." I said simply, because I didn't want to wonder as I left when the last time I'd said it had been.

"I love you." He replied, with that smile as though we both knew this and saying it made it more than true. Without another word we turned and parted.

The walking was worse now, and the frustration was worse than the walking: I could smell Bracken. I could feel the vampires. They were *here*, dammit—they were *here*…I ran among the vast warehouses like a rabbit running around tomato trucks—everything I wanted was inside, but I couldn't figure out how to get in. I brushed against every pedestrian I could without attracting attention, hoping for an added scent, a stray vibration, but there was none. I touched every door with my bare hand, hauled Nicky from side entrance to side entrance, until finally, I smelled something besides Bracken.

"Oh Goddess." Nicky breathed, trying not to retch.

"Sweet bleeding Jesus." I coughed. "Where is that coming from?" I asked, and a man wearing a threadbare coat and a tattered watch cap stared at me and looked away as he passed, as though the stench of death weren't rolling through our nostrils, our clothes, our hair, clawing its way into our lungs.

"A couple of dogs got hit by a car—over there—" Watch Cap pointed down an alley across the street. "They're in that dumpster over there." And with that he wandered off, looking back at us over his shoulder as though he couldn't put his finger on what was wrong with us.

Nicky and I squinted at him, but I pulled Nicky away because I could smell the magic here as well as the death, like incense and rubbing alcohol. Anyone who could smell the magic would know what we did—that it wasn't just dogs, and it wasn't just a couple.

When we got to the dumpster and took a good look inside there were five bodies, some more dead than others, piled haphazardly on top of each other. They looked as though they had been disemboweled by razors, and they were naked.

"Orson's werewolves." I said, knowing that if my stomach hadn't been so empty right then, everything I'd eaten would have come right back up. Nicky wasn't as lucky with the empty stomach—he knelt in front of the dumpster and lost his last two hot dogs, then stood with his head between his knees, breathing hard through his nose. I sympathized—I'd lost a lot of lunches this summer, while Bracken had held my head. I swallowed hard, squared my shoulders and closed my eyes.

The bodies themselves had nothing—inert matter, the souls that drove them departed for better realms, I hoped. But there was sheen of light around them— queasy, baby-shit yellow colored light, meant to deflect the natural occurring processes of decay and surrender, meant to mask them in triviality. When I opened my eyes the bodies shifted, and for a moment I saw two largish dogs, pitiful, with bony rib-cages and matted hair, mouths gaped in death. I wanted to rip that sheen of deception from them and let them be recovered and mourned over, but I couldn't. For one thing, as soon as the bodies could be seen for what they were, there would be a thousand people in the area, and I knew first hand that crime scenes were no place for the Goddess' children. For another, I was running on Green's borrowed strength, and underneath the stench of death was a weaker, sweeter smell—copper-brine, musty like stolen breath and borrowed blood— vampires. And underneath that was garlic and cream pie—our mama vampire, asleep with her brethren. And then the smell that had traveled across the car exhaust, the concrete and steel, and even over death—rock, sun, and foothills bracken. My Bracken.

I wanted him back.

"The bodies are coated in magic." I told Nicky, who was wiping his mouth and trying to look cool. I could have told him there was no way to look cool after tossing your cookies like that, but he needed all of the self confidence he could get. "They're coated in magic to keep the smell from spreading—but Bracken's been…thinking about us…it worked."

I pulled out my cell phone and looked anxiously west, where I could see the sun, just hitting the water on the horizon. "Max? Put Renny on." I said. Nicky looked at me surprised, but I couldn't explain—if I called Green he'd beg me to wait and there was no time to wait, but I couldn't say no to Green, and then if anything bad happened, I'd hate us both. "Renny? Can you smell death?"

I heard her, snuffling like a cat in girl form, which was even odder over the phone, and then I heard the snarl when she caught scent of the dumpster in front of us.

"Got it." She said exultantly, "Where are you?"

"Follow that smell and call Green." I said succinctly. "Tell him to call Orson—there are dead werewolves near the warehouse. We're going in." I snapped the phone shut, ignoring Nicky's startled squawk, then moved to the door a few feet beyond the dumpster. It was unlocked—Nicky was surprised but I wasn't. The wall of magic on the inside was horrific in its intensity—I was betting that the minute we entered it would snap shut behind us like a fucking rat-trap.

We opened the door and the smell of vampire temporarily overpowered the smell of death. I stood at the doorway and looked around—like Green had said, the windows had been sealed, but even though our doorway was on the East side of the warehouse there was just enough foggy light left outside to give us a sense of what was inside. The warehouse itself was almost empty—pallets were scattered here and there, the occasional one still holding a stack of wooden crates with what looked like cheap dishware in them, but for the most part the floor was thick with dust and old canvas bags and pieces of wood. I knew as soon as the door closed behind us, the darkness would be stygian so I lingered there, in the doorway, scoping out the territory by the weak daylight before I committed Nicky and I to what would happen when the magic wall closed

On the far side of the warehouse, to our right, nearly twenty vampires lay, in the various poses of vampire death. For some reason, it was impossible for them to die unattractively—their heads tilted back, their lips parted, their eyes closed gently, their arms stretched languidly above them or even against a cheek. I guess if you don't breathe, you don't snore, drool, or squash your face against the pillow, you get to look like this as you sleep. These vampires looked hollow cheeked and shadowed, even in sleep, and I felt a little shudder. They would not be happy when they woke up.

But I'd seen vampires in day-death before—even hungry ones. My eyes were searching that darkness frantically for something else, and there, up against the wall, crouched on a raised pallet of dusty tarps, I saw what I was looking for.

Grace was asleep in day-death, collapsed in front of the pallets—she had died threatening the starving kiss—I could tell, because her fangs remained extended, even in sleep. She had fallen, not lain—her fingers were very nearly still cramped in their threatening, claw-extended pose, and her arms were bent at the front. Her knees were bent, as though she'd been caught in a crouch by daylight, and had simply toppled sideways. Bracken was behind her, glowing so faintly with his own elfin luminescence, a huddled figure with his arms wrapped around his knees. He saw us, and sat blinking from his now shaggy bangs as though we were his last best hope and the rock at the bottom of the pit of despair. With a yank on Nicky's hand I started trotting across the warehouse, relief giving me strength I didn't know I had.

"Dammit, Cory, don't come in…it's a…" And at that moment, the magic wall crashed behind Nicky, throwing the both of us forward on our faces in a cloud of dust and grime.

"Trap." I said, picking myself shakily up and dusting off my jeans to cover for my trembling hands. "I know." I paused then, words shivering on my lips, apologies, declarations—I wasn't sure which—and then our gazes locked, in mute exchange, in appeal, and honest longing. That's when I saw the blood, welling through a vicious wound in the down the back of his shoulder. He was clutching it, and his hand was coated in his own blood. He was bleeding. He was hurt. Suddenly I was furious.

I strode across the warehouse fumbling under my coat and sweatshirt for the T-shirt underneath. The ripping sound echoed in the vast, musty, dark space, even more than my furious footsteps. "You got hurt." I hissed, tripping over a pile of wood that I couldn't see. I put out a hand to still my fall and cut my palm on a nail, but it hardly slowed me down. His night vision was better than mine, so he saw me biff myself in the dark, and my anger was so unexpected he almost smirked in surprise.

"Well excuse me." He replied, our words at odds with the anguish in our eyes. "I assumed you'd be bringing along someone who could help with this."

"He's on his way." I snapped. "I thought it would be more important to get a little back-up your way and I didn't think you'd be stupid enough to get hurt."

"Gees, Cory, harsh." Nicky said from behind me as I neared Bracken. He was pale. Of course he was pale, dammit—he'd been sitting there *bleeding* all day as I wandered around the fucking city so desperate to know he was alive I could smell him over a cartload of death and an acre of water. Bracken could heal most wounds—for the wound to not be finished bleeding yet, it must have been deep…down to the bone and beyond, deep enough to tap into Bracken's heart-blood, where his own power would keep it from healing.

"Harsh?" My voice was shrill but I didn't care. "Harsh? Harsh is a broken promise, Nicky." I was ripping my T-shirt into strips as I spoke. "Harsh is some-one who tells you he'll be there, and you see forever in his eyes, and he goes out and gets himself shredded by a fucking velociraptor, or blown into summer driz-zle."

"Cory…" Bracken murmured, and I could hear the heartbreak in his voice but I couldn't, *couldn't* stop to listen. I was busy. I was tying those strips around his arm, trying to make a pad of them on his shoulder. I was trying to stop his *god-dammed bleeding.*

"Harsh is when you think that nothing can take love away from you, and you find out that people are *plotting* to steal it…and that they've reached into your brain and scraped it out with a fucking ice-cream scoop…" It was bleeding. He was a redcap and things bled around him and I couldn't stop it because he'd been bleeding all night and blood was who he was. Goddamn it. Goddess blight it *all.* "Harsh is when Bracken's own talent is ripping the fucking life force out of him as we speak goddammit all…" I grabbed Nicky's wrist with my right hand as I said it, working on instinct and anger and grief, enough to add some oomph to the swing of my left hand as I smacked it against Bracken's wounded shoulder, "*Heal* dammit—*HEAL.*"

And with that there was a buzz of blue light under my hands, and Bracken said "Ouch, *fuck* Cory, what in the hell are you trying to…"

And I let go of Nicky and fell to my knees.

"Do." Bracken trailed off. "You did it." He murmured, straightening, feeling his whole shoulder underneath the sticky bandage of my T-shirt. Then he turned and saw me, crouched and shivering on the concrete. "Goddess blight it." He snapped, and knelt next to me, looping an arm around me and rocking me towards him. I made a reluctant, keening sound, but remained crouched, trying to resist his comfort.

"I'm not going anywhere," He promised soberly.

"Pretty words." I replied, without heat. I felt empty, shaken, aimless.

"They're all I have." He said quietly, making a hash of my resistance with a kiss in my hair.

"I made sure Green will call Orson." I said, a little more briskly so I didn't fall apart, and tried to stand up. My knees shook, though, and I fell gracelessly on my ass.

"Moron." Bracken murmured, and bent down to pull me up. I leaned against him for a second, a sweet second, and I heard him suck in his breath.

"I'm a moron because I called in an inexhaustible food supply?" I asked mildly, because that had been my intention when I'd had Renny call Green—we would have to break out of this prison, I knew, and if the vampires were to live, we would have to do it after the sun went down, or risk exposing them to the light. And if we were to live, we'd have to do it mighty fast, or we would be hot lunch on the hoof. And if the vampires were to eat, and not commit mass murder, there had better be reinforcements ready.

"You're a moron because you've exhausted yourself." He said harshly, ignoring the brilliance of my strategy. "Because you think life comes with guarantees." He went on, picking me up and moving to sit us both on the stack of pallets I'd found him on. "Because you think Adrian's death means you'll lose everybody. I can't figure out which one makes you more stupid."

"Like you're any smarter." I snapped back, sitting up irritably. "You got caught, dipshit, or hadn't you noticed? You told me to worry about you and then you went and made me fucking frantic all goddamned day and you think I'm not going to be tired?" I sighed and blew out a breath. "Fucking asshole."

"Ah…Green's children—always such a joy." Said a voice from across the dankness, and I let out a little yelp, and would have been embarrassed, but Nicky screamed like a girl so I felt better.

"You know who we are?" I asked, standing up and trying to sound as tough as I'd sounded with Brack.

"I can smell Green's children from across the city." The voice said gently, with humor. "They smell like wet hay in the spring time, clean meadows, wildflowers, and lovers rolling around in those meadows and wildflowers. I can smell your sex from here, Green's children, and I could hear your foreplay when I woke up, but I'd say you have more pressing concerns, now don't you?"

"Andres." Bracken whooshed out in a gust of relief. His vision really was better than mine—I could barely see *him,* and we were sitting so close as to be touching. "Brother, I didn't see you this morning—it all happened so fast."

"Yes—you found us right at sunrise." Said the voice, and the person attached to it was staggering, it sounded like, this way. "Which is good, because Green's children or no, I don't think I could have kept my people from ripping you apart."

"You're up early." I said flatly, hoping it was true.

"Yes." And I could see him now that he was only a few feet away from us. He was smaller than I had imagined, and his voice was courtly, pleasantly accented Latino, with dark curly hair, sloe eyes, and precise Latin features to match. On any given day, I would have said he was pretty yummy looking, and the irony didn't escape me. "When I realized that the two people who had stumbled in here last night and then fled across the room were Green's people, I made it a point to rise early—some of us older vampires can do that, providing it's safe enough." He finished, and drew closer, giving an elegant, if shaky, bow. Bracken hopped off the table and extended a hand, but Andres put his own hand up and demurred.

"All of that lovely blood, and not a drop to drink." He apologized smoothly, but he looked haggard and gaunt, and I realize that if he could barely bring himself to touch one of us because of the temptation, then the others would be in far worse shape. Goddess.

"How old are your vampires?" I asked suddenly, thinking about what he'd said. He blinked in surprise, and even took a breath which he didn't have to do. "Are they old enough that a few swallows would do them—keep them off our backs until I could smash through the wall?"

Andres tried not to laugh. "A few swallows might very well 'do them' as you say—but, providing that you could actually do what you promise, and smash through that magic barricade, I'm not sure I could guarantee that we'd stop at a few swallows." He looked away then, and his throat worked, and he took a few steps back. "You cannot starve a wolf, my dear, and expect it to behave like a lap dog."

"They don't have to drink *from* us..." I began, but he interrupted.

"You cannot expect us to drink it cold!" And I could have laughed, because it was a connoisseur's horror.

"It doesn't have to be cold if it dances across the room." I said quickly, looking at Bracken, who nodded grimly.

"What then, Cory?" He asked levelly. I wanted to touch him, I realized. His face was so close to mine, in the dark, that I could feel his breath stirring the fine hairs around my eyes. "After I've fed them our blood, what next? You're weak. Everything you had you spent healing me."

"Well go ahead and tell the hungry vampire that!" I snapped, irritated because he was right and because I was trying to hide it. "I spent my anger—but that's not the only way to rev my battery, Brack—you know that. It's not even the most powerful way."

Bracken's expression was furious and incredulous at once. "So first you're pissed at me, and now you want to fuck me?"

"I'm always pissed at you." I shot back, although it was hardly true. But I did want to make love to him, and maybe the irritation would help keep me awake when I was dead on my feet. "You're arrogant, you're overbearing, and you don't see what's in front of your face. But you're also tender, protective, and as hurt inside as I am. All I ever wanted from you was a little time, asshole, but now we don't have any, and I don't know about you but I'd like to live to see where we might go."

"So Nicky and I make love to you and you blow up the wall?" Yeah. It sounded really stupid when he said it.

"Not Nicky." I said quickly, remembering what Green had told me about Avians. I looked over my shoulder at Nicky, who nodded, stricken. "He mates for life, Brack—he comes once, and he's in my bed forever. He needs to touch my hand, that's all—as soon as we blow the wall, the vampires leave, we get up and go."

"That's it?" And his voice cracked oddly. "I feel you up, 'charge your battery' as you put it—we get up and go?"

"Children," Andres pointed out gently, "It sounds like a plan—one I look forward to seeing put into action—and since I just saw one of my own twitch a little, I think maybe we should be quick about it."

But not so quick that I shattered a beloved's heart. Mindful that even Grace was showing signs of life, I put my hands on Bracken 's face, touched my forehead to his, spoke gently for the first time since I'd entered that cavernous trap, furious and frightened. "Have I ever, from the time I first kicked you in the balls, been able to just get up and walk away from you?" I asked.

"I will never let you go." He whispered, his brackish, shadow colored eyes smoldering and intense. "If I touch you, I will keep a part of you that Green will never have."

I swallowed. "Then we're even, the three of us." I said roughly, and he nodded, as though we'd struck a bargain, and his intensity changed.

I knew it was coming—we were standing well, chest to torso, nose touching nose, and we had just pretty much announced our intentions to get very friendly in the immediate future, but...but his mouth which had been so sweet the night before was harder, now, more possessive, and so, so much sweeter. Bracken surrounded me, his hands, long-fingered, were large enough to span my midriff and almost touch fingers across my back, his arms were almost crushing me against him, but even crushed, I felt enfolded, and so, so safe. This man would hurt me, I thought, in the corner of my mind that could still think, this man would fight with me, and challenge me, and make me angry, but he would never leave me, as long as breath was in his body or will was in his heart.

I heard a sound, a startled yelp and a stretch, and then Grace's voice in front of us. "Jesus Christ on crutches, do you think there could possibly be another time to do that, you two?"

"Not really." Nicky answered for us. He had come up behind us, close enough to touch me if I needed him, but not close enough to intrude. Of course, the way my body seemed to be swelling up inside my skin, he would have needed to climb inside my capillaries to intrude. "We're going to feed the vampires, then Cory's going to blow a hole through the magic wall and let them out."

"Are you sure that's what she's going to blow?" Grace asked dubiously, as Bracken thrust his tongue practically down my throat. I gasped, fighting my need to thrust my hands inside his shirt, and pulled back for a moment, trying to clear my head. If Grace was awake, that would mean...

"Ohhhhhhh...." I heard a voice from across the room groan ecstatically. "Finally, room service."

"You have no idea." I gasped. Bracken, beating me to the punch, had found his way under my sweatshirt. Since my T-shirt was tied around his now healed shoulder, the contrast between his chill, rough skin, and my heat-warmed fleece sweatshirt was enough to make me shudder. "But if you want to eat and get out of here, you'll give us a minute, here."

"Fuck that." Said another voice, roughly. "I'm too hungry to get off watching you two—get out of my way, Andres—this could be the only food we get."

"How very short sighted of you, Robert." Andres said mildly. "These people are trying to help us."

"I'd rather help myself to them, thank you very much." Said Robert. He was getting impatient, I could tell, and Bracken's clever, clever hands found my breasts, doing their best to drive away fear.

"We'll feed you!" I panted, and then, to Bracken, "Do you mind—I'm trying to save our *lives,* here."

"And I'm trying to live." He hissed wolfishly, and I found myself smiling back at him with stupid eyes.

"I'm *starving.*" One of Andres' vampires cried, and I could hear it, that ever present hunger in his voice, and thought of Adrian's own drive to feed. Things would get desperate in here awfully damn fast, and I wasn't sure if Andres could control them.

"Andres!" I called, gasping again as Bracken's long and nimble fingers found my pointed nipples and rubbed. "Andres..." I moaned, and I heard him chuckling in appreciation, because it sounded as though I were calling to him in passion. "Lord Vampire." I said, as formally as I could seeing that I was being ravished in public view. "Lord Vampire, do I have permission to kill?"

"Indeed yes." He replied. "If you feed me and set me free, you have permission to kill anyone who tries to stop you."

"Thank you, sir." I said, and Bracken moved his mouth to the corner of my mouth, to my ears, to my throat. "Grace!" I gasped, and she looked behind her enough to grin at me. "Grace, you need to open our wrists." I said, hating the thought. Bracken's hands, his mouth, were making my heart pound and my blood course through my veins—but even as my fingers tightened convulsively in his hair, I knew that I was weak, not with passion, but with exhaustion. Making love could make you strong—but at a price later.

I heard Nicky behind me, wincing, then she pulled my hand reluctantly from Bracken's shorn hair, and there was a gentle pain in my wrist. Bracken pulled his own hand from my waist, running his thumb under the waistband as he did so, and I almost sobbed in reaction. His other arm wrapped around me for support as Grace bit him, and then the three of us held out our wrists, and Bracken leaned his head against my collarbone and began humming under his breath.

My own breath caught in wonder, as my blood began to spurt, pulling in little balls from my wrist. Then from the flesh of the three of us, our blood began to dance, small mouthfuls of it catapulting rhythmically from our coursing veins and arcing across the dim interior of the warehouse, to the wide open mouths of the ravenous kiss of vampires. The dark was so complete that Bracken's magic glowed from the globules like diamond sugar sparkles on red licorice, and the little sounds the forty or so vampires made when each swallow of wonder hit their open mouths was childlike in it's glee. I could hear them gulp from where I stood, clinging to Bracken in arousal and weariness, and prayed that it would be enough. I wavered against him, lightheaded, and the dancing blood stopped its flight, and the wounds on our wrists closed as Bracken called our blood back to our bodies. He could do this now, I thought, because we gave each other strength. As the vampires sighed at that tiny taste, his mouth found mine, as ravenous for my taste as the vampires had been for my blood. I grabbed Nicky's hand with my own, a little static zip rippling through me as the circuit of power that was me closed, and my lust for Bracken and attraction for Nicky began to build power in my blood.

"Sorcerer..." One of the vampires said in wonder. "Elf..." Another moaned. "I haven't had elf in heavens know how long..." And then, Robert's impatient voice—"Goddammit—all I got was shapechanger...and not enough...I want some fucking *food...*"

"Well, Robert," another voice said dryly, as Bracken's hand slid underneath the waistband of my jeans and cupped my bottom, "It looks like you're about to get your wish."

Nicky's hand squeezed mine in fear, and I knew without looking that Robert's face was undergoing that scary thing that happened when vampires were super hungry, and super aroused, where their foreheads bulged and their teeth extended from their hollow-cheeked jaws. Adrian had been wearing that face when he'd flown to my rescue and died. I hated that face, and right now, I was pretty sure Nicky wasn't too fond of it either.

"Stand back, Robert." I gasped, trying hard to stay standing, to stay clutching Nicky's hand, to stay sane. I was charging—the combination of fear and pure animal desire was working, and I could feel it, the thrumming through my loins, my breasts, and up into my throat. I needed more control than that, I thought, and blessed Green for teaching me that handy little power-in-the-hand trick the night before. Bracken's fingers traced the line of my bottom, and I made a little groaning/gasping sound in my throat as I closed my eyes and my mouth and forced the rising static in my body into my free hand, which was no longer clenched in my lover's hair. Not a minute too soon. As I opened my hand to the glowing ball that was my love and life-force, I heard a collective gasp from the gathered kiss of vampires, and the shrill scream that meant that Robert's slender thread of self control had snapped.

I heard cries of "Robert, no!" "She can kill you, man!" And "Dammit, Robbie—look at her hand!" Before I felt the big whoosh of air as he hurtled into the air and rushed us from above. I felt him more than saw him, but it was enough for me to open my hand and launch. Pure sunshine, brilliant, angry, aroused and in love, burst from my hand, and Robert was caught mid-air. I even saw the agonized surprise on his face before he burst into flames and drifted down on the upturned faces of his kiss in a mist of ash.

I felt like shit. He'd been hungry, and trapped, and he was loved. I hated what I'd done, and the ball of light in my hand flickered.

"Don't." Bracken said against my throat. "There's no sin in wanting to live. There's no sin in wanting to save our lives." His head dipped lower, his mouth cupping around my breast through my sweatshirt, suckling through the thick fabric, making it wet and weakening the quivering muscles in my thighs. I whimpered a little, felt in my body all of the reasons I wanted to live and knew by the strength in my arms and the brightness behind my eyes that my pulsing ball of glow was stronger.

"Every vampire I kill will make the wait to get out of here longer." I said between my teeth. "Give me a little time…" Dammit—time. Time with Adrian. Time to get over him. Time to love Bracken. No wonder immortals were so willing to move forward over their grief. The one thing longevity had taught them is that there is **never** enough time.

"Co…Cory?" Nicky's voice was quavering, with fear, with desire, and I realized I had to cut him loose, or his heart and body would be lost, but not to me— just lost.

"One more minute, Nicky—think of sports scores or something." I panted.

"I hate sports." He said tersely, and his hand tightened on mine again, but this time in desire. He was molded to my back now and I felt his erection through my jeans.

"Back away…" I hissed. "Back away but keep hold of my ha—aand…" Because Bracken had moved from my breast to my midriff, which was bared by his hands, and his tongue dipped into my belly button, began a slow line down the open zipper of my jeans. Busy boy, Brack—I didn't even know my jeans were undone.

"You know I was half-in-love with you before this." Nicky groaned. I squeezed his hand back, and, Goddess help me, leaned against him some more as he leaned on the pallet of tarps.

"Hang in there, Nicky." I whispered…My world was rapidly narrowing, from the cavernous warehouse, to the kiss of vampires, to the people I was trying to protect, and now, it was down to Bracken and his clever, clever hands and diabolical tongue, and the opalescent glow of fire in my hand.

"Ahhhh…ahhh…" Oh, Goddess, his lips brushed my pubic mound, not even the swollen button of flesh which was still covered by denim, but just the fur, and the skin, and…

"NOW, NICKY…NOW!" I commanded, and hurled my force like a freakish tennis ball into the East-facing wall. At the same moment, I jerked Nicky away from me and released his hand to clench my fingers convulsively in Bracken's hair. Keening, breathless, pleading sounds were coming from my throat, and still, in the back of my mind, I knew that even when we were alone there was something I **must not** do.

A gaping rift the size of an RV opened up in the side of the warehouse, followed by a swarming kiss of starving vampires, followed by a poor little Kestrel falcon, with a hard-on that could be seen even as he flew, and as soon as they cleared the wall, they ceased to exist for me.

I fell back abruptly against the pallet onto the soiled bed of tarps, and then I was centered on Bracken, consumed by him, caught in the conflagration that was and always would be the two of us making love. His hands caught roughly at my hips and pulled my jeans down to my knees and he was burrowing between my thighs. I cried out, washed again by a building climax, and another, and the power that was the two of us crashed over me like a climbing tide, and again, and again, building inside of me to a peak that felt like it would crack the world. The teeny-tiny pea sized part of my brain that was still sane was afraid. There was a reason, I thought, that I couldn't allow that to happen, but I couldn't remember what it was. I clenched against the sexual incursion, determined not to let the madness inside of me erupt. It was hard…Goddess, it was hard, because his tongue was clever, and my body was swollen and begging for his touch and for his sex and I wanted him inside of me so badly it was like pain…it was pain…

"Nooo…" I gasped, digging my hands into the grimy tarps that were our bed, and the same teeny-tiny part of my brain spared a neuron to wish that we were some place glorious, for our first time, and then Bracken moved up to cover me with his bare body. He wedged a knee between my thighs and then I spread them willingly. I would have held my knees to my ears if it would have eased this terrible, awful ache of wanting in my sex. He poised his body above mine, touching my swollen, slick sex with his own, and I almost sobbed with the effort not to impale myself on him. "I don't…I don't remember…something bad will happen…" *Goddess,* I needed him.

"It's okay…" Bracken whispered, his shoulders shaking with the effort not to sheathe himself inside of me. "Green's here. He'll catch you. Let go."

And only then could I feel Green, outside, surrounding the warehouse with his power, readying himself to catch whatever burst from me in aftermath.

I cried out and arched my hips, taking Bracken inside of me in one thrust. And then he was moving, and he was engorged and awesome, and pounding so deeply I thought I could taste him in the back of my throat and I craved him. And still he drove me, higher, higher, until I thought I could see the heavens, and I had one last breath to wish again that we were doing this somewhere, anywhere, but here in this dank warehouse, and then there was no room for anything but

Bracken, and my body exploding around him, surrounding us with power that spilled around us, washing against Green and flowing back, and something awesome and huge gave way inside of me and Green caught that too. Then it was only Bracken and me, clutching each other, crying out, and a his trembling arms clenching as he spilled himself into me, and for one perfect moment, we were everything.

GREEN

Unexpected Edifice

The air around the warehouse was like being inside a storm cloud before the first charge of lightning. It was thick, and expectant, and static, and even though Green had a pretty good idea what was going on inside, his chest wanted to explode with the agony of waiting.

Renny came up beside him and leaned, cat-like into his circle of warmth. "What do you suppose is happening in there?" She asked quietly, her breath pluming in the cold winter wind from the bay. The fog had blown away at sunset and it was so clear that Oakland looked close enough to leap to, and the Bay Bridge looked unreal overhead. But the wind, Goddess, the wind, was cold enough to fog the mind when there was no fog to speak of. Renny had been running around in bicycle shorts and a T-shirt all day—if she hadn't been a were creature, with a lightning speed metabolism, she would have been too cold to speak.

Green shivered and looked carefully at Renny. She'd been spitting mad at Cory when she'd called, and he couldn't blame her. All the effort they'd put into keeping his little sorceress alive, and she'd gone and put herself in this sort of danger. But after he'd called Orson and given him directions and an order to get as many healthy were-beings in the area *immediately,* he'd had time to think through Cory's reasons for walking into the trap, and he couldn't fault her logic. And now, standing outside the window-less warehouse that was a literal as well as a preternatural dark-spot among the other, well-lit buildings, he could admit that

Cory could do from inside what none of them could do from the outside. And given that the sun had set just as he caught sight of the place—and its grisly marker—he also knew that if she had waited for him, Grace and Bracken would have died. Judging from her quiet, he could guess that Renny had come to the same conclusions.

"If we're lucky," He told Renny, keeping his voice light, "Cory's getting laid."

"Again?" Renny asked, incredulous. "Didn't she get enough last night?"

"Renny!" Max said from her side, aghast. He had pulled himself together well, Green thought, for someone who had just lost his lunch at the sight of the dumpster on the East facing wall. Good—they would need Officer Max to smooth things over with the local police. Or at least to drag them over to where, Goddess hoped, some by-then very active and recently fed vampires might smooth things over for them.

"Well it's not as though they were quiet!" Renny argued.

"What can I say," Green told her mildly before Max could say something he either didn't mean or would regret meaning later, "She's developed quite a taste for elf."

"Well you're very good at what you do." Renny told him, wrapping her arm around his waist. For the weeks after Mitch had died, when Green hadn't been with Cory and Adrian, he had been with Renny. It was nice to be remembered.

"Thank you, dearest." Green smiled at her, kissed the top of her head, and turned towards Orson who was moving shakily towards him. The bodies in that dumpster were his friends, his comrades—his people. "I'm so very sorry, Lord Werewolf." He said formally, moving away from Renny to bow. "You have whatever help we can offer you."

Orson was still dressed for work, but the knees of his wool suit were stained from when he'd kneeled on the street in honest mourning. He passed a shaky hand over his mouth, and tried to pull himself together.

"They were ripped apart by birds." He said. "That fucking Goshawk—he ripped my people apart so he could starve the vampires out. And we never would have known it if…" He looked at Green. "We owe you, Lord Green." He said formally. "You have our loyalty and our aid in this fight, to the last were." He sat down abruptly, and took up Green's look of staring at the warehouse, as though that one declaration had used up everything he had. "What do you suppose is happening in there?" He asked, and even Max laughed.

"We've got someone inside…" Green began, and Renny burst out with more giggles while Max slapped a hand across her mouth. Orson didn't notice but Green looked at them both drolly. "I think she has enough power to break through that metaphysical wall." He finished, shaking his head at his precocious children.

"That would take a hell of a magical charge…" Orson was respectful.

"Fortunately she's got a couple of batteries." Green said dryly. Renny convulsed against Max's hand.

"Large enough to do give her that big of a zap?"

"They're portable." Green supplied, wincing as Max, exhausted and stressed, finally broke into giggles of his own. Cat and cop sank to the ground, laughing hysterically and leaning weakly on each other. He smiled with them, but…he felt something…he knew that storm feeling well…but it wasn't quite…He blew out a breath and Renny looked at him questioningly. He shook his head. "Premature." He murmured, and that set them off again.

And then they could all feel the build up, and the pressure grew so great it clogged their lungs and made laughter impossible.

"Holy God." Orson breathed.

"Are your people ready?" Green asked, and Orson stood up, laboring to breathe against the cloud of static charge in the air, and began to organize his shape-shifters—about sixty in all, in a group thirty or so feet from the small door towards the East side of the warehouse—there was more room on that side then on any other except the side facing the street. For a static, breathless moment, everyone stood, staring at the warehouse, waiting for the storm to break. Suddenly, from the East side of the warehouse, there was a screech so shrill it should have warped the metal siding and shattered the grimy brick. Without warning, a bird so big it almost looked like a vampire in flight arced over the structure and rushed in, screeching and rending the wall with his claws while Green and the were-folk looked on in horror.

"My God, that thing's huge!" Max burst out, and before Green could tell him that it wasn't *really* a condor, it happened.

There was a silent explosion, followed by a shattering of brick, wood, and sheet metal that blew out of the North side of the East-facing wall. The metal itself peeled away from that part of the building so suddenly that the were-condor was hit by the edge of the sheet, rent in two from wing shoulder to claw, and taken down while the debris obliterated the body. The explosion was followed quickly by a frantic swarm of flying people, moving in that eye-blurring fashion that Cory called hyperspeed, terrifyingly quick, coldly purposeful, starving dogs at the hunt. Orson's people had flattened to the ground in fear, first from the explosion, then from the vampires.

Into that moment of stillness, before the wave of vampires could crash against the frightened were-folk, Green called out in powerful words of old elvish that pulled at the swarming vampires. The effect was electric—in a heartbeat, the vampires stilled as one, and, with a controlled slowness, continued their advance towards the willing blood supply. In a moment several arms had wrapped with taut urgency around several bodies, and the age old dance of blood seduction was conducted en-masse. But it wasn't uncontrolled, and it wasn't frenzied, and as it became apparent that none of the alarmed sacrifices would, indeed, be torn to bits, Green and those waiting with him blew out a general sigh of relief.

"What in the hell did you say?" Max wanted to know.

Green, who was as surprised as everyone else at this urgent self-control, had watched the whole display with raised eyebrows and surprise. "Death to those who violate the tender sacrifice." He translated, baffled. "They're ritual words— from a vampire's first feeding. Its how they learn not to kill unless they want to— that if they kill a willing sacrifice they owe a debt to the family." He looked at Max and Renny and shrugged. "It doesn't usually work so well, which is why we tend to keep new vampires near a prison population, or a nasty back alley." He shook his head again. "I have no idea why they listened to me."

"They listened to you because you choose your lovers well." Said a voice emerging from the cluster of feeding vampires. Green noticed that the vampires had enough self-control to release one 'victim' before moving on to another, and he thought that maybe the owner of that voice had a little more to do with it.

"Maybe they listened because their master is good and wise." Green replied, and stepped forward to shake hands. "Good to see you well, Andres—we were worried."

"Well, my Lord Green, you should have been worried—if not for your little sorceress, there would be many dead by morning, in one way or another."

Andres came forward then, bowing slightly, and Renny looked at him with surprise. "I thought you said he was freaking scary, Green?" She asked—this slightly built man with the fine nose and sweet eyes appeared cultured and kind.

Green chuckled weakly. "I said I had to negotiate with a freaking scary vampire, dearest." He answered, bemused. "Andres usually sends someone else to do his business dealings."

"Yes." Said Andres, a trifle grimly. "In that way, at least, I'll miss Robert."

Green's smile faded. "I'm sorry, Andres?"

Andres smiled ruefully. "Do not be too sorry, brother—if your little sorceress hadn't killed him, she would be dead now and so might we all—we wouldn't have made it through another night without tearing each other's throats out."

"Oh…that explains that little burst of…" Green began, but Renny interrupted him.

"Hey—Green—where are they?"

Andres laughed outright. "Finishing what they started, I would imagine."

Green winced, trying hard not to show, but Andres and Adrian had been fledglings in the same kiss. Green had been there, for both of them, when hungers had run rampant. Andres had been a terrified lover, at first, and then a creative one, and finally a friend. Now, it was the friend who clapped a hand on Green's shoulder. "Don't worry, big brother." He said gently. "They…came to an understanding, I think, about your place in their lives. It was in your favor, if I read things right."

Green flashed a grin. "I have a feeling you're understating things a bit."

Andres joined him. "You would be right." And then he stepped back and bowed. "And now, if you would forgive me, your sorceress and your red-cap gave us an appetizer before she freed us, but I really must dine if I am to hold on to my manners."

Green blinked, put the facts together, said, "She really is brilliant, isn't she?" But before Andres could answer, Renny stepped forward.

"Lord Vampire." She said formally, a slight girl with bare feet and a T-shirt that reached below her knees, and apparently not much else on beneath it, "It would be my pleasure." She raised her chin, exposing her neck for his pleasure.

Andres smiled, and bowed again. "The pleasure is all mine." He murmured, stepping forward, while Green put a restraining hand on Max's arm. It was a generous—and politic—gift, from Renny, and Green wouldn't interfere with it for the entire world.

Andres' incisors grew, and his jaws lengthened, but the rest of his face retained its quiet control, up until he was close enough to smell the warmth of Renny's skin.

"Ah, Goddess." He murmured, looking at Green with heartbroken eyes. "It's bad enough that all your people smell like you, Lord Elf, but it breaks my heart to be near so many who still carry Adrian on their skin." His lips twisted bitterly, then, over his retracted teeth, and he changed to kiss Renny on the forehead. "Thanks, my dear." He murmured, "But I can remember him from your sorceress and red-cap, who practically filled that warehouse with his ghost. His smell on you just hurts too much. I will dine somewhere else tonight." And with that he turned and faded into the night, where weakened were-folk and sated vampires had sunk to the ground in what could only be defined as a food coma.

Green would have followed him, to embrace, to commiserate—even to make love, for old times sake, since he would be alone this night—but at that moment, several things happened consecutively.

The first was that another bird veered out of the night sky—this one much smaller than the dead condor whose body lay unlamented in building debris. In an explosion of feathers and sobs the little hawk landed at Green's feet and became a distraught Nicky, bent practically double and crying "Goddess, make it stop…"

Green stepped forward to gather the boy in, and as Nicky pressed up against him, Green could feel the boy's arousal through his jeans, and cursed himself. Of course she would have needed Nicky's contact—she couldn't have made that hole in the magic wall on fury alone—not in her condition.

"Shh…" Green whispered. "She let you free like this so you could forget her…"

"How can I forget her?" Nicky wept brokenly. "She was wonderful…and he touched her and it was…Goddess…and she's…she's…"

And then Green felt the second thing. Everybody felt it. The vampires and were-folk rose from their somnolence, looking in surprise at the warehouse. The police, alerted of strange activity were now pulling up in a fury of sirens and lights, emerging from their cars and looking at the broken warehouse in suspense, as though wondering what the next explosion would be like. And Green felt the agony of an explosion unwholesomely suspended, waiting…waiting for…waiting for him.

He had Nicky against him, which was too bad, because neither of them would have planned on what happened next, but he drew on Nicky, drew on Renny who came up and put her hand on his back, even drew on Max, who had touched Cory in the past, and now clenched Renny's hand, and using this strength, he threw up a barrier, a bowl of his power, felt her touch it, felt her love him, felt her come. In a heartbeat, there was a brilliant wash of silent light against his shield. Nicky, feeling Cory in that wash, convulsed against Green in orgasm, coming, mourning, sobbing at his lost innocence and freedom.

The light subsided, and Green picked Nicky up and cradled the young man against him like a child, and looked in awe at what had once been the warehouse. What stood in its place was still glowing with magic, and breathtaking in its beauty. It was also starkly, woefully, shockingly out of place in the middle of the warehouse district.

"Well—it's a prettier building…" Renny said, flummoxed.

"It is that, luvie." Green said, bemused and stunned.

"It's a good thing I never got in her pants." Max said—almost to himself. He looked at the others defensively when they opened their mouths in astonishment and reproach. "I'd be dead!" He said, still looking bemusedly at what Cory and Bracken had wrought. "Hell—I probably wouldn't have survived our first kiss."

Nicky turned his head for a moment, took in the new edifice in place of the old one, and laughed through his sobs. "It was pretty nasty in there, for a wedding night." He said, his voice muffled and congested. He leaned his head against Green's chest then, resigned, comforted, and Green nuzzled the top of his newborn's head. Poor Nicky, he thought, aching for him. Cory had saved his life, only to enslave him, although that had never been her intention. He looked in front of him, shaking his head. He doubted this had been her intention either.

Andres came back then, wiping a trickle of blood off his mouth with his thumb and then licking his thumb for the last drop. "What the hell am I supposed to do with this?" He asked, incredulous, gesturing at the gleaming structure of wood, marble, brass, steel, and glass.

"You own this property?" Green asked, and as Andres nodded, "I'll buy it from you."

"You have it as my gift, big brother." Andres told him, "But what you're going to do with a smallish Ritz-Carlton hotel in the middle of this district I haven't a fucking clue."

It was the same shape as the original warehouse—a plain square, and although it was taller, it was still was only six stories high—too small to need lights—with a car port and a red-carpeted entrance. The sides were gleaming tan marble, and there were green banners strewn from the squared top. It wasn't a real Ritz-Carlton, but it looked like one of the finer hotels of San Francisco, as Cory might have seen one when she and Renny had knocked about the city. It even had the insignia, Ritz-Carlton, emblazoned on the entrance. A honeymoon suite indeed, Green thought, his mouth turning up at the ends in spite of himself.

"Andres," He said thoughtfully, "I think your people need to escort the police into that nice hotel…and have them wake up back at their original beats, do you think?"

"I'll help with that." Max said, regaining some of his own composure and fishing his neglected badge out of his back pocket. "I'll take them inside, you meet us there, Lord Andres…uhm, Green…" He turned towards Green, not sure how he wanted to say this, because it would be painful, for both of them. "You don't think we can…that they're…out in the open, do you?"

"Don't worry, Max." Green said gently, wryly, "I'm sure they've got their own room."

Max relaxed, shook himself a little, like a man letting go of a long held dream he hadn't known he'd had. "Me, Nicky..." He looked at the building again, looked back. "We are so out of our league." And then, as weary as he was—as they all were—he gave an awkward, mortal, military bow, and Green decided then and there that the man could eat at his table at any time. Max turned then, and hadn't gotten more than a few paces when Renny gave Green's waist a squeeze and then ran to catch up, taking Max's hand in her own as she caught up, and bringing it to her lips. She ignored his startled look, and together they walked to the gathered group of puzzled policeman standing with their backs to the Bay Bridge to stare in astonishment at the newborn hotel that had sprung out of the pavement like a pretty mushroom.

It was after midnight when Green, Nicky, Grace, Renny and Max huddled in the back of the town-car that Andres had so thoughtfully called for them. Nicky had been inconsolable for most of the night, caught in the agony of being mated both to a woman who was so obviously in love with someone else and to Green himself—even Green could feel the dual connection, and although he knew that there was probably something profound in the idea that he and Cory had acquired another lover, he was just too damn weary to decide what it could be. Green finally had to roll Nicky's mind and wish him to sleep, and his heart ached again for the ravages of the boy's lost innocence. Goshawk would have so, so much to answer for, in the matter of Nicky Kestrel, he decided grimly.

Max had done his job well when he convinced the other officers to come inside the hotel. With Renny at his side, he pleasantly introduced them to the now calm, powerful vampires who had, as a kiss, rolled their minds smoothly and then made certain that both cops and cop cars were placed strategically around the city. Being familiar with call signs and assignment sheets, Max was invaluable in that area as well; Green was particularly impressed with the way the young officer didn't even flinch when some of his compatriots ended up half a pint low with a sore spot on their necks.

The bodies had been harder to account for—but even then, Max had come in handy by saying that they had been caught in an explosion caused by improper chemical storage. It was a weak story, and it never would have been believed if Max hadn't dispatched several vampires to the morgue with the ambulances (and the unconscious drivers) who would smooth things over with the mortal world and it's need for times, dates, and paperwork. There would be holes, certainly, but Max had dealt with those holes as a cop, before he knew what caused them.

"People will believe in incompetence, in freak chance, in brutality—but a magic hole in the wall and vampires?" He'd shaken his head then, slightly-crossed blue eyes weary and cynical. "They'd rather believe in human monsters than inhuman ones."

Grace had fed from one of the grateful weres, although she'd been in better shape than the other vampires having only been captive for a day. But she was shaken from her face off with an entire kiss of older vamps, from the attack at the beginning which had nearly killed Brack, and from finding the bodies of the werefolk in the first place. Grace had only been dead for twenty or so years—not nearly long enough to grow accustomed to seeing life thrown away so casually. She was also heartbroken for Nicky, and for Green, and even for Bracken and Cory. "It hurt to watch them." She told Green later, leaning into him for comfort. "They weren't ready for this dance, neither of them—last night, Green. Last night, she actually *thought* about it, thought about this new relationship. Tonight, she's…"

"Balls deep in it." Green had supplied dryly, and Grace rolled her eyes and gave him a weary smile.

"Do you ever have to remind yourself that she's not old enough to drink legally?" Grace asked at last.

"It only occurs to me when she's not here." Green told her honestly, wanting the night to be over with so he could curl up in a corner with this thought to keep him warm. "I can't imagine making the choice she made tonight." He shook his head in wonder. "What was it like, the fountains of dancing blood?"

Grace laughed, shook her head as he had. "It was pretty fucking amazing." She murmured. "In a thousand years, I wouldn't have thought about feeding vampires like that." Suddenly she giggled. "You should have heard them bragging about who they got…" And without warning she sobered again. "Poor Nicky— not even the vampires were happy to have him." She reached over Green then and kissed the sleeping Nicky on the forehead with all of her maternal instincts at the forefront

But the ordeal—and the exhausting day—had taken its toll on everybody in the car. Renny and Max were curled against each other, sleeping soundly. Even Green was nodding off, dreaming of his own home instead of the San Francisco apartment and thinking, in his haze, that all of his dear ones needed peace, desperate, desperate peace.

They had a few scant hours of peace in the end—enough to stagger out of the car into the apartment building, and make it to their rooms. Max went with Renny, Green noted, for comfort not sex, but he was sure the other would come in time. Grace went to the darkling, but he saw the light blinking on the apartment phone when she left, so he was pretty sure Arturo was getting an earful. Nicky went with Green.

The boy was traumatized, Green knew. A borderline homophobe, he'd been aroused not just by seeing Cory and Bracken make love, but by Green's highly sexual presence as well. His first sexual experience had been bizarre and careless— Nicky had been introduced into the world of sensuality by brutal necessity and bitter remorse on the parts of all parties involved. And unlike others in his situation, he wouldn't have the luxury of finding a soul-mate to make that initial pain go away. He was stuck, for better or for worse, with Green, and Cory—provided she were willing to take yet another man to her bed. If anyone needed healing at this moment, it was Nicky Kestrel.

And, Green had to admit, he was feeling a little bereft himself. Healing was what he did. Healing Nicky would help heal the ache in his heart that came with sharing what had never been wholly his to begin with.

Nicky was awakened gently, with hands on his body, a whispering voice, pleasant sensations in sensitive areas. He was so wounded, so heart-weary and aching, that when he finally came to his senses enough to question gender, he was deep in Green's mouth and spasming euphorically, hands clenched in Green's hair, body rocked with honest passion and sweet desire. After, Green held the boy, spoke to him lowly about being cared for, about being loved, about what it would mean to be a part of Green's household, and with people who would die before they failed him. Nicky wept a little, talked about Cory a little, and his hopeless, pure, adolescent love for the girl with the sarcastic sense of humor and haunted eyes that he'd met in computer class at college. Green told him about his first meeting with Cory, about Adrian, about loss, about love. They fell asleep together, Nicky curled up for solace, and Green thought, as he listened to Nicky's gentle breathing, that yes, they had their peace.

Just after dawn Cory cried out again. She was exhausted, sick, and under siege, and once again, nobody in Green's place could help her.

CORY
Wounded Redux and Backatcha

We slept, a little, Bracken and I, and I awoke on my side, curled into his chest. As impossible as it sounds, Bracken was still inside of me. Both of us were covered with a blue and red comforter richer than anything I'd ever seen.

"Uhm, Brack?" I ventured. "Bracken..." He murmured something and clutched me tighter, and I would have indulged in his heat and his smell a little before I started fretting with trivialities, except..."Bracken—who in the hell is Dewey Anne, and where in the blue fuck are we?"

"Wha?" And suddenly, naked from the waist down and half asleep, he was standing on the mattress, crouched in a fighting pose. I was so surprised I fell off the bed. Note to self—don't wake this man in mid-sleep or he may kill you with his bare hands.

"Where the hell are we?" Bracken asked from his crouch on the bed.

"That's pretty much exactly what I asked you!" I giggled. Bracken looked down at me, flushed, and hopped off the bed so lightly I couldn't hear his feet thud on the floor. He bent down and offered me a hand, and I stood, clutching the comforter to my chest. It was stupid really, because I was still wearing my sweatshirt and my bra, and even my jeans weren't off entirely, but wrapped around one foot, the one with the tennis-shoe still on it. We were in a well lit, spacious, beautiful hotel room instead of the icky, grimy, filthy warehouse. The walls were done in light oak paneling and burgundy and forest green wallpaper— the kind with the raised, velveteen curlicues, and there was matching burgundy carpet under my feet. We were in a freaking rich-man's paradise, but I was still dressed in the dusty stained clothes I'd put on that morning.

"We just made love." Bracken said, stripping off his ruined sweat-shirt—there were giant bloody rips in the back where one of Goshawk's people had almost rent out his life, and my eyes fixed on those in fear for a moment. Bracken took my attention gently back to his living self by reaching his long-fingered hands out and covering my own hands with his. Then he pried my clenched hands away from my chest, and forced them to relax, so that the comforter fell to the floor. Moving stilly, he bent down and took off my shoe and then helped me step out of my jeans and panties. I stood and let him, but I couldn't stop myself from clenching my hands under my arms when he went to take off my sweatshirt.

"Where are we?" I asked stubbornly, and a smile quirked at his hard, thin-lipped mouth.

"If I look to figure out where we are, will you take off that damned shirt?" He asked patiently.

"That depends on where we are." I told him, not meeting his eyes. The smile bloomed, and he bent and took my mouth with his. His hands ran up my hips then, in one smooth stroke, and, as I put my hands on his ribs (his shoulders were pretty high up, no matter how he bent down to kiss me) he continued the caress under my shirt, and deftly removed it when I was too lost in his kiss to demur. He broke from me briskly, grabbed the comforter and wrapped it around my shoulders, sat me on the bed and walked towards the windows, which were shaded with heavy green drapes and tinted glass. Carefully he looked outside, and then turned to grin at me.

"What?"

"We're still in the warehouse." He said, incredulous, admiring.

"We're not in the warehouse." I told him patiently. "This is *obviously* not the warehouse."

"Okay, okay. We're not *in* the warehouse, but this building is *where* the warehouse used to be. Come look, Corinne Carol-Anne—they can't see us." Because I continued to stare at him as though he were speaking old elfish.

Still dragging the comforter behind me, I got off the bed and did as he told me, peering gingerly around the thick velvet drape. The building was beautiful—I could see from the sides that it was clean, beige marble with brass and wood trim. In front of it was the now familiar warehouse-dot.com district, and distantly, over three blocks of squat brown buildings, I could see the faint twinkle of the Bay Bridge off the water. Our room was a corner suite, so we could see the alley where the entire kiss of vampires we had just freed was crowded, but they were feeding in an extremely civilized fashion from a group of what I presumed to be were-folk. On the other side of the window, standing across the street I could make out Green, carrying Nicky like a baby, standing next to a smaller, slightly built dark haired man that I thought might be Andres. Next to them stood Renny, Max, and Grace. They were grouped together, looking slack-jawed towards Bracken and I, staring up at my new building in awe. In front of them in the street a mass of cop cars was converging with ambulances as well. It looked like we were about five stories up—in a penthouse suite—and we couldn't hear the sirens at all.

Abruptly I sat down.

"We're in the Ritz-Carlton?" It came out as a question, but I knew the answer.

"How do you know it's the Ritz-Carlton?" Bracken asked, looking down at me.

"Because the last thought I had, after I knew Green was there, was that I wished we were doing this some place nice, like the Ritz-Carlton hotel."

Bracken chuckled appreciatively, and then the laugh grew and became a full-throated whoop. He laughed so hard that he slid down the wall next to me, and looked at me, his eyes twinkling, to see if I saw the joke. I was giggling weakly, but something in my face must have been sobering, because he quit laughing and bent and kissed my bare shoulder.

"You wanted us to be together some place nice." He said softly. "That's sweet, Corinne Carol-Anne. There's no shame in that."

"It's frightening." I said, leaning against him. This I knew how to do—I leaned against Bracken all the time. "I didn't know I could do this. I could have hurt somebody."

"You didn't know…" He trailed off, incredulous, thinking. "Of course you didn't know." He said at last. "There's been no time to tell you. You know that Goshawk stole three first from you. Your first kiss with Adrian. Your first sex with Adrian. And your first time with both Green and Adrian."

"I did this before?"

"With Green and Adrian." He smiled then. "You don't remember the Goddess Grove?"

I could see it in my mind, oak trees, lime trees, thorn-less rose trees, twisted into figures, graceful, erotic people. I knew one of them was me.

"I do remember." I said soberly. I had to—it was how I could respect the mark that Bracken had placed on Mist—the oak leaf, the lime-tree leaf, and the rose. "I just don't remember making it."

Bracken blew out a breath. "It was something, that night, to be there. The whole house glowed with the three of you. I swear, by the end of this year there will be a litter of sprites the likes of which the world has never seen—it's why they're so devoted to you, you know."

I smiled a little at him. "I could have hurt someone." I repeated, still horrified.

He shook his head. "You waited for Green." He reminded me. "You waited until it was safe. Eventually, you'll be able to control it yourself." He kissed my shoulder again, and, in spite of everything, I shivered. "Don't worry, *due'ane*," He murmured lowly. "Trees will still grow, rain will still fall, and you will have lovers again."

It sounded like a song. "Who's Dewey Anne." I asked him, voice gruff. He was so familiar, this Bracken, but so strange, naked next to me. I could touch him, I realized with wonder. I could run my hands from his flank to his shoulder, and he would welcome the touch because he was mine.

"You are." He whispered, and I met his eyes. "It's elfish, the feminine noun for 'other equal half'. You are my other. My everything."

I stared back at him, heart in my throat. I couldn't claim the same thing, I knew. I would always want Green, in my heart, in my bed. But now I would always want Bracken too. I swallowed, and it hurt. "Is there a masculine?"

He nodded. "*Due'alle.*"

I felt a pressure then, in my chest, in my eyes. "Can you be that, my *due'alle*, when I have another? You can be my *due'alle*, and then…" And then Green could be my Green, and all that he was in my heart. Except that I couldn't say it out loud, not with Bracken, who had just made love to me, and called me his everything. I couldn't bring Green into our bed, or it would never be ours.

"There is a word for you and Green, in elfish." Brack said, taking the burden from me. "The leader you share your bed with, whom also shares with you—the sidhe lord to his beloved."

Fair enough. "What's the word?"

"*O'ue'hm.*"

It sounded like *owe we him,* and I couldn't think of a better word at all. "Okay."

He raised an attenuated finger then, to trace my collarbone delicately from the center of my neck to my shoulder, and I shivered once more.

"I'm filthy." I demurred.

"So am I." And in one smooth movement, he stood up, then bent and gathered me in his arms.

"Why do you people insist on carrying me?" I grumbled, as he made his way to the bathroom.

Bracken grinned down at me, and I touched a grimy finger to the divot in his cheek that I had never noticed because I had never seen him this happy. "You make it so easy for us," He said, "When you waste away to nothing but chicken legs and cherry pits."

I blew a raspberry, and he frowned at me.

"No—I am serious. I told you once that you'd miss your boobs eventually." He stopped in the doorway to what can only be described as a truly palatial bathroom and swung me down so that my bare body took that long slide against his and my naked feet touched the blue-tiled floor. I shivered, from his body, which I had never felt all soft and hairless against mine. New. Everything about him was so new. Curious, I leaned forward to see where my mouth would touch, and found that it met in that hollow between nipples, where chest met stomach. His skin was like soft marble, without even the pale green cast that Green had, and his muscles were smooth underneath. He shuddered when I kissed him, and I felt his sex, rousing again, grow heavy against my stomach. I blinked. Looked down. Stepped back.

"God and Goddess." I said, my eyes huge. He arched his eyebrows and turned towards the golden tap of a red-tiled bathtub that could have sat six. Well, six of me—maybe two of Bracken. If he was erect, one and a half.

"What?" I was still wrapped in the comforter, and he pried gently at my fingers. The comforter fell, and he scooped it up and tossed it out the door towards the bed. I stood there, naked, torn between holding my hands up to shield myself and putting them behind my back like a school child to stare at the floor. I did neither. Instead I reached out, and my grubby fingers brushed the line between his stomach and his pubis. I tickled the furz there. I could see that even lower, his hair grew no coarser than that on the back of my arm. It was not an elfish thing, I thought, because Green had a wealth of curly blond hair at his groin. It was a Bracken thing—distinct to the species he descended from.

He was perfect. He was *huge*. If I had really looked at him, the few times I had seen him naked, I probably wouldn't have, in a million years, gotten near him naked again because all reason said he couldn't fit. He was beautiful and unblemished. I moved my hand to his hip and before he could hold me, moved behind him and touched the shoulder I had healed. Faint, and fading even as I looked, I could see three scars from where something with a talon had raked him deeply.

"The scar will be gone by morning." I murmured.

"That's not what you were going to say." He murmured back, and turned, this time taking me in his arms before I could move away. He picked me up against him, my toes dangling, and stepped into the tub, then sat down on the step under the foaming water. I looked determinedly behind him and saw that there were bottles of bubble-bath—not the tiny ones you usually see in hotels, but big ones. It was cedar-rose—my favorite scent.

"I thought of everything." I said then, a smile in my voice. I was held against him, my knees on the bottom of the tub and my head against his chest.

"That's not it either." He returned in grim amusement. He pulled burgundy washcloth from the side of the tub, lathered it up and started to rub my back. I shuddered against him, and he turned me and slid down to the bottom of the tub, so that the water was up to my chin and I was leaning against him. His erection was pressed into my lower back, and I found I almost couldn't breathe, knowing this.

"I don't see how you fit." I told him baldly, after a minute of feeling it throb against me in time to my breathing. "You weren't lying about being super-sized..." I leaned my head down so he could lather my neck, and he rinsed me and tipped my head back, scooping water onto my hair, which was probably a complete disaster anyway. A little soap, and eventually long fingers massaged my scalp. I sighed, and relaxed a notch more.

"And you're perfect." I sighed, able to speak now that I couldn't read his reaction to my words in every expressive line of his grim face. With difficulty I held my left ankle out of the water. A jagged, wide white band of scar wrapped around it, where a combusting vampire had nearly charred my flesh in two. "I scar." I lowered my ankle and closed my eyes, and warm water washed the line of my hair. And again, until my clean hair lay against my scalp. I felt a shadow over my eyes, and opened them to see Bracken, upside down, leaning over me. He had a tiny, sober smile at the corner of his lips. "I was there for that one." He said. "And this one too." And he straightened and touched my shoulder with warm soapy hands. I shuddered. My shoulder looked like a grenade had exploded through it and then had been reconstructed by a mad scientist. Bracken had almost killed me when I was wounded that time, because after the bone shrapnel had ripped through us both, his talent had called to my blood and I had almost bled to death. He had almost killed *himself* then, as well, when he'd cut off his connection to his talent—and his own life force—in the effort to keep me alive. It seemed like a bad omen for our relationship, this scar.

He bent, pulled me up, and placed his lips to the back of my shoulder, where, Goddess knew, things could only be worse.

"You learned your power from these scars." He said reverently. "I was fortu-
nate enough to be there. Never apologize for being mortal, and brave."

His white arms were around my waist, and my own hand rested, tiny and
trembling, against the massed muscle of his thigh. Beautiful. Everything about
him was beautiful. "I'm not particularly brave at the moment." I confessed, feeling foolish and small.

"I fit just fine." He said into my ear. Our skin was touching, I was surrounded
by wet, soapy, hot, tender man, and I could barely breathe with the perfection of
our touch. I could tell, even though he wasn't facing me, that the corners of his
swamp-colored eyes were crinkling. "I'll prove it to you after you wash my hair."

I turned and wrinkled my nose at him, because I didn't want my awe of him
to go to his head. "You're still perfect." I accused, and he tipped his head back
and laughed.

"I thought I was an asshole." He told me, and I smiled reluctantly.

"You are an asshole." I assured him affectionately. "You're just built like a
god."

"I," He said smugly, "Am built like a sidhe." He maneuvered us some more,
and I let him, feeling very content to be passive, now that we were safe and speaking civilly, and maybe not going to rip each other to shreds with our sharp and
pointed love. I sat now, up on the step, with my chin resting on his shoulder. In
spite of the scented water, I could still smell stone and pond and sun. Bracken.

"And I am built like a human." I murmured into his ear. "A flawed, scarred,
frightened human, with too many great big lovers in her bed."

"Adrian was not that big." He said levelly, running his hand up my calf. So
now we had spoken of the other thing that would always hurt.

"I guess he was plenty big, to be my first." I responded, massaging his head
with shampoo. I did this for a long time, because it had felt soooo good when
he'd done it. "And more than big enough to leave a shadow." I finished, after a
moment.

Bracken tilted his head back as I rinsed his shorn hair. "He was my first too."
He told me unexpectedly, then grimaced. "My first love, anyway." He turned his
head sideways to let me look in his eyes. "I let him think he was my first man
besides Green—Adrian was…reluctant…to compromise our friendship at first.
But I was relentless—I had to be. He was my first love, and my friend, and my
rival, and my brother. When we had nothing better to do, we made love. When
we had someone better to do, well, we usually competed over her. And when he
died, I wasn't sure what hurt more." He paused, his voice grew gruff and clogged

and sad. "I wasn't sure if it hurt more that he was gone, or that I was so, so glad that you were still alive."

My fingers stilled in his now-clean hair, and I wrapped my arms around his shoulders, and my legs around his waist. "I would never have known." I told him, overwhelmed.

"I would have gone to my grave before you did." Bracken said seriously.

I tightened around him, wanting to take him in my heart and make sure nothing ever hurt him again. "Trees will grow." I murmured at last, "Rain will fall, and we will be lovers again."

And so we were. And it was wonderful. He touched my scars, deliberately, first with his fingers, then with his mouth. His tender hands cupped, and rubbed, and smoothed over me, making that skin-slick sound that makes your sex shiver, when you're in bed and the lights are dim. And when the time came, and he poised his body over me again, I ran my hands over his amazing chest, and felt tears start that he would want me.

"*Due'ane.*" He said roughly, capturing my mouth, ravaging me breathless.

"*Due'alle.*" I returned, and the word had grown, and now meant more than lover, more than friend, more than all, and was now synonymous with Bracken, it was his name, his title, his being. He sheathed himself in my flesh, and the world ceased to move and it was only the two of us, moving, moving, the blessed dark within us and the light of each other without.

He fit just fine.

I was dreaming. Bracken's fine long body was wrapped around me, and I dreamt that a man came into our room. He was swathed in dark robes, in the style of the middle East, and I could not see his face, but he was not that tall— not as tall as Adrian, certainly not Bracken's height, and very much shorter than Green. Adrian lay, sleeping and senseless, in his arms.

I stared at Adrian, hungry for the sight of him, even in a dream, and my hands hurt, wanting to run my hands through that soft, fine, white hair. *Open your eyes, beloved,* I thought, *open your eyes and see me.*

"Give him back." I told the man in the black robes, and my voice sounded brave and noble and proud—everything we want to be in our dreams, but somehow don't sound like in real life.

"Mine." He said, and I couldn't really hear him. He cradled Adrian in one arm, as though he were a package, and reached for me with the other. Except he wasn't reaching for me, he was reaching for Bracken, whom I was now (in the way of dreams) clutching with one arm. I stood –no longer naked, but wearing a swirling sky-blue robe that glowed with the magic that coursed through my veins—and held Bracken tightly, and knew, without looking, that Green slept behind us and that they would sleep and that I would never give them up.

"Mine." The man said again, and I was suddenly furious.

"They're all mine." I told him clearly, and I could feel myself putting power into my voice. "They're all mine, and you can't have them."

He didn't seem to be listening to me. He kept reaching, and I knew that if I didn't wound him, he would take them all—Adrian, Bracken, and Green.

Fuck him.

I did what Green taught me—I forced my power into my hand and then I reached that hand towards the hand that was reaching for me. The scream that reached my ear was not dream-like at all—it was human, and it was real, and it was furious and in pain and I didn't care. Adrian was still sleeping in the stranger's arms as the man struggled against my nuclear-fusion hand, and I reached for Adrian with my other arm. He came, and yet he didn't. I held him, and yet I didn't. And then the stranger broke free, by breaking off his arm in my grasp, so that I was left holding charred flesh and bone, and the jagged end of bone protruded from my enemy's robe. He wielded it in front of him like a lance, and I deflected him with my arms, clutching my lovers before me, but not before he scratched my chest, leaving a poisoned, bleeding wound.

I hurled what was left of his flesh at him as I screamed obscenities, and my voice was just my voice, and I clutched them all—Green, Adrian, and Bracken to my heart, and only my death could have torn them away.

I was abruptly awake, standing on the bed, screaming "You can't have them, mother fucker, I'll die first." Bracken had rolled off the bed and was crouched forward, his hands out, and I could feel him using his talent towards the smallish, dark-robed man bleeding in front of us. He was waving the charred, broken stump of his hand and shrieking in pain and horror. It was real. *Goshawk* was real, even though he looked very different than what I remembered of him when I'd met with Nicky. Goshawk was *here*—he'd snuck in here as we'd been sleeping and had tried to *steal* them from me. My power was there, in my hand, and it was real, and my blood was real as it seeped from a brand new wound from my shoulder to my chest. All I could think was "you *fucker*," but I was wounded and still half dreaming, so I screeched at him like a broken gear, which was all the warning he needed.

Abruptly he launched himself at the drape covered window, and in a crash of safety glass and an explosion of feathers flew away, a half-hearted ball of light following him, because I knew that he'd escaped, and I didn't want to hit anything out there—including the Bay Bridge, and all of its oblivious innocents.

When he was gone, I crumpled like a Kia fender in the now freezing room. "My Goddess, that fucker was strong." I gasped, surveying the damage.

The air was rushing in through the window, and it was ice-fucking cold, and there was glass all over the beautiful room, and blood, and some of it, I thought, feeling towards my aching, raw and bleeding chest, was mine. Bracken closed his hands and stopped calling Goshawk's blood, and gathered me in his arms, and even though my wound spilled as soon as skin met skin, the touch of his flesh was like the smell of blackberries from home, Green's home, and I closed my eyes and...

I was standing in the Chevron station, perched on top of a blackberry covered hill. Adrian was looking at me, his bright blue eyes so, so serious, his head lowering towards me. He was going to kiss me, I thought, thrilled, or kill me. Either way, I was his. I was lost. I was in love. And then his mouth touched mine, and it tasted like summer nights, and blackberries, and a little like blood, and a lot like bubble-gum, and I was drowning, drowning in his kiss, and I wanted him to bite me, take me, make love to me then and there, and I quivered because I knew that it would come...

I came to again, and Bracken was shaking me and calling my name.

"Bubble-gum." I sobbed against him. "I have him back—our first kiss...I remember now...Oh, God, Adrian...how could I ever forget?" And I wept, weak and inconsolable, until Bracken shifted me in his arms and I felt—really felt— that charred rip on my collarbone. I whimpered, a low, keening grunt, and felt what I always felt when I was hurt and broken: nausea. Bracken knew the drill— he turned my head and I threw up with the white pain of the wound, and a long fingered hand went to my face to pull my hair back as I spilled stomach acid and not much else on the pretty rich green. I could have stayed like that, I thought blurrily, for a little while longer, but Bracken's hand had touched my face and now he was running his cold skin all over my forehead in fear, and he was making me shiver.

"Goddess, Cory—you're feverish. You're bleeding all over the place and you're burning up...where the fuck are my pants, dammit..." How the hell should I know where his pants are? I wanted to ask, but he'd set me down gently on the bed and it felt both queasy and freezing to be under the comforter in the spinning room and I didn't want to have to say anything because Bracken and I were so new and what if what I said was wrong?

One of the last things I heard before I lost consciousness the first time was Bracken, his voice broken and desperate, calling Green on the cell phone.

"Green's coming." He said to me, after a moment of darkness. He had found his pants, and was cradling me against him, stroking my hair and pressing his forehead to mine.

"Goshawk can't have you." I said distinctly. "He can't have any of you. You're mine." This seemed important—it seemed *vital* that Bracken know this. I repeated it again and again while Bracken held me close against him and whispered shushing noises at me, but he had to know that I'd fought for him. That I'd fought for all of them. There were more dark moments, and then both of them, Green and Bracken were peering down at me, and my eyes were hot and dry and both beloved, beautiful faces seemed to grow and distort before me. "I'd die for you." I said distinctly, and then I had to close my eyes altogether.

GREEN

Deals with a Kiss

The evening knock on the door was not entirely unexpected, but Andres' first words were.

"Goddess Green, you look like hell." Andres himself was neatly dressed, his hair coiffed and gelled, and he smelled lightly of cologne. He had obviously fed well, recently—his cheeks were warm and rosy, and the only sign of his adopted species was the hint of incisor that he flashed with his smile. If it weren't for the honest concern on his face, his very health would have been insulting.

Green was not quite too weary to grin at the thought. His own hair was unwashed, dragged from his pale face in a disheveled queue. Even he knew there were hollows under his eyes. He didn't have the heart to tell Andres that he himself looked better than any of the people in his impromptu embassy. "Good to see you too, Lord Vampire." He said dryly, but formally. However, he didn't step back. "Honestly, Andres, I'd let you in, but we're knackered—I have no hospitality to grace you with, and my people are too weary for politics and strategy."

The concern on Andres' face was real. "I have dined tonight, my brother. Do not worry—I am in your debt, and I've always been a friend. The word is out about Goshawk's attack—please, let me in. Any help I can give the wounded is yours to have."

"How do you know…"

"Goshawk?" Andres' expression was fierce and triumphant. "Your people killed one of his captains at the warehouse—did you not know that?"

Green remembered the condor, rent in two by the exploding sheet metal and nodded.

"And Goshawk himself was wounded—badly." Andres continued. "He's been sending people in to make treaties with all of us. Only the elves have been receptive."

Green's face went taut. "I will drink his blood first, my brother."

Andres nodded. "And I will pour it for you." He said with equal force. Then, knowing the answer simply by reading Green's face. "Who was hurt?" He asked quietly.

Green backed up, and Andres entered. The sprites were efficient—there were no dishes in the sink, no dirty tissues, no clothes on the floor. But there were three exhausted people crumpled on the pillows in front of the couch, and whimpers coming from the room down the hall.

"Goddess." Andres said, blowing out a breath. "What happened here?"

"She's sick." Came a voice from the crumpled people on the floor. It was Nicky, with his head on Renny's stomach, and his own stomach covered by Max. "Goshawk wounded her, and…" He trailed off, as though the words themselves had wandered away.

"Can't you heal the wound?" Andres asked Green, still uncertain how one sick sorceress could so badly damage what should have been a thriving household.

"I did cure the wound." Green said, sitting exhaustedly down at the table. "The wound is closed and scarred—but…" He looked away, his expression desolate. "She turned twenty in June, you know." He said after a moment. "She turned twenty, and came into her power and lost her lover, all in the span of about six weeks. And she was shredded and wounded and weak. And Friday night, Nicky attacked her. Monday afternoon, she could barely walk. Tuesday, she was tearing across the damned city, trying to find Bracken. She found him, she saved your people, and then the fucker attacked her again." He looked at Andres, rubbing his face with a trembling hand. "She won the attack—but she's feverish and weak. It's Friday again, and the only way we can keep her alive is to lay down with her, feed her our life force, and she's so weak, she'd kill us all if she let herself, but she won't." And that, perhaps, hurt most of all.

"Goddess." Andres murmured, stricken. "And you'd do it, all of you—you'd kill yourselves to keep her."

Nicky dragged himself out of the people pile, and Max and Renny shifted to lay on top of each other. His dark-rust colored hair was lank and flat to his head and dark freckles stood out on sickly white skin. He wore a pair of boxer shorts and one of Green's T-shirts. Nicky had been living with Goshawk's enclave since he came out from Montana—everything he owned, including his textbooks was now gone forever, and he'd been wearing other people's clothes all week, but he hadn't complained once. Slowly, like his muscles ached, he made his way to the table, and Green automatically shoved a bowl full of trail mix his way.

"There's meat in the fridge, brother—eat it." He said, tired authority still ringing from his voice.

Nicky nodded. "She forgave me for attacking her." He said as he moved, trying to explain to Andres, and even Green why he'd give his life for her. "She welcomed me here, with her people." He sat, putting a hand in the bowl. "She even tried to save me from falling in love with her." He said through a mouthful of trail mix. "She practically threw me out of that warehouse; she tried so hard to keep me from bonding with her." He swallowed, hard. "It's one of the things that weakened her to this. How do you repay that kind of love?"

Andres nodded, not really understanding, and Green met his eyes. "If we could, we'd bring her over to you, but we can't." He said after a fraught moment. "She's so weak, feeding her blood may be the only way—she's got three of Adrian's marks, still riding her. She's a hair's breadth away from being one of yours."

Green could see Andres digesting this.

"Would she welcome that?" He asked.

"She'd grieve away her immortality." Green said bluntly. "Her power is sunshine—she'd have to cut herself off from her power to survive."

"Not an option." Andres acknowledged. "Who is she feeding from?" He asked thoughtfully. "Can just anybody give her strength?"

"Only the men." Said another voice from the floor. Renny picked herself up, and, much like Nicky dragged herself to the table. Her hair was actually tame, but that was only because she was the one who shopped for them all and Grace practically dragged her into the bathroom to groom every morning before dawn. She was wearing one of Mitch's old T-shirts, which went down past her hips, and a pair of men's boxer shorts over her own cotton panties. When she went out, she put jeans over them, but she hadn't had the energy to leave the house today. She stopped at the refrigerator on her way to the table, and soon she and Nicky were dumping cubes of cold steak on cold tortillas and eating steadily.

"So the only requirement is that it be a man?" Andres asked, and Green thought he sounded semi-amused. Renny had been quite bitter.

"They have to touch her skin to skin and they have to want to get in her pants." Renny said through a mouthful.

"Renny!" Max murmured, the last body on the floor. He might have blushed, Green thought, but he had no strength left for shame.

"Well it's true!" She said, looking at him and shaking her head. "Pretty much every man in here has wanted her—yes, Max, even you."

"I wasn't denying it." He said, humor glinting dully in his eyes as he pulled himself up. "I was just saying that maybe it doesn't have to be sex—maybe it's just because she's our friend."

"Well then I could heal her too, and I can't, and it's not fair!" Renny burst out, still eating. She swallowed, and looked up at Green for validation. "Mitchell died, Adrian died—I swear to Goddess, Green, I was looking at my own open goddamned grave. And she made everything so fucking normal. Go to class. Chase some pigeons. Bail me out of the park. Call you. Go visit home. And normal day to normal day I walked away from that fucking grave and all I can do now is…"

"Keep us alive." Max said gently. He too had migrated to the kitchen for food and now he wrapped his arms around Renny. "You cook, you feed us, you shop for Grace, you keep us dressed. You haven't been a cat for days. We would have fallen apart without you, puss." He murmured, and Renny leaned into him. "I could feed you too, you know." He murmured kindly in her ear, just loud enough for Green's hypersensitive hearing to pick up, and Renny smiled weakly. Max wasn't talking about food, and maybe he had learned something after all.

"Well I want her." Andres said into the suddenly still room.

Green laughed outright, and everybody else looked at Andres in surprise.

"She saved me, she saved my kiss—she's lovely and brave—I'd take her on any fog-lit night. Do I qualify?"

"What will you want in return?" This came from Bracken, who was stumbling in from the hallway, wearing a pair of sweats and nothing else. He looked, if possible, worse than Green. His shorn hair was sticking out in clumps, and he was having trouble focusing his eyes. "Grace is bathing her." He said to the others who looked at him accusingly for leaving Cory alone. Then: "What would we need to give you to save her?" He asked again, looking at Andres like a drowning man might look at a rope made of straw.

"That's a fair question." Green said. "I love you, brother vampire, but we are Lords of our people. You and I both know that. Your strength would save us all—what can we offer you to gain it?"

Andres nodded his head. "One thing: a permanent alliance between us. No more treaties. I want to be part of you."

Green laughed. "Of all you see here?" He asked ironically, indicating the cheerless apartment and its exhausted anguished denizens.

"You are alone here, brother." Andres said gently. "This is not your faerie hill. And yet you've managed to save my kiss, save Orson's folk, acquire the loyalty of the lesser fey to the extent that they mutiny against their employers—yes." He added, because Green looked surprised. "The sidhe wait their own tables and do their own laundry these days. No sprites will attend people who betrayed the man who fought their enemy. Alone, you have shaken our communities to their core. Surrounded by your own people, you are a power no one has reckoned with. I will stand or fall with you."

Green inclined his head, moved. "How will you seal this alliance?" He asked.

"With your sorceress' blood, of course." Andres said.

"Done." Bracken broke in, and Green looked at him sternly.

"No." He said. "You cannot bargain with her blood when she can't speak for herself."

"I'd bargain her into marriage with the other himself, if it would save her." Bracken said brokenly, sinking into the chair next to Green's. "She's dying." His voice fractured, and Green pulled Bracken's head to his shoulder and kissed his temple, comforting them both. "She's dying, and I can't…Goddess help me, I can't seem to give her more of me."

"She won't take it, Bracken." Green told him, knowing it was hard truth. "She's just strong enough to not strip us to nothing. We may die of grief because of it, but she won't let us die because of her."

"Take my blood, then." Bracken murmured. "Take it all, if you must, but…Goddess, I can't lose her—not so soon after…"

"And she can't lose you after Adrian." Andres broke in bluntly. "No. I would not hurt your people, Green, for all the world. If nothing else, I owe you a debt of gratitude for *my* life, if not the lives of my people. We will bargain to seal the alliance when your sorceress is whole and well."

Green knew there were tears trembling in his eyes, but he did not care. "Goddess bless you." He said, his voice shredded and bleeding. He stood and gave Bracken a hand up.

"Come, brother, let's see what he can do."

Green led the way to Cory's room, knowing that between Grace and the sprites there would be no sickroom smell. But there was no joy either, in Cory's room with its bright movie posters and tumble of stuffed animals. The old-fashioned Irish chain quilt that Cory loved was there, and her hands moved over it restlessly as she lay, half dreaming. Grace had asked Arturo to send it after Cory had been brought back to the apartment, still bleeding and feverish. She lay against the sheets, freshly bathed and dressed in one of his old white T-shirts. Grace had kept her in Green's or Bracken's cotton shirts—it seemed to calm her down, when the two of them weren't there. She was so thin, she was almost transparent. Her hair, clean now, lay lifeless against her still face, the strands free of the dye she'd worn until Adrian had courted her, it was a color between red and brown, and still pretty for all that she looked nearly dead.

Abruptly, her eyes opened, unfocused hazel. "You can't have them." She said abruptly, to no one. Her eyes closed, and she whispered to herself, "They're mine. He can't have them. Adrian come back, you're mine...he can't take you..." She continued murmuring, quietly, but her body was too weak to toss back and forth.

Grace was next to her, smoothing her hair from her face and stroking her forehead with a cool cloth. When the men walked in, she looked up briefly and took in Andres presence. For a vampire who'd been eating regularly, she looked nearly as bad as the others in the apartment. Worry had worn her long-boned features even longer, and anger that her people were under attack etched a fierce look in the bridge across her eyes. But her mouth quirked when she saw Andres, and something softened in her, and her incisors, which had been prominent with her anger since Green had brought Cory home retracted for the first time in days.

"Another conquest?" She asked wryly, and looked back down at Cory, smoothing her hair from her face. "Good." She murmured. "Cory can handle another man, if another man can handle her."

Cory responded by murmuring again. "Mine. They're mine."

Andres bowed slightly at Grace. "I will do what I can." He said modestly, but when he looked at Bracken and Green, he must have seen something hard and painful in their faces, Green thought, because his own expression changed.

"What is she saying?" Andres asked gently.

"When Goshawk gave Nicky the power to attack her the first time," Green said, steeling himself for the explanation, "What Nicky did was take her memories. Apparently Goshawk's people feed on those memories like a robin feeds on worms—it's human essence, pulled from it's native element, and according to Nicky, Goshawk's people fed very well."

Andres thought. "So that magic wall—the one that not even forty vampires could crash out of..."

"That was the lost virginity of over two thousand women." Green said bitterly. "Nicky was only one soldier out there stealing for Goshawk—we sat down and did the math, the other night. I don't know why Goshawk chose that memory—at this point, I don't much care. But for Cory, when they took her 'firsts' from her, they took Adrian."

It was Andres' turn to close his eyes. "Ah." He said, wiping a bloody smudge from the side of his nose.

"Adrian was her first kiss." Green continued, inexorable. He had thought this through in his head, during the long hours of watching her life trickle out of her wasted body, but he had never reasoned it aloud. "He was her first sex. And the night she came into her power—all of her power—was the first night she spent with the two of us. When Nicky stole her memories last week, he had no idea what it was he had done."

"But Goshawk most certainly did." Andres said grimly. He looked at Grace and asked politely, "Allow me?"

"Good Luck." Grace wished him sincerely. She looked up at Green and Bracken. "I'm going to go make something really tasty, like feta/ricotta lasagna. And you two are going to go eat every last fucking bite of it—do I make myself clear?" She asked firmly.

Bracken and Green nodded dumbly, and Andres chuckled as he moved past Grace and sat down to take Cory's hand. He looked at her tenderly, Green realized, and knew, of course, why. Any one who had been beloved of Adrian would be beloved of Andres.

"Yes," Said Green roughly, answering Andres earlier question, "Goshawk knew exactly what he had gained from her memories—Nicky said he looked like a heroin addict, getting a hit, when he took them from Nicky. And the other night, if, as you said, she'd taken out his captain when she took down the building, he wanted revenge, and he wanted more of her."

"So he came looking for the other memories of her firsts." Andres supplied. "How did he get into the building?"

"He must have been there already." Bracken spat. "The lower fey checked out the hotel—there's a giant garage—they think it was a basement before Cory did her..."

"Terra-forming." Green murmured, choking on his own dry laughter. "She calls it terra-forming—it's from Star Trek or something."

"Anyway," Bracken went on, lost in his own bitterness, "The gnomes think Goshawk was under the warehouse, maintaining that magic wall. After Cory blew through it and then transformed the building, he...he crept up into our room like a fucking cockroach and attacked her while we slept." His legs folded beneath him, and he sat angrily on the deep brown carpet of Cory's bedroom. "I don't think she was awake for half of it...her eyes were unfocused...she was talking like some sort of old-fashioned book hero…she didn't really wake-up until he stabbed her with his…" Brack swallowed. "With his bone stump, after she broke off his arm…"

Andres listened, amazed. He had not heard the whole story—nobody had. That Goshawk had been wounded badly, that they all knew. But that Cory had fought him off in her sleep? *That* was a story worth telling. "Goddess!" He exclaimed, and Green saw him squeezing Cory's tiny hand in his as he stood by her bed. "I can feel her feeding from me, even from my hand. She's so tough."

"That's almost what did her in." Bracken said, his voice tinged with bitterness. He moved next to the bed and reached out to take her other, tiny-boned hand. "Goshawk came not just for memories of Adrian and Green, he came for me too—and she fought him back, and took back Adrian's first kiss as well…but it cost her. She was defending the three of us, at least in her mind, and she kept saying…" His voice broke, and Andres looked at him, wanting to hear the rest.

"What?" He asked, looking between the two men.

"She kept saying she'd die before he took us." Green murmured, heartbroken, saying what Bracken couldn't. It had probably been what Adrian had been thinking when he swooped in from the sky and clutched his death. "We've spent the last three days trying to convince her body that that's not necessary."

Andres let out a shuddering breath. "She's extraordinary, your little sorceress." He said at last, "And she smells so much like Adrian that I can almost taste his skin."

With this, Andres gently released Cory's hand, stood, and began unbuttoning his shirt. His chest was pale gold—his natural skin tone, deprived of sunlight for more than one hundred and fifty years—and covered with dark, curly hair. Green thought that, as cures went, waking up next to Andres wouldn't be the worst thing that ever happened to Cory. With a minimum of fuss, Andres stripped down to his silk boxers, draping his suit gracefully on the chair. When he was done, he bent to place a tender kiss on her hot, dry forehead, inhaling lightly, smelling Cory and her lovers. The two who weren't Adrian, had loved him, and Andres could smell that too. He closed his eyes then, and Green could see it all: pleasure, pain, and remembrance.

Andres shook himself to the present and looked up to Green and Bracken kindly. "Go, my brothers." He said gently. "Shower. Eat. Be with your people. Sleep." He pulled back the comforter, slid in next to her painfully tiny body, and pulled her into the shelter of his arms. "Let me see what I can do."

ARTURO
Meanwhile, Back at the Ranch...

There was a thick coating of frost on the ground around the protection of Green's faerie hill, and Arturo had to stomp through it with authority, or he would find himself on his ass. It was hard to stomp with authority and move quietly, but Arturo had been an Aztec god, 3000 years before, and he could handle a little frost. He didn't like it—in fact, the frost pretty much reminded him of why he missed the jungles of South America badly, on occasion.

He looked around. Green's place dwelt on that invisible line that separated the Auburn scrub oak and straw grasses from the red dirt and pine of Foresthill. Past the confines of Green's hill, the Northern California landscape reverted from a fairy tale English garden, capped with the Goddess Grove, to the native growth—red dirt, straw colored grasses, and Joshua Pine trees on the Eastern side, and the occasional scrub oak to the West. He was standing to the North West, behind the sprawling house that dug into the hill itself, where the view from the side of the hill was unencumbered by houses in any direction. He was in a thicket of trees, and his bait was in the clearing itself.

She didn't look like bait—she looked like a tall, pretty, dark-haired woman. She was one of Adrian's saved. Since Adrian's passing, Arturo had truly begun to tally the number of these people. Drug use was fairly high among the bright, uneducated young in Northern California—too often promising lives wasted away into that quest for a little rent and one more hit. Adrian had looked the part—he'd been pale in life, and almost marble colored in death, and he'd appeared handsome and wasted and lost. He had often slipped under the radar at parties—both the rich ones and the poor ones—and collected lovers and broken hearts by the score. But he'd had a weather eye for people like Leah, the girl in the clearing. He'd come to the parties, chat up the lost, and occasionally he'd offer them a choice.

Vampire or Were—which would you be?

The logistics were simple, even if the choice was hard. You are dying, he would say. You are spilling your life with every hit, with every drink, with every puff…I can help you change. Because the blood process that changed a person into a were-animal, or a vampire cleansed the body of the drugs, and kept it clean. Instant sobriety. Your life was your own again, with a few, teeny, tiny wrinkles that it was up to you to iron out. Mitchell Hammond would have been the first to say that besides Renny, the infected needle that had made him a were-animal was the best thing to happen to him. Leah, the were-puma in the clearing, prayed to the Goddess every morning in thanks, and—very sincerely—referred to Adrian as her patron saint.

Every one of Adrian's saved under Green's command did.

And Adrian had a talent for spotting the ones that *could* be saved. Arturo would suggest this one, or that one, from his own wanderings through the foothills underclass, and Adrian would say, sadly, "No, brother, he would go mad." Or, "She would waste away without a child…she may pull herself out yet." Or, "That one, that one would eat our throats as we slept." And as Arturo watched, frustrated, he would eventually see that Adrian was right. In the matter of saving the lost, Adrian had always been right.

Arturo had been hard on Adrian for over forty years. He'd seen the playboy, the partier—the little kid that Green had never asked to grow up, since his actual childhood had been so, so cruel. Arturo had even forbidden Adrian from seeing Cory, until she'd lied for him to the police and he'd realized that the two of them were inevitable. To this day, Arturo marveled that Cory—little Corinne Carol-Anne Kirkpatrick, who'd had the dyed black hair and the five thousand earrings and the massive hostility—had possessed the wisdom to see what Arturo hadn't seen until she'd showed him Adrian's fineness through her own eyes.

And he had been fine, Arturo thought mournfully. Throughout the years, the number of Adrian's saved had mounted to the hundreds. Grace had been one, although it had been cancer that almost killed her, and not drugs. So he had been fine, and good, and in the way we tend to minimize the qualities of our own family, so Arturo had waited until the last days of his wayward brother to tell him that he was a good leader—and a good man.

So here was Leah, Adrian's last saved, if one didn't count Cory, and she was stretching her were-puma muscles as bait.

Arturo was nervous—he wished like hell for a cigarette, a habit he'd picked up when he came to this country. He was sidhe, a god, and his body didn't form demeaning addictions—but that didn't mean his fingers didn't twitch inside his pockets. Leah was barely older than Cory, and he didn't want her hurt. He took a deep breath and scanned the surrounding area one more time, thinking "hawk". No hawk replied.

This alone was a problem—Arturo had a thing for hawks, since he had once been the condor god. But that was long ago, and although he had given up the ability to change into a condor when he'd left his native land, he still had the ability to talk to them, and, as a result, they tended to populate Green's land and the surrounds fairly heavily. If there were no hawks around, something was definitely amiss. If things larger than hawks were swooping down on the heads of your were-creatures, events were more than amiss, they were in chaos.

He missed the hawks. They had been like little cousins, when they'd been allowed to thrive. In his spare time, he would sit in the sun during the spring and fall and watch the hawks play on the wind.

Of course, he mused bitterly, he very possibly missed Grace even more.

He was god, he thought again, irritably, but it was no use. Grace had been amusing at first—foul mouthed, quick tempered, well read on everything from Elizabethan poetry to how to fix a motorcycle engine. But it hadn't been until he'd seen the way she mothered Adrian and Green that he'd really started to love her.

The sidhe of South America tended towards brutal autonomy. No one wanted to share godhood, so a sidhe rising from obscurity had to either kill the more powerful beings around him or go find a place to rule alone. That had been Arturo's intention when he'd come to America. The yawsatawni of the Native Americans had dwindled with the humans they'd come to depend on, and North America had been ripe for the plucking. Arturo was tired of watching his humans get massacred by the rich, or by the careless, or by themselves. America, he'd come to believe, would be more stable, and had so few fey that he'd be able to come in and rule where he ruled.

That had been his plan, until he'd met Green.

He'd first seen Green when he'd driven his baby-blue Edsel up Green's driveway. Green had been working his garden, casually throwing out power like a father would throw a slow softball to his child, and Arturo had actually smiled at the lovely, lovingly crafted gardens that had bee carved out of this inhospitable soil and climate. He'd hid the smile, as he climbed out of the car and bowed stiffly to Green, announcing his intentions to take over as the reigning sidhe of the area.

Green had blinked, then smiled, and offered a hand. "That sounds like a hard task you've set yourself, friend." He'd said equably. "Why don't you come inside, have some food and wine, and tell me why it's my land you want, yes?"

Arturo had gotten drunk, although any sidhe would have said arrogantly that this was impossible, and had enjoyed Green's company very very much, because the other elf had a dry wit, and a sharp mind, and a surprising fierceness when his own people were threatened, and in spite of himself, Arturo had warmed to the sidhe who was supposed to be his enemy. He'd woken up the next morning, in a bed full of very satisfied wood-nymphs who, they had confessed, had learned how to bed a man from Green himself, and had asked himself if, were he in charge, he could possibly make a better, safer home than the one Green had.

The answer had been no and Arturo had stayed on, but as Green's lieutenant, and not once had he wished for Green's status or his power. Twenty years later, when he saw Grace, with all her surprising fierceness, caring for Green and Adrian, who had made the security of their family circle sacrosanct, he had found himself falling for her hard, as he couldn't fall for Green and Adrian, but would have if he'd been at all as liquid in his sexuality as almost all the other fey were. It didn't matter—Grace was everything he loved about his home, and his leader, and the young man he'd thought of as a son.

Feathers and wind interrupted his thoughts, and he nearly turned into a euca-lyptus tree (one of his remaining powers, and deadly to him in this climate) in his quest for instant quiet.

Leah, whose senses were nearly as sharp as a human as they were when she wore fur and claws, heard that sound and smiled to herself, giving her long, dark hair a careless flip, knowing it would come.

A hawk larger than a hawk came screaming out of the sky, talons extended, ready to take out Leah's throat. Closer it came, closer, and Arturo was almost screaming with fear for the girl when, between heartbeat and breath, too late for the bird to stop it's dive, she changed into a giant, black-furred, snarling predator who gracefully dodged the bird's dive and, with careless ease knocked the bird to the ground with a massive paw. In a bound, Leah was on top of the hawk, her jaws locked around its throat but not penetrating feathers and skin. Arturo was by her side almost before she had stilled.

"Nicely done." He told her, and she wrinkled whiskers and fur around the burden in her mouth for what passed as a feline smile. In an easy hop, he straddled the bird, and pinned its wings with his knees.

"Now listen up, my friend." He said conversationally, pretending that the bird wasn't struggling furiously. "You have two choices here. The first is that we can keep fighting, and I would have to break your neck, and that would be too bad because I like birds. The second is that you change yourself, and we go back to my basement and you join your fellows, and we give up this idea of attacking my people because it doesn't work." His voice rose in exasperation, because the damnedest part of the struggle was that it *wasn't* working. So far, Green's people had sustained negligible injuries, and Arturo had captured four furious Avians. Of course, that didn't count the missing hawks that had fled the property from the larger predators, but Arturo was fairly certain they'd come back when the Avian threat had cleared.

The Avian shrieked again, loud enough to bend metal, and Arturo remembered enough about being a bird to shout a warning to Leah. In a ten foot standing leap she bound upward into the air, and came down hard on the soft-brown feathered mate to the hawk in his arms. The mate had been streaking towards the both of them, claws extended, murder in her eyes, in defense of her male, and Leah—working on adrenaline instead of planning—landed on top of her neck, which then bent sharply when the bird's head was driven into the ground. They landed with an ominous crunch, and Arturo's heart fell.

"Aww…damn it…" he said, and looked over to where Leah was nosing the still body of the giant bird and emitting little growl-whines when it didn't move. Slowly, oh so slowly, it turned, and there was the naked body of a brown-haired woman, who had been beautiful in life, and now was only pitiful, lying on her stomach with her head cocked at an unnatural angle and her eyes wide open as her body fought for, and lost it's last breath.

The bird beneath him shifted, changed, and the voice that came from the fully clothed human beneath Arturo was anguished, devastated, and bereft.

No man, vampire, or elf, could have stood still and heard that cry without being moved.

With a sigh, Arturo moved his knees from the fallen Avian's arms, and was too saddened to be pleased when he didn't struggle to escape, but stayed, face buried in the frost, and howled his grief.

"Was it worth it, my brother?" Arturo asked softly, not expecting an answer. "Was it worth it, to follow a false promise of power?"

The man only howled again, and sat up to his haunches, then sank, weeping, into the frosty ground. His hand reached out, made a helpless, stroking gesture towards the dead woman, and then he sobbed again.

Arturo sighed. Grace might know what to do, he thought, but that was probably because he missed his lover, and wanted to lose himself in her and away from this sadness. The truth was that he needed Green. Goddess, did he miss his leader. They had four already, held prisoner in the basement, away from sunlight and wind, and pining to death. He had a house full of weres—mostly feline—who were just dying to sink their claws into these giant nuisances and maybe munch on a little California fried were-condor as well. And now he had this one, bereft and heartbroken, and he had no idea how to comfort him. Green could do it. Green would do it well, Arturo thought, frustrated with his own limitations. No one understood heartbreak and the will to live like Green.

But he wouldn't trouble his leader with this, not today. Grace called him every night, and he knew how to lead well enough on his own. But, Goddess, did he pray, every minute, for Cory to come back to Green, and Green to come back to his hill where he belonged.

CORY

Cory, don't go.

I was suffocating. I was burning. I was naked in the snow and freezing. I was alone, all alone, oh *Goddess,* so alone. I was surrounded by lovers, and someone was trying to rip them out of my arms.

I'd die first.

I kept trying to tell people that, and they wouldn't listen.

A new body, a different taste—cool, spicy, sweet. I didn't know this one. I'd never had it inside me. But it knew me. It called me Adrian.

And Adrian answered, and told me that I needed to wake up.

"But you just came to bed." I told him, teasingly, holding on to his cool hand as he moved away from me.

"Things to do, luv." He murmured. He leaned over me, autumn-sky eyes bright and clear, and I could feel his lips on mine, taste him in my mouth, smell him, bubble-gum, clean vampire, copper-penny blood, me. Another kiss on my hair and he was gone.

"Adrian, don't go!" I sat up abruptly in bed, feeling like I'd said the words, but suddenly aware that my throat was parched and I couldn't say anything. Green was lying under my grandmother's quilt with me, naked, on my right, and Bracken was lying, also naked, on my left. And Adrian had been gone from all of us for a long time.

"Shit." I murmured through a cracked throat, and fell abruptly back into bed, feeling as though I might crumble into dust at any given moment.

"Jesus, Cory." Said a soft, female voice over by Bracken, "You're awake."

"No I'm not." I croaked. "I've been taken over by the undead. This is an illusion."

Renny made a courtesy laugh in the back of her throat, but it didn't sound happy.

"That should have been funny." I told her weakly. Why couldn't I sit up again? I peered over towards Renny, and Max and Nicky were asleep on a green and red brocade couch next to her. Since when was there a couch in my room? I squinted towards the clock, but it was covered up by water bottles, one of our crockery soup-bowls, with something in it, which was odd, because normally the sprites would have cleaned something up like that.

"It's only funny because you haven't been here for the last six days." She muttered, her voice choked. What had made Renny cry, I wondered. We had all been so careful not to make her cry, these last months.

Six days? "What's wrong, puss?" I asked. Suddenly she loomed over me, holding a thermos of something in her hands.

"Here—drink." She muttered. Her flyaway brown hair was more of a mess than usual, and she had bags under her eyes I could ship to Paris. She looked like hell.

"What is it? What's wrong…shit…" Because she'd dumped it down my throat and it was chicken broth with some herbs in it that were probably regulation elf and it was all I could do not to just spit it up, sans dignity, all over me. I swallowed instead, and some more, and then I pushed it way. "I'm full." I said after a moment. "What happened to you?" I looked around at all of the unconscious men. "What happened to everyone?"

She made a sound between a laugh and a sob, and put her hand over her mouth. "You happened to us, you stupid dork." She said after a moment. "Jesus, Cory—do you have any idea what you've put us through?"

"Tell me?" I said gently, letting her lay me back down. "What day is it?"

She nodded faintly. "It's 4 a.m., Monday morning."

"No…" Impossible. Tuesday night did not turn into Monday morning. I tried to put that into words, but Renny shushed me.

"You've been sick. Goshawk attacked you, when you and Bracken were alone—he tried to take your memories again."

"Adrian." I said, in wonder, tasting that kiss as though it were yesterday—which apparently I didn't remember. "I got him back…" Part of him, anyway.

"Yes, Adrian." Renny said, gentle and bitter at once. "You fought Goshawk for *all* of them. You won. It almost killed us all."

I felt foggy, far away. "The men…fed me." I said after a moment. "They were so tired."

"Yes." Renny murmured. "You wouldn't drain them completely—they would have died to save you, and you were dying to save them—we would have lost you if Andres hadn't showed up."

Andres. "The head vampire here? In my bed?" Then, to myself, "Bracken must have had a fit." Because Bracken was possessive, and he was mine.

"Bracken would have sold you to marriage with the other if he thought that would save you." Renny said dryly, her voice getting closer to normal.

And finally, I was beginning to see the desperation, and what it had cost everyone. "Green's weak." I said with wonder, realizing that although he was next to me, trying to give me strength, there was an electricity that usually coursed under my palms when I touched him and there was barely a ripple of it to my touch now. Both Green and Bracken were barely thrumming with the vitality I'd come to treasure.

"Everyone's weak, sweetie." Renny said at last, seeing how upset I was, I guess. "We're the walking dead here—the men slept next to you in shifts, to keep their energy up."

"Max and Nicky?" I asked, and saw her nod. She was mad at me, for almost leaving her I thought, as Renny's tiny, shaking hand came to brush my hair from my eyes. I fought the urge to cry. "I'm sorry." I said weakly. "I've hurt everyone…I didn't mean to…" Tears leaked down the side of my face to the pillow. "Poor Nicky." I said after a moment, struggling to look at him to see if he was okay. I remembered flinging him away from me to keep him from bonding with me because that could only end up hurting him, and he'd been trying to feed me his life energy for a week. This last week must have been awful for him. For them all.

"Shhh." And Renny was no longer angry at me. She ran her hands over my face, trying to calm me down.

"I have to pee." I said after a bit.

"That's good." She said. "Your kidneys almost shut down—you weren't giving them anything to work with."

"That's bad." I corrected her. "I don't think I can sit up." I felt wretched, helpless, and pitiful. And I felt worse because I had reduced all these people I loved and cared about to the same state.

"I'll call Grace then." She said, and to my complete mortification, Grace had to hover over the bed and scoop me into her arms so that I wouldn't wake the sleeping men on either side of me. And then she had to help me go potty, and that was even worse. The only good part was the bath, because in spite of the fact that she assured me that I'd been bathed once a day, I felt grody and full of sweat and the stink of my own sickness. Apparently, I'd been living in Bracken and Green's T-shirts, which was sweet, because the smell of either one of the men had calmed me down as I had tossed in fever. That probably boosted their egos, I thought dryly, to be so loved that even their smell was a comfort to someone they cared for. Although, any emotion more sensual than 'care' was somewhat of a stretch, I guessed mournfully, looking down at my wasted body.

"They're not even cherry pits any more." I complained to Grace, without meaning to complain because I had lots to be grateful for.

"I'm pretty sure that's not why all those men climbed in bed with you, honey." She responded drolly.

"Speaking of which," Renny said, standing by Grace with a towel, "Can I keep one?'

I was so happy for her; I felt those stupid weak tears come back again. "Max?" I asked roughly, "Sure—since my dance card seems to be filling up right now, go ahead."

"Four men isn't 'filling up', Cory—it's pretty packed." Renny said dryly. Grace hoisted me, dripping wet, out of the tub, and I lifted my arms like a toddler while Renny wrapped me up in the towel. Both women were preternaturally strong, I knew, but I also knew that there was very little of me to woman-handle.

"Four?" I said, surprised, as Grace toweled my hair. "My last count had two." *I'm a little out of it, and everyone gets delusions of grandeur* Han Solo was saying in my head, and I knew I had very little time to talk before I was physically compelled to sleep.

Grace shot Renny a look and the two women grew very still. "What?" I asked, feeling dopey.

"Nicky." Grace said after a moment.

"No." I denied. "I threw him out of there." Horrified, I tried to remember, as I'd leaned back, if Nicky had done more than just want me. "I wouldn't have done that to him." I swallowed hard. Nicky—with that terrible, brilliant, hopeless smile before he went to Goshawk. Nicky, who had held my hand that whole awful day while we tore-assed over the city, searching desperately for my other lover. Damn. I looked to Grace and Renny, hoping it wasn't true—that he hadn't bonded with me for life. They wouldn't meet my eyes. Damn damn damn damn bugger fuck it all. "Aw, Jesus…" I murmured.

"It's not just you." Renny said after a minute, as though this were the good news. "He bonded when Green was holding him, right when you created that totally awesome hotel." Goddess—I guess that wasn't a fever dream either. "Either you or Green can satisfy him." She said, as though hoping.

"That wouldn't be fair." I said automatically. "He's in love with me." Just saying it hurt. "No." I looked at the two women, smile twisting. "I'm part of this now—he's mine too. I can't just forsake him." My throat went tight, and my eyes pinched. "I love Green because he doesn't do that to people. If I let Nicky down, I let Green down—I can't do that." I didn't even want to think about the act itself. Not now, not when my body felt like it might shatter if I sat down too hard. I swallowed past the lump in my throat, and risked the next question. "So, that makes three." I said carefully.

"Andres makes four." Renny thought this, at least was funny.

"But not in her bed!" Grace interrupted with exasperation. They glared at each other for a minute, and I didn't have the strength to ask about it while Grace brushed my teeth.

"I'm so confused." I murmured later, sitting on the toilet seat while Grace blew my hair dry.

Grace sighed, shut off the hair dryer and finger-combed my hair around my face. She was comfortable, I realized, grooming me. It must have been a long week for everybody. "Andres healed you," she said at last, "On the *hope,* mind you, that you would give him blood when you are whole and well. He wants you to be a representative for Green—to sign a treaty to bind his people to Green's people, and your vampires."

"They're really yours." I said, because leaving the vampires without their Queen had been a niggling little guilt at the back of my mind since I'd left the hill in August.

"No, darling," Grace said gently, "They're still yours. They follow me, and they understand, but you've got three of Adrian's marks, and they miss him terribly, and you're their only sunshine and they miss you. But don't worry about that now—don't even worry about Andres now." She had scooped me up into her arms again, and because she wasn't Green or Bracken, I could fully relax and be mothered. "He's a good man, and he loved Adrian, and he'll take no for an answer." We entered my room again, and the men hadn't moved.

"And I can't tell him no." I said, knowing it was the truth. "Besides—a little blood—really—I just agreed to sleep with Nicky for, like, ever. What's a little blood intimacy in exchange for my life?" I looked at the unconscious men, all of whom would have given their lives for me, and maybe would have had to, if Andres hadn't showed up and offered them that way out. "For all of us." I added. "He saved all of us."

"You saved him first." Grace reminded me dryly, "And his whole kiss. Don't let gratitude give him a free pass into your bed."

"I thought you said he only wanted my blood."

"He only *asked* for your blood. He wouldn't have been able to help heal you, if he hadn't been pretty excited about the other thing."

"I don't even know this man." I said wearily. "And, quite frankly, I think dealing with Green and Bracken is going to be difficult enough—especially now that Nicky and I are pretty much married by Avian standards. Why don't we just let Andres suck on my neck, and try not to piss Bracken off any more than necessary?"

Grace chuckled, and Renny managed a tired guffaw. "I've seen you two dance, sweetie." Grace said when she could. "If you and Brack aren't pissing each other off, you're just not living."

Dimly, swimming in exhaustion, I looked again at the men who had given their lives to me—even Max, who would love Renny, had become part of my household. "And we want to live, don't we?" I asked myself, but Grace gave me a gentle hug in response.

At last I was clean and dry and wearing one of Bracken's old baseball shirts—the Rivercats. It occurred to me in a vague sort of way that Bracken was something of a sports enthusiast, and Green was not. This could be good, I thought fuzzily, because it would make sleeping with two men in the same home a hell of a lot easier. The last lucid thought I had was that I shouldn't go back to sleep with Bracken and Green.

"They're so tired." I said weakly to Grace.

"So are you, baby." She told me briskly, doing that hovering thing and placing me between the two of them as though I'd never left. "And they've prayed for your health for so long, I'd hate to rob them of waking up and seeing that you're better."

I wouldn't have argued with that, even If I'd had the strength.

When I woke up again, it was light. I reached for Green or Bracken, and found instead the slighter, more mortal body of Dominic Kestrel instead. I wanted Green. I wanted Bracken. I was surprised by how equal these wants were. But I saw Nicky, expecting to be rejected, and I refused to do that to a friend.

"Hey, luv." I murmured, remembering all the times Green had greeted me with this, and how I had felt instantly better, "I understand we're married." I leaned into him then, and even Nicky, for all of his inexperience, knew how to hold a tired, sick woman when she asked for comfort.

"I'm sorry." He said.

"I'm sorrier." I said back. I looked up and saw his face pale beneath his freckles. His hair—usually gelled and perfect—was a complete messy disaster. I felt a tug in the direction of my heart. "You know," I said softly, "In a whole other world, it would not have been a hardship to spend my life with you." He looked at me with sorrow-filled eyes, and I smiled a little. "It's still not." I told him, and he tucked his slight body next to mine as though he were learning how, and I felt him shudder. Once, twice, and then he was weeping silently, and I was shushing him.

"We'll be okay." I told him softly. "I won't let you down."

"You'll have to have my child." He said, voice choked with tears. "How can I make you have my child?"

I closed my eyes tight, opened them, digested. "I promised Green a child first." I said, feeling my way. "Bracken will want his child too." I couldn't hardly believe I was saying this. Of course I had always wanted to be a mother, but I wasn't old enough to buy beer. I wasn't *well* enough to walk to a bar. But Nicky had to know if he could live. "But I could have your baby, Nicky." I promised with a lump in my throat, hoping there could be another way. "Do we have to start today?" I meant it to be a joke, and was relieved when he laughed a little through his tears.

"We've got about ten years." He said.

Good—I had some time then. I could at least finish college before I started pushing babies out like gumdrops from a pretty glass ball. "And then what would happen?"

He looked at me seriously. "The same thing that will happen if I'm deprived of love for any length of time. I molt and pine and die."

I nodded, feeling like I was going to fall asleep again in very short order. "Green and I will take care of you, Nicky." I said from far away. "We don't let people down."

I woke again, and it was dark, and, thank Goddess, Green was holding me and Bracken was feeding me soup.

I was so happy that it was the two of them—Green, who I loved with all my soul and Bracken who I loved with all my heart—that I actually started to cry into my soup.

Bracken was appalled. "Goddess, Cory!" He sputtered, putting the bowl precariously on the bed and starting after me with a napkin, "its just soup!"

I felt a rusty chuckle rumble in my throat, and heard Green's gorgeous laugh softly in my ear. I smiled at Bracken, and as awful as I was sure I looked, it must have held something in it, some promise of beauty, of health and of strength, because he leaned forward and placed a chaste kiss on my lips. "Go ahead and cry then," He said softly then, "As long as I'm not the one who made you."

"Oh fine, take that out of the relationship why don't you." I tried to snap. It was hard when I was all choked up, but it got another smile from Bracken, and I could feel Green's chest shake beneath me, and I thought that maybe we could get through.

After a moment, I grabbed the hawk by the talons, so to speak, and said, "I'm sorry about...everything." I was going to say, "About Nicky," but it just seemed too cruel.

"Don't be sorry, luv." Green said quietly, at about the time Brack said, "You should be sorry, genius!" The two of them locked eyes, and Bracken had the grace to look sheepish.

"You worried me to death, Cory." He said, sort of like a little kid remembering his words. "And we would have had other firsts—you could have let me go."

"Not possible." I said quietly. I found I was looking longingly at the soup and hoping Bracken would pick it up again. "Not possible for me to let any of you go. And how dare he come in and try to make me. But I'm sorry for almost killing us all—I'm sorry I forced you guys to make that choice. I'm sorry I hurt everybody."

"What you should be sorry for," Green said acerbically, "Is the same thing you should have been sorry for these last five months—you wouldn't let any of us heal you."

"That's not true." I told him back, standing my ground. "I just wouldn't let any of you die for me."

"It would have been our choice if we did." Bracken snapped sullenly. "You just need to remember that if someone chooses to die for you, it's because they can't live without you."

I didn't know what to say to that. His name hung in the air, and nobody would say it, but we all knew who this argument was about. Suddenly Green, of all of us, started swearing. "Goddamned buggering goat fucking bastard fuckwit!" He burst out, and Bracken and I didn't even have to ask to whom he was referring.

"If he were here right now I'd beat the living shit out of him." Bracken agreed. He moved the soup to the floor and wrapped his arms around my middle, laying his head on my chest. Green reached around to clutch both of us to him, and I could feel us all vibrating with laughter, with anger, with grief, and with, hardest of all, relief.

I started to laugh, and it came out faintly hysterical. "What an asshole." I agreed weepily. "Do you think if he knew he was going to fuck us up this bad, he might have found a way not to die on us?"

"Bleeding Jesus, I hope so!" Bracken said against me. "I'd hate to think we've been hurting so bad, so long, for someone who didn't give a shit."

"I give a shit." I murmured into his hair. "I wouldn't die if I could help it."

"Just don't leave us behind." Bracken begged. Then, looking wry, he looked over my shoulder to Green. "Okay—you can leave him behind. But you can't leave me."

"Show off." Green said wretchedly, and I laughed in the same vein.

"I'm sorry." I had to say it again, I felt it so badly. "I'm so so so sorry." And it was the last thing anybody said for a while as we sat on the bed and held each other.

Eventually we pulled apart, and Bracken fed me soup in a murmuring silence as I dozed off in Green's arms. When I woke up again, there was only Green, which was fine, because I had so much to talk to him about I couldn't put it all in one sentence.

He was laying next to me, watching me sleep, and when my eyes opened, his face creased in a sweet smile.

"You're awake." He said, and he sounded like a happy child.

"You're here." I responded, and I must have sounded the same.

We stayed like that, smiling for a moment, and then I said, "I seem to be married to Nicky."

Green nodded ruefully. "So do I." He replied. Then: "Can I tell you how proud I am, about how you handled that?"

I looked away, embarrassed. "We have to take care of our own." I mumbled. "You wouldn't let him pine away and die—I couldn't. Anyway," I added, "It's the least I could do after all the other ways I screwed up."

He kissed my forehead. "And what ways would those be?" He asked.

"I got sick. I almost killed everybody I loved." I gave a half laugh. "I just flunked out of school!"

Green's eyes grew hard. "No you didn't." He said flatly.

"Aren't I supposed to be taking finals right now?" I asked in surprise.

"You took your finals. You passed." He said, his face implacable.

"Green…" I protested, and for the first time ever, I saw that he was angry, really angry, with me.

"You passed your finals." He said fiercely. "You won't take those classes over again. You won't *ever* take that many classes again. And we won't talk about this again."

"Green…" I said again, but this time I was hurt. He had never been angry with me before.

"You were punishing yourself." He said, still angry. "You were punishing yourself with work, with leaving, and I didn't see it." His eyes, every shade of green, turned towards me, and, in spite of his great age, and his agelessness, he looked very young. "You were worn down before Nicky attacked you. You were exhausted. You were weak—everything that happened afterward happened because you've forgotten what it's like to live, and live happily. That won't happen again." He looked away for a moment, and I lay quietly, in his arms, as he tightened his muscles as though to get up.

"I didn't earn my grades." I insisted, still hurt, but unwilling to be afraid of his anger. He loved me. I knew this. What was fear?

Green swore, rudely, succinctly, with heat. "Tell me, Cory," He said after, "I've seen your courses—a business computer course and six poly sci or European History classes—what exactly you are training yourself to be?"

I flushed, even laying next to him, neither of us in the mood for anything resembling love making, and then I mumbled an answer.

"What was that?" He demanded, grasping my chin and making me look him in the eyes.

"Your Queen." I said, not feeling this hostile since I wore 20 earrings and a black-Goth hair cut. "I'm training to be your Queen."

He nodded, still looking bad tempered. "Well, Corinne Carol Anne, you've just fought to save the memory of my people, fought ferociously to save an ally's entire court, and agreed to bed a young man that you are not in love with simply because he's one of ours and you will not let him die. I'd say you aced your god-damned final, wouldn't you?"

I flushed even more, feeling foolish. "So what're Nicky and Renny studying for?" I asked acerbically, not willing to concede just yet. But I'd lost—Green knew it, and he replied with the kind laughter crinkles in the corners of his eyes.

"They're studying to be your subjects, luvie—I'd say they passed with flying colors, yes?"

"Fair enough." I begrudged, only, I told myself, because I wanted to see that smile lurking in his eyes blossom. Goddess, did I need the healing of that smile.

I was denied. "No, not fair." He said quietly. "Nothing about your first year with us has been fair."

I had no answer for him, and one agenda. *Smile at me, Green, please smile at me.* "Did I really make a hotel?" I asked, out of the blue.

And that did it. "It's a five star masterpiece." He said, beaming wearily at me.

"We'll have to stay there some day." I told him. "After the sprites fix up the honeymoon suite."

"We'll make it a priority." He agreed, then, still chuckling.

"Thank you." I murmured.

"For what?"

"Smiling at me."

He nodded. "It was the least I could do." He waited a beat. "I have to leave for a couple of days. Will you be okay?"

No. No, I would not be okay. I needed him. "What happened?" I asked instead.

Green sat up in bed and sighed, leaving me, still weak and struggling, prone and helpless. "Attacks at home." He said bluntly, and I was so surprised I struggled to sit up. He put a firm hand on my chest and waggled a finger at me. "No one's been hurt—on our side at least." He told me, and I relaxed against the piled pillows.

"Their side?"

"We've captured five, with one casualty. The mate of one of the captured Avians. Arturo is afraid they will die in captivity, and he doesn't know what to do with them."

The unsaid hit me—that Arturo would have killed them immediately, but he knew Green wouldn't agree to that at all. Green was needed. Green knew how to make people want to live. "You have to go." I said unwillingly. I'd been training to be a Queen, right? Well, Guinevere had been unable to let Arthur go. I had to be able to do better than that.

"I'll leave Launcelot here to champion you." Green said wryly, and I told him to stay out of my head—he only laughed. Then I told him to take Nicky, and he agreed.

"And Officer Max will drive us up—his vacation is up at the end of this week, anyway—he needs to go back to work."

"He needs to change his job." I said thoughtfully. The reason Max and I had never been an item is because he'd been more cop than hero. I'd guess that his steadfastness in the last few days now made him more hero than cop.

"Very probably." Green agreed. "And I've let him know that if he does, we have a place for him. But for now…"

"For now, he'd probably like to get out of the place where the pigeons shitting on your car really *do* have it in for you." I finished dryly.

"Indeed." Green murmured, sitting back down on the bed again. I could feel it coming on—nappy time. I felt like such a loser, having to fall asleep every fifteen minutes. I realized that I had lost track of the day again.

"Wednesday morning." Green said gently when I asked. "I should be back by Friday evening, Saturday morning at the latest."

"So Grace stays here?" I asked. Poor Grace—I'm sure she missed Arturo.

"And Renny." Green nodded. "And to baby sit the lot of you, Andres will be here in the evenings."

To my absolute horror, I blushed, and Green laughed at me outright. "It's not funny," I groused, mortified. "He's seen me helpless—he held me as I slept, and all I know about him is he's got a very sexy accent and good manners—I couldn't even pick him out of a line-up!"

"You're right, of course." He answered gently, "But that's not why I'm laughing." He took one of my fretful hands, as it twisted my grandmother's quilt—someone must have mailed it here for me, because, as I remembered, I'd left it at Green's. "I'm laughing, because you're thinking that you'll probably have to sleep with him too—and you want to say no but you don't know how."

This wasn't helping the blush, and I said so.

"Look, luv," He told me kindly, "I'm not denying that the man would like to be your lover, but he very much understands that you're spoken for."

"Boy howdy, am I." I retorted, and Green laughed again. And because I'd made him my other college course for the last seven months, I saw the sadness behind the laugh, and I finally realized that for all of what he believed, about monogamy and love and the Goddess, that it had not been easy on him to decide that we would live like this. Without another word I took the hand that held mine and kissed it gently.

"*Ou'e'hm.*" I said, hoping that was right.

For once, it was Green who looked raw and vulnerable and distraught, and it was all I could do not to take it back, when I had said it for comfort.

"Thank you." He said after a moment. A single tear rolled from his cheek to my hand, became crystal, tumbled down onto Gran's quilt and spread, making the whole quilt glow as though threaded with light, which is how it looked forever after. Oblivious to the small miracle of elves, Green touched his cheek to my hand. "Thank you, my *Ou'e'eir*. It is a fine title for a lover and a leader. It is everything we are, and everything we can become. Thank you."

And now I wanted to cry. When the tears started to leak from between my eyes, I knew that I *really* had to sleep soon, and then I *really* had to eat again. Damn, I was a slave to my physical person—and for the first time I understood that when someone had their health, they had a hell of a lot.

"Will you be gone when I wake up?" I asked, feeling foolish and helpless to ask it.

"Yes." He murmured, gathering me into his arms again. "But I'll be here as you fall asleep."

"When can we make love again?" I murmured, feeling that faint hunger underneath all of the other bodily pulls that commanded me at the moment.

"When you can be awake for more than five minutes at a time." He responded, his voice still clogged from the one moment when the words *due'alle* and *due'ane* remained unspoken between us.

"I'll work on that while you're gone." I told him, and buried myself in his arms and his smell and the feel of his hands in my hair until oblivion rolled me under.

GREEN

Hazy shades of winter.

Traffic up I-80 was vile—two accidents on either side of the freeway had cars backed up from Vacaville to San Rafael. Green was crammed in the back of Max's '69 Mustang, because fitting his long legs into the front was not a possibility, and this way he at least got to sprawl on both seats. He spent the time listening to Nicky and Max talk in the way of new, fast friends and reflected that he hadn't minded December so much when Adrian had been alive.

"Favorite recent movie?" Nicky asked, about midway through the traffic back-up.

"*Lord of the Rings,* one through three." Max agreed promptly.

"*Ocean's 11!*" Nicky disagreed. "You, sir?" He looked in the mirror, soliciting Green's opinion. Nicky's affections towards Green fluctuated between hero-worship and blatant infatuation these days—Green was never sure which would be shining out of his eyes at any given moment.

"*Lost Boys.*" Green said dryly, although on most days, he pretty much agreed with Max about *Lord of the Rings.*

"Favorite band?" Max asked. It was his turn in the game.

"Current or classic?" Nicky wanted to know.

"Both." Max returned.

"*Blink 182* and *Pink Floyd.*" Nicky returned smartly. Green almost cringed at the contrast.

"*Maroon 5* and *Def Leppard.*" Max answered back, but that seemed to fit. "Green?"

"*Metallica* and *Linkin Park.*" Green said, still looking out at the iron grey sky.

"Cory said it was *U2* and *Dave Mathews.*" Nicky said, unexpectedly. "That day we were looking for Bracken—I don't know why I remember that, but she said she'd never been a fan of Mathews until she saw that you had every c.d."

"Today, it's *Metallica* and *Linkin' Park.*" Green responded, keeping his voice light.

"They weren't your favorites." Max said, and his eyes in the rearview mirror were suddenly old—older than Green. "They were Adrian's."

"True enough." Green conceded. "But I'm in that sort of mood today, so today they're mine—go on with the game."

The boys in the front eyed each other, and Max spoke next, even though he'd taken the last turn. "Heroes." He said, meeting Green's eyes with purpose.

"Movie or real?" Green asked.

"Real." Max responded levelly.

"Cory." Nicky said promptly. "Max?"

"My old trainer." Max replied thoughtfully. "He's retired now. He loved his ex-wife madly, adored his kids—but never, never, ever could say no to the job. But God, what a solid cop. Tough, smart—never got jaded, you know? Worked vice in Oakland for 15 years—moved his family to our area when his partner ate his own gun."

"Ouch." Green acknowledged from the back.

"Yeah." Max affirmed. "And Mickey, he used to say, that dying was easy—it was wading through what was left that was hard."

"Smart man." Green said gently, wondering where this was going.

"Yeah—I used to think he was the best man I knew."

"Until?"

Max's face firmed up, resolved itself into a new manhood to match his old eyes. He met Green's eyes in the mirror. "Until I met you."

Humans, Green thought as he swallowed the lump in his throat, could continually surprise you. "I'm not much to my people." He said rawly, surprising even himself. He hadn't planned on revealing how much that hurt, and certainly not to Officer Maxwell Johnson.

"They're not your people." Max responded. "We're your people. And we'd die for you."

Max meant it. Green hadn't seen, in these last days, how Max had changed from skeptical outsider to one of his. He should have seen it, but he, like all of them, had gravitated around Cory's bed like planets around a sun.

"I'm honored." He said softly, now fully in the present.

"You're beloved." Nicky said, looking embarrassed. "We were afraid of Goshawk. We worshipped him. We were mesmerized by him. We didn't love him. He..." And now Nicky looked away, looked surreptitiously at Max, who pretended not to see the look, and then just spoke. "He wouldn't have understood about...about me bonding with you." He said at last. "Not even when it was an accident."

The other men were quiet, waiting, because there was a wound, a hidden one, that they could see about to open up before them.

"There was a boy, when I first came to the city—he was like me, from the Midwest somewhere, and so bowled over by San Francisco—he fell in love with another boy..." Nicky's breath hitched, then, and Max kept his eyes fixedly on the car in front of him that hadn't moved in the last three minutes. "It's a death sentence anyway, you know...unless mates produce a child, we die within ten or fifteen years as it is...but Goshawk said it was a sin against God—he told Seth that God would forgive him but he had to prove he could fight his nature..." Tears now, open ones, and Nicky dashed them away with the back of his hand. "So Seth flew to the top of the tallest building in the city, and changed into a human. Then he jumped off, and fell to the ground."

"Jesus..." Max breathed, and Green murmured "Goddess!" And the car was silent for quite a while.

"You'd do anything to keep me alive." Nicky said at last. "Cory will have my baby, even though she doesn't love me like she loves you. And Goshawk wanted us dead if we weren't just like him." He shook his head then. "I'm glad you're alive, Green." He said at last. "I'm so, so glad you're not Adrian. I need you to be glad too."

Green shrugged off his melancholy abruptly, saving his mourning for another rare and private moment with Cory, and smiled gently. "How could I not be glad to be loved like all of this?" He asked wryly, and was pleased to see Max roll his eyes and snort.

"And I am now officially entirely too straight for this conversation." Max said dryly, and the somber mood that had haunted the car was officially lifted.

"Favorite food?" Green asked, pulling them back into the game.

"Anything!" Nicky piped up—like all of the men, feeding Cory his life force for a week had left him perpetually hungry.

"Too right." Green agreed. "Max, the next time we start moving, let's take the off-ramp here—I think I own a restaurant somewhere nearby."

The place was little, tidy as a grandmother's kitchen, and fragrant with odd and homey smells. It had maybe ten tables—few of them occupied at two in the afternoon—with a menu that spoke in code for the preternatural clientele that it often served.

Green had the *Pasta Desperation*—which had a sauce made from pine nuts and feta cheese, and was particularly packed with the carbohydrates that needed replacing after expending any sort of power. Nicky had the *Protein Shred,* which was exactly what it sounded like, browned just enough to not make Max's gorge rise, and seasoned with sage and basil and other things that a wild rabbit or field mouse might have eaten to make it tasty to a predator. Max had the cheeseburger, but not before he'd asked Green if there was anything in it he should know about.

"No." Green replied, "But I understand they're addictive."

Max had to agree, and ordered two more to go from the tiny, genderless confection of piquant features and purple hair that waited on them.

"You know," He said after a watching the sylph disappear behind the counter, "A month ago, I wouldn't have noticed that she probably isn't human."

"She's not really a she, either." Green said dryly. "Sylphs choose their gender after they fall in love."

"What if they fall in love with each other?" Nicky asked, enchanted.

"They don't." Green answered simply. "They're the preternatural leveler— sort of the Goddess' way of making sure that there really is somebody out there for everybody."

Max laughed a little. "Even if it's not who you think it's going to be."

"Too right." Green agreed. "Have you and Renny come to an agreement, then?"

Max scowled up at Green in reply. "If you weren't who I know you were, I'd say that's none of your damned business." He said after a moment.

"But you just accused me of being a good leader, and so it is." Green answered back easily. "Besides, I'm not asking for details, Max—I'm just wondering if you've reconsidered my offer."

Max took another gulp of his chocolate shake—his second. (Nicky was on his third, and even Green had ordered one.) "I like being a Sheriff." He said unhappily. "I could do things for you there—now that I know about you—about all of you, I can make sure that, say, people like Renny and Mitch never get rousted before the full moon, right? I could make sure that someone like that sylph never gets harassed. I mean, if you think about it, if Nicky had someone like me to turn to, he might never have found Goshawk."

Green nodded, impressed. "Good points all." He said, "And I appreciate it. But you need to know that if it ever gets too hot for you, working in two worlds, that ours is open. And we need investigators of our own, as you've probably figured out by now, right?"

Max nodded. "Right." He smiled then, slyly. "Of course, I understand that rent's free if I ask…"

Green laughed. "It is indeed—in fact, the lycanthrope wing has been a little empty since this summer."

Max sobered. "Uhm…that brings me to a…. weird-assed question…." He trailed off, obviously unsure of how to ask.

"Do you have to turn furry to date the furry?" Green supplied, before Max could blush any more.

"Right." Yup. Red to his toes.

"Depends on how serious you get." Green said meditatively. "Renny's been furry for quite some time—she's got enough control not become a giant house-pet at, shall we say, delicate moments of your acquaintanceship." Max blew out a breath, and Green suppressed a grin. "However," He warned, not smiling at all, "Things get trickier with time."

"What do you mean?" Max asked, and Nicky listened intently.

"Well," Green blew out another breath, and tried not to add his blush to Max's. "Accidents, for one. Renny's bite is contagious in any form—sort of like preternatural herpes. Enough contact over a long enough period of time, and you're bound to contract giant-house-cat-itis." Max almost snorted shake out his nose, but Green went inexorably on. "And children, for another. Renny's primary reason for seducing Mitch into biting her, as I recall, was that she wanted to have his children. Neither mother nor child can survive long, unless all parties involved have the shape-changing capability."

"So," Max said carefully, "There's no such thing as a mixed family in Renny's world."

"Not for long." Green agreed. "But there are some benefits of being furry."

"Such as?" Max asked, trying not to look crushed.

"Longer life." Green said promptly. "Shape-changers age at about one-third to one-quarter the rate of human beings. It depends on how much time they spend in their other form."

Max blinked—it had not occurred to him that this would be a factor. "So that explains why Renny still looks like she's sixteen…" He breathed.

"Well, she's not much older than that." Green responded. But the space between sixteen and twenty was a big one, in human terms, he realized. Sidhe and lesser fey didn't think like that. They became sexually precocious around the age of twenty, and there they remained, beautiful, young, and fully sexed, for the rest of their lives. The Goddess was funny in that way—most of her creatures tended to keep their youth and their appetites.

"Anything else that's different?" Max asked, still looking a little dazed.

"They easily replace lost blood volume—but you know that." And Max nodded with him. "Do you also know it makes them very hard to kill? Even if you amputate a limb, or even a head, if the body and appendage are within any distance of each other, the lycanthrope will find a way to join—the only reason Goshawk could kill Orson's people was that he used the power from the memories he stole to stop their metabolism. Elves do the same thing." He added, seeing Max's look of disbelief.

"Avians don't." Nicky said glumly, and Green looked at him without surprise. He knew now how very mortal Nicky's people were. "We're extra strong and everything, but once you get past the strength, it's as easy to kill us as a regular bird—but we do age differently. In fact" and he looked up at Green a little sadly, "Once we hit our age of sexual maturity, we sort of stick there, until we find a mate."

"And then?" Green asked, interested. He had known Avians existed, but Nicky was the first one he'd ever known personally. It appeared that they were a rather secretive branch of the Goddess' get—which was too bad, because it had probably made Goshawk's work easier. It was easier to isolate a group from morality that had already isolated itself from its moral center.

"And then we age with our mate." Nicky smiled then, a sweet, heartbroken smile that told Green exactly what the last two weeks had cost him. "I have no idea what will happen to me." He said after a moment.

"I think you're in luck." Green said kindly. "I don't age at all, and since you and I will probably have a little more bonding than you and Cory, you'll probably have a long, full, happy life."

"What about Cory?" Max asked abruptly. "Bracken seems to think she's…" He frowned, looking for words, "Something more than mortal."

"She could be." Green conceded. "But it takes a great deal of power, channeled very very often in order to make that happen—and usually some sort of rite of passage, that all involved will recognize." He gazed past Max, and his look was

happy. "It's coming." He said after a moment. "There will be something, I can feel it. The Goddess does not just drop a Cory into the world, and not give her a way to stay here a while." He smiled then, as well, the kind of smile that seemed to ease the aches in both men's hearts. "It would be wonderful," He said after a fraught, sunbeam moment, "To have a love that will not leave my side." They were all quiet, and the wish was so strong from all of them that it almost hung, visible, on the brown formica table before them.

"I do believe your food is done, Max." Green said pleasantly as the waiter set it down in front of them. "Just allow me to pay our bill, and let us see if traffic has cleared up, right?"

Traffic *had* cleared up, and the rest of the trip was uneventful, if dreary, under a sky the color of a sweat sock washed with jeans. The trees, which had had some color on Green's way down to the city, were now completely naked, bare, defiantly dark against the sad sky. Only the bright lights that lit the strip malls lining the freeway gave any sort of liveliness to the view, but those had palled by the time they blew through Davis, and twilight had set in. The conversation had quieted a little, not a bad silence, but as yet another Christmas light strewn store appeared, Green surprised everybody by swearing viciously.

"Buggerfuck! What in the hell are we going to do about Christmas?" He asked rhetorically.

"Do you believe in Christmas?" Max asked cautiously from the front. "I thought the Goddess was all about Yule and Imbolc and Litha and shit that I've never heard of…"

"Of course we believe in Christmas." Green said absently. "The sabbats are a part of the year too—they celebrate the year as the Goddesses body, really—youth, fertility, death, rebirth—those really magical human times that she delights in. But since She birthed the son of God as a human on earth—hence the worship of the Virgin Mary—there's no reason we shouldn't celebrate the one time God and Goddess actually got along, right?"

"Right." Echoed Max somewhat dazedly.

"It didn't happen in the winter, though…" Green continued, his mind still on the celebration at the house. "My Da' said it happened in spring."

"I don't even want to ask." Max murmured weakly. "So, what do you usually do?"

"After the Yule solstice—sort of Elvish New Year, we do the regular Christmas stuff. We decorate the house. We feast. Give gifts. Celebrate. I just…" He looked embarrassed. "I usually spend a couple of weeks shopping for my people. Adrian

took the vampires and shape changers, I took the greater fey, Arturo took the lesser—what are we going to do this year?"

"I don't know." Max said, at a complete loss. "Who's in charge of the vampires now?"

"Cory nominally, Grace actually." Green muttered flatly. Then: "Wait a minute...yes, that'll work. Nicky—the people sent to attack my home—that was sort of a suicide mission, wasn't it?"

"Yeah." Nicky nodded. "I'd left by then, but Goshawk would have sent people who needed to atone for their sins or something. He might have sent a captain with them, but Cory killed Eyeass, and I don't think he'd risk Osprey so soon afterwards—he tends to keep his strongest people close by."

"Right." Green acknowledged, "And do all of Goshawk's sins fall into the same sort of category?"

"Uhm...yeah..." Nicky replied, as though really thinking about it for the first time. "Bonding with a mate he didn't approve of, or with someone without his permission. Socializing with any other Goddess' get." A pause. "What Goshawk called sexual perversion of any kind."

"I thought so." Green murmured thoughtfully. "Good. So we've got something to work with." And suddenly he knew what he would do with the prisoners Arturo held in the basement, particularly the heartbroken one who would not eat.

They were in worse shape than he'd first thought, he realized an hour and a half later, as Arturo brought him down into basement part of the darkling. The darkling itself was a cleverly engineered section of the great house designed to never expose itself to sunlight. The basement of the darkling was a fairly comfortable place—couches, carpeting, a wide-screen TV, etc. It was often a private meeting place for the vampires, but it had a steel door and frame with a wheel and bar lock on the outside for new vampires, who were not necessarily easy to control.

Today it was home to five pale, shaking men, who, it appeared, were shedding their hair at an alarming rate. As angry as Green was to be under siege, he could still feel compassion for these five, these misguided souls, these lost brothers, starving for space and the wind on their bodies. When he entered the room four of them turned their faces towards the door like suppliants towards an altar. The fifth sat in the farthest corner of the room, facing the wall, and rocked himself silently, lost in his grief.

"Well." Green murmured, sick in his heart. "Anybody who's having second thoughts on your current life path, please raise your hands."

There were no smiles and no irony when slowly, four sweating, trembling hands reached for the ceiling.

Green nodded, unsurprised. "Here's what we're going to do, gentlemen." He began, and gestured to the ten vampires crowding the hall behind him. "These people behind me will take your blood. Has anyone here shared blood with a vampire?"

Sober shaking of the head. No. They weren't allowed to fraternize with other preternatural beings.

"Vampire feeding is both very emotional and very intimate." He told them. "A vampire who feeds from you will be able to, for a short period of time, know what you are feeling, but not what you are thinking. If you are planning to escape, attack, self-terminate, whatever, your vampire will know. And will take you down, feeding from you until you are too weak to move."

"We're too weak to move now." The strongest looking of the five men snapped sarcastically.

"Yes." Green agreed compassionately. "But you won't be after we take you outside, you feel the air on your skin, the wind in your face, and you are allowed to hunt."

The collective intake of breath sounded almost like a sob. "Hunt?" One of them said, the longing of a lifetime in his voice.

"Yes, hunt. Within the confines of my property, and with your vampire shadow, of course."

"You would let us do that?" This from the same man who had possessed the spirit to speak up before. Green took a closer look at him. Slightly built, African-American, young—younger than Nicky, which meant he hadn't hit the age of maturity yet, but with sober, grave brown eyes. Good, thought Green—he was hoping someone of this lot would be thoughtful enough to see what was best for his people.

"If you will let our vampires feed from you, I will let you hunt." He saw them shift, look at each other, hardly daring to hope.

"How intimate?" One of them asked fearfully from the back. This too, Green had anticipated.

"Your clothes stay on, if that's what you mean." Green said, a little bit of humor in his voice, "But other than that, it can be quite...arousing." A flash in his head, the last blood he'd ever given Adrian, their bodies arching, thrusting against each other, and Adrian's final giddy release. "In a good way." He finished off weakly.

"I'm not a faggot." One of the men said stiffly, and Green looked closer at him. He was another farm-boy, it appeared, like Nicky. Tall, white-blonde hair, casual muscles from work, not the gym.

"No one said you were." Green conceded. "If you wish, there are female vampires here as well."

"We'll...we can't." Their leader said, painfully. "We might bond..."

"I honestly doubt you can bond with a vampire." Green said frankly, "Because of the simple nature of your bonding. It's all about mating and life—I would imagine you can't bond with someone who is neither alive nor procreating. But as for the extent of the arousal, the vampires can control that." Green said gently. "They usually make the experience pleasant, sensual—and yes, orgasmic. But they can be clinical about it as well. Still, it's another person's mouth on your body. The choice is up to you." He watched them pause, in an agony of hope and indecision. "If you like," He said at last, "We can go outside and you can make your decision there."

There was a faint moan of relief from the back, and Green thought with satisfaction that he had them. "I do warn you," He said after a moment, "That anyone who attempts to escape will be captured, and the blood taking will not be voluntary." The four men facing him nodded, and he stepped aside and gestured for them to precede him up the stairs.

"Marcus, Phillip," He called, "Take them to the Goddess Grove." He wanted the air sexually charged, he thought. These men had been deprived of mate or choice to mate—he wanted them to feel what they'd been missing. As the last one passed through the door, Green moved to the back of the room to the bereft and heartbroken Avian who had lost his mate. He was a big man, muscular, probably proud of his body and its ability to protect. He had the milk and coffee complexion and strong features of a second or third generation Mexican immigrant, and a look of such blank and total loss on his face that Green's power, both sexual and genderless, came to life just looking at the boy. With a sigh, he hunkered down, and laid his hand on the man's shoulder. Another young one, he thought, but then realized that he wouldn't know. It didn't matter. Green knew from experience that grief made all creatures young, vulnerable, and alone.

"I've asked around you know." He said conversationally. "Avians don't have to die when their mate dies. They may even mate again."

The shoulder beneath his hand jerked, but he didn't let go.

"Yes, I know you feel that way now." He leaned closer, into the man's peripheral vision, and his demeanor was no longer casual. "I know that feeling, brother." He said. "I am nearly two thousand years old, and not once have I truly loved my own kind. Believe me, I know your loss. I know your loss again and again and it never gets easier. It never feels better. But you have two choices." Those eyes, dark and colorless from this angle, darted towards Green's face. Yes, he was very interested to know what his choices were.

"The first is what you are doing." A scowl. Anger. This was not a very attractive option. "You can stare at the wall until your body fails you, and you pass away." That jerk against his hand again. *Go away, sounds fine to me.*

"And the second option is to live."

"How?" This surprised Green. He hadn't expected words this early into the lecture. Good. There was a will to live. His reply echoed in his head—he heard the words he'd first used the morning he and Cory had awoken and realized that Adrian would never awake at twilight and love them again. They echoed back to him, in their simplicity, and their inadequacy, and he could almost weep with the irony.

"Stand up. Go outside. Eat. Breathe in and out. Repeat the next day. Eventually you don't have to remember to do these things, and you will be able to remember the rest." He murmured.

A minor shake of the head. "I don't deserve to live." He said. "She was protecting me. I was sent here because we bonded without Goshawk's permission. She came to keep me safe."

"Ah." And this pain was even more acute. Green could still feel Cory against him, Bracken weeping into her lap, the three of them raging against Adrian, who had died, after all, to keep them safe. He couldn't speak to this when the man's head was turned. He reached forward and grasped a stubborn chin, forcing the red-rimmed brown eyes to meet his.

"Listen to me. I will spill my insides for you once only. We were three—I am the green, the growing, the day. I loved the moon, the silver night, and he loved the sunshine, fierce and hot, and she loved me because the sun must love the day. And the sun and I stood in a valley of stone and faced death, because we wanted to spare the night, who had suffered a thousand deaths already, and we didn't want him to bleed any more. But he would not allow it. He swooped from the sky and clenched death in both hands, and we wore his blood like skin."

The Avian gasped then, in horror, in sympathy, it didn't matter which.

"Yes, my brother, I suffered loss. My beloved, the sun, has suffered loss, and she, again, almost gave her life for me, and I again for her. And it has taken me eighteen-hundred years and my own blood and tears to learn this truth, and here I am, just giving it to you for free." Green leaned forward until their foreheads nearly touched. "If someone gives their life for you, it is because they can not bear to live in a world without you. This is a great gift and a terrible burden, and if you are going to live, you need to be grateful for the gift and prepared to bear the burden. Can you do that, my brother?"

A tear, then another, down a golden cheek. "I don't know."

Silence. Breathing, both of them, in and out. *Fair enough*, Green thought, *let him know I heard*. At last, the stiff shoulder under Green's hand relaxed a little, accepted the simple animal comfort of touch. It was time. "Let us go out under the moon," Green said into the stillness, "And maybe the gift will seem greater and the burden less, right?"

The Avian nodded then, and Green wrapped his arm around the man's waist and helped him onto wobbly legs. Together they made the long walk from the darkling up to the Goddess grove.

The fog, which had made the day dismal and oppressive had burned off, leaving the stars so crystal clear they almost cut the skin. The Goddess grove was surreal and holy in the sharp starlight, and the Avians waiting by the pool in the center already appeared healthier from the fresh air and the loveliness around them.

Green supported the weight of the Avian he had helped up the granite staircase, and waited for the others to figure out what shapes the trees made as they bent, twisted, contorted around each other.

This was, in fact, the second grove of trees consecrated to the Goddess on Green's property. The first grove was a simple intersecting of lime trees and rose bushes that he and Adrian had planted a hundred years ago. It was where he and Cory had waited, one balmy summer night, for Adrian to come to them, so that they could love each other. That one was still cared for, but now it was private, a tiny haven in the garden below that only Green visited when he was feeling most alone.

This grove, the newer grove that Cory had created with power she'd forgotten she had, encompassed the entire crown of the hill which housed Green's giant house. Until this summer it had been made of the long straw grasses and the Sentinel oak trees that grew native in the area. Then Green, Cory, and Adrian had lived their first night in each other's bed—Cory's power had erupted, and Green had barely managed to keep her from blowing the top off of his Faerie hill. The result of the three of them was here, and the trees—Green's lime tree, Cory's native oak, and a sweet thorn-less rose for Adrian—twisted to form the three of them as they had been that night, making love in the truest form of the words.

Suddenly there was a chorus of "Oh my God!" And "Sweet Jesus would you look at that!" And Green knew that the young men had figured out what they were seeing.

"How in the hell did you do this?" This first young man—the youngest looking one with the cocoa colored skin and grave eyes—said directly to Green.

"Magic." He replied, enjoying their reactions very much. They'd been taught that sex was bad, eroticism evil, and that their leader had a right to control these things for them, dictate their behaviors as he felt to be true. Green wanted them to see something very different. In fact, by the time the vampires came to feed, he wanted them to *feel* something very different—in a very intimate, personal way.

"Whose?" The young man replied, and all the others turned, waiting for an answer. Their eyes, he noticed, moved from one stand of trees to another, making out the forms, the positions, and, he hoped, the tenderness and true melding of body and spirit imbued in the wood.

"The oak tree—the woman—it was her magic, fueled by the lime tree, and the rose." Green answered. "Throw it all together, shake it until it explodes, hold up a canvas of magic shielding, and this is what fell out. Lovely, don't you think?"

"They all look like they were enjoying themselves." Said the young blonde farm boy. His voice, Green noted, was hushed and awed, and not judgmental in the least.

"It was the best night in a very long life." Green replied truthfully. "I would not trade the experience that made this grove for all the heartbreak that came after. Is that what you needed to know?"

And now he could see their recognition—him. He was the lime tree. The awe in their eyes was both touching and reassuring. It was good, he thought, to know that something you valued could touch other lives.

"We are the enemies that your leader has chosen." Green said after he'd measured that look of awe in their eyes. "The last group that tried the same thing no longer exists—at all." He added brutally. "We didn't plan that—but when you take people who love passionately and justly and then interfere with that love for no reason, things can spiral beyond control very quickly." Oh, he had their attention now, yes he did. They all seemed to know about unjust interference with love. "So, yes, you will need to make a choice, eventually. But not tonight. Tonight you have only the choice of letting the vampires feed. You have an hour to decide—when you're ready, approach the vampire of your choice, and he or she will do the rest. When the hour is up, you may either fly with your vampire as a shadow, or return to the darkling basement. If you choose to fly, an hour before dawn, you will return, we'll let you have a sleep and then we have things for you to do, both outside and in rooms lit with sunlight."

"When can we hunt again?" Farm boy asked, blatant longing in his voice.

"At night, with your vampire, of course." Green replied pleasantly. "Here, all of you, don't make this decision in isolation. Talk amongst yourselves, talk to the vampires—don't hold the fangs against them, they're nice people on the whole—and by all means come introduce yourselves to me. I've had a rough day myself—I'll be sitting down right over there," He indicated a stand of trees in which a lime tree and a rose tree simply wrapped limbs around the oak, and she around them, in an embrace that, even in the abstract, was painfully tender, "Having some dinner. Come say hullo, if you like, but I warn you—Elves are vegetarians, so my dinner won't interest you all that much." He managed to make them smile a little, and that was good. He summoned a sprite to ask for food, and then did exactly as he promised: sat down in the cool moonlight and ate.

It took less than half an hour. They grouped together for a moment, whispering, absorbing the ambiance and impact of the grove itself, and casting longing looks into the night. Then they wandered to the vampires, struck up conversations that would have been awkward if the vampires hadn't been Adrian's lost who knew about compassion and making other people comfortable, and finally they came, with their chosen vampire, and introduced themselves to Green.

The young African-American was LaMark, from Seattle, the Farm Boy was (fittingly enough) John, from Nebraska, and the poor, lost boy without his mate was Mario, who had been born and raised in Los Angeles. The other two, plain, freckled, brown-haired boys, had been friends since the first grade, Danny and Tommy, from the little town of Twain-Hart, east of El Dorado county. Green met each one graciously, clasping their hands, and, in Mario's case, grasping a shoulder, and if he thought it was extremely interesting that, of the five, only Mario chose to venture into the dark with a female vampire, he kept that observation to himself.

When, at last, both vampire and Avian had moaned, and sighed, and shuddered in their dark corners, and the Avians changed with a flutter of strong wings and taken off over the grove, the other vampires who were left faded into the night to look for food. Green sat and stared up into the night, feeling Cory and Adrian breathing through his skin in this holy place, and missed them both so much he could practically hear Adrian's voice in his head.

"I loved to fly." He said, admiration in his voice for the shapes playing in the trees. "But I was always sad because you couldn't come with me."

Green felt a weight lift from his chest and a knot bind up his tongue. Oh, Goddess, if it wasn't real, he didn't want to know. "I was always glad you had someplace of your own." He forced out past a rough throat.

"You're too sad now anyway, and our girl's too thin." Adrian told him bluntly, like Adrian could, and Green didn't dare look over his shoulder, but relied on a flicker of moonbeam hair out of the corner of his eye, and the sound of the beloved voice.

"We almost lost her." He said instead, concentrating fiercely on the loveliness of the dark shapes against the crystal air. He didn't know what to say about the sad comment. How do you tell a ghost in the garden that you're sad because he's a ghost and the garden is his only memorial?

"I know mate," Adrian's voice was real. The shadow and memory that made up his body were thin and translucent, like a picture on wax paper, but Adrian's voice could still send shivers of desire up Green's skin. "She tried to follow me here, you know but I made her stay. You owe me for that."

He knew. Of course he knew. She'd called Adrian's name in her delirium, just as she'd called his name, and Bracken's. Green couldn't stand it anymore, and risked a look over his shoulder. Adrian's eyes, autumn-sky blue, were the only color left in the moonlight. Then he smiled, flashing a little fang, and Green felt his expression answer, even if his heart was breaking.

"We owe Bracken and Andres too." He said gently, wondering again if it really was Adrian, or if his sorrow of the day had summoned this vision and made it true.

"Well, Brack loved her as soon as I did." Adrian said wisely, and a pale, transparent hand reached out, and Green felt a breath of wind pull a strand of sunshine hair from his mouth, "And I couldn't have loved her nearly so much if she hadn't loved you too."

Green closed his eyes tightly, wondering if he could stand this, oh please Goddess let him be able to stand one more moment…"Hope you don't mind if I would have loved her without you, my beloved…"

Arturo came up through the door in crown of the hill and plopped next to Green, sighing with relief.

"I don't know how you do it, brother. If I had given them this choice, they would have died first."

Green took a deep breath and watched the shadows of Avians and vampires flicker from tree to tree and back. Arturo was next to him, waiting for an answer, and Adrian was a flicker of moonbeam and a smell in the trees and a touch of tenderness on his savaged heart. He forced himself to breathe, to breathe, to live, and to answer.

"Not true, Arturo." He murmured after a moment, "Not true at all."

"You're right—first they would have gone for my throat so I would have *had* to kill them." Arturo finished with a laugh, and Green laughed too, because Adrian was gone and it was time to sit in the present, and Arturo was probably right. Arturo had way too much pride to be able to offer the sort of amnesty Green had just given.

"Do you think they'll take me up on this?" Green asked after a bit. It was easy, so easy, to get lost in the wheeling, diving dance of darkness and thin starlight but just as Adrian had found him, so he must find himself.

"It depends." Arturo murmured. "What do they get to do when they wake up?"

Green laughed then. "Decorate the house, shop for presents, start the baking, do the same for the businesses…" He trailed off when Arturo dissolved into what sounded like a macho version of the giggles.

"You're joking…" He gasped between laughs.

"Not at all…" Green said, humor engaging his smile—it was moments like these that the ever so hetero Arturo could almost fall in love. "Adrian and I," And his voice grew sober here, but not too much, "We used to start all this shit during Thanksgiving…and it took us both the whole six weeks to get it done…we're behind schedule here, mate—we need the help."

"You know," Arturo said kindly, "No one would think less of you if we had a quiet Christmas this year."

Green plucked a clover from the grass—a miracle of the temperate climate that existed on this hill and nowhere else in the area—and blew on it, watched it grow, even with the shattered stem in his hand. "I would." He said after a moment. "Cory has known us less than a year. In that time she's lost her first lover, been forced to take on others for various reasons, rearranged her entire future, and remade herself in our image. I've lost track of how many times she's almost died for us." He peered into the night, watched a large falcon flirt with his vampire shadow, saw the vampire wheel and dive, a darkness of death against the living starlight. "I want to give her something beautiful. A Faerie-tale kind Christmas, if you will. I want her to see us as we can be—full of joy and light and lovely shadows…" He looked down at the flower in his hand, placed it back with its smaller brethren and willed it to grow roots and prosper. It obliged him by immediately blossoming, spreading the scent of sweetness and summer through the air.

"I want to give her a good memory to make up for all the bad." He said at last.

"You want to give her something Bracken can't." Arturo replied, seeing all too clearly what his leader would not say.

"Well," Green murmured in self-deprecation, "I am her *Ou'e'hm* after all."

"Of course you are." Arturo murmured, all of the compassion in three thousand years of living weighting his voice. "You know she'd probably love you if you were a human flipping burgers on the McJob."

"Yes, of course." Green brooded, "But then she wouldn't be a target of three quarters of the preternatural community, now would she? And then, she'd get my total attention—I'd fucking worship her, wouldn't I? I'd be with her right now, helping her heal, instead of here, helping everybody else."

"But we need you here." Arturo retorted, helplessly. He knew. They all knew. They knew that Green loved Cory, and Cory would throw herself in traffic for Green. They knew that Cory needed—almost physically demanded—a full time lover, and that Green had things he needed to do and couldn't, *couldn't* be there for her. And they knew that Bracken could. In fact, although Green wouldn't admit to it, Bracken was the perfect choice, because he loved his leader, and would step aside if necessary for the *Ou'e'hm* of his *due'ane*.

"So Arthur needs to lead, and Gwenyfar gets to have Launcelot, and that's all well and good." Green replied, pulling himself out of his funk. "But that doesn't mean that Arthur doesn't get to have moments when it's good to be King." Briskly, he stood up and offered his hand to Arturo. "I'm going to go call Cory before she falls asleep for good tonight—keep an eye on things here for a few, right mate?"

"Always do." Replied Arturo, his voice mild.

"I never forget it." Green returned sincerely, and then turned back into his hill.

CORY

You can't jail sunshine

It was Monday evening, and Green wasn't back yet. I was now up for six hours at a stretch without a nap, Grace had taught me how to knit, Bracken had bought every DVD under the sun for my viewing pleasure, Andres had me hooked on classical music, Renny and I had perfected Scrabble, Chess, and Monopoly, and I was going out of my *mind* with boredom.

I sat in bed, dressed in sweats and one of Bracken's well laundered, purple *Kings* T-shirts, knitting a scarf for Green in, well, brown and green, and nagging Bracken senseless.

"Please." I said hopefully.

"No."

"Please?"

"No."

"*Pleeeeeaaaaaasssssseeeeee!!!!.*"

"Yes. Wait…No."

I smacked him upside the head with the hand not maintaining a tenuous and deadly grip on the knitting yarn. "Don't be an asshole." I snapped. "You know, I can play the 'please' game until you're ready to strangle me—why not give in?"

Bracken looked up from the historical romance novel I'd begged him to go out and buy and then finished in an hour and a half. There were stacks of them in the apartment, and to our amusement, Andres and Brack were always on the list to read the next one after Renny, Grace and I. "Because I can play the 'no' game for just as long, and I'm right and you're not. So there."

"You are *not* right!" I squeaked. "C'mon, Bracken—it's 4:30 in the afternoon in December—the birds are in, the vampires are out, and I can't think of a safer time for us to go outside! Andres will come with us—we can go shopping somewhere really touristy and fun like Ghirardelli or the San Francisco Mall—I don't have any of my Christmas shopping done, how am I supposed to get you something?"

"You could make me a scarf." He said mildly, and I stuck my tongue out at him.

"How do you know this isn't for you?" I asked, and he merely rolled his eyes. I had, in fact, ordered (with Grace's help) some really snazzy dark purple yarn, with sparkles, and white yarn to match, and was hoping to make him a really awesome scarf in the color of his beloved basketball team, but I wouldn't tell him that, not even to soothe what appeared to be ruffled feelings. "Cooommmmmeee oooooonnnnn!!!" I wailed, and, in spite of his gimlet eye, I put down my knitting and got up and paced around the room.

Renny wandered in and noted with slitted-eyes that Bracken was reading the book that it was her turn to read. She smacked him on the back of the head and snagged the book, and before they could have a showdown I appealed to her sense of reason.

"Renny, we've got to get out of here!" I said, desperate. "You and Bracken are fighting over *The Cowboy's Bride*, Andres has me humming *March Slav* and if Grace gets another crack at me, I'm going to figure out the difference between intarsia knitting and Fair Isle, and I'm not ready to be that good! Let's go shopping! Let's go to Ghirardelli Square and ooh at the lights and drive across the bridge and see the city all sparkled out…let's shop at the Embarcadero for shit we're not sophisticated enough to buy…c'mon, Renny—you're a were-cat for sweet Goddess' sake—let's get out of this rat-hole!!!"

"I do go out." Renny replied smugly. "You may have been playing Sleeping Beauty, but I've got all my Christmas shopping done, *and* Andres has taken me to dinner and a play."

I'm pretty sure my eyes bulged out of my head. "You *bitch!*" I squealed, and she laughed easily and dodged me as I lunged in what was sure to be the most violent tickle tackle of all time when Bracken caught me about the waist. "You're not supposed to be out of bed." He said quietly, and my eyes narrowed.

"I'm feeling much better." I said, as though suitably chastened, and turned in his arms with a sweet smile.

"That's because you sleep most of the day." He replied, seriously. So serious. Bracken had become quiet and reserved and sober, since I'd woken up from my six-day nap, and now *I* was the one worrying.

"I'm not sleeping now!" I answered tartly, and then brought my hands up to his ribs and proceeded to tickle. His body went rigid, as though trying to fight off the urge to laugh, but I had known his body. His ribs were sensitive, and so were his underarms, and the backs of his knees, and the back of his neck. It took only a minute for a laugh to be forced out of him, along with the obligatory "stop it, Cory…dammit, stop it…"

I only laughed some more and tickled him until he backed up on the bed with me straddling him, enjoying myself more than I had all week. But he was fighting it.

"Cory…no…wait…stop…" I might have had him there, but I had been laughing, and that started the latent cough in my throat that would jump out and grab me at the absolutely worst times and when I buried my mouth in my shoulder, Bracken took his advantage. He clamped his arms to his sides and trapped my hands, then brought his own hands up to capture my wrists, and pulled me down close to him, looking, dammit, serious all over again. "You're getting over being sick." He said. "You were really sick for a really long time. You can't do this right now, okay?"

"I can do this right now." I told him kindly, through watering eyes. "I *am* doing this right now. Why don't we just see what I can do and draw the line where I wind down?"

"Because…stop it!" I had taken a nip at his chin, now that we were this close. This was as personal as Bracken had allowed himself to get all week, and I was going to take advantage of it.

"No." I said, but kindly, and went for his neck. "Why?" His skin was warm, and a little salty because he usually showered at night—right before he slid into bed with me, wearing sweats and a T-shirt, and held me in a warm, brotherly way that would have been fine this summer, but now, after what we had done and been to each other, felt like a slap in the face.

"Because," he continued with gritted teeth, "You don't know when to stop before you kill yourself." In a move of sheer frustration he rolled over, pinning me to the bed, and I grinned up at him without repentance. This was now *very* personal. He lay on top of me, his body pressing against me from my breasts to my thighs, and our groins were in close proximity. And now his groin was in close proximity with a lot more of me as he grew hard and weighty through his jeans.

"I don't want to kill myself." I said, with feeling, "I want to live." Smiling wistfully, I peered up at him. "You remember how to live, don't you Brack?"

He jumped up as though I'd slipped an electrode down his pants, and I almost wept with exasperation. "Dammit, Bracken..." I began, but he cut me off.

"No, dammit *Cory.*" He snapped. "Why do you always have to push things? Recuperate, get better and healthy or go outside and run yourself into the ground, and you choose run yourself into the ground. Wait for Green to help or come in and get me yourself—and you come in yourself and almost get killed. Take a break in school to let your heart heal or grind yourself into paste, and you grind yourself into paste. Stand in the background and let Green deal with a psychopath with purple hair or set the psycho's hair on fire—and you set his hair on fire. Why can't you just, for one goddamned minute, take it easy and let things be?"

I looked at him, wounded, immeasurably hurt. "Because then I wouldn't be me." I whispered. "But I guess you wanted someone else." And in that moment, leaving that fucking apartment was right there next to breathe-in/breathe-out on my list of things I absolutely had to do.

At a run I reached into my closet and grabbed my shoes, then sprinted through the hallway and for the door with Bracken so close to my heels I could almost feel his breath on my neck. I grabbed my coat from the rack and was reaching for the newly gorgeous front door when it swung open and I stepped back by instinct, right into Bracken's arms. With a grunt I brought my foot down the side of his shin and stepped hard onto his own bare feet at the instep, then wrenched myself out of his arms and ran straight into Andres, who was the one coming in the door in the first place.

"Goddess *fuck* it." Brack swore behind me, hopping on one foot, and Andres caught me in his arms and held me firm, relying on the fact, I guess, that I liked him too much to hurt him and didn't know him well enough yet to risk the indignity of wiggling out of his arms and crawling away on all fours like an infant. He was right, on both counts, damn him, because I *had* come to like the soft voiced, sly humored vampire in the last few days. He was funny and cultured, and remembered and spoke about the past as though it wasn't a grief that it had gone but a joy that he had lived it. At any rate, I had too much respect for him now to just blow past him, no matter what my temper.

Renny and Grace had been in the kitchen, ordering stuff from a catalogue on the laptop on the table, and both of them came over to watch the show.

"Jesus, Cory," Renny said from the kitchen landing, "I was only kidding about dinner and a play..."

"I don't care about a fucking play…" I all but sobbed. "I just want to get out of this goddamned apartment and *live.*" I turned to Bracken then, and Andres wisely let me. Hurt and fury were probably making a mess of my face but I didn't care. "You remember what it was like to *live,* don't you Bracken? It's what happens when you're more afraid to lose love than you are to lose life."

"Ah…" Andres made a noise behind me, and I turned miserable eyes towards him.

"What?" I asked, wiping my face messily with the back of my hand.

"I think," He said carefully, a kind half smile on his almost delicate, latte colored features, "That Renny, Grace and I need to go do something. Right now." He looked up at the two women who both exited the kitchen at a run and, I assumed, went to pretty themselves up for a night on the town.

"But that's what *I* wanted to do." I wailed.

"Now why would you want to do that?" Andres asked, ever so wisely, "When what you really want is going to be here in this apartment with you?" With that, and a platonic little push, he backed me up against Bracken, whose hands came to my shoulders in what I assumed was another gesture to make sure I didn't try to get away.

"And you." He said severely, aiming his sweet brown eyes towards Bracken, "Whatever it was you said to her to make her risk running out into the night unprotected is something you didn't mean and need to take back."

Bracken made a protesting noise in the back of his throat, but Andres cut him off. "Don't think Cory's been the only one to notice, Master Elf—I saw you two, that night in the warehouse. If you haven't bedded her yet it's your own stubborn fear that's getting in the way. You cannot keep her safe by keeping her in a glass coffin—in fact, you've apparently done almost as much damage as our enemy."

I could feel the tension draining from Bracken's body, a shrinking, a quietness that I disliked almost more than his quivering anger.

Grace and Renny whisked out of the hallway behind me, then, and they must have moved in hyperspeed because they were dressed and I saw Renny struggling with lipstick as she walked. Great, I thought sourly—she barely brushes her hair for six months, and now she's dressed in my best jeans and a gold sweater that Grace knit me only a month ago. I watched them move past Andres into the hallway with wistful eyes. Andres saw me, and smiled. He was only 5'6", or so, so he didn't have to bend down much when he placed a chaste kiss on my forehead and touched my cheek. "Don't worry, little Goddess." He murmured. "Tomorrow I will come get you and your champion, here, and we will go shopping in the square, and out to dinner some place lovely, and see the city all prettied up for Christmas, yes?"

I looked at him with shining eyes, thinking that I really loved Andres and that it was a shame my bed was full enough as it was. "Yes, please." I said graciously. "That would be really wonderful."

He gave me another chaste kiss, his lips cool and sweet on my cheek, and a little bow in Bracken's direction, and with that they were gone, and the two of us were alone in the now vast apartment, and the lacerating sting of Bracken's words still had my heart beating, skinless and flayed.

"You can let go now." I said, in a stony little voice. "Andres is gone."

"Look, Cory..." He began, but I didn't want to hear it. I broke away from him and dropped my shoes and coat in the hallway where I stood and stalked to my room, slamming the door and locking it. Then I collapsed on the bed and cried until, Goddess blight it all, I fell asleep.

I woke up when Bracken wrenched the door open in a splintering of wood and screeching of broken hinges. I sat up in bed, sure we were being attacked and summoning power for all I was worth. When I saw Bracken, standing there holding the broken door by the handle and looking baffled by it, I was a hairs' breadth from throwing a power ball right at his chest. With an angry sigh and cough I tried to hide, I let the power ebb out of me, felt the instant weariness it brought, and still had enough in me to get pissed off.

"Jesus, you moron!" I cried, "I almost killed you—what in the blue fuck do you think you're doing?"

"You locked me out." He said, as though that explained it. Gingerly he lay what was left of the door on the ground with hardly a clatter.

"You did it first." I said, through a tight throat.

"Well," He swallowed, running a hand through his shaggy, shorn hair, "You've said it yourself. I'm not that bright."

"You need to listen to me." I told him, a few tears sneaking out of my scrunched up face, "I'm fucking brilliant."

He met my eyes then, and a smile trembled at his grim mouth and an apology trembled in his shadow colored eyes. "I've noticed you're right a lot."

I sighed and opened my arms, and he rushed to me, hugging me so fiercely he picked me up off the ground and we stayed there, my feet dangling and my arms wrapped around him as though we were carved from stone.

"I am so terrified," He whispered after a moment, "Of losing someone else I love."

"Then love me." I demanded, looking him in the eyes. "Love *me*...the person who jumps in with both feet and will die before she lets anything happen to you and who set that asshole's hair on fire because he desperately deserved it. I'm me—I'm not Adrian." I said that last softly, because it might hurt but it needed to be said.

To my relief, he smiled. "Corinne Carol-Anne Kirkpatrick, I've been getting laid for over fifty years—believe me, I know the difference."

"You asshole." I murmured. "You want to keep me in this fucking apartment then you give me a reason to stay."

He kissed me then, his firm, grim mouth coming down against mine gently, as though he were kissing cotton candy and trying not to get any on his lips. I groaned in the back of my throat and clenched my hands in his thick, silky, coarse hair. "Kiss me, dammit." I demanded, and turned my head and ravished his mouth with my own. I heard it then, a long, drawn groan from the bottom of his chest as though he were taking a breath that he'd held for two weeks. Goddess, he'd wanted this, I thought with wonder. He'd wanted me so badly he was mean with it, and angry, and afraid.

Good. He was afraid, I was terrified. It wasn't until I'd started falling in love with beings who were supposedly immortal that I'd come so close to death so often, but it wasn't my own death that frightened me anymore. Grace had said that I needed two lovers to keep me safe in case something happened to one of them, but she was wrong. I wasn't twice as safe, I was twice as vulnerable: if I lost either Green or Bracken, I thought my heart would shrivel up and die. And now Bracken was here, in my arms, placing rough and vital kisses down my throat, pushing his hands down my sweats so I could feel his smooth cool skin against my thighs, and pulling my legs around his waist so I could feel him through our clothes. His want coursed through both our veins—it was our lifeblood and I could taste it. It was so, so sweet.

The fear disappeared, and so did everything else except Bracken, who had me on my back on the bed now, and whose hard, long-fingered hands were sliding my sweats off my hips. He placed nibbling, sucking kisses up the outside of my thighs, missing the apex on purpose, and working his way up to my hipbones which now jutted out more than they had ever done. Those hands—engulfing, swallowing, maddening hands—moved his own T-shirt up my body, and suddenly modesty kicked in and I clenched my arms at my sides unreasonably.

Bracken knew it was unreasonable, and his eyes met mine with exasperation and humor. "I've seen them before." He said, tickling my ribs with kisses. Between Bracken and everybody else I'd probably been fed every two hours if not more unless I was sleeping, but my body was still healing, and the weight was slow to come back.

"You've seen more of them." I stated the obvious.

"I told you that they'd be missed." He laughed, and instead of forcing my shirt up, he moved his head to my breast and placed his mouth over it, which wasn't hard to do since it was practically all nipple. With a groan, he suckled me through the thin cotton until I cried out and buried my hands in his hair again. He chuckled and took his opportunity to lift his head and whisk the shirt up over my head. I made another whimpering sound in my throat when his mouth closed around my throbbing, tender skin. He moved his head then, to the newly healed scar that ran from left collarbone to right armpit and kissed it tenderly too.

"More scars." I demurred. I was completely bare, underneath him, and here was one more embarrassment next to the A-cup breast size and the prominent hip bones.

"You took this scar defending me." He murmured, his eyes suddenly very near, and very bright. "You defended the very memory of me. There's no ugliness in honor, Cory."

"You're wearing too many clothes." I replied, more uncomfortable with the praise than I had been with the hurt vanity.

He kissed my neck, and once again I whimpered and clenched against him, feeling that underlying hunger that had made my skin itch all week finally erupt. "Clothes." I remembered breathlessly. "Oh, please, Bracken, nothing between us, not even clothes."

He stood and removed his shirt as I bent to take care of his jeans. He never wore underwear, I realized. Or at least the two times we'd been naked together, I hadn't seen them. But then he was naked and I had other things to worry about besides the underwear he never wore and wasn't wearing now.

"It's still intimidating." I murmured, stroking his cock with my thin little hand.

"It does the job…Goddess!" Because I had touched him with my mouth, and I kept on touching, stroking, and worshipping until he pulled me away from him so his knees could buckle and he sank to the floor. Kneeling on the floor he was nearly as tall as I was kneeling on the bed, and he captured my face with those big long hands and crushed me to him in a kiss that was tender and brutal and everything I had ever wanted in a kiss but didn't know to ask.

And then he was on top of me, and our skin kissed and slicked and kissed again, and our mouths too, and he blessed me with his mouth again and again, my breasts, my thighs, the sweetness between and within, and once again when he covered me with his body and slid deep inside of me I was so insane with him, so drunk on the wildness that was us that I couldn't imagine for a moment that I might have lived a lifetime without that power surging, riding, taking me to heaven with the sweetness of thrust and cock and give and take and come…

Later, I lay on top of him and moved up and down with his breathing, and touched him, randomly, with tenderness, skimming my fingers down his triangular jaw and around his pointed ears, and on the ripples of the trim and narrow muscles of his chest. He was built like a sidhe, taller and more angular and more fluid than most humans, but Bracken was broader in the chest and had more mass in the arms and thighs than Green. His father was a true red-cap—short, squat, and built like a forgotten corner of a rock quarry, spider webs, spare earth, scratchy skin and all. That's how Bracken came to smell like warmed rock, and feel like smooth stone beneath my fingers.

"So you've been getting laid for fifty years, huh?" I asked, smiling down into his eyes.

"Give or take a few." He murmured. He liked to play with my hair, and for the hundredth time I blessed that I hadn't cut it when I was in temper with him. I would have to remember that, in the future. He looked so arrogant, so cock-sure, now, that I didn't need to know he was supernaturally beautiful to know women had been falling into his bed like apples from a tree.

"You're being modest." I laughed. "You've probably had T&A beyond the dreams of mortal men."

"T *D* and A, if you must know." He smiled. "And since I'm not mortal, I'd say that's a fair assumption."

I was a little slow on the uptake, but when I figured out what the D stood for I flushed red and laughed into his chest.

"Does it bother you?" He asked, knotting his fingers in the hair at my neck.

I buried my face in his neck and flushed some more. "I don't know, Bracken—you've seen the highlights of my sexual history sculpted in living wood—which I still don't remember making, by the way. Do you think it bothers me?"

"*That's* what bothers you." He said wisely. Had we both said that he wasn't bright? What were we thinking? "And even though you don't remember making the grove *that* night, the three of you spent weeks running off together to make love, and I know you live those memories every time you think of Adrian."

I blinked and flushed. How had Bracken felt, then, as Adrian and Green and I had honeymooned? Had he wished he'd been there with us? Would it have hurt him too much? Or had his desire for me, his love for Adrian, been as poignant and as painful as it was now that Adrian was gone. "I'll never regret what the three of us did together." I told him sincerely, knowing that some pain could never be taken away. "But…" I looked away, because that didn't change the truth. "It would have been nice, I guess, to save a few secrets for you."

His expression was wry, and accepting, and all of the things I hadn't felt when he'd yelled at me earlier. "Well," he began, "Like you said, I love all of you. You jump in with both feet, right? You weren't planning on losing anyone the night you made the Goddess grove, am I right, little Goddess?" I looked up because Andres called me that, and Bracken never had.

"I don't imagine so." I murmured, sarcastically. Goddess, I wanted that memory back. I remembered the grove. I remembered the three of us together on other nights, lovely, powerful moments of bodies coupling and tripling and the two men I'd loved best warm and cool and hard and wanting against me and inside of me and the warmth of them, splashing on my skin and running down my thighs and my chin. But I didn't remember that first night. I didn't remember the combination of love and sex and power that had created those memories etched in wood, and had begun the odyssey of perfection that had been the three of us. We had been so sure nothing could take that away from us.

But now Bracken couldn't meet my eyes. "You just keep on thinking like that, baby. Don't plan on losing me. Don't hold anything back from me. Don't save any part of yourself for the next lover." And now he looked at me again, and his eyes were fierce and as burning as pond shadow could be. "Because there will be no next lover without me." He said grimly. "I will live—Goddess, I will live, but I will have as much of you in my bed and in my heart as you can give."

"You have a part of me that I never knew existed." I told him truthfully, shaking off the anger of not remembering, of having been violated and stolen from. I was in Bracken's arms right now, this moment. I would have this moment, and I wouldn't let memories or lack of them steal it from me. "And no one else has ever had that part of me, and if you leave me, that piece will die and no one else will ever know that it was there."

"So we love bravely, right?"

I laughed, warm, kind, and very in love with the dark haired, short tempered sidhe filling my arms. "Yeah. Love bravely…" I trailed off, and a random question, intimate and curious, struck me. One I had not felt comfortable asking either of my other lovers, perhaps because they had been making love to each other as often as to me. "How different are we?" I asked, "Men and women?"

"Well…" He thought, not surprised by the question in the least. "Men are thrusting, aggressive—even making love together, they're both shoving their parts into something…" My mouth quirked and he kissed it and then kept talking. "Women are…well men try to shape things, shape love making by thrusting into it, women try to shape things by accepting them, and then changing their shape with their acceptance—you're a woman, you know what you do, physically, in a man's bed—that's a power in itself, but it's a different nature, right?"

"I should hope so." I said dryly, wiggling my body over his and making him laugh. For a moment, I was captured by his laughter, and my hands moved up to touch his dimple, trace his jaw line, and then, best of all, play with the sensitive curve of his pointy elfish ears. But something was busy in my brain, striking me from nowhere. "Goshawk doesn't fight like a man." I said after a moment.

Bracken frowned. "I'm sorry?"

"Goshawk—he doesn't do anything bravely—he thrusts, but in secret. He asserts himself upon the world, but he does it slyly, without face, or, well, honor. He steals women's memories after he's stolen their trust. He sends his men into the field when he won't go himself. I mean…when we finally met face to face it was because he attacked me while I slept." I shook my head, trying to figure out where I was going.

"He's a coward."

"Yes." I agreed. "But there's more—he's attacking women, making hidden alliances…" I chewed my lower lip—there was more, there, but I couldn't wrap my brain around it. "What do you think he would do if we just invited him over and confronted him?"

"Run like hell." Bracken said on a snort of disdain.

"But he can't anymore, can he?" I asked. "He's lost too many people. He's pushed too many people to do things they didn't want to. He can't run. He'd have to face us…but he'd want to do it when he thought he had the advantage."

"So…" Bracken reasoned, "We'd want to meet him when he thinks he's going to win…"

"But we need to surprise him with something and not give him a road out." I murmured, losing myself in the idea until Bracken grasped my chin and forced me to meet his eyes.

"Later." He said implacably. "Later. Sleep. Eat." A quick grin then. "Make love to me. But heal. We'll face him. We'll win. But I want you to be strong and healthy, and able to cut that goat-fucker off at the knees."

I smiled in spite of how completely serious he had become. "Awwww, sweetie, you have such a way with words." I chided.

"You think that was good?" He asked, and he put his mouth by my ear and whispered such an insanely erotic suggestion while brushing my ear with his breath and his lips that my body went boneless and my thighs ran slick with wanting.

"That's better." I said through a dry mouth. "Do you think we could manage that?"

And as it turned out, we came close.

GREEN

'some'

Even Andres' voice was neat and cultured, and perfect.

"Right." Green responded. "I'm working on something right now to deal with that—you'd better believe I'll call you when I've got it figured out." Green, who had been pacing around the kitchen that sat next to his moon-lit study, slanted a smile at Arturo, who was sitting at the desk next to him. Arturo raised his eyes and grinned—they had, indeed, been busy planning something rather nasty for enemies since Green had left the city.

"Oh?" He said, and grimaced, still in good humor. "Oh dear." Rubbing his hands over his eyes, Green shook his head. "Probably the best course of action." He agreed, "But I suggest you send someone in there to repair the damage to the apartment before you get back…No, I'm not joking…you've known her for a week, you figure it out—if she doesn't break something, she'll drive him to do it…" Green chuckled then in earnest. "No, but then, I'm an entirely different fish, aren't I? And so would you be, but it's not us in question, now is it?" Green grew quiet then, but his good humor remained. "Yes—yes, I did know the three of them. Bracken is very like, indeed. But Cory's stronger than she was—and I'm not Arthur. We'll be fine." Another head nod. "Thank you, indeed, thank you Andres—and yes, by all means take them out tomorrow—it would save every-body's sanity if you do. Yes, blessing on you. Tell Grace that Arturo wants her to call him when she gets home—and watch Renny. She's like a two-year old—if she's not disappearing around a corner herself, someone's snatching her around it…no, I'm not kidding—she weighs ninety-five pounds, she's more snatch-able than the sylphs. Right. Tuesday, then, Wednesday at the latest." And with a final shake of his head, Green hung up.

"Trouble in San Francisco?"

Green grinned wickedly. "Let's see if I can sum it up: Cory's doing better, but not as well as she's trying to make everybody think she is, Bracken's treating her like Snow-White—girl in a glass coffin—Cory wanted to put Bracken in a real coffin until Andres played me for a minute, took the other ladies out on the town and left our two contenders home to make-up. He assures me they are probably doing so right now and says I might not want to call."

Arturo nodded, amused as well. In the last few days Green had recovered himself from the melancholy that beset him earlier. Part of it, Arturo was sure, was just being home, but part of it was the action they had initiated in the meantime. It is one thing to feel attacked and powerless, and quite another to feel like a predator, laying a trap for an unwary bird. "And the other?" He asked.

"Well, word out among the lesser fey is that Mist is forging an alliance with Goshawk—but since the lesser fey are still boycotting the sidhe and the high elves, we only get shadow reports of how deep the alliance goes.

"It won't matter, if this works." Arturo said smugly.

"And it will work." Green agreed. "But we need to wait for Cory's full recovery—or as close as we can get, at any rate."

"So—we take care of Mist and what about Goshawk? His power will be broken, but he's still an enemy we can't afford to let wander around."

Green nodded thoughtfully. "You're right." He said, "As usual. But right now, I'm not all that sure what we want to be doing with him." Green grimaced. "I hate the idea of out and out war—we both know how wasteful it is."

Arturo nodded and Green knew they were both thinking the same thing—Crispin's vampires had been a rough crowd to begin with, which made, for some reason, their complete annihilation somewhat easier to swallow. But Goshawk's followers…Green shuddered. Children. Lost, miserable, misguided children, who only needed a good leader, a safe haven in which to be themselves.

"They will fight to the death for you now." Arturo said with satisfaction, referring to the still supervised but much happier Avians who were currently engaged flying little lights around to the tops of all the trees in the hill, and Green agreed.

"I don't want to ask them to fight." He said soberly. "Their friends are all still in Goshawk's group, and that's such a horrible choice to make—no, when we take Goshawk down, we need to take him down alone, and then leach the poison out of him so it can spread to no one else."

"They will need to make a choice sooner or later." Arturo warned.

"Maybe not—not if we take Goshawk out by himself instead of as a general."

"Assassination is always very effective." Arturo agreed, eyebrows raised. "Any ideas on how to do that, brother?"

"I'm working on it…" was the mild reply. Green frowned, mulling something over. "How showy do we want to go with this take over?"

Arturo frowned in turn, considered, ran his fingers through his shoulder length black hair. Unlike the sidhe from the British Isles or Western Europe, long hair was not a birthright or a sign of status for his people, and he was a practical elf. "We could do it privately, I suppose…" He murmured, "But I don't feel like doing it privately."

"Me neither." Green stood up and wandered from the computer desk in the corner of the living room to the huge bay window that, in one form or another, wrapped three quarters of the way around the hill. The house tunneled through most of the hill, its outer layers built of rock and solid, bewitched earth. That covering was about all that remained of the original hill, so thoroughly had Green and Adrian—and later Arturo—utilized the space to create their haven of safety. The cap of the hill, where the Goddess grove sat, had once been the same oak tree/pine scrub tree that made up the rest of the area, but after that one night when sun and day and night were one, it had become the sacred place where the Avian's had first seen the power of the Goddess. So many types of preternatural creatures called Green's house home that even Green lost count.

"Everything so far has been so underhanded." Green murmured, almost to himself. "Mist's people didn't bother to attack us outright—they sicced some nightmare from Adrian's past on us. Goshawk's people didn't use their own weapons—they mind-raped women for nearly six months in order to get their strength. Our world functions on instinctive traditions, unspoken laws…and when the world was bigger, that was okay…" He turned away from the moon-lit silver lawn that contrasted with the snow falling in the lands beyond. "But the world is smaller now, Arturo." He said with a sigh, "And we need the trappings of civilization—the real ones. Laws—spoken, if not written. Accountability. Public forum."

"Democracy?" Arturo asked ironically.

"Christ no." Green laughed. "I'm not that progressive."

"Not that stupid, you mean." Arturo agreed. Democracy would be a disaster. The Goddess was not egalitarian with her gifts, and the fey were expected to follow a certain pecking order—the sidhe were born with powers that the lower fey didn't have, the high elves were born with gifts and beauty that the lesser fey didn't want. No—a ruling hierarchy was genetically encoded in their DNA, but that didn't mean they had to be barbarians about it.

"I served under Titania and Oberon for a bit." Green said musingly, referring to the legendary rulers of the faerie underworld. "They were pretty autocratic, but not bad really." He thought for a moment, lost completely in the past, in another land, with other loves—practically another Green. "They were cold." He said at last, turning to Arturo. "Chill, like a room that's not been used in a long time. No—we don't want democracy, with the almost constant fight to be top dog, but we don't want that either."

Arturo laughed outright. "That's the *last* leadership trait you have to worry about, brother."

Green smiled faintly back at him. "Thank you, I think. But that's not my point…"

"Your point, leader," Arturo said shrewdly, "Is that you're going to overthrow a power that's been in place for nearly two hundred years—even longer, if you count the fact that Mist and his ilk were big back in the old country a few centuries before that. But you don't want to 'teach bloody instruction', isn't that how the quote goes?"

"'And commend the poisoned chalice to my own lips'." Green agreed. "Right. I want to be the sort of power that people don't *want* to overthrow."

Arturo pinched the bridge of his nose and let his shoulders shake for a minute. "You are the best leader and the most insecure sidhe I've ever met. If enough fey didn't love you already, you'd never be able to do this."

Green looked at Arturo from the side of his wide-set eyes, and twisted his sensual lips into a grimace. "You laugh, but you were a god and you were worshipped from your birth."

"It got old after a few centuries."

"I imagine it did." Green returned dryly. "But I, on the other hand, started life as a wood elf, and when I finally *did* join the court, for obvious reasons my function was very different."

Arturo had the same wide set eyes as Green, but suddenly they sharpened, looked fierce in a way Green couldn't achieve. "You were a courtesan?"

"Oh yes." Green murmured, trying to keep it light. "Delivered to Oberon, courtesy of Mist, and Morana, you remember—the two people we're about to piss off in a big way."

"But you've never…never…"

Green turned his back to the window, and its enticing view of the snowy canyon. "I wanted out, Arturo, I got out." Thinking about his confrontation with

Mist, Green cringed. That was perhaps the understatement of the millennia. He hoped he had leached it out of his voice, but he wasn't sure you could eliminate that sort of pain, that betrayal, and the doubt of everything you'd ever believed about love and compassion and your own abilities to protect yourself from your person, much less your voice. He tried anyway. "It wasn't as though I were enslaved, or beaten." He deliberately left out the word 'imprisoned'. "I just had a particular gift, and I was expected to use it as they saw fit—that was all."

Arturo snapped his jaw shut, biting back something particularly nasty that he was going to say about the sidhe that were currently holding court in San Francisco. He could hear what Green wouldn't say. He could only imagine what the people who were responsible for Adrian's death could have done to his beloved Green. But Green wouldn't want Arturo's pity—all these years of being a rock, a touch stone for his people, Arturo realized with a groan, and the last thing Green would want would be pity. So Arturo didn't say anything about what he could read between Green's silences. What he said instead was, "So, this takeover is all about Adrian?"

"Yes." Green said unequivocally. "What they did to me—another place, another time—another way of life. What they did to Adrian—that was sheer spite, Arturo. Pure malice. They didn't like my court, fine, they should deal with me about it. But to send Sezan to take out Adrian?" Green's voice grew rough and tight with the unshed tears of a century and a half of companionship. "I will not live with an enemy who can betray me and then laugh at my grief not two hours away from my home."

Arturo stood, as though he needed to do something and had no idea what. "Fair enough." He said, his voice also rough. "You go ahead and you pay them back for Adrian. But while you're doing that, I'll be paying them back for you." He whirled and stalked out of the room, leaving Green, touched and bemused in his wake.

The next two days were frantic—there were visits to be made and employee meetings to be held at every business Green owned—and there were quite a few of them. Gas stations, craft stores, fast food and restaurant franchises—even a boutique of fey- and vampire-made handicrafts that Grace had set up and ran during her spare time, all needed a visit, an exchange of power, and a ceremony and sealing. Every visit was accompanied by the same thing—a shaking of hands with every employee—and occasionally, depending on the fey employee and his or her allegiance to Green, a great deal more—a sowing of salt around every perimeter, and a surprising, often forgotten flash of green light as Green and Arturo left.

It was a tremendous use of raw power, and it couldn't have been done without the consent and help of everyone who owed their allegiance to Green. And curiously enough, everyone had been happy to give that allegiance and consent.

"It's a great sacrifice." Green had said gently to the wizened gnome who ran the almost invisible garden store tucked behind a development in Foresthill.

"You'll keep me safe, sir." The little man had replied. "A mark like this—you'll know, if something's hurting me and mine—you, being you, you won't be able to turn away from us. I'm glad to do it." And with that, he'd reached up and pulled Green's head down to his tiny withered lips and placed a kiss upon the clear pale brow. The flash of green at the perimeter of this particular store had been laced with earth brown and the peculiar red dust of the area, and the store disappeared from all but fey sight. This was not the only business to benefit personally from Green's touch, but when they were done, Green and Arturo collapsed on their respective beds and slept like the dead.

Green was awakened the next morning by Nicky, who had slept with him since their return, moving his naked cleanly muscled young human body against Green's older, longer, more muscular sidhe body.

"Mmm…how are you feeling this morning, darling Nicky?" Green asked, enjoying the young man's boldness as his hands explored.

"Better than you, Green." Nicky said dryly. "It's nearly afternoon."

"Shit!" Green sat abruptly in up in bed and was surprised when Nicky pushed him back down."

"We've already called her and told her we'll be late." Nicky murmured, amused. Obviously Green hadn't forgotten his promise to Cory to be back in the city by Wednesday. "But you need food and a little more rest and probably some…" The boy blushed. "You know, some…"

Green grinned, wicked and gentle at once. "Yes, Nicky—I know 'some'…"

Nicky laughed. "Will it be different, with a wom…with a girl…with Cory?" Nicky's sexual education had progressed steadily in the days since they'd left the city, and Nicky's reaction was, amusingly, much like Adrian's. Sex with another man was good, if it was both sensual and consensual, but, given that, sex with a woman was going to be *spectacular*. As little as Nicky complained about his situation, Green knew that he'd started to look forward—with great eagerness—to Cory's promise that she wouldn't forsake him when he needed her.

"It will be different because you've loved her for quite some time." Green said wisely. "And because *she's* different." He grimaced, not wanting to take away Nicky's fantasy any sooner than he had to. "Cory isn't like me, you know that Nicky? Sex doesn't just come to her…"

Nicky was lying on his stomach, propping his chin up on Green's stomach and looking up into Green's emerald eyes with his own, bird-like brown and gold spangled gaze. "You mean it will be awkward, because she doesn't know how to make love to people she's not passionate about." He said with certainty.

"Yes." Green agreed, surprised. "That's exactly what I mean."

Nicky smiled, also old and wise. "Will you help me? That first time? Maybe, if you help, she can learn to love me, just a little."

Green ran a hand through the boy's downy, rust-colored hair and smiled gently. "She already loves you like a friend, Nicky. But I'll help you—because you deserve for it to be wonderful, and it's what I do best."

"Thanks." He replied. With a sigh, and a movement that suggested nothing more sexual than animal comfort, Nicky turned and rested his cheek against Green's long, flat stomach and reached out to grab his leader's hand. "I'll go get you some food and stuff in a minute."

"Take your time." Green had already resigned himself to a longer wait to see his beloved. It was easier, that way, than yielding to the cold itchiness of anticipation. Goddess, he missed her, now that he'd had her back for a couple of weeks— even when she was lost in fever dream, he could still touch her, feel her heartbeat against his hands. He found that he needed her, in a way that was new and fresh and exciting and frightening to a being that was old, and even used to being in love.

"Oh!" Nicky sat up abruptly. "When we were on the phone Cory told me I had to bring something when we went down—maybe you could help me find it?" At Green's nod, Nicky frowned. "Good—but it's sort of scary—why would she want me to bring her gun?"

Green was no longer drowsy or resigned or content—and breakfast and sleep and 'some' with Nicky were now the last things on his mind. "That, Nicky is a very good question." With a sigh and a heave he swung up from the bed to head for the shower. "Shall we change our plans and hurry to find out?"

CORY

'Buckwheats'

The play was excellent. Andres had lived up to his word after all and Tuesday night I sat next to him in a darkened theatre and we lost ourselves in the absurdity of *The Producers,* Bracken throwing off heat like a nova sun next to me. Quite frankly, I was surprised we managed to talk Brack into it—he'd stopped *touching* me like I was made of glass, but he was still a little leery about letting me out in public.

"We can stay here tonight!" He'd suggested brightly, throwing himself on my bed half-dressed in black slacks and a white tank shirt. "Watch a movie? Make love?"

"I can go psychotic and blow up the building, too!" I snapped back, fluffing my weird red-brown hair in the mirror and trying not to make a face at the thin, sickly looking creature looking back at me. My nose was even bigger when I was skinny enough to have a chin. "And wouldn't that be fun?" I was wearing a long-sleeved turtle-necked knit dress with a full swirling skirt to both keep me warm and disguise the fact that in recent weeks I'd lost boobs, hips, thighs and musculature in the bargain. For the first time in my life I was more worried about putting weight on than losing it, and stuffing my face continuously did not seem to be satisfying that goal.

"What are you going to do if we run into someone?" He asked, the false brightness gone. "Mist and Andres—they run in the same circles you know…for all we know, they'll be in the same restaurant, or we'll see them in the theatre—what are you going to do?"

The automatic answer—blow them to hell and back—trembled on my lips, but I managed to lock it down. "Nothing that would embarrass you in public." I said instead.

Bracken had sighed then, and stood behind me, wrapping his long, long arms around my waist and meeting my eyes in the mirror. It was hard to look at all that inhuman beauty, when there was only plain little me next to him. I ignored my own reflection and concentrated on his instead.

"You've been sick...no, no, hear me out..." When I would have protested because I'd heard *that* before, he tightened his arms and went on. "Your temper is uncertain at the best of times, Cory." He told truthfully. "Even more so when you're afraid, or not feeling your best. Now, think about it—what are you going to do?"

I did think about it. "I'm Guinevere, right, Launcelot?" His mouth twisted sardonically. "Well- if I'm a queen, I'm damn sure not going to shame my king, am I?"

He'd nodded against my shoulder, a painful truth between us. "You won't do it for me, but you'll do it for Green?"

"I'll do it for you because you asked." I'd whispered into his ear. "I'll do it for Green because he's Green." This, I thought darkly, pretty much summed up the difference between loving your *ou'e'hm* and loving your *due'alle*.

So now here we sat, laughing breathlessly in orchestra seating through the antics of the two con-men on the stage, and scenting, like sea-mist and sandalwood sachet, something preternatural with us in the intimate, richly appointed theatre.

When the first act was over, and I stood to go use the bathroom, Andres stood quietly to my right and Bracken to my left to follow me out of the theatre into the lobby. I was conscious enough of how worried they were not to say anything nasty about it either. I fought my way through the press of nicely dressed women to the miniscule bathroom and back out into the bar of the lobby where the men were waiting for me when I realized that the smell of sea-mist was getting stronger, behind me, and to my left. I whirled quickly and took a step, and ended up face to neck with Mist. As my eyes narrowed and he tried not to look surprised that I knew he was there, I smelled sandalwood as well.

I had promised to behave—a promise I fully intended to keep, but Mist's expression had turned hard and calculating, and Goshawk was moving behind me, and I figured a little bit of trash talk would buy me some time while Bracken and Andres fought their way through the crowd. "What's the matter, Mist—couldn't you go out in public without your pet bird?" I asked nastily.

"I'm not here to talk to you." Mist said, as though from a lofty height. It was hard for me to take him seriously, though, when I was used to dealing with Green and Bracken and Arturo, who were not only taller than Mist, but greater as well. Mist was dressed nattily in a tuxedo with a crème colored cashmere thing around his neck, and his hair was tied back in a leather queue, but no amount of sophisticated clothing could change that shadowy look he had, like he was not wholesome enough to move in true light.

"Too bad." I returned sweetly, "Because I wanted to ask you how it felt to wear my lover's mark on your skin." It was as sharp a barb as I've ever thrown, and I was not surprised to see as petty an emotion as disgruntlement pass over Mist's glamorized features. I had a moment to wonder, if you could use glamour to alter your appearance to look like *anyone,* why could you choose to make your face as uninterestingly handsome as Mist had made his? And as soon as I thought it, the glamour went away and I saw Mist for all his treachery and shadow beauty, searching for a comeback. But before he could reply, Goshawk grabbed my shoulder and pulled me away from Mist, saying "You will not address him, woman."

I turned to face him, and knew that Bracken and Andres' subtle fight to get to me was gaining overtones of panic. Without flinching I reached up and grabbed the Avian's hand, feeling poly-something skin and metal bones, as well as an advanced magic covering to make the hand both function and appear real.

"Nice prosthetic, Goshawk." I smiled knowingly into his bird-like gold eyes, and had the pleasure of watching him flinch when I had not. Up close, he was much shorter—a little taller than myself—and fairer skinned than he had appeared in that nightmare moment of attack and defend. His hand—the real one, not the prosthetic—wasn't black or dark brown, it was tanned, and his face had the high fore-head, wide-set eyes, and long chin of European descent, rather than Middle-Eastern. Whereas Bracken, Andres, and even Mist looked sophisticated and lovely in their evening clothes, Goshawk looked blocky, like a peasant in his Lord's clothes. As I spoke to him my mind ran circles trying to figure out where he was from, and what was familiar—and unfamiliar—about his features. "Almost as good as Luke Skywalker's—did it take you long to recover from the fact that I *broke your arm off with my bare hand?*"

Goshawk's face began to twist, and I simply gripped the hand on my shoulder and allowed a teeny tiny bit of heat to seep into the skeleton. It would, I knew, seep into whatever part of Goshawk's arm that remained eventually. "I'll melt it clear into your remaining flesh if you don't get it off my person." I continued evenly, and he dropped the hand and moved his shoulders into my space instead. To an observer it might have appeared as though he were interested in what I was saying—Goshawk and I knew better.

"Now Goshawk," I murmured, smiling at him under the burgundy ceiling of the Orpheum theatre, "Wouldn't it be better to play nice in these surroundings? You don't want to draw too much attention to yourself, do you? Isn't that where you work best? In the shadows?"

I saw his jaw harden, and his expression contort with rage, and knew he was both chastened and infuriated. I was right. We both knew it. Making a move here—now that I'd spotted the two of them—would be disastrous for all of us—but him in particular. He had no legitimate identity, no human alibi—and no subtle way of exercising any power we knew him to have. "In my day, we would have you *flogged.*" He hissed sincerely, and suddenly I knew why he had looked familiar.

He was *old.* Not as old as Green, but far older than Andres—my guess, was that he was a European, who had survived the crusades. It would explain the Middle Eastern clothing, the accents—even the attitude towards women. Many Middle Eastern men do venerate their women—but Goshawk had chosen to imitate the ones who think everything female is contemptible. His complete disdain was like a mix of the worst of both worlds. Green and I had been on the phone for hours in the last five days, discussing everything from my favorite color (Adrian purple, Adrian blue) to Nicky's people. There could only be one way for an Avian to be as old as Goshawk.

I giggled. I couldn't help it. I was afraid, and Bracken and Andres had just arrived, so things were now *extremely* dangerous, but he was just so *frustrated.* So seriously angry at my sex. So everything he wouldn't be if he'd gotten laid any time in the last six-hundred years. The next thing that popped out of my mouth almost ended my life.

"You're a virgin who can't drive." I quoted, and giggled some more. Behind Goshawk's shoulder I saw Bracken close his eyes and Andres actually cover his with a slender, latte-colored hand. I thought Goshawk was going to turn into a bird right there, and, glancing at Mist's face I saw panic and a bone deep knowledge that Goshawk was not quite the ally he might have wished.

"I will see you die screaming…" Goshawk ground out.

"I don't possibly see how." I returned, keeping my voice low and sweet. I kept repeating the name *Guinevere* in the back of my mind, trying to look dignified and queenly when what I really wanted to do was turn into a walking nuclear meltdown. "Unless you're attacking me vulnerable and sleeping, the closest you've come to hurting me was through Nicky—and he's on our side now." I leaned in confidentially, "By the way? When we bring you down, I'm going to make it extra painful, just for making Nicky be the bad guy…"

"He was a strong, honorable man before you corrupted him with your foul mouth and your foul sex…"

Bracken was turning red. I suddenly realized that I had to keep the banter going until the lobby light blinked, or Bracken, true to his Launcelot's soul would step in to defend my honor. "You only think it's foul because you've never done it." I said, trying to be gentle. "What happened to her, by the way? The one you broke your heart over, who convinced you that sex was bad?"

It was a guess—based on my own experience of waking up next to Green one morning, feeling wonderful, and thoroughly used by Green and Adrian, and then, suddenly, remembering all of my training, all of my mean-minded inculcation to that damning Puritanical fear of anything sexual, and feeling shame. It was a memory Goshawk had tried to possess and the thought that he might have lived that moment in my mind made my stomach curdle.

As it was a series of emotions passed over his broad features, difficult to read, but, unsurprisingly settling on defensiveness, and anger. "My beloved was beautiful and pure you…you…*whore.*" Bracken was right behind him now, and I saw that Andres had a hold of his arm when he would have lunged. Oh, swell. It was a sad day for us all when *I* was trying to keep things civilized and *Bracken* had to be forcibly restrained.

"Whores do it for money." I said, still pleasant, although a little girl in my heart was absolutely devastated. "Sluts do it for pleasure. Goddesses do it for love. Where does your heartbreaker fall in all of this?"

"She was *forced.*" He spat. "A Saracen princess…her fiancé discovered our letters and…his men, a whole squadron…" Damn it. Damn it damn it damn it all to hell, I did *not* want to feel sorry for this asshole. I did not want to feel sorry for the woman who did this to him I did *not* want to think we had a fucking thing to do with each other, but I remembered that horrible feeling of violation that I'd had when Nicky had attacked me, and I could feel for her, this faceless 'Saracen princess' and her anguished lover. Fuck.

"I'm sorry." I said quietly, and even Bracken subsided in sympathy, "Did they kill her?"

Goshawk was too lost in this ancient memory to realize he despised me. "No." He said, proudly, "When it was over they gave her to me, and we both agreed…" His voice failed for a moment, and then he glared at me, and it's a good thing he didn't have my power because the hatred in his eyes would have killed me on the spot. "Something that soiled can only be pure in death." He hissed. "She wielded the knife herself."

Oh Goddess. Oh Jesus. Oh God. Bracken and I met eyes above his shoulder in absolute horror. The lobby light blinked, and it was weird, how strongly this beacon of ultra-civilization seemed to call to the lot of us. Mist and Goshawk both took a step backwards, Bracken and Andres did the same. Only I, lost in the shock and horror and pity of what it was Goshawk had convinced his beloved to do, could not seem to remember Guinevere after all.

"She's well rid of you." I said with a rusty voice, and didn't flinch when he moved as though to grab me and haul me out the doors. I couldn't be afraid of him now, not when, really, he was such a pathetic specimen of *any* species. He wouldn't attack me. Not here. Not when I could fight back. He was a fucking coward whose only gift, apparently, was the ability to steal memories and to talk the young and impressionable into self destruction. The light blinked one more time, so I grabbed Andres hand with the hand that Bracken wasn't clutching, and took a step away from Mist and Goshawk. As I turned to speak to them—dismissively, over my shoulder—and I saw both men were in their spiffy dark suits, I realized that, maybe, like us, they'd been out on the town, enjoying Christmas time in the city, when they'd seen us and decided to fuck up our night.

"You know," I said with some consideration, "I'm glad I didn't kill you when you attacked me like a coward in my sleep." Goshawk's face tightened one more notch, and I hoped he got a headache from all that tension. "Magic's too good for you—too clean, too blessed for something like you." I shook my head, allowing Bracken to usher me a few more steps towards the entrance to the theatre proper. We'd been watching movies all week, as well as reading books and driving each other batshit. My favorite thus far was *Things To Do In Denver When You're Dead*—it had given me another horrible, painful death to add to my list of ways I didn't want to go. "The next time I see you," I promised, "I'll have my .45—and then, buddy, it's buckwheats for you."

"Buckwheats?" Andres asked later, after we'd sat through the second half of the play with the men on either side of me, clutching my hands and lighting me up with power like a Christmas tree.

"Do we have to talk about this when she's eating half a cow?" Bracken asked painfully. We had gone to the restaurant at the Renaissance Park, and, at Bracken's insistence I might add, I was eating the largest piece of steak on the menu. He was right, of course—I'd been channeling power for the last hour and a half, not to mention the fact that I was still recovering, so I needed the protein, but he didn't get to complain about it if he's the one who gave the order to the waitress.

I pointed this out to him, and when he didn't seem repentant I finished up with, "And by the way, pal, the next time you decide to give me a lecture about my temper, I get to seriously fuck you up."

Andres, sophisticated, polished Andres, actually snorted. I had the feeling that, if vampires still ate or drank anything besides blood, he would have sprayed wine all over the table. "*He* lectured *you* about *your* temper?" At Bracken's rather sheepish scowl of assent, Andres started to laugh some more. "My God—you do realize that if you'd been mortal, I would have broken your arm with the force it took to restrain you?" I stuck my tongue out at Bracken over my water and he snarled at me in return.

"He called you a…"

"Shh…" The laughter was gone now, and I leaned over the table to press my fingers against Bracken's lips. "He's a coward. He's a crap-eating cheese-weasel, and we all know it, right?"

Andres laughed again. "So—what do you think they were doing there?" He asked seriously after a moment.

"I think they were there to see a play." I answered truthfully. "But we were there, and they saw me alone, and…" I made motions with my hands.

"And, like you said, they're cowards." I nodded, and Andres continued. "Okay, fair enough—what made you guess his secret?"

Damn. I flushed, so hotly that Andres' nostrils flared as he scented the blood beneath my skin. I felt Bracken's hand, under the table, resting on my knee, and both blessed and cursed him. He knew everything I had to be ashamed of, every moment of violation—I couldn't decide if he was a comfort to me, or if my embarrassment was more acute because he knew me so well.

"Well, for one thing there were the memories he chose to feed off of." I said, buying time and composure. "Nicky said they were all…first times. I think he meant the memories of girls losing their virginity—he told me that the memories were painful, and awkward…and I think that's what Goshawk wanted." I grimaced. "It would make sense that he wanted confirmation that sex was painful and awkward and that it was just fine that he wasn't getting any."

"Anything else?" Andres asked, nodding.

I shrugged. "Well, Nicky—being born and raised in a permissive time, didn't just take my first experience *period*. He took as many of my firsts as he could— and he said Goshawk looked like a heroin junky getting a fix when he got my memories—I have a..." I smiled, my flush intensified, and I ploughed on, "I have a couple of memorable firsts." I finished lamely. "And probably not the kind Goshawk was expecting. In fact," I murmured thoughtfully, "I think that's why he attacked me that night after...after the whole warehouse hotel...thing. If he read my memories right, he knew that I did...well, spectacular things with my power on my first nights..."

"All first nights?" Andres asked, curiosity a living thing, arcing out of his eyes.

"Well..." I murmured, thinking, "Maybe not my *very* first, with Adrian..."

"Adrian swallowed her power." Bracken said casually to Andres, shaking his head.

My eyes widened. "No..."

Bracken shook his head yes. "I would have thought he would have..." But my mouth was still open and my eyes were still wide, so no, Adrian had obviously not told me that our first night together had been more than special. Bracken sighed with resignation. "You have no idea what you almost did to all of us that night. Adrian glowed with power for the next three days—he must have looked like a solar flare when he was inside you..."

"How could he do that?" Andres asked, curious. "Green told me that her power was sunshine...couldn't she have killed Adrian with her power that way?"

Bracken looked thoughtful, then. "I think..." He said, looking at me, and I could almost read his memories of us, flashing over his beautiful features, "I think when she was with Adrian alone, his power was the moon...maybe it's only with sunlight creatures that she gets her sunshine power..."

Andres nodded his head thoughtfully, and I was still fumbling with the idea that, even then, even that first, innocent, lovely night with Adrian, my power, this freakish explosion of energy in my body with no clear origin, would have blossomed to the point that Adrian would have had to control it. But I couldn't remember that moment, I thought, panicked. I could remember the night after, when he had seemed to glow with love for me, but I couldn't remember that moment of pain, or of pleasure, when I had first lain with Adrian and welcomed him into my body. And to know that the glow that had seemed to cover him in those first days that I *did* remember...

"I thought that's just what a man looks like..." I murmured, too shocked to even flush that Brack would imagine that moment. "When a woman loves him..." I'd had no idea. My little mourning song for Adrian kicked up a notch; how unbearably sad that Bracken should be the one to tell me this, when Adrian would have wanted to tell me eventually.

Bracken was helpless beside me then, until Andres captured my chin between his fingers and smiled gently into my eyes. "Of course that's what a man looks like when a woman loves him." He told me gently. "But with you, Adrian probably looked like that for the world to see, and not just in your heart."

"That's really sweet." I sniffled, and Bracken put a frustrated hand on my shoulder, squeezed once, hard, before he stood abruptly and stalked away from the table. I watched him go, feeling miserable. "You'd think," I said after a moment, "That we would have other things to worry about besides this."

Andres laughed dryly, and said, out of the blue, "You know, Cory, when I was young, before I was a vampire, I was desperately in love."

"Who was she?" I asked, unthinkingly, but I was right.

"We were peasants in the same village in Mexico. Goddess—I can't even remember where the damn place was now. But we grew up together, weeded fields, fetched water, learned our letters from the local missionary—I thought she was the most delicate and lovely creature to ever grace the face of the earth."

"She must have been beautiful." I said kindly, seeing in my mind's eye someone who looked like a cross between a Catherine Zeta-Jones from Zorro and Kate Beckinsale from, well, anything.

"Not at all." Andres replied, surprisingly. "I have traveled the world since, you know, and have seen beauty—Latin beauty, Nordic beauty, beauty from the heart of Africa—and Lucita, she was none of these things. She had square palms, and a broad face, with small eyes and a low forehead...if she were a movie star, she would be cast as comic relief—the homely sister, in need of a man."

"But you loved her!" I protested, looking beyond Andres' shoulder to where Bracken stood. He had moved outside of the restaurant, onto the balcony of the hotel, and against the manic lights of the city, he looked like a dark angel, ready to descend.

"Indeed I did." Andres affirmed tracking my gaze to where my definitely beautiful lover stood. "I still do, in some secret, human part of my blood-lusting heart. And to me she was more beautiful than any model or starlet, or any socialite—or any lover, for that matter, that I have been blessed enough to have since."

Damn, I was going to cry again.

"With one exception." Andres continued, and, Oh Jesus, I knew where he was going with this. Even here, in this alien city, the table linens and the crystal glasses whispered his name.

"Adrian." I said, closing my eyes very very tightly.

"Oh yes." Andres agreed. "And Adrian kissed you on your virgin night, and swallowed the moon for you—and as beautiful as he looked to you, Corinne Carol-Anne, you must have looked a thousand times lovelier to him."

My throat clogged, because whether it was Andres' age, his innate sensitivity, or, Goddess love him, his poetic Latin soul, he had found the perfect balm for a wound I didn't know I had. I just wished I could remember what Adrian had looked like at that moment, so I could put even this pain into perspective.

"What happened to her?" I wanted to know.

A clutching grief passed Andres features, and I wished I hadn't asked. "Before her independence, Mexico was a place for petty tyrants, small Don's, Lords who could not make it in Spain and enjoyed the conquests here." He said after a moment. "Much as it happened in the Dickens's book, Lucita was killed by a carriage roaring down a tiny street, carrying the cloth for her wedding dress in her arms."

Was there no end to the wounds that would be uncovered tonight? I thought, painfully. Goddess, couldn't one of her creatures make it through a lifetime whole?

"What did you do?" I asked, seeing this story to its end, no matter what it cost me.

"Came to America." Andres forced lightness and irony into his tone, to spare us both, I think. "Where money and power were for the taking, looking for vengeance. I disembarked the same day a haunted ship came to harbor, and ran into a fine English Lord more beautiful and compassionate than any man I had ever met."

"Green." But of course. "And did you find vengeance?"

"Oh yes—my first act as a vampire, you know. As it was, I died, though Green tried to talk me out of it. Tried to talk Adrian out of it, for that matter, but I think he tried a little harder with me than with Adrian."

"Adrian was very suited to be a vampire." I said thoughtfully, remembering Adrian's almost child-like joy of flying through the night.

"And Green wanted an immortal lover so badly." Andres added levelly. I looked at him quickly, but could detect no censure in Andres' voice—but there was…something. In his turn, Andres shrugged, looking uncomfortable, which was a first for the short time I'd known him.

"Adrian…" He shook his head. "You see, little Goddess, those first few months as a vampire are not…comfortable. You are always hungry—hungry for blood, hungry for flesh of any kind." He looked away. "I was a peasant in a Catholic country...the first time I fed from a young man, and desired all of his flesh...it was..."

I thought of that moment I woke up in Green's bed, smelling of Green and Adrian, damp and slick with the both of them, and I knew exactly what he was saying. This first, Goshawk hadn't stolen from me. "Unnerving." I supplied dryly, putting my hand on top of his.

"Very much so." Andres smiled. "It must always be so, I think, to go in one moment from being one of God's favored ones to a child of the Goddess. But Adrian and I—we roomed with Lucian's brood of new vampires. We were of an age, you know, but Adrian...the darkest I ever saw of human nature was the death of my Lucita—and that was a callous, impersonal darkness, although it was enough to kill me in the end. But Adrian had seen darkness in a much more personal form. And he knew—better than anyone I've ever known besides Green— that love and desire and sex are both very much the same and very very different. He knew how to *make* them different, with a touch."

My throat had closed, because I could remember, now, my first touch of Adrian, our first kiss, his head lowering, his nostrils flaring with my scent, the reverent way he'd brushed our lips together before pulling me against him. Yes. Adrian had known how to convey love with just a touch. And Goshawk had tried to take that memory from me. "He learned it from Green." I said, with an effort.

"Of course he did." Andres agreed, wiping a bloody tear from the corner of his eye. He leaned in to me then, so close I could smell his aftershave, and the coppery alive smell that was, paradoxically, the hallmark of the vampires I've loved. "But he was Adrian—our Adrian, and nobody will ever touch just like him. He taught me, truly, about love, and touch, and about no shame. Vampires say it all the time, you know. They use it to justify things like killing children under the mask of the plague, or mindwiping victims of their lust, but those are actions of the other. We *should* be ashamed of those. Adrian taught me any touch, any tender, consensual, respectful touch could carry no shame at all. Since he taught me that, I've killed on occasion and had many lovers, but no shame is my most important lesson—that's the principle that has guided both actions. I've become the leader of my people by that principle, and I tell you this truly—your hot tango with Bracken, your stately waltz with Green, these are the heartbeats of motion that rock cities, ravage countries, beleaguer our entire confused planet. Goshawk's attacks, Mist's cruelty, the court's arrogance—all actions, fair and foul, stem from the dance of hearts."

Oh Goddess he was right. I nodded, swallowing hard, and Andres' cool hand came up to my flushed cheek. Our foreheads were almost touching now, and I could see, close up, that his eyes were really a spectacular brown/gold, and that his lashes were extraordinarily long, and that his lips were sensual and strong. "You will go outside then, and make your dance with Bracken right, will you not?" I nodded, still beyond words. "Good. Because when you are done, you will eat more steak, taste a desert that is sheer sin, and since, were you any other woman I would take you home on a night like this and touch your warm flesh with my cool hands, I will instead take your blood, because *that* hunger I can satisfy. And your great, frightened, terrifying lover will watch me, and he will want you more because of it, do we understand?"

He was whispering, but I would imagine everyone in every table could see the tenderness with which he was touching me. Even the blindest of God's mortal children would understand.

"Yes." I murmured, and leaned in to kiss his cheek. The touch of his caramel skin to my lips was electric, and as I turned blindly and made my unsteady way to the door to the balcony I could imagine his strong mouth on my neck, and Bracken's hot eyes on us both. It was an intoxicating idea, almost heady enough to drown the sorrow of the night's conversation.

It was forty degrees outside, but Bracken was—like most of his species save Arturo—impervious to the cold. Heat bothered them, but cold, not so much. He was staring out at the skyline, and since the hotel was towards a top of a hill, there was quite a bit of skyline to see. To our left was telegraph hill, in silhouette, and quite further beyond that was the gaily lighted Golden Gate, with its vast promise of whale-road beyond. To the right was the Bay Bridge, also twinkling merrily, and beyond that Oakland, like the same alien ship Sacramento would be, if we were standing on a hill top back home. But we weren't home, and if we could look through the hotel, I imagined, we would see the warehouse district, and the new hotel that Green assured me was up and running with the help of the disenfranchised lower fey of San Francisco. It was a beautiful world, vast and rich, like cold dark velvet, but it didn't hold my attention as much as the man who was taller than normal, with the subtly alien features and the ruffled, uncomfortably cut hair and even more uncomfortable love for me.

I was behind him, and gently, so gently, I wrapped my arms around him, taking in his body heat to help battle the awful chill of the air.

"I'm sorry." He said distantly. "That was unforgivable of me."

"It's a beautiful night." I said, leaning my cheek against his back. "Nothing's unforgivable."

He turned and wrapped his arms around me and I was warm again. "It's a beautiful woman, who would forgive me." He said simply.

"Do all of the Goddess' children wear love-goggles?" I asked him with tender wryness. Andres to his beautiful Lucita, Adrian, Bracken and Green to me—how else to explain the attraction?

"Green's children are born with them on." Bracken murmured thoughtfully, "But we don't need love goggles to find you beautiful." Such blindness was, I supposed, the very nature of love-goggles. "What were you and Andres talking about?" He asked roughly.

I didn't take offense to the question. I imagined there were still ravages of the truths that the conversation had left on my face. "We were talking about love goggles, and how our dance—with Adrian and without—makes the world go around." Our bodies had started to sway, gently, and we did, indeed, dance on the balcony overlooking a chill, brightly lit night.

"No wonder it's such a mess." My lover cracked grimly.

"Give it a chance!" I laughed up at him. "You realize of course, that in actual time, we've been lovers for like…a week and a half…"

"For you it's been a week and a half—for me it's been forever."

I'd been sick for a week, but it seemed to have left a lifetime of hole in his heart. More woundings to heal. I raised my hand to his face, much as Andres had done for me. "Don't worry, baby." I said softly. "Rain will fall, trees will grow, we will be lovers again."

He smiled, then, warmly, with no hesitation or irony. "I must teach you the whole song someday."

"Where did it come from?"

"Green wrote it." He replied, in a voice that was free from pain, or double meaning. "Adrian told me once that he has a voice that makes even the mortal's God weep." A tiny part of me flared, with hope. We could do this, I thought for the first time. We might not destroy ourselves in our dance.

I laughed. "You can't blame me for loving a man who is so much that is good, then can you?"

Bracken his body still swaying mine in time to the music looked at me like he'd swallowed the sun. "I can't blame you for loving any man, Cory, when you turn your love to me." I was warm, blazing hot where my body touched his, and his large hands smoothed down my back, covering, it felt like, almost the entire surface with their heat and their want. Every time we touched, I thought with a sort of awe. Yes, it happened with Green, every time we touched. It had happened with Adrian, every time we touched. Who knew I had enough passion in me to spark and go liquid every time I was touched by these men?

"Then you won't mind hearing this." I said, wanting to get past the moment when all our words led to tears. "Andres wants to take my blood tonight—to seal the pact, you know?" Bracken nodded, his glow never dimming. "He wants you to be there..." But I didn't have to finish my sentence. Bracken had grown up loving a vampire—he knew.

He glowed so brightly then, I had to turn my eyes.

CORY (Again)

Blood and Tiramisu

Andres was good to his promise, and the tiramisu was something spectacular. So was the second steak with mushrooms that he pressed upon me, much to the incredulity of the twenty-something waitress. She had a nice rounded bottom and a decent chest and an eye for Bracken that had me glaring at her and digging into that steak like my once-larger boobs would grow back in an instant.

"Where are you putting all this?" She asked, as she cleaned up my plate and presented me with sin and chocolate.

"I wish I was putting it down my shirt." I said dryly, and she smiled then, a wry, sarcastic smile that had me forgiving her for eyeing Brack. Wouldn't anybody?

"Honey, with what's going down your shirt tonight, I don't think you need tiramisu." She cracked straight-faced, and I laughed, and flushed and giggled through the dessert course until Andres said drolly that he was going to have to over-tip the woman just for giving him that mental picture. And then I only flushed, and I think Andres over-tipped her anyway.

The night was cold but—that rarity in San Francisco—very clear, and the hotel was a block from Geary, and not so very far away from Green's building with our top-floor apartment, so we opted to walk. (Well, Bracken opted to carry me for part of the way, but I did two entire blocks all on my own.) We knew Mist was out there, and Goshawk, but they were day creatures, we reasoned, and how much safer could you get at night than being escorted around the city by the head vampire of the local kiss?

Walking between Bracken and Andres was like having your body rubbed by invisible cats. My body was heavy electricity, crackling with desire, and my thighs were liquid, conducting shivers of what was to come to my dancing stomach, my sinuous breasts, my galvanized skin. A little before Green's apartment building we stopped, and Andres led us down a tiny alley—but not an unpleasant one.

Most alleys smell of wet metal, garbage and piss, but not this one—it was like a quiet side street next to the building itself. There were several low windows with tidy window boxes—in this season they boasted little more than hopeful crocuses that would only bloom because the heat of the street rose up to greet them. There was a low door that apparently lead underground, and although it was scarcely a block from Green's door, right on Fillmore, I could swear I'd never seen this place before.

"It is one of my darklings." Andres said with bemused pride, as I blinked rapidly and tried to place a memory of it in my mind. "We don't all hole about in one place, but some of my sweeter, more conservative brethren share this place—Green has subtly and heavily shielded it for us as a courtesy." Oh—I could see it now—subtle was right. I was so saturated in Green that I could barely see the sheen of his power as it hung over the rather magical little alleyway.

Before I had time to even comment on the place Andres whirled me to face him, pushing my back up against Bracken and forcing Bracken's back against the stucco wall of the building. I could feel Bracken, all trembling tense muscles and terrifying erection at my back, and Andres, silken want at my front, and wondered if this was what the books were talking about when they said *swooning* with desire. Tension was thick around us, a cocoon, filled with threads of hunger so fine, they caught and expanded with the roughness of our breathing.

Andres' face began the frightening change of the vampire that seemed, regardless of *which* gender, the epitome of the sex of the vampire. His jaw and chin jutted with masculinity, his forehead wrinkled with virility, and his fangs thrust outwards, proving themselves. I couldn't take my eyes from his mouth, which was now all teeth, and which was preparing to nurse from my carotid like an infant's naked lips nurse from his mother. Another delicious tingle, this one starting at my toes, shivered up my body, and against Bracken. His arms tightened convulsively around my middle, and a whimpering sound, the kind a man gives a woman when he *really* wants her, vibrated against my cheek.

"Give me." Andres commanded, and his voice rasped in his altered throat, deeper, sexier than his normal, measured accents. Although I could have said no at any time, it would have taken an army of sidhe to keep me from obeying.

I raised my chin, tilting my cheek against Bracken's, and knew that Bracken could see *everything. I remember this,* I thought breathlessly, and now that I had won back some of my first times from Goshawk I *did* remember Adrian's first feeding from me—the anticipation, the helplessness, the power of offering something on a crème pale platter that the recipient desired with every particle of matter in his heart, soul and sex.

Andres bent his head then, and our bodies were locked now, in an embrace as intimate as any I'd shared with Bracken, and he licked just a tiny line along my throat in foreplay. I groaned, pleading with him in one tortured syllable, and ever the gentleman, Andres complied. His teeth sank into me with hardly a twinge, and it was the three of us, arching, heaving, convulsing against one another until Andres' body clenched with the completion of feeding, and stilled in my arms.

I whimpered then, because he had finished early. He did it for Bracken and I, I knew, so we were still knife edged with desire, and I heard Andres' chuckle on my neck, and it resonated clear down to the ache between my thighs.

"You two will have a very good night." He assured me, and I made another inchoate little grunt, and heard Bracken next to me. With a turn of my eyes I could see Bracken, watching Andres with raw hunger on his face. I looked back at Andres, and could trace my blood, still running from his fangs and down the corner of his mouth. He gave a casual lick of my neck, and my wound closed (fortunately for all of us, with Bracken touching me, the Goddess' gift to vampires was that powerful) and he grinned. A grin is a feral, vicious expression on the face of an aroused vampire.

"You want this, don't you, red-cap?" He asked slyly, making as if to lick the final drop of blood from his chin.

Bracken whimpered. Oh, yes. My red-cap lover wanted to taste my blood more than words could say.

Andres smiled even wider. "Take it, then, red-cap. Take it all." He shifted his stance around my body, grinding his swollen groin into my stomach as he did so, and now he was face to face with Bracken, around my shoulder, exposing his still dripping fangs for Bracken's attention.

Brack leaned forward, eyes half closed, and delicately, like a cat, lapped my blood from Andres' fangs, and then from his chin, down the chin to catch the tiny river of it on our vampire's neck before it reached his immaculately white shirt, and then, as Andres writhed against me, he moved up again along that same slow, painstaking path, and, still delicately, thrust the tip of his tongue into Andres' mouth and swabbed, looking for whatever taste of me he could find. It was delicious torment, to watch that touch of tongue and skin, to smell the sex of the three of us, and the feeding, and the want. It must have been sensual agony to endure, and when Andres had endured enough, he groaned and forced me back against Bracken with his body, and cupped the back of Bracken's head with his small boned hand, pulling my lover in for a kiss of raw animal need, a kiss that Bracken returned. In my turn, I ran my hands down Andres' back, found his tight flank muscles, and pulled him against me, where he groaned again and reached that other, more human climax, spending himself inside his slacks and grinding against my body with desire.

The two men broke the kiss, and the three of us were suddenly individuals again, not part of the whole, writhing one, and we were panting with the force of our need into the cold night.

"Go." Andres whispered hoarsely. "The two of you go now, or I will take you to my darkling, and ravage any chance of balance you have from your bodies before you can come up for air."

Bracken didn't need to be told twice.

His shoulders and his arms shielded me, and my eyes were on his tautened, pointed features, but I could feel the burst of the world as the wind hit my face and he blurred through the streets of the city. No one could see us, even if they looked, only feel a shrill blast of air as we passed, and it was still not fast enough.

I had forgotten the arousal of a vampire's kiss. I had forgotten how it made my breasts tingle, down to the nipples, and my thighs ache, and everything between my legs go swollen and slippery and ready for a lover. I was empty and painfully aching, and I needed someone, and not just someone, not even Green. Tonight I needed Bracken, my warrior, my blood-taster, the solid, angry, companionable mass of testosterone who had just kissed the delicate Andres and stirred my blood to boiling by doing it.

So I urged Bracken on, my lips just at the hollow of his ear, "Faster...Oh, Goddess, Bracken, faster...I want to be home, with you inside me..."

And faster we went, so it was my fault too, when a line of power snaked out around Bracken's knees, and we went tumbling, sprawling, exploding into a ball of speed and lost skin on the sidewalk.

Bracken tucked, when he lost his balance, or our speed alone would have killed me when I hit the pavement. As it was I tumbled against him, sheltered in the massive flesh of his shoulders and heavily muscled arms as we spun and thumped against the ground, and more than once I heard a sickening thud when

Bracken's head took the brunt of the momentum. It would have killed a mortal man, and as it was, when I caught my breath and pulled shakily to my knees next to his still breathing body, he was inert and unconscious underneath my hands.

And that was when I saw Mist, twenty feet behind us, still glowing with the power that had tripped Bracken's feet up, like the preternatural clothesline of a school bully. He was advancing on us as if I were no threat at all, and Bracken was still not moving.

I had seen his wounds heal under my hands, I told myself, frantically. He was a sidhe, and a red-cap, and he was strong and young and his wounds would heal again. He just needed time. If I could keep Mist at bay Bracken would wake up and the two of us could either kill him or get the fuck off of this deserted residential street.

I looked at the sidhe, moving slowly, with an arrogance that told me that he had measured me and dismissed me, and my mad ploughed through my chest like a goddamned wrecking ball. I've never had any problem spewing filthy words into the air like a vomit of sound, but as my power surged through me and into a shield around myself and my fallen lover I was surprised the air in front of me didn't burst into blue flames.

"Goddamned fuck-faced cunt-mouthed bugger-assed cock-sucking piece of shit-eating goat-fucking son of a bastard's ***whore!!!*** " I spat out, and Mist actually recoiled from my words alone. Good. I could appall him—I appalled myself sometimes, but this was not one of them. He tripped us—like a fucking coward he ambushed us and tripped us and now Bracken was laying still at my feet and I was damned I was thrice-Goddess fucking *damned* if this stupid vain little cockroach was going to touch my lover, my beloved, my *due'alle* with his foul-assed hands.

Some of my violence must have shown on my face because Mist realized he didn't have much time to wreak whatever havoc he had planned. His face contorted and he started to run for us then, and I don't know what he intended to do, but when he bounced off the shield of magic with a sound like a ringing church bell, the satisfaction that ripped through me was grim and vicious.

"Yeah, goat-fucker!" I jeered, wishing he was close enough to spit at. "You just try to dick with us. You just fucking *try!*" And the shield glowed brighter, and larger, and Mist's body, prone on the ground, was actually rolled a little by the force of my protection. And still Bracken didn't get up. *Christ, Jesus, God, Goddess, Bracken get up…oh Bracken, please…*

Mist pulled himself to his feet then, and wiped the red ichor that elves bled from his nose, because slamming into my metaphysical shield had been like slamming into a brick wall.

"How..." He began, and shook his head, looking at me with a mixture of disdain and fear.

"How what, dick-weed?" I returned evenly. My breath was coming in pants and my mad was still like a snow-plow slamming against my ribs.

"How are you doing this?" He asked, gingerly putting out a long-fingered hand and hissing when the shield repelled him. "You're nobody. You're a child—an ugly *human* child...why would the Goddess put this much power in your hands?"

"You're so stupid..." And to my horror, I felt tears coming on, because he was dumber than tits on a bull, and his stupidity had caused so much heartbreak and because he would never see. "You're such a stupid fucking asshole...I don't know why She gave me this power—don't you get it, it doesn't fucking *matter!*" Mist looked at me in surprise, but I wouldn't shut up. I was mad, and my mad would keep Bracken safe until he *for chrissakes moved* around my feet. "It doesn't matter...what matters is that you don't *fuck* with people who don't fuck with you...we weren't doing anything to you and you go and sic Sezan on us and maybe the Goddess gave me this power because that was stupid and wrong and mean and she doesn't like it when her people are stupid and mean..."

"That's not for you to..." He tried to interrupt, looking confused, as though these ideas had never crossed his mind.

"The *fuck it isn't!*" I screamed at him. I wasn't doing this pretty. I was crying, and there were tears and snot and spit running down my face but I didn't give a fuck because this asshole took everything from us once, and he was trying to do it again. "You want to know how I'm doing this? You really want to fucking know?"

He nodded, slowly, big eyes, and I felt a breeze coming through my shields and a determination that the next time we met face to face I'd have every weapon at my disposal to wipe that smugness and that look of bewilderment off his face because if a breeze could make it in, then a bullet could make it out.

"I'm doing this because I love him, like I love Green and like I loved Adrian and you don't get that because you think you're too good to love anybody, and a lot you fucking know about any of it..." I was sweating with the force of maintaining the shield, and I shook my head, short hair flying across my eyes, and there must have been something in them to frighten Mist, because he backed up a step and still, like a dialog of diarrhea I just couldn't stop. "You've fucked with us all one too many times. I swear to Christ, asshole, do this again—go ahead, ambush us again, because the next time I'm going to have my fucking.45 on me and I'll fire it through my shields and I will ream you up the ass with that fucking cannon because mother fucker that's what buckwheats means and that wouldn't kill you but my lover here is a red-cap and he loved Adrian too and he will pull your blood out of your body and you'll be sucked dry and die screaming in a pool of your own goddamned blood because God and Goddess and Jesus H. Christ you just don't get to *fuck* with people like this!"

Mist backed up another step then, and I realized I frightened him, and disgusted him with my bleeding heart and my bleeding knees and elbows and my bleeding humanity, gushing forth from my mouth like verbal viscera.

"I thought Green's children were all about sex and peace...you're weak with it!" He protested, still backing away from me in revulsion. "He's a concubine—a sidhe *whore*...I've had him a thousand times—what else could he know?"

"We know his *love.*" I groaned, and my mad and my grief coming out in that one word made him stagger, almost to his knees, and I hurt so badly I almost joined him there on the pavement. Oh, Goddess, this fucker had *had* Green? Oh, Green, oh my beloved, my *ou'e'hm,* you never said a word...all the anger for Adrian, and not a heartbeat for yourself...and I wept some more with the old wounds I'd never known my beloved had bled. And I wanted this elf dead some more, so much so that my blood ran thick with the hating of him, this arrogant, ignorant fucker who would kill or defile the men I loved. As She was my witness, if I wasn't made to be the Goddess' retribution for these sins, there was no other reason for me to be.

There was a silence there, punctuated by our ragged breathing and by, thank the Goddess, oh my God *thank you* Bracken's small groans of pain as his tissues re-knit and his harder-than-rock head repaired itself in that queasy slide of flesh I'd felt before with Green's help. Mist was stuck then—he couldn't hurt us, and he didn't want to just run away and leave us there, soon to be whole and healthy and really pissed off. Maybe he was hoping my shields would die—maybe he was hoping Bracken really was dead and that his death would unmake me. We'd told him what I was capable of when I grieved for a lover—maybe he just didn't believe I was capable of it. Maybe he just didn't know that grief and love were more powerful than arrogance and disdain.

"Do you know how Sezan and Crispin died?" I asked out of the blue, into the morning bell silence of the black a.m.

"You killed them." Mist said, looking lost and confused. "Morana told me—everybody knows that." Lost and confused—hurray, and bully for Mist—humanity at fucking last.

"Everybody knows wrong." I told him viciously. "My anger killed the vampires…but not Sezan and Crispin—Green did that."

"With what?" He was genuinely shocked. He was wearing Green's brand on his skin, and he was shocked? Everything about him made my anger bubble inside my chest. "But Green can't *use* weapons," Mist's incredulity was building to a sort of whine that I usually associated with fourth graders. "Cold iron, steel, too much contact makes our flesh shrivel." Like I wouldn't know that. I'd asked Bracken to holster my gun once, in an emergency, and had cringed when Green had been needed to heal the blisters on his hands. "His magic can't hurt anyone—how could he kill another sidhe?"

"With grief." I replied to Mist, feeling a falter in my shields that I hoped he wouldn't. I was pouring all I had into them, and suddenly wished I had thought to just blow this bastard up before I'd erected the fucking barriers in the first place, because what we had here was a Mexican standoff. I had been so worried about Bracken, I thought now, watching Mist trying to wrap his head around what I'd just said, all I'd thought about was protecting him. Now I knew how Green had felt last summer, and how horrible his grief had been when he'd failed.

"Grief is an emotion—a human emotion." Mist said, looking at me sharply.

"Grief is the Goddess' gift to all creatures." I said with certainty, still in tears. I could still scream and blubber at him, but I restrained myself even though nothing was going to dim that horrible, fatal sense that Mist's problem was that he was blind, and I could make him *see*. "Grief avenges wrongs and cleanses wounds to heal…without grief, nothing is worth defending." No one had told me this, but, Christ, if I hadn't been learning it the hard way this last year I don't know what my living had been for. "Adrian died." Again and again and again I had to say this and it hurt and it wept and it bled every time. "Green grieved." That sound pouring from his throat, the one that would have pulled water from deserts and blood from brick walls, the wail that shredded nerves and hearts flooded my skin, and I could hear it all, *feel* it all again. "He grabbed Sezan and Crispin by the throat and his grief tried to rip their own grief from them."

"They didn't have anything to grieve for!" Mist interrupted his exasperation plain in his voice.

"Which is why they died!" I shouted. "If they'd been able to feel just a little, a little remorse, a little sadness, at what they did, that would have been it…I mean, I would have killed them with my own anger in a minute, but that at least was clean…no, they went out vomiting blood and guts and little black crappy things that stuck to Green's hands because they didn't have enough in them to *grieve…*" And my voice was rising in passion, and Bracken was pulling himself to his knees and Mist was backing up now, with an expression on his face like someone who thought he'd been catching a tuna fish but who'd caught a twenty-foot Great White instead.

"Yeah, that's right mother-fucker…." I spat, my mad coming back to me, fed by the fear and uncertainty that rolled off the no-longer arrogant elf in greasy waves. The fact that Bracken was wrapping his arms around my waist and feeding me whatever strength he had in his still healing body didn't hurt either. "You go figure out where you screwed up by dicking with us, and I'm going to sit here and plan our next encounter when I've got that big fucking gun and my red-cap here is going to give you the mother of all buckwheats…" And he must have remembered what that meant because in a flicker of mist and fog he whirled and blurred away, leaving me and Bracken, still wrapped in my shield like a big magic bell, shaking in reaction in the chill pre-dawn.

Eventually we staggered back to the apartment, and I longed to cling to him, to let him carry me, because the strength that had carried me through the evening was gone and the exertion hurt my lungs and I couldn't stop coughing; but my palms were bleeding, and my knees and elbows too, where my dress and tights were shredded, and every time he touched me, my wounds ran slick with blood.

When we lurched through the front door, we saw Renny asleep on the floor, and Grace awake on the couch, so intent on her quiet knitting that her hands were moving in hyperspeed, and her upper body and head were quietly focused on the movie in front of her—still and breathless as only vampires can be. She turned to smile at us as we came in, and the chagrin that crossed her features was not at all comical.

"Holy blue fuck, you two—what do we have to do to let you have a real date?" She put her knitting down in its basket and came up the landing towards us, pulling me away from Bracken's side.

"Kill that cocksucker Mist." I answered back, grateful that Grace wouldn't flinch from my language. Last summer, 'cocksucker' had been Grace's favorite word.

"Goodness…" She clucked, assessing what amounted to road-rash. "I was sure that coming in and looking like this you would have done that yourselves."

Bracken gave a grunt then, part self-disgust and part exasperation, and I turned to him, leaning up close enough to touch. Grace yelped as the blood began to seep and I felt her, frantically licking my palms to make my blood congeal, even as Bracken pulled it from my skin. "I'll be back in a second." I said seriously, "But don't you dare go to bed thinking that. Take a shower, chill the fuck out, beat off, do whatever, but don't blame yourself." I sounded shrill to myself, and took my own deep breath. "Give me a minute, okay?"

He wouldn't meet my eyes.

"Please, Bracken—please?" They were the exact words I'd whispered in his ear only a half-an-hour before, urging him back here, home, to bed, and that bitter, grim twist to his mouth let me know he remembered too. He nodded, once, and shouldered his way down the hall, thank the Goddess, to my room which had its own shower.

"Mist tripped us." I told Grace later, sitting on the same toilet I'd made Nicky sit on when I was bandaging his wounds. "We were…well doing that blurring thing home, and Mist tripped him and probably fractured his bloody great thick head…"

"And all you could think about was protecting him, which is why Mist is still alive." Grace filled in between laps at my elbow as she made the blood first run clean, then stop flowing altogether. It was a useful little vampire quirk that they could do both at will—like their own existence on the planet, it was a power purely at the will of the Goddess.

"And now he blames himself for it because he's Bracken and he's stupid and he loves me." I finished up with a laugh, standing up and stripping off my cloak to take stock. My wounds we're now all scabbed over—Bracken's touch alone wouldn't make them bleed.

"So…" Grace asked, leaning against the doorjamb with only a faint twist of irony at her mouth.

"So what?" I found I was fluffing my hair, and rinsing the marks of make-up and grief of my face—making myself presentable for my lover who was waiting for me.

"So what made Mist run? You didn't kill him. You didn't get killed. What made him leave?"

I thought about it, unsure myself. "Well…I did threaten to shoot him up the ass with a .45 and have Bracken make him bleed out…" I joked lamely, but Grace laughed anyway.

"That's a pretty potent threat…" she considered. "Anything else?"

I shrugged. "Well…I was telling him how Crispin and Sezan died, and then Bracken woke up and grabbed me about the knees, and there was a power-surge in the shields…and he got all weirded out and ran into the night like a little girl…"

Grace smiled then, and suddenly she looked like a vampire, not like a very pale housewife with fangs. "I saw them die…" She murmured appreciatively. "I'll just bet he ran away."

"Grace…" And my voice quavered, because I remembered what Mist had said, before that happened, and it hurt badly, and it was not what you told one lover about another.

"What, baby?" She asked gently, laying a maternal hand on my shoulder.

"Mist told me something…something Green never told us, that doesn't matter anyway, but…"

"But now you know?" She must have been a wonderful mother, I thought, because she had that mom-the-mind-reader thing down to a science.

"Do I tell Green?" I asked, from my heart.

"Why would you do that?" She asked, and I thought hard.

"Because…" I sat for a moment. "Because you remember the night that Adrian told…well *everybody* about his past…about Sezan?"

Grace nodded, closing her eyes. Everybody who'd loved Adrian remembered that night. Talk about reliving another person's pain and making it your own.

"We were linked then, right? And all he could think about was Bracken, and would Bracken ever look at him with that same hero worship in his eyes that he'd always had…"

Grace laughed. "Nothing could kill that, sweetie—not even you…"

I had to roll my eyes at that. "Well, when Adrian realized that was the truth, it was like…it was like almost as good as the night I healed him. He felt free, and like he really deserved that love for the first time."

Grace looked at me sorrowfully then. "So our Green has this kind of secret in him?"

"Yeah." I murmured, blowing out a breath.

"Well, then, you do what you can to make him feel better about it."

I smiled at her then, my full out blinding smile, but she wasn't a man, she was my surrogate mom, so it didn't make her stupid. I gave her a heartfelt hug and then practically ran down the hall to greet Bracken.

Bracken was emerging from the shower, stark naked, and gingerly rubbing his scalp with a towel. The towel was coming back pink, probably because he hadn't taken the time to wash all the blood out of his hair and not because he was still bleeding, but I knew my face puckered anyway.

"I'm fine." He said kindly, and came forward to take my scraped palm in his big hands.

"So am I." I murmured back as he pulled my palm to his lips and brushed it with a barely-there kiss.

"I know." He flashed a grin that actually made it up to crinkle his eyes. "You haven't barfed once."

My laugh was unforced and I easily found myself in his arms, my shredded dress probably scratchy against his hairless, soft skin. He bent his head that impossibly far distance down to my neck and his tongue traced my new bite marks, and just like that, all of our hunger from earlier in the night flooded through me. My tender upper thighs ran slick with wanting him in such a rush that I actually gasped with the pain of not having him inside of me.

"Please, Bracken, please…" I murmured again, and the next thing I heard was my already ruined dress, being ripped in pieces and falling around my ankles.

Later, much, much later, after making fast, hard, and painfully tender love until the gray light of dawn started to creep down the hallway and edge under my door, we lay quietly. My head was pillowed on his upper arm, and my hand lazily skimmed the distinct and hard muscles of his chest and abdomen. I hoped, with all of my female heart, that all was right in Bracken's world, and that there were no wounds left to heal about the fact that I'd been protecting him while he'd been out cold.

"Bracken?" I asked, before he could fall asleep, but so softly he didn't wake up fully, "How much did you hear, when I was talking to Mist?"

He was not quite too tired to smile. "I heard you say 'fuck' a lot…"

"I say 'fuck' a lot anyway." I murmured, trying not to fugue into dreamland.

"Not so much these days." He was almost gone.

"What's the first thing you remember? Because I was terrified for you…"

He rolled a little to his side, to look at me through veiled eyes. "I remember you saying that grief is the Goddess' gift to all of us. I thought that this was pretty wise of you, and that I was sure Mist was too much of a prick to get it. And then I figured that it was the reason you hadn't killed him right off, that you'd protected me instead and then I got pissed because I was out of commission and you were there, by yourself, and I was supposed to be protecting you."

So much for foolish hopes, I thought wistfully. "Your life is more important than our revenge." I said with feeling, and then I wrapped my smooth, bare limbs around his body, like a vine around a tree, and burrowed my head into his chest. "If it wasn't, then we'd be just like Goshawk." He chuffed out a breath, as though he hadn't thought of that, but Green's secret was safe, and Bracken would live with the idea that he was precious to me too, and I didn't want to talk any more.

"Go to sleep, Bracken." I murmured, hoping I hadn't ruined his chances of doing just that. "I'll still love you when you wake up."

"Me too." He returned, smoothing my hair against my head with one hand, and pulling the comforter over us with the other. I heard his heart beat, steady against my cheek and then I was asleep.

GREEN

The Secret of the Stately Waltz

Green was later than he'd planned because he'd had to argue with the Avians first about whether or not they should come back to the city with him.

Goddess help him, Mario, the man who had lost his mate, sank gracefully to one knee in the middle of his living room, in front of the brand new white leather couch and the newly decorated Christmas tree, to ask to be a member of his guard.

"Please, Lord Green," He said quietly, all of his lost heart in his eyes, "We owe you lives, freedom, self-respect—everything. We won't betray you. I promise on my life."

Green had needed to blink back tears, because he was truly moved. In a very short time the lost and discarded Avians had come to love Green's land like the bird sanctuary they'd never had. The landscape beyond Green's hill was falcon country—hills, trees, sweeping canyons—and that alone might have had something to do with it. But in their time at the faerie hill, Green had learned that it was not geography that clenched the Avians like a rabbit in a falcon's claws, it was theology.

Goshawk says...he'd heard that so often in the last week that he was almost sick with it. *Goshawk says* Avians must not mix with other of the Goddess' species. *Goshawk says* the Goddess is weak without her God. *Goshawk says* you mustn't love another man. *Goshawk says* female Avians are weaker. *Goshawk says* women are corrupt.

"Goshawk can go fuck himself with a pretty white stick!" Green exploded, the last time Tommy had used that refrain to try to explain to Green why it had seemed like such a fantastic idea for him and his best friend Dennis to launch themselves at the were-coyotes in a suicide mission, which is how the two boys had been caught. "His prejudice is not more important than your life!" Tommy had been rendered speechless at the time, and had sat down abruptly, and then burst into tears. Dennis—always ready to run to Tommy's rescue—had been there next to him before Tommy could even sob again, and had looked at Green with gratitude in his eyes.

"I'll take care of him." Dennis said, rubbing his friend's back. "It's just...his life at home wasn't...and then Goshawk was, like, a god, except he wasn't...and..." Dennis had a keen sense of irony, and his lips quirked, acknowledging that the things he wasn't saying were much more important than his actual words. "No one has ever said anything like that to either of us. You have no idea what it means to know we matter—and you haven't even known us that long."

Green had been torn—he wanted, more than almost anything, to take the boy into his arms and comfort him, because that was what Green *was*, but Dennis seemed to be doing the job, and Green wanted the boys to trust him even more than he wanted to comfort them. "You matter to me." He said quietly. "Anyone who puts himself under the protection of my hill matters to me. You can come to me anytime, and I will give you what you need." And then he turned away, and left the two friends weeping against each other in relief, and pain, and healing.

Arturo had watched the whole thing, from the other end of the living room. "Can you really fuck yourself with a pretty white stick?" He'd asked, trying to lighten the mood as the two of them vacated the room. "And would it hurt less than with an ugly blue stick?"

"I have no idea." Green replied, taking the humor gratefully, "But you're welcome to try them both out and see." Arturo had laughed then, but now, watching Mario on one knee begging to serve Green, he wasn't laughing at all.

"If I thought you'd betray me," Green said now to Mario, "I wouldn't leave you here, of all places, with my people who believe they're safe. Do you understand? My people's safety is everything to me. I won't sacrifice one more life than I have to—every life leaves a hole—you of all people know that, don't you?"

And silent tears slipped down Mario's proud face. He was still mourning for his beloved. Of course he knew. "I want to help." Mario whispered. "I don't need to kill him...but I need to help bring him down...can't you understand that?"

Green sighed and pinched the bridge of his nose. He'd said from the beginning that he didn't want Goshawk's people to have to make this exact choice. But Mario had already made it—who was Green to stop him? "He will want you dead as soon as he sees you, you know that, right?"

"I'll stay with you, Green." Mario whispered. "I won't leave your side, no matter how badly I want to go after him…"

"But that's not the way he works!" Green snapped, holding onto his patience by that thin grasp on the bridge of his nose. "He'll talk to you—tell you how much he admires your courage, and how there's a way to redeem yourself for your failings…The next thing you know you'll be on top of the Bay Bridge, jumping without your wings!" He needed to leave, he thought, just a trifle desperately. Cory needed a gun. Nicky had packed it for Green, since Green couldn't even touch the damned thing, but it was there, contaminating Nicky's luggage with its cold steel and death. And he was here, arguing with someone who had barely healed about leaving the safety of Green's hill…

The way Green should have argued with Cory before she'd left, bugger fuck it *all.*

Mario turned compassionate eyes up to Green, then. "We're not all as lost as Seth was, Green." He said quietly. "Some of us just needed you to light the way."

Green sighed, a sound that came from his toes on up, and nodded. "Just you or all of you?" He asked after a moment.

"La Mark and I." Mario replied, his voice a little less tense, now that he sensed capitulation. "We want to tell Goshawk that he's evil, and that we quit, and we want to see him lose. The others agreed that we can speak for them." The others were terrified to face Goshawk was what Mario meant, but Green let that slide.

"You've got five minutes to pack, then we're out the…"

"I've got our stuff…" La Mark called, running into the room. Green looked at him sharply, and the young man grinned with hopeful white teeth. La Mark, of the five, was the most beautiful—and the smartest. Green wondered exactly what it had been about Goshawk that had enticed the young African-American into his camp—it would have taken some pretty fast talking to get past La Mark's sense of fun and honor to make him stalk young women for their memories. "Just in case." He said, a smile lurking in his eyes.

Green laughed a little, weakly. "Tell Nicky to move our stuff to the other Suburban." He said after a moment—he was actually running out of vehicles that weren't down in the city. "The others can take the hearse…" There was a contingent of vampires—Phillip, Chet, and Marcus, who were going to join them that night, and sleep in the darkling with Grace, and under ordinary circumstances, Green would have fret about leaving his hill so very very empty of leaders.

But all of his work of the last week had more than one purpose. His people would be guarded by one of the tightest spells that had ever been wound on this side of the ocean—hopefully a spell that would not only keep his people safe, but, if everything worked out, augment his power by a nice geometric proportion when he was done. And the spell couldn't be destroyed unless Green himself was destroyed, and then all of the binding would flow into Cory, and then into Bracken. He would rather it all flowed into Arturo, but since he and Arturo had never shared a bed, the magic wouldn't work that way. But if that happened, he guessed it wouldn't matter. If he were dead, Cory would need that power in order to keep her will to live, pretty much, and Arturo assured him that being a second to this operation was where he was happy. It was a certainty that the tall, dark skinned sidhe hadn't so much as demurred when Green had made the power-flow proposal to him, so Green was simply going to have to trust in the fates. But the fates had betrayed them before…

As the younger men ran off to throw their stuff in the car and grab some sodas from the fridge, Green turned to his second. "Arturo…"

"No." Arturo replied imperturbably, grabbing his keys from the counter and throwing Green's knapsack over his shoulder with his own.

"You didn't even know what I was going to ask…"

"You were going to ask me to stay here in case this doesn't work. It will work. And if it doesn't work, I'll fight to the death to kill them all, and the hill will still be safe." Arturo was walking to the door, waiting for his leader impatiently. Behind him Green knew, there were twenty or so high-elves, nymphs, sprites, and sylphs, waving good-bye, Bracken's mother, Blissa among them. A tiny, maternal sex-kitten of a nymph, she had come to Green earlier, all happy tears, and given him thanks for his blessing on Bracken and Cory. Until that moment, Green had not realized how worried she had been for her child, who had taken Adrian's death so very hard. She had confirmed what Green always knew—sometimes the hard decisions had the best results, and he took this lesson to heart now.

"We'll be fine, leader." Blissa said, and Corge and Gref and Cocklebur and Sweet who were his sidhe high elves and lieutenants all nodded, making shooing motions with their hands.

"Go!" Corge laughed, and although there had been friction between the two of them in the summer, he had sobered quickly with Adrian's death, and the overt display of sheer destructive magic that Cory and Green put on afterwards.

He had been happy in these last weeks, excited that he was working for a powerful leader, and Green wouldn't show weakness to him now if he could help it.

"Be safe people." Green said at last, in benediction, and then turned and walked out the door behind Arturo.

They had a couple of stops to make into the city—places of business to seal with power as they had done in the foothills and through all of Sacramento, so it was late afternoon and nearing full dark as they took the Mission Street exit and made their way cross-town to Bay Street. It was all Greed could do not to claw the upholstery off of the sides of the car as they neared the long, beige colored building the held his apartment; his movements, as he helped the other men gather their luggage, were nearing on desperate.

He burst into the apartment abruptly, with the others on his heels, and saw Cory, perched on Bracken's lap, reading a paperback romance out loud to him. As Green entered, he saw Bracken lean forward and brush a lock of hair out of her eyes, right as she raised those eyes to see Green. A smile split her face, making her humanly plain features radiant and lovely.

"Green's here!" She burbled, giving Bracken an abrupt hug and a kiss on a bemused cheek out of sheer joy before catapulting herself out of his lap, across the room, and into Green's arms.

"You're here!" She repeated, wrapping her arms around his neck and her legs around his hips. He'd dropped his bags as she'd ran, and now he cupped her bottom in his large hands, noting how tiny she still was after her sickness, and how the little weight she'd gained back made her look almost elfin as opposed to emaciated. His heart gave a giant thump, all the way down from his chest to his stomach, and as she smiled up at him he lowered his head and devoured her mouth, smile and all. Her lips were just as warm, and just as soft as he remembered, and her mouth tasted like peaches and cinnamon and Corinne Carol-Anne and without thought he pushed her back against the hallway wall and kissed her and kissed her and kissed her as though all their time apart would disappear in that frantic mating of tongue and lips and teeth. He wanted to take her into himself, all of her, and keep her warm and safe and happy, just like this moment when she burst with joy, just to see him. Oh, Goddess, how could he have stayed away so long?

He pulled back from the kiss only to have her burrow her face in his neck and nibble. "I missed you." She murmured. "I missed you I missed you I missed you I missed you…" And with that something he didn't know was broken in his chest fixed itself and he gathered her to him in one all encompassing embrace and they stood there, embracing and kissing and murmuring to each other until the others came in.

"Hell, you two, get a room." Nicky complained because they were causing a bottleneck at the entrance, and Green didn't need any more encouragement than that.

Leaving introductions and hellos to Arturo and Bracken he carried Cory, their mouths still locked, into his own room, and shut the door behind him with his foot. Panting, groaning, dying to reclaim her for his own, he laid her on the bed and between her busy fingers and his desperate hands they were naked in moments, and he was hot and hard and inside her mere seconds after that.

He didn't just make love to her; he possessed her, took her, mastered her body and in turn was mastered by hers. In that moment he was as he had wanted to be from the beginning: her one, her only, her everything. When he felt her shudder around him, clenching her teeth and crying out in the ecstasy of come, he grunted **Anyaen** before he poured himself into her. *Anyaen. Mine.*

It was the only time he'd ever claimed a lover as *Anyaen*. She was the only lover he'd ever completely given up any claim to be just exactly that.

"Anyan." She murmured, as he caught his breath, still inside her and leaning on his elbows. His hair was braided, but falling out of the braid at his brow, and she was busy, worrying the strands free so that she could run her fingers through it. "More elfish wedding words?"

Green swallowed. Yes. It was an elfish wedding word exactly. He nodded his head, using the pretense to taking a breath to keep from answering.

"You know," Cory said conversationally, pulling his hair from his face and touching his cheek with tender fingertips, "If you and Adrian and I hadn't done the whole "three" thing, I would have been in a hell of a mess."

"Really?" Green met her eyes then, smiling a little. Sometimes he could tell where her mind was going—often in fact—but not always. She had the pleasant ability to surprise him, say unexpected things, *do* unexpected things that he thought might always keep him enthralled.

"You're getting hard again." She murmured, and wiggled to make it happen faster.

"And you're teasing me!" He rolled then, keeping her with him, until she ended up straddling him, and he could tell by the sudden look of concentration on her face that he was hitting new and exciting places inside her body.

"What does Anyan mean?" She asked, moving, ah, Goddess, just a little, just right.

"The word is *Anyaen,*" *He* groaned.

"What does it mean?" She moved again, and he was fully hard again,

He couldn't look at her, for shame. He'd practically thrown her at Bracken, and praised her for inviting Nicky into her bed to save his life, and then, after all of that, to name her…when he couldn't—even now, with all he'd done to protect his people…*especially* now, with all he'd done—wouldn't ever be able to live that promise. It was unforgivable.

She was still moving, clenching her muscles, riding him, enjoying him. She leaned over, but she was tiny, so she couldn't loom over him—in fact, she gazed up from the middle of his chest, meeting his eyes as gently, he knew, as he sometimes met hers.

"I would have had to choose between you, you know that right?" She murmured, and he blinked, because he never would have thought of that. She nodded, and kept moving in a gentle rhythm, smiling that secret woman's smile that told him she knew she was making him crazy for her. He gasped, and she nodded. "You came and held me that night, after Mitch died, and I thought, what horrible kind of woman am I, that I could love Adrian and want this guy too? And every day after that, you bloomed in my heart, and I kept waiting for you to push Adrian out, but it didn't happen—my heart just got bigger. And if you two hadn't loved each other as well, I would have had to choose one of you, and that would have cut my big heart into two big bleeding halves…" She moaned a little, shuddered, just a little around him, clenched tight between her spread thighs, and moved some more. "So tell me, *ou'e'hm*, what does *Anyaen* mean?"

"*Mine.*" He groaned, grabbing her hips and thrusting into her with fury, mad to possess her one more time.

They really did need to rest after that, and she pillowed her head on his shoulder and made a study of touching him for a few quiet moments before speaking again. "Why was it so hard to say?" She asked quietly.

"Because I have no right to say it." He was playing with her hair, smoothing it back from her face, and he could tell by the way she leaned into that touch like a kitten, that she enjoyed it when he did that.

"You more than anyone." She told him seriously, making sure he could see her eyes. "I know, okay? I get it—I understand why I need Bracken." She looked down and flushed a little. "There's something in me…when I use power, I **need** to be touched. I **need**…well…" She flushed a lot this time, and then sighed deeply, and then coughed.

"Some." Green supplied dryly when the coughing was over.

"Lots." She corrected her voice equally dry, but husky with the cough. "And then *some.*" They both laughed a little, and she continued. "And you absolutely can not stop sleeping with your people. Other supernatural creatures use force and violence to rule, you use love. I couldn't love you the way I do if you ruled differently, and that is just how life is on the faerie hill. So I get it. No monogamous single Prince Green Charming for Cory. No Penelope Carol-Anne for Green-dysseus. It's not going to happen."

"And you love Bracken." He supplied gently, because honesty was essential.

She wrinkled her nose at him. "Of course I do." She responded, and then she put her chin on his chest and made sure she had his complete attention—as though that had ever been in doubt. "But here's the thing, and it's important, and I've decided that if my lovers don't like sharing each other then I'm not going to share one in bed with the other, so this is the one and only time I will ever say this and you are going to have to hold it to your heart and keep it there, because hurting people I love is not what I want to do, okay?"

Goddess, she was magnificent. "Okay." Of course it was okay. With her looking fierce and lovely, with the sheen of tears in her eyes because she loved him, there was nothing else it could be.

"Bracken and I are combustible." She said after a moment of searching for words. "We're fire and gasoline, plutonium and fission, we're a continuous explosion waiting to happen. But we could have stayed in our own separate little containers for several thousand mortal life times and neither of us would have known that it would happen that way. You understand?"

He felt a smile that didn't quite reach his eyes. Yes. He'd seen them together—they were everything she said, and possibly more that she wasn't saying, and he couldn't pretend it didn't hurt.

"You don't." She blew out in frustration, but continued on. "You and I…" She put one hand over his heart, and the other between her own small, bare breasts. "You and I were *inevitable*. If Adrian hadn't been your lover too, I would have had to leave, with him in tow, and even if I went to the whole other end of the earth I don't know if I could have avoided you. If I had died, after living a long happy life with Adrian, I would have come back, been born again right in my home town, because God and Goddess would not have been able to keep me from surfacing at your side. I am young, and stupid, and basically white trash with a preternatural sexual fusion ray gun at my disposal, and I am not worth the dust at your feet, but if I were dust I'd still cling to your feet and you couldn't get rid of me. Do you understand?" There were silent tears slipping down her face now, and suddenly he did understand, and he was shamed that he, of all people would need her to expose her soul like this.

He pulled her into his arms, and her tears slid, briny and warm against his chest. *"Anyaen,"* he murmured, *"Anyaen…"* Mine.

The storm passed, they slept a little, and then he murmured something about food and padded naked out into the kitchen. Everyone else—the Avians, the vampires who had arrived without his knowing, Renny, and Nicky were all in the front room, playing Cranium and watching a movie. He noted drolly that Grace and Arturo were absent right before he noted that Bracken was scowling at him from a corner of the kitchen with a painful mixture of frustration, jealousy, friendship and admiration in his eyes and he sighed, looking about the rest of the kitchen. Sure enough, Grace had left two hot plates for them—Cory's obvious by the giant cut of medium rare meat. He looked at the meat and grimaced at Bracken.

"Whatever we're doing it's not working." He said to break the tension. "She's still much too thin."

"And she's still not well." Bracken said gloomily. "She had to walk two blocks the other night, and she almost keeled over from the work-out. She tries to hide it but she has a cough. Why can't you heal her of that?" He demanded.

Green shrugged, resigned and not a little unhappy about it himself. "She's still missing her memories." He said simply, thinking that Bracken's worry was both infectious and irritating. "She's missing a part of herself that I can heal—she's incomplete, and will never be truly well until she gets it back."

Bracken grimaced. "How awful is it that," He asked, shaking his head, "So much has happened that I keep forgetting she's still suffering from that wound…Nicky's attack is what started this whole mess, and now he's one of the family."

"It's been a rough month." Green understated dryly. "But it had to happen, or she never would have healed as much as she has."

"She was heading for worse before all this happened." Bracken agreed, then, wistfully. "I miss how…substantial…she used to feel."

Green looked the young sidhe in the eyes sorrowfully. "Once Adrian brought her home, not by the three headed One could we have stopped her from changing." He said after a moment.

"Or stopped us from changing." Bracken added softly, nodding when Green did. Then, abruptly, "I want to claim her."

Green breathed deeply through his nose, surprised when he shouldn't have been. "Impossible!" He said, too shocked to be angry.

"For her to claim me?" Bracken nodded, "Yes. It's impossible for her to be mine only." His lips twisted wryly, the Bracken they'd all known a year ago surfacing for just a second. "She'd kill me in a week." He said, and they both knew he wasn't talking about guns, knives, or preternatural sexual nuclear fusion.

"But not impossible for me to be faithful to her." Bracken continued, and Green frowned, trying to figure Bracken's motives. Claiming was such a rare thing for his people—and Bracken was so young to even speak about it. Green said as much.

"I know." Brack said simply. "Do you think that hadn't crossed my mind? But…" He gestured helplessly—words had never been his strong suit. "My parents claimed each other. You may not have claimed Adrian, but…but you could have. If you hadn't been needed as our healer, as our leader, you and Adrian would have lived a quiet and happy eternity together—don't think your people don't know and appreciate that."

"And then he never would have met Cory…" Green tried to interject.

"And you would have bound yourself to her if you could…"

"But in the way of our people I can't!" Green argued, a trifle desperately.

"But I can!" Brack shot back, then ran his fingers through his hair spiky, unkempt hair.

Green realized that they were both standing, feet spread, shoulders back, staking claims to their beloved in the way he was absolutely sure they could not afford to do. He took a deep breath, then deliberately relaxed his shoulders and held his hands up.

"I'm sorry brother." He said formally. "We both love her. She physically needs someone in her bed every night. You've felt it, I've felt it. When she channels power the way she'd done this month she needs our life force—she feeds off of us the same way she feeds our hearts. You, Nicky and I may not even be enough to feed her. That's hard truth, and it's a tricky balance to walk—I just need to know why you would make it trickier."

Bracken sighed and inclined his head to acknowledge Green's peacemaking. Then he moved closer to Green so they couldn't be overheard, even though every being across the open space in the living room had ears that could probably hear this conversation if they were in the downstairs apartment wrapped in wool.

"She needs this, Green." Bracken said helplessly, and Green could tell the boy was trying not to beg. "With all the changes in her life, wouldn't it be good to know that one thing, me, isn't going to change?"

Ah, gods, Green thought, this was too close to his own sore spot regarding Cory, and his knee-jerk reaction was to say *no* ferociously and unequivocally, when, in fact, the boy was making sense. "Have you asked her?" He said instead, buying for time.

Bracken looked away uneasily. "She'd want it to be you." He prevaricated, and Green felt like he was eating one of those sour candies that had become so popular in recent years, the kind that made your mouth pucker but that you couldn't seem to stop savoring.

"You'd be binding yourself to her mortality—you know that?" Bracken would age as Cory would, and whether the Goddess granted her immortality as he suspected, or kept her mortal, which was also Her wont, Bracken would have to live and die as Cory did.

"It may not come to it, but yes, I know that. I'll take that chance." Bracken said, so proudly that Green wanted to kick him. Yes, he was a sidhe and they were seldom monogamous, but Green had never been like his brethren. He had never minded being bound to another creature, saved from loneliness by the shelter of another being's arms. Cory was supposed to be that person for Green, and Green alone, and *Green* wanted to take that chance. *Green* wanted to claim her and bed her so thoroughly she would never need to explode with Bracken. Who else better to be a battery to a sexually powered nuclear fusion generator than an elf whose power was born in sex? But Green had set his path a hundred and fifty years before, and he wouldn't forsake his people now that he finally had a bona fide way of keeping them safe.

"Ask her." He said after a moment when his heart thundered in his ears. "Explain it to her—all of it. I'll think about it, okay?"

Bracken nodded seriously. "Thanks, leader." He said after a moment, stepping back. "And Green?"

"Hmm?" Because Green was already padding back down the hall, to his bedroom, holding the two plates of food in front of him.

"I'm glad you're back too."

Green could tell he meant it.

CORY
Elvish Wedding Words

I put on a shirt when Green went to get food, because although I had no problem when the men wandered around bare, I was just not that comfortable naked. I was careful to put on the one Green discarded, and not Bracken's shirt, which is what I had been wearing before Green burst through the door.

Goddess, I was so glad to see him I was almost weak with it. And the really really strange thing was that I knew that if Green and I had been together, and Bracken had been the one gone, I would be just as weak with longing for Bracken. A month ago I barfed down the sink and cleaned the entire plumbing system of San Francisco; I gazed at the sky, and every bird for miles got horny; I came with my lover and altered the structure of reality; but none of those things had actually convinced me that I was *that* different than any other mortal I knew of. But this *longing* this complete soul defining *yearning* after two completely different men managed to do it. I needed them both, physically, magically and in a lot of other ways I had never thought of, and if that didn't make me something slightly other than human then I didn't know what did. My mindset had gone from *Goddess, I hope we can do this,* to *My God, we have no choice* in a few hours alone with Green.

I was in the middle of this thought and climbing back on Green's wooden four-poster when I heard a knock at the door. We were in Green's room, which made me wonder where Nicky was going to sleep this night—probably on the couch in my room next to a pissed off Bracken, if I had my guess—but it did put in the back of my mind the idea that musical beds was going to get dizzying unless Nicky had his own room at Green's. Of course, Green had probably already taken care of that.

At that moment, Nicky popped his head in the door and I was surprised at how happy I was to see him. I smiled, my genuine smile that would make most men without some sort of preternatural power completely stupid (I still think that's the ultimate of ironies, since I myself am not all that attractive ordinarily) and was rewarded by Nicky's un-beguiled but very sincere smile in return. He looked behind him, and slid inside the door.

"The big guys are having a fairly intense discussion." He said, "So I thought I might get a word in edgewise."

He really was cute, I thought as though noticing for the first time. He had that reddish brown hair, tipped in black and those All-American boy freckles, and even the smallish, beak-like nose added to his appeal. Suddenly I was remembering that, until he'd attacked me (which I'd almost forgotten!) I had seen him nearly every day for the last four months and that Renny and I had really enjoyed his company.

"I'm glad to see you, Nicky." I said with absolute sincerity, and was rewarded by another shy smile.

"I wasn't sure if you would be." He murmured. "I mean…" His eyes took in the rumpled bed, and I was suddenly conscious that I probably looked like walking sex in a man's button up shirt.

"Well, I was *very* glad to see Green as well." I quipped, and was rewarded by a flush that practically took over his face, and then, of all things, spread to mine.

"I think lots of people have been very glad to see Green." He said, not making eye contact.

I knew what that meant—it meant that Nicky and Green had been spending a lot of time together, and spending it naked, which, considering my past experiences with Green and Adrian was really sort of a tingle. And I had lost my jealousy of the others who shared Green's bed a long time ago. Besides—*Only I'm his Anyaen,* a part of me sang out in my heart, but, like my conversation with the man himself, it was a part that was only meant for Green. "He's pretty wonderful, isn't he?" I said instead, smiling gently.

Nicky nodded emphatically, and then cast his eyes down the hall. "And he's coming this way…gotta go." And with that he slipped away—presumably to hide in the bathroom and pretend we'd never had this conversation, as if Green wouldn't figure that out! But it had been good to see him again. It reminded me that, for me as well as for Green, not all of the responsibilities that came with power were unpleasant.

Green came in, holding plates of food and of course I was ravenous. We ate companionably, sitting across from each other on the bed. I had one leg tucked under the other, and when he was done eating, Green reached out and brushed the road-rash on my knee with a gentle finger.

"So, luv—you going to tell me why Nicky had to pack your gun, or do I have to ask Bracken for the 'I'm so stupid and I hate myself' version?"

"Anything but that." I returned with as much acid as I could manage, considering my mouth was full. I took my time and swallowed, then wiped my mouth with the napkin he'd brought and sat quietly, gathering my thoughts before I spoke. "It's weird, actually." I said after a moment, "Because I would have thought you'd have been in on it from the very beginning—you knew when Nicky attacked me, you knew when Goshawk attacked me—but when we woke up this morning and you hadn't called, I figured that maybe the paranormal phone lines or whatever had shut down." He raised his eyebrows and I launched into a narrative and analysis of last night's series of disasters and near misses. I tried to brush over my conversation with Andres, and then the part where I gave blood, but Green, being Green, demanded details, and by the time I had finished with that there was an unmistakable gleam in his eyes. It was quickly erased when I got to the part where Mist tripped Bracken, and we went tumbling across the pavement like dolls from a moving van.

"I don't remember everything we said." I lied, and then there was the arching of his brows and the clearing of his throat and suddenly I couldn't make eye contact.

"Okay." I said at last, toying with the remains of some very fine pasta on my plate. "I do remember everything we said. And I'm sort of mad at you, actually, because Mist told me something last night that I didn't know, and I'm remembering last summer, when I told you that you shouldn't fight because that's not your specialty, and I can't believe how much that must have hurt you—truly, bone deep, heart deep hurt, and you didn't say a fucking word to me, and I might have made that mistake again and hurt you again because you didn't tell me."

"Well, first of all," Green said briskly, clearing our plates from the bed and brushing off invisible crumbs. "I know why I didn't get my 4 a.m. psychic wake-up call." He was evading me and I knew it, so I just sat there with my arms folded, waiting for my usually unflappable beloved to get this part over with. "You had things handled, luv—can't you see that? Those other two times, you called for help—you needed me. This time you had things well under control—

no call for help, no Green in shining armor." He met my eyes and smiled and I nodded in return, a bland expression on my face.

"And about that other thing?" I asked sweetly.

And now Green wouldn't meet my eyes. "It's over and done with." He said after a moment. "It's just...it was just the way things were done, right? The Goddess gave us gifts, and I was...exceptionally gifted, and that's where the court saw fit to use me." He swallowed for a moment, and looked me in the eyes then, the picture of equanimity. "And I wanted to get out, and I did, and now I do my best to see that none of my people are anywhere but exactly where they want to be."

Green, my beloved, my night and my day, the most wonderful, honest and strong man to ever walk the earth, was lying to me, as much as elves could lie to anyone. I could almost laugh, if it didn't hurt so much, that he felt he had to hide something—the pain, the embarrassment, the *anything* at all from me. From his *Anyaen*. From his wife.

"I'm not Adrian." I said after a heavy, hanging moment, and he flinched, those lovely green eyes so wide spaced that they almost seemed to move independently. "And even if I were Adrian, I'd still be able to deal with it. What do you think, Green? Do you think that if you told me, or Adrian, or Bracken or Arturo or Grace or Nicky or *anyone* who loves you that it would change fuck-all about how we felt about you? Like, oh, yes, you are the sun and the moon and the stars but once upon a time you were forced to have sex against your will so now you're only the sun and the moon?" And now I was crying—for, like, the billionth time in a month. I'd shed more tears this last year than in the entire nineteen that preceded it—and I was reasonably sure I wasn't done weeping by half.

Green reached across the bed to me, to wipe a tear off my cheek with a sensitive thumb, and I glared at him. His smile was a little watery, but it was a real smile, a "hang the moon and the sun and the stars just for you" smile, so I tried to rein the glare in a little. "This," He said, tasting my tears from the end of his thumb, "This is why I didn't tell you. This is why I didn't tell Adrian. This is why Arturo only recently guessed." He took a deep, cleansing breath and let it out shakily. Abruptly I launched myself at him to burrow in his arms.

"You can't do that to me." I charged, when I'd knocked him flat and sobbed on him for a minute. "You're my *o'ue'hm*—and I'm your *Anyaen*—and I don't know everything those words mean, but I know that they do mean that I get it all...like marriage, right? I get the good and the bad and the painful and the beautiful and I know I don't get it all at once because you're, like, old and by the time you finished telling me from beginning to end, I'd be withered and dead but something like this, that affects us...I mean..." I stopped myself for a minute and instead of collecting my thoughts blurted out the first damn thing that came into them. "I mean *Jesus,* Green, is there anything in your past that could hurt me more than when we lost Adrian together?"

He stopped then, and thought very carefully, and the silence of the room was almost louder than my torrent of words. "No." He said after a moment, almost surprised. "And yes…" He frowned for a moment, his lips quirking as though he hadn't thought of it before. "Adrian definitely heads up the top three." He said, almost wryly.

Goddess! "Will I ever find out about the other two?" I asked, feeling about as brave as I've ever felt in my life.

"Yes." He said gently, and then moved me up so he could kiss the tears off my cheeks. "Yes, Corinne Carol-Anne, I promise you that, someday, when our lives are quiet and we are not healing from many different wounds, or when something is hurting me that you have no knowledge of, I do promise that I will tell you about my past."

I smiled at him then. "It's a fair promise, *o'ue'hm,*" I murmured, my fingers once again finding those irresistible, inhuman ears and stroking gently. "I'll hold you to it." And then I kissed him, a messy, salty kiss, and before I knew it I was naked and we were making love again.

When we were done we talked some more—he told me about his reasons for coming back to the city instead of just bringing me back home, and he told me what he had in mind for Mist. The audacity of the plan alone had me catching my breath.

"Can you really *do* that?" I asked, nearly blinded by the promise of it.

"I've done a lot of it already." And I could see, in that one moment, how tired he was. He had worked hard, very very hard indeed, to get back to San Francisco, and back to me, by the time he'd promised. I touched his cheek with my hand in silent acknowledgement, and he kissed my hand and tucked it against his chest. "But I will need you—I will need you and Bracken and Arturo and Andres and even Renny, Nicky, and Grace—all of you there by my side when I seal the whole thing off."

"Are you sure they don't suspect?" I asked. I mean…Green's magic, what he had planned involved every business he owned in California. He'd spent a vast amount of time either on the road or blurring from one place to another, creating this 'circle of power' among those he protected. Between Green, Nicky, and Arturo, they had either shook hands with, kissed, or slept with the owner of every fey establishment between San Francisco and Crescent City.

Green shook his head, looking fierce and very proud of himself. "Mist and Morana don't *do* businesses. The sidhe in their order send the lower fey out to do whatever they need to do. And since their sprites and brownies have been either boycotting Mist for the last two weeks or working for us..."

"The sidhe would have no idea that the peasants were rebelling..." I murmured.

"Exactly."

I grinned back at Green fiercely. Give him power to help make our people secure? I'd probably lie on my back and give my body to every sidhe in our hill to make sure another nightmare like Sezan or Goshawk never descended on us again. Of course, the more human part of me was extremely glad that my lover did that part for me.

Green finally put me in my own bed a few hours after midnight, exhausted, spent, and so full of his sex and his seed that I probably glowed with it. When I protested, he told me, wryly and honestly, that the Avians and the other vampires and even Nicky might need him sometime in the night, and he had to be available to them.

"And you didn't see Bracken's face, luv, when you jumped off his lap and into my arms." He murmured. "It will help ease things a bit, I think, if you share a bed tonight."

Goddess! How can anyone be so very right and wrong in the same breath?

Bracken crawled in with me a few hours later, smelling a little like beer which, if I'd been truly awake, would have surprised me, because the sidhe rarely drank. The were-creatures and vampires didn't abuse alcohol or chemicals because the changes in their blood that happened when they went over from one world to the next effectively cleaned out any mind altering properties—the only thing that really made the vampires drunk, actually, was elf blood. The sidhe, however, were a little different. I'm not sure if it was a cultural thing, or if they'd all just had too much of alcohol and chemicals in the 60's, or if alcohol and chemicals were sort of an anti-climax to a being fueled by magic, but one of things that kept Green's hill, well, green, was that although there was plenty of wine and beer (Arturo used to buy a six-pack every other night) it was consumed for taste and not to kill any pain.

So Bracken staggered in and spooned me from behind, which is sort of like saying a giant polar bear spooned one of those little arctic bunnies because he really is huge—as tall as Green with more mass to his chest, and more muscle to his arms. But it didn't matter, because he made me feel safe and loved and I was sated and happy and exhausted, and all was right with the world when I fell asleep.

I awoke on my stomach, hiding my face from the pale winter sunlight streaming in from the window above me. Bracken was nibbling a series of soft, aggressive kisses, starting at the inside of my knee and working their way up my thigh. I must have made some demur of protest, because he said gruffly, his breath tickling the skin of my inner thigh, "Don't hide from me. Don't hide him from me. I know both your tastes…don't hide…"

And then he was kissing and licking and tasting and I was sensitive and tender from the night before, and without warning I was *coming,* I was falling apart, I was exploding, and Bracken was up behind me, inside of me slickly and hugely, clutching my breasts in both hands and whispering harshly in my ear.

"What's my name…"

"*Goddess!*" I grunted, as another climax ripped through me like a claw.

"What's my name?" He demanded, and there was nothing at all that was gentle about him.

"*Bracken, oh, God, Bracken…*" and still he pounded at me, relentlessly sexual, a consensual assault, with the force of his will and his great heaving body.

"Bracken Brine Granite op Crocken." He ground in my ear, "Say it."

"*Bracken…*" I began, but my body was exploding, my *universe* was exploding, and I could barely see the red stars behind my own tightly shut eyes I was so overwhelmed with the brutality of the pleasure he was inflicting.

"*Bracken Brine Granite op Crocken.*" He repeated, and I was biting my hand to keep from screaming in orgasm, and power was roiling through me so deeply I could feel it in my vitals, in my womb, where Bracken was thrusting inside of me, and I was helpless to deny him anything.

"*Bracken Brine Granite op Crocken…*" I shrieked, and suddenly the power that was within me was enveloping us, as we lunged against each other, and he was saying words, more elfish words, including *due'ane* and *due'alle,* and then, just as a final, mammoth climax rolled over us with the slow, hurtling force of a glacier with jet-thrusters, he said my full name.

"*Corinne Carol-Anne Kirkpatrick.*"

And my power surged around the two of us, making a soundless sound, and every light bulb in our room exploded, although none of them had been on, and I could feel it, a bond, forged by, damn him to hell, my magic and our sex and my helpless, painful love for the sidhe, for the *man,* who was currently collapsed upon me bonelessly, his breath coming in sobs, his sweat soaking us both.

"Jesus, Bracken." I said into the sudden, frightening hush that followed the roaring in my ears, "what did you do?'

GREEN

A Few Straight Things

Green was doing business on his laptop at the kitchen table when he felt the power surge from Cory's room. All of the light bulbs exploded in the power surge, and he had just enough time to throw a shield of power up around the entire apartment before the binding was completed, and then he was left, gasping in shock in the dark, as Renny, Nicky, and the other Avian's looked up from their places in the living room saying things like "What in the fuck was that?"

Before he could even think to answer, Cory pounded out of her room, simultaneously pulling on a sweatshirt, snapping a pair of jeans and putting on shoes.

"What do you mean you didn't mean to do it?" She was shouting, so loud that the people in the living room had no choice but to gather, with interest, into the entryway.

"I...don't know how it happened..." Bracken sounded genuinely distraught, and it was the only thing that kept Green from lunging for his throat. That power surge was unmistakable—it had been an elfin bonding in progress, and *fuck it all,* Cory had obviously not known it was coming.

"How can you not know, goddammit—you were there!" Cory's voice rose hoarsely, and she looked at Bracken, bewildered, and with a solid layer of hurt beneath the anger. Her breath rose and fell with her anger, until a fit of coughing overwhelmed her, forcing Brack to wait, helplessly, until she finished to answer.

"I wanted it…" Bracken was still naked, but as usual, he didn't care. He looked shell-shocked, like a man awaking from a fever dream to find out that his house had fallen down around his ears while he was under.

"Goddess knows I wanted it…but…" He reached out and grabbed Cory's shoulder and swung her around to face him. "Goddess, Cory, you have to know I would have asked you. You have to know I would have waited for Green's permission…you have to know that…you know that, right?"

Cory looked up at him from miserable eyes. "I know that you're possessive," she murmured, and he looked away. "I know that you're possessive and difficult and impulsive and you fly off the handle more than any person I've ever known and I know that if what you say is true and we're bonded now, for life, for ever and ever and ever that means that it was something you wanted…and I know that you smell like a distillery and you never drink, and that it wasn't Green or Nicky in that bed with me, forcing me to scream out his name."

Bracken looked like a man who had been slugged in the solar plexus, and he sank slowly, despairingly to his knees about the time Green heard himself saying, dream-like, "He smells like what?"

"Beer." Cory spat, tears still leaking down her face. "He's just made himself my master and commander and he smells like *beer.*"

"No, no no no…" Green murmured frantically, finally finding he could move across the kitchen without hurtling towards Bracken with death in his hands, "he doesn't smell like *beer*…he smells like *magic…*"

Bracken's eyes were red and swollen, and his face was streaked in tears, but his usual intelligence peered up at Green from under his thatch of mutilated hair. "Magic…" He echoed, "Magic…*Goddess….*"

"Bracken—what did you do last night after we talked?"

"I went outside." Bracken murmured, still on his knees and staring at his hands which were dangling limply between his thighs. "I went outside, and there was a…a sylph?" He asked himself. "Yes…a sylph…it…it kissed me, and it…" He looked at Green in horror. "It kissed me and it *changed,* it *bonded,* and changed into a girl, right before my eyes, and I could feel her change and then…" Bracken shook his head, as though trying to shake away cobwebs. "And then I came up and lay down next to Cory…and this morning, I…" He flushed a little, "I wanted to make love to her. That was me. Yes. That was me." He looked up at his leader again, certain. "I wanted to make love to her. But the…the binding words…the binding words—Green, I would have had to ask you what to say…the binding words weren't mine…"

"They were the sylphs." Green said harshly, his eyes glittering. "And they cost her life."

"Killed her!" Bracken murmured, at the same time Nicky said "Does this mean Bracken and Cory are married?"

Green swallowed. "Yes—they're married—that's what killed the sylph."

"How?" Renny asked, and Nicky was asking "Does that mean Cory and you and I can't…" And Bracken was pulling himself up to his feet, breathing hard to hold in his anguish and Cory was standing there, stricken, bewildered, and distraught; confusion threatened to engulf the now-tiny apartment.

"Enough!" Green roared into the noise, and everybody turned their frightened faces to him. "Bracken was bespelled." Green said, measuringly, reasoning as he spoke. "He smells like sylph magic—it's the smell Cory thought was beer." He looked at her sympathetically. "I can see why you would, luv." He said quietly, and then went on. "Not everybody here knows about bonding—even Bracken, apparently, was cloudy on how it was done. It involves words and intent, spoken with pure emotion and physical contact—touch, blood and song, the way all magic is done, right? Well, I think what happened…" He looked at Renny suddenly, "Renny, how long was Bracken gone?"

Renny thought about it. "An hour, maybe." She said quietly. "Yeah—we were watching *Ladyhawke,* and Bracken left right when the hawk got shot, and then he came back with the ending credits."

"Impossible." Bracken burst out, still confused and hurt. "It was a minute…maybe two, to clear my head."

"It was probably an hour." Green said gently. "And you've probably forgotten the part where you got laid."

"He got what?" Cory burst out, at the same time Brack said "I did not!" and any lingering resentment Green might have had towards Bracken evaporated, because never in his long life had he seen a man so devastated and so beleaguered at the same time.

"He doesn't remember it." Green interrupted flatly, because Cory looked like she was going to rip his lungs out, and she turned a disbelieving face towards him. "It's an old battle tactic—it was used a long time ago, when the Tuatha de Danaan reigned with an iron fist, and the sidhe and the high elves were looking for an advantage. Sylphs are neutral—they always have been. Their sole purpose is for companionship. Usually they determine their companion, right? But, because they're weaker, they can be forced…"

"But don't they decide their gender?" Nicky asked.

"Exactly." Green replied, anger and disgust lacing his voice. "They are compelled to choose a victim—usually an enemy—and the sylph bonds with him or her immediately, choosing a gender to seduce the enemy." Green blew out a breath. "A lot of things happen at once, then. Yes, there's sex. And since the victim wasn't bonded with his free will, he won't remember it—it's part of the compulsion. And then the secondary compulsion is transferred…through touch, blood, and song, right?"

"So…" Bracken looked like he might burst into tears again. "I did?" Cory put out a hand then, to touch his arm, to apologize, to give solace and sympathy, but Bracken shook her hand off as though she might contaminate him. Cory's tears overflowed from her already bright eyes instead.

"I'm afraid so, Bracken." Green murmured, with infinite tenderness. Then, "Come here, brother." And Bracken stepped towards his leader trustingly, like a lost child. Green took his hands and looked into his eyes, and saw, and saw, and saw…

"You were supposed to kill us." He murmured. "Me and Cory—you were supposed to kill us in our sleep." Green smiled gently, still reading the magic around Bracken like a soiled book. "Like that would ever happen." He murmured reassuringly. "You wanted her far more than you wanted me dead…and we had just talked about binding, and now you knew the words—you heard the sylph say them as you bonded…and when you woke up, Cory was there…and she smelled like me…and you wanted and you wanted and you wanted…and binding her would hurt me, and that was as far as you'd go…"

Green broke away from Bracken and touched the other man's brow gently. "You did good, Bracken." He said seriously. "You were told to kill us, and you got married instead."

"What killed the sylph?" Renny asked, as though her curiosity had gotten the better of her.

"She was bound to Bracken." Green took Brack into his arms and let the sidhe shudder against him, as the compulsion cleared and the fear and disgust and guilt took over. He murmured into Bracken's hair, softly, and then, when the other man had calmed he continued, because they all needed to understand. "When Bracken took Cory, and bound her to him, the breaking of the first ritual…well, it probably broke her too. Poor thing," He added, "Odds are great this wasn't her choice." He looked around and swore to himself because Arturo wasn't there— Arturo was out inviting the enemy to a fucking banquet, and all hell had just broken quietly loose in Green's own ground.

With a grunt of frustration he caught the eyes of Mario and La Mark. Not his first choice, he thought grimly, since it put them in Goshawk's path, but it couldn't be helped. "Gentlemen," He murmured, "Since you're here, could you go find her body? It's probably in an alleyway or dumpster not far from here—I would imagine Bracken didn't have much time to…bind…to her before he came back up. And…gentleman?" They both turned to look at him seriously. "Don't talk to anybody—especially not helpless looking young people. She might not have been the only mind-wiping time-bomb Mist compelled." They nodded gravely, but Green was far from reassured.

"So…infidelity means death?" Cory asked, before breaking into a panicked coughing. The two young men passed by her, laying supportive hands on her shoulder as they went. Later, Cory would remember that, because she hadn't even met the two of them yet, and that contact steadied her enough to calm down her coughing fit. Green smiled at her a little in reassurance as the door closed behind them.

"It's okay, baby." He said, in a voice meant for her alone. "You and me, and you and Nicky…we happened before you and Bracken…The sylph's spell is encoded with her genetics—it's a part of her very soul. I doubt this spell is like that—even Mist and Morana wouldn't even know how to eliminate previous connections. Most bindings are done without any. I'm pretty sure you're still safe with us."

"Thank the Goddess." Nicky said unashamedly, and Renny pat his shoulder in an obvious show of sympathy.

"However," Green added, with a glare at Nicky, "Anyone else—Andres, for example?" And she closed her eyes at this, "He would need Bracken's approval and permission—maybe even his presence and…well, his participation. Other-wise…well Bracken's fate would be like that of the sylph."

"Oh Goddess" Cory choked, and she looked at Bracken, and reached out a helpless hand to take his in comfort. She cringed, with a little moan in her throat when once more he shook her off as though he couldn't bear her touch. "We're bound…I'm married…his life depends on me? Bracken didn't even have time to ask me…or me to say yes…or…" She looked at Green, still helpless. "Or you and me to say yes, or any of us to choose…and now…is this for always? For my life?"

"Both of your lives." Green replied, "But one sided. When you die, Bracken will die, but you can survive his death."

Cory turned white, and swayed on her feet for a moment, and if he didn't have an armload of despondent elf, he would have reached for her. "Oh, Jesus. Bracken, you *wanted* to do this?" She asked devastation clear in her eyes.

Bracken was enmeshed in his own private hell, and couldn't answer her, but Green could. He met her gaze levelly, tenderly, and murmured, "He'd already asked me about it. If you said yes, I was going to let him."

Cory took a deep breath, closed her eyes tightly, and opened them as Bracken looked painfully over his shoulder at her and nodded. Oh, Goddess, Green could see her thinking as she opened her eyes, the pain of it all was still here. A third time she reached out a hand and a third time Bracken burrowed into Green, looking for solace and redemption. Cory took a stumble back into the wall and looked blindly at Bracken's hand, and then met Green's gaze with her own tortured eyes. "I've got to get the fuck out of here." She whispered hoarsely. Green didn't try to stop her—none of them tried to stop her, and after grabbing her purse and her jacket, which were hanging in the entry way, she did just that.

"Fuck." Green swore succinctly, in the silence left by the slamming door, "Renny, Nicky—follow her—do you have your phones? Great." The two of them were already grabbing jackets and halfway down the hall. "It's full fucking daylight, there's not a vampire in sight to protect her...bugger-fuck it all..." He swore as they disappeared, and Bracken staggered against him.

She needed to be alone—anyone could see it, but of all the fucking worst times...he swore again, and assisted Bracken to the living room. Cory had already proved she could take care of herself, he prayed, and if Bracken had a chance of making it through this with his soul intact, Green had to stay with him now.

"You know," Green murmured, when the silence of the nearly empty apartment had descended on them like the crashing of symbols, and was still ringing in Green's ears, "The human military has a word for a day like today."

"Please share." Bracken asked, hanging his head between his knees and forcing himself to breathe evenly.

"Clusterfuck." Green all but spat. He kept rubbing Bracken's back, like a parent would a child, because Brack was more than a rival, he was one of Green's children, and Goddess it hurt to see him hurt like this. So it was an immense relief when the rusty sound that followed the dirty word was Bracken's pained laughter.

"Okay, brother," Green soothed, feeling hope as he leaned his temple against Brack's, "How many languages do I have to use to convince you that this was not your fault?"

CORY

Blood and Ink

My lungs hurt and my legs shook, but I still practically ploughed over Arturo as I pounded down the stairs. When I hurtled off the stairs and down the street I heard Renny shout "Follow us!" But I just kept right on going; the three of them trailed me like a rock star's entourage.

"What happened?" Arturo asked Renny, as she dragged him along.

"Drama." Renny said tersely, and I was practically running now, and they were jogging to keep up, and a part of me was thinking that this wasn't fair; they were trying to protect me, and I was taking my...well my every emotion under the sun, actually, out on the three of them. And I couldn't do it for long, I knew, because my breath was coming in gasps and my side hurt and my whole body felt like the brief jog down the hallway, down the stairs and halfway down the block was akin to getting beaten by hammers because my body just wasn't that strong yet.

"What sort of drama?"

"Well," Nicky gasped behind Renny, "Apparently Cory got laid too much— and that's gotta be drama, right?"

I missed Arturo's disgusted look, but I could practically hear it, I knew him so well by now. And I'd missed him, too, this last month when he'd stayed at home on Green's hill.

"Goddess, *mija,*" Arturo panted at me, "What drama could have happened in the time I was gone to warrant this?"

And something in me broke. I'd wanted Green or Bracken to hold me, as everything—the violation Bracken endured, the binding I'd never asked for, the being so desperately in love with two men at the same time that something like this, out of the blue, was all but ripping me apart—as it had all exploded, I had wanted to be held, and Green had—rightly so, I knew, and I blessed him for it— Green had needed to comfort Bracken, who felt like he'd betrayed me and wouldn't take my own comfort, no matter how much it hurt me when he refused. And here was Arturo, who didn't need me, or want me, or love me sexually, like Green or Bracken or even Nicky. Arturo was simply big, and male, and he loved me like a favorite niece and now he was three feet behind me, honestly concerned about my welfare, and I hadn't seen him in a month and right this second he was the most beautiful being—supernatural or human—on the planet.

I pivoted on my right foot and did a 180 degree turn, past Nicky and Renny who almost fell down they were so confused, right into Uncle Arturo's startled chest. "Oh Jesus, Arturo…" I sobbed, and I couldn't even finish the sentence because I was coughing and crying at once, and because it was all such a mess of pain in my chest that all I could do was collapse on him weakly and cry.

I don't know how long it took him to calm me down. I have a hazy recollection of crying on him as he carried me down Bay Street and then took a left towards the warf and I was so emotionally exhausted that I couldn't even hate myself for being weak. I know we ended up, all four of us, in a Starbucks in Ghirardelli Square and Arturo was pumping caffeine and pound cake into me like gas into an RV. However, I didn't really come to until Renny showed up with four giant hamburgers from Friday's which was in the square itself, and I was wolfing two of them down with the pound cake and caramel latte. Renny and Nicky had been forced to give Arturo the details, because every time I tried to talk about the bonding I started to hiccup and blubber and cough, and about all I could do without freaking out was refuel my overtaxed body.

When it had all been said and Arturo had asked every relevant question under the sun *and* the moon, the big elf used one hand to wipe my mouth with a napkin, and another hand to cover my hand in his own.

"No drama now, *mija,*" He said after a moment, and captured my gaze with his own. Arturo had copper-lightning eyes, and he was the first elf and the first sidhe, and the first preternatural being I had ever recognized, and I realized, gazing into those strangely tranquil eyes, that I trusted him, and his steadiness, more than I had probably trusted any one else on earth. Arturo would help me, I thought with a brain growing more rational by the moment. Arturo could. He nodded, as though just with thinking the word 'trust' I had done something good.

"Good, *mija,*" He murmured, and he smiled at me with silver capped teeth. "Now, without all the drama, I want you to think very carefully, and I want you to ask yourself, what is it about this binding that hurts you most of all."

And it was like saying 'without all the drama' allowed my mind to trace that tangle of emotions back to each separate skein. "Bracken was violated." I said clearly, and knew this to be true. Bracken had been forced to so something against his will, and something that should have been beautiful and poignant had been invasive to me, and a major mindfuck to him.

Arturo nodded, and pat my hand in sympathy. "Yes. This is true." He murmured. "We can't change it. I'm sure Green is doing his best to help Bracken as we sit here and drink coffee."

Which brought me to the second thing that hurt worst. "He wouldn't let me help him, Arturo..." And my voice rose, because this one was a doozy. How could he not let me help him...if he loved me enough to marry me, shouldn't he let me help him, like Green had let me help him, and Adrian? Maybe the problem was, I thought in absolute misery, that I had been married, in one way or another, to too many men with too many problems, at too young an age. But there wasn't anything I could do about the bindings, I thought irritably, except be there for the people I was bound to.

"He couldn't, *mija...*" Arturo was saying gently. "Do you not understand? On some level he wanted this—which means that he wanted to be your rock, your absolute test of steadiness. How can he do that, if you have to pick up the pieces all the time?"

"How can *we* do this if I'm not allowed to pick up the pieces ever?" I countered, and Arturo actually grinned.

"You'll tell him exactly that, after Green has cleaned up the magic and the self-loathing it left behind, right?" I nodded, and Arturo continued to hold my hand. "But these are Bracken's hurts, for the most part, aren't they Cory?"

"Yeah."

"So what's Cory's biggest hurt...no, no, hush hush..." When my face crumpled for the umpteenth time. "Without the drama, remember?" Goddess, he was good...I felt it then, his magical attachment to that one phrase that kept me from losing my composure whenever he said 'without all the drama'. Clever, Arturo, clever and necessary, and the reason you're Green's most trusted friend.

"I never got a choice." I choked out. I looked at Renny and Nicky and they both took the hint and left—presumably for more sandwiches, because I seemed to have eaten three of the four they brought back. They have high metabolisms as well, I scolded myself, but it was too late now. It was all too late.

"I would have chosen Green." I said, looking up at Arturo, and I hoped he didn't read the absolute truth in my eyes, that meant I would have chosen Green at the beginning, if it had come down to a choice, because that would hurt beyond words and the world was too much hurt already. "Bracken was a choice, but it was one forced on me, and Nicky was another choice forced on me, and, before the shit storm hit, I would have chosen Green. *I* would have done the one way binding to *Green.*" My tears were falling again, but they were quiet, sob-less tears, and it was okay. "I don't think I can regret the things I've done, Arturo, but…now that I have two husbands, with fragile, breakable hearts, how do I choose Green?"

Arturo grimaced, sat back, and took a long draught of his cooling coffee. "It figures, Cory." He said ruefully, "The one thing that hurts you the most really is the one we have nothing to fix…"

"It feels like I haven't made a choice since I raised my neck to Adrian." I said bleakly, thinking it was the truth, but that it sounded cowardly to say it.

"You chose to come here." Arturo gestured around to this beautiful city that I had hardly seen because I'd been so immersed in misery.

"That was really for you guys, you know." I said after a moment, and he looked surprised. He should be—I hadn't confessed this to anybody, even Green.

"I was so lost, and you and Green and Bracken and Grace and even Renny were looking at me like you were so afraid I'd never find myself, and Bracken told me that it sounded like going to school was the one thing that was constant in my life…" I shrugged my shoulders. "I wanted you to feel better about me." I said simply. "I wanted to take that worry off of everybody's face, that fear that I'd never be whole again…I wanted you to grieve without worrying about how I'd grieve…" Arturo's hands came to cover mine and a weird little laugh forced its way out of my tightened lips, "And it's like all this shit that's happened down here is the only thing that's let me grieve for Adrian after all." And this was true as well. You could only say *My beloved is dead* so many times before deep in your heart you believe it, and you make peace with the idea that you'll never see his autumn-sky blue eyes, or touch his delicately planed face, or answer his love-it-or-lay-it smile or ease his soul-deep pain or make him laugh that naughty-little-boy laugh again.

"I'm sorry, little Goddess." Arturo said after a moment, grooves creasing his paranormally beautiful face. Since Nicky attacked me, and I'd seen Professor Cruickshank morph before my eyes, I hadn't had to look too hard to see past glamour to realize it was being used. Something in my experiences allowed me to see straight to the truth. I wondered what Arturo looked like to everybody else in the coffee shop, but whatever they saw, it couldn't be as beautiful or as dear as his expression of kindness was to me right now. "Green was afraid, you know, of using you as a weapon." He said after a moment of profound sorrow. "I told him to do it. I told him that the Goddess wouldn't have dropped you in our lap if that wasn't your express purpose." His sadness was a palpable thing. "In our wildest dreams, we never dreamed that Adrian would be a casualty of that decision."

"Adrian was a casualty of being Adrian." I said after a moment, bleakly, feeling like my soul was naked on an operating table in a vast theatre, and the doctor making the incision didn't give a shit if it hurt. "Only Adrian could have loved us all so much, and been so blind to the whole rest of the world, to fly out of the sky and grab death with both hands to save us from it." I shook my head, wishing for tears now, because I felt empty and drained and exhausted. "If I was supposed to be a weapon to protect him, it didn't work, but then, he didn't let it, did he?" I shook my head of that, because I was tired of being mad at my beloved for dying. I wanted to just love his memory instead.

"I don't mind being a weapon." I said after a moment. "I certainly didn't mind it the night that Adrian died—and that was clearly a decision I made on my own…I don't even mind being Queen of the vampires—although I've been running hell-be-damned away from that responsibility, God knows. It's just that…" ouchie, "Adrian marked me, and I never knew it. I've made my peace with it, but it still hurt, when I found out I wasn't even given a say. I still haven't embraced all the possibilities of it, and I can still see his purple aura, glowing from my neck when I look in the mirror just so. Nicky bound me, although I risked all our lives to avoid it, and we've all been pretending that I don't have to sleep with him eventually to keep him alive. And now Bracken…even though it was against his will…" My voice was rising, somewhat hysterically. "They don't mean to, Arturo, but they did…" I took a deep breath, but it didn't help. "I was never asked, it was never a choice, and even if it had been, and I probably would have said yes, but we'll never know now because I was never given a say! These men, these men who love me, they've marked me!" I exclaimed, before lowering my voice because it sounded like I'd been the victim of a Tom-cat incursion. Well, I guess, in a way I had.

"Just once, I would like to make my choice and do the marking…" I shook my head. It was ridiculous. The sidhe did magic, they didn't do jewelry. "I would just like to have it public that I had a say in who I am and who I love and that I have some sort of control over the absolute weirdness that has become my life."

Something I said caught Arturo's attention. "Marks...so...it's all about marks? And choice." He added that last part because I was about to protest. It was sort of an understatement, but it was close, so I nodded. "You know," He began, looking thoughtful, "One of the tribes that used to worship me...they had marriage, and they had divorce...it was a custom for them, that as for every lover they had, they put a mark on their body...one that represented their lover, or spouse..."

"Like a tattoo?" I asked, liking the idea so much it actually made my shoulders straighten and my chest lighter.

"Yes." He nodded, catching my mood, and we shared a slow smile. "Exactly like a tattoo." We sat there, grinning to each other for a moment, caught up in the idea like children. "I know just the place." He said, and, sure enough, Uncle Arturo had made everything all right.

"I'm jealous." Renny said frankly, a short time later as we trotted after Arturo through a series of turns and alleyways that would have, I was sure, left even the most comfortable city dweller completely lost. I was panting with the effort of keeping up with Arturo, and my knees felt watery. I was still not up to full speed, and it was irritating that my body kept betraying me when my emotions were one-hundred percent, but I was too proud and too excited about what we were doing to ask him to slow down or stop.

"That I'm getting a tattoo?" I asked, breaking out into a cough that I tried to smother. I had caught fire with the idea. I knew what I wanted. I wanted *Green,* and me and even Adrian, but definitely *Green.* I wanted him on my skin, for the world, preternatural or otherwise to see. I could never wear his wedding ring, and there were no elfish wedding words for an *o'ue'hm* who could have no *Anyaen,* (I know, I'd asked Arturo before Renny and Nicky got back) but I wanted *something* on my skin to prove that Green had marked my heart forever. On someone else my age I would have laughed, or mocked, or even earnestly begged her to reconsider. It was ridiculous, right, that a twenty-year old girl would know who she was bound to for eternity? But I was supernaturally married to two other men already, one of whom I might never love as more than a friend. I knew the meaning of "Til-Death-Do-Us-Part", and unlike the things that had been done to me, this was not a forcing of my will on Green's. It was a choice made by me. This alone made me feel free, and giddy, and powerful in a way that I had not felt since...well, I couldn't remember when. I wondered how many people could see me, a walking supernova, tear-assing down the street, drunk on my own free-will.

"I've always wanted one." Renny was saying, animated in a way I probably hadn't seen since we were in high school, and she was hanging with the academic crowd and talking about SAT scores or something. She was wearing an oversized man's T-shirt and Nicky's running shorts and a jacket that probably belonged to Grace because she was swimming in it like a kitten in the ocean. Her hair, which used to be kept in a perpetually perky pony-tail in high school, was now barely combed, wild and fly-away. She looked like a tawny cat I once had, whose coat got thicker every winter until the fur on her ruff stood up around her head like a halo. I was no longer a punk goth chick, and Renny was no longer an honors student—between the two of us we'd met somewhere in the preternatural no-man's land in the middle.

"You've wanted a tattoo?" If we wouldn't have lost Arturo I would have stopped and turned towards her, because this was interesting. Renny and I had been rooming together for months, crying in each other's arms on a regular basis for our lost lovers, eating pizza, watching movies, building a friendship based on the soul deep bonds of knowing loss and knowing that we lived in an exclusive little world that few other women our age would ever see. But Renny had been an honors student, and I had been a Goth chick, and those preconceptions based in high school are hard to lose, even two and three years after high school had spit us out on the shoals of a weird, bleak, and beautiful shore.

"Yeah…" Renny smiled sadly. "Mitch and I would have gotten ones that matched, but…" she shrugged. But were-animals healed very fast, and a tattoo would only last a few days, and two changes at the most into your alternative form. Renny had two tiny holes in each ear to hang earrings, but she had gotten those when she was a child. The only real wound she carried anymore was the one on her heart.

"What would you get?" I asked, genuinely curious.

"Now?" She thought for a moment, as Arturo took one more left, and suddenly we were faced with a dead end of brick wall, and sandwiched between a giant, graffiti walled building, and a neat, tiny, and very Celtic tattoo parlor. Renny's face twitched in a way I recognized—it was a twitch of grief being tabled for a time when someone wasn't watching. "Mitch as a cat, curled around a flower." She said with a quirk to her mouth.

"A flower?" My voice was neutral.

"He bought me a flower every night after we got off work." They had worked at one of Green's many tiny foothills restaurants, and had stopped off at the Chevron I'd worked in at the time. Mitch had bought those flowers from me. Renny laughed shortly. "Adrian would have given us all the money we wanted, but Mitch wanted to keep it real, he said, so we were just sort of scraping by, and I don't know how Mitch managed to get me the most beautiful roses…"

"Rolled pennies." I said roughly, hoping she wouldn't guess the rest—that I had bought the flowers for more than Mitch had paid for them, knowing that Mitch was buying flowers with the love of his heart and not a hell of a lot else.

"Really?" She asked, thankfully oblivious. "But…it was just that…I loved knowing he loved me enough to be that thoughtful…you know? It was like, any struggle was worth it, to have that particular man bring me flowers…as long as I live, I'll associate Mitch and flowers in a vase…I may move on…" and she flushed now, thinking of Officer Max, I was sure, "But that image, the big tom cat and his vase of flowers…I'd love to be able to show that to the world some-how…"

"You may get your wish." Arturo said gently, gesturing us into the tidy white shop. "Ladies, Dominic, meet Lloyd."

Lloyd was shorter than Arturo and taller than Nicky. He was young, but had laugh lines around his eyes that came with his genes, and not with his age or even his disposition, although he seemed good tempered. He had a bold, rather hooked nose, long pointed ears, and shoulder length hair that was black dyed over spring green. To someone not accustomed to the fey, they may have thought the dye job was the other way around, but I knew. Lloyd seemed to be friendly, and judging by the quality of the artwork on the sterile, white walls he was very talented, but he was obviously not human.

He turned and greeted Arturo with bird-bright eyes and a very toothy smile. "Arturo, buddy, how's things—what are you doing here?" He held out a long-boned, blunt fingered hand, which Arturo shook, and took in Nicky, Renny and I with that same toothy grin. Abruptly his gaze shifted back to me and nar-rowed, and to my intense discomfort he bowed, long, low, and deep.

"*O'ue'eir.*" He said reverently, and I blushed. So I guess the whole preternatu-ral world knew who I was.

"Lloyd." I smiled, nodding a little in return, and hoped Arturo would break awkwardness.

"Oddly enough," He said, bless him, "That's exactly why I've brought her here."

A remarkably short time after that, Renny and I stood, our shirts over our heads with our middles leaning against a counter and staring sheepishly at our own reflections in the wall-length mirror behind it. We would have had to unhook bras, but I had dressed too quickly to remember one, and Renny had always had the body of a sylph and had never needed one. The tattoo needles buzzed like rabid bees, stinging our skin swollen, but I guess one of the perks of knowing preternatural beings (and, well, *being* one, really) was that the needles were bespelled. Although their hands *blurred* in that heady, supernatural hyper speed that was about to make a three hour job into a one hour job, Renny and I could barely feel the touch of the needle.

Renny's artist, a terrifyingly tall, willowy elf of indeterminate rank, worked in the silence of her own head, I guess, because Renny was chatting nervously with me, Lloyd (who was busy with my back), Arturo, Nicky, and anyone who would listen. Considering how mouse quiet she had been with other people for the last few months I was both relieved and worried by this sudden storm of breeze and banter now.

"You're sure it won't come off, right?" She was saying to Lloyd. Everything was still about her except that fuzzy, straight, fly-away head of hair and her fine brown eyes.

"Do I look human to you, little were-cat?" Lloyd responded in good humored exasperation. "I'm full sidhe, Spider is full sidhe, and that is our hearts blood in this ink. Do you think we'd spill it if it meant we had to do this *again* for every were-creature who walked through our doors?"

"I'm sorry." Renny would have shrugged, but we were both frozen in a magical immobility. Like I said, the supernatural world has its perks. "It's just that..." her eyes caught mine in the mirror. "Mitch didn't even have a body to bury." She whispered. "Our apartment was unsubstantial, all the books were mine...This is his memorial, on my back, right?" I nodded, knowing to the deep flesh of my nerve endings what she was trying to say.

"We're human." I murmured, with a quirk of my lips because not one of us, Nicky, Renny, or myself, really was human. "We want that proof, that our lovers lived, and that their lives mattered, and that our sorrow isn't their only marker in the world."

Renny nodded, and a little of her manic energy dissipated. "You do that." She said after a moment. "It's like...I remember the two of us, checking out the same books in high school," Although we hadn't been friends, at least not then, "And I always wondered if people really talked like that—and when it's important, you do. You sound like a Walter Scott poem."

"I do not!" I protested, but flushing because my words were still ringing in my ears and maybe it was true.

"Sure you do." Nicky said from his side of the store. People who weren't getting their flesh rendered into art didn't get to cross the line—although Arturo was an exception, I guessed, because he was two steps behind Lloyd, viewing the white skin of my back with a critical eye and nodding approvingly. It would figure, I could almost sigh, that this too would be one of Green's businesses. "You

do it practically every time you talk about Adrian, Green—even Mitch sometimes. Even Bracken is starting to get the Biblical diction treatment."

"I don't." I denied again, but they had me and I knew it. "At least not on purpose." I mumbled.

"Its okay, Corinne Carol-Anne." Arturo reassured. "You do it for the same
reason Adrian loved you—there's a great heart beating in your chest. Poetry
always comes with a great heart."

"Oh for crap's sake!" I exclaimed, "Can we just change the fucking subject?"

And that made everybody laugh, as it was supposed to, and they obliged me
by talking about what Green would think about my tat. But Renny's words hung
in my ears. Adrian didn't have a body to bury either. All he had to prove he had
ever existed was the Goddess Grove, and I didn't even remember making that.
Even the mark on my back was Adrian, Green, and me, all intertwined, like the
trees in the grove. For the first time it hit me, that the only part of Adrian that
had existed without the two of us, was the part that had flickered through the
night like black flame, and come out of nowhere to grab death in both hands. It
was a sad and awful thought to have about your beloved, and then Lloyd spoke
up behind me and made things worse.

"So, there's for your beloved, and your *o'ue'hm*. Now how about your *due'alle*,
and your *ue'alle*. " He gestured towards Nicky when he said this last one, and I
crossed my eyes trying to put the new Elf word into my steadily growing lexicon.

"'ue' means allegiance owed." I murmured. "'alle' means male lover. He's the
male lover who owes his allegiance to me?"

In the mirror I could see Lloyd and Arturo nodding approvingly.

"And I know that *due* means 'equal other' right?" And they nodded again. I bit
my lip, thinking about it, because my meditation on elvish grammar had basically
been to buy me time. "I don't know…" I murmured. "I mean—the whole point
of this exercise was to…well, to make a mark for Green…for my *o'ue'hm*, right?
Nicky and Bracken…well they've sort of had their say on me, preternaturally
speaking." I tried very hard to make my voice wry and understanding because
Nicky was standing right there, and Goddess knows he felt bad enough already.

Lloyd nodded, kindly, and put his hand right above the new ink-and-blood
wound that sat on the small of my back, as though feeling something that was not
there yet. "I do understand, little Goddess." He murmured after a moment. "I
understand, that your first instinct, as a human, would be to feel violated, to feel
as though your life was wrenched from your grasp, and you want to make up for
that…this mark on your back is symmetry, that is what you are thinking?"

I nodded my head slowly, trying not to blink with the emotions behind my eyes. "You're very astute." I managed through a shredded throat.

"But the heart has no symmetry." He had moved very close behind me, and when I looked into the mirror, I could see his eyes. They were over large, without the glamour that other humans would see, so large in fact, that they almost overtook his face, spreading, like still pools of water on concrete, black and fathomless.

"But I need balance..." I replied somewhat desperately. His eyes were growing larger, I thought muzzily, aware of his hand on my back, and the fact the skin beneath it was throbbing against him, as though there were something in my body trying to beat its way out.

"Balance is not symmetry." Lloyd continued, still kind, but implacable. His voice was a fading hum in my ear, and still I was mesmerized by the giant, still, glinting pools in the mirror, and the picture I could almost...I could now see..."Tell me—if you think you can balance your *o'ue'hm* and your *due'alle* so logically, what would you do..."

His voice receded, and it was me and Bracken and Green and Nicky, all on a cliff. I could smell the wind in the air, smelling like ocean, and hear the cry of gulls overhead. The sea itself was grey and green and angry, and the precipice was frighteningly high, with a brutal drop and terrible, eviscerating rocks below. Not even a sidhe could survive that drop. I don't know how I would know that—as far as I knew they could survive anything, but as surely as I could feel Green's hair whipping in my eyes, and the vertigo from being so close to the sheer drop, I knew it would be fatal.

Green smiled at me kindly, told me not to worry, although I don't remember speaking, and I could smell his peculiar mix of animal and wild flowers when he touched my face, and Bracken brushed his lips against my temple and I could feel the heat of his lips on my brow. Nicky said something wise-assed behind me, and I could feel my relief that he was there to ease the moment, and the whole scene shifted, like a movie with lost frames and the lovely tableau went to hell.

Without warning, the men pitched over the edge, falling helplessly, arms flailing, fear on their faces, and I threw myself stomach-down on the edge of the cliff, catching Green's arm in one hand, and Bracken's on the other. Nicky changed, quicker than everything else, and flew overhead, shrieking like his heart would break, but my elbows were cracking where they were hyper-extended, and my arms were jerked so hard it felt like they'd been yanked cleanly out of their sockets and still my lovers dangled below me, Green and Bracken, my *o'ue'hm* and my *due'alle,* and I could save one of them, Goddess help me, I could save one of them, but I could not save them both.

They read it in my face, they could see that I was slipping, and that if I kept hold of both of them, all three of us would die. Green wanted to let go...it was agonizing, how much he wanted to make that sacrifice for us, to let go, to shatter on the soul-chewing rocks and know sweet oblivion and afterlife with all those he'd loved. But he couldn't. He couldn't let go. I couldn't let him go. I needed him too much...*We* needed him too much, and he had to live or all our lives would be for nothing and Bracken looked at me and looked at his leader, the man he'd loved and followed for all his life and he knew this too.

I saw his lips move, benediction, blessing, farewell? I couldn't see what he said, but I knew his intent, and with all the slow motion of horrible memories he let go of my hand himself, and hurtled sluggishly to his death, as Green's other hand sought my now empty one, and we started the scrabble to safety. Nicky shrieked and dived, catching Bracken's arms in his talons, but Bracken was too heavy, his momentum too great, and Nicky's wings, outstretched and heaving, snapped like a broken umbrella in mid-fall. I could hear his bird's shriek of agony just as his and Bracken's body hit the rocks below and were swallowed by the green-gray sea which receded...

...to a pool of gray water which receded...

...to a pair of sympathetic sidhe eyes, staring back at me in a mirror with more compassion and understanding than I could have possibly imagined.

I sucked in a breath to keep from screaming and threw myself forward against the counter, shoulders heaving, trying not to sob. My shoulders and elbows ached dully, the pain receding much more quickly than the memory of what had not happened.

"You bastard..." I wept, trying to gain control of my voice, "I trusted you...why did you make me live that...why did you make me make that choice...."

"What choice?" He asked quietly, and Renny and Nicky were looking at me as though I'd lost my mind.

"What the fuck was that?" "What the hell happened?" And from Arturo, with a calmer, wiser voice, "What was it you saw, Corinne Carol-Anne?"

"They were dangling from...off a cliff...I couldn't save them both..." I looked up at Arturo, eyes streaming..."Bracken...let go...to save Green, to keep me from making the decision...from having to live with it myself...Oh Jesus..."

And because Lloyd was closer than even Arturo, he's the one that caught me when my knees buckled and he's the one who helped me into the dentist's chair nearby, and he's the one who stroked my hair.

"So your *due'alle* died, rather than make you choose between him and your *o'ue'hm*." He summed up quietly. "Why would you have chosen your *o'ue'hm?*"

"We need him." I choked, hating the bitterness. "He's my *o'ue'hm* instead of my *due'alle* because we need him. Because everybody needs him and not just me, and that's why he had to live." Of course, a big aching voice in my head was saying. Of course Bracken would have to make that decision. After all was said and done, it was the same decision Adrian had made. Oh, Goddess…and I started to cry even harder, that was truth. Adrian hadn't just died to save me and Green. He'd died because Green was the leader and I was the weapon and he knew that we would live without him and he could not have lived without us.

"It's a hard truth." Lloyd agreed, still stroking my hair like a long beloved uncle. "Do you imagine it's something your *due'alle* doesn't know?"

My breath came to a shuddering halt in my chest, and I saw a series of Bracken's most vulnerable expressions—before we'd made love, in the warehouse, when he thought I was just using his lust to charge my supernatural batteries; when he told Green and I that he'd follow me to the grave because Green couldn't; and, most recently, when I'd left him sitting on the couch because Green was home, and I couldn't wait for just a moment of propriety to go embrace my *o'ue'hm*.

"No." I murmured, hurting for Bracken all those times in memory as I had not ached for him at that moment. "He knows." I choked again, trying not to sob outright. "He's always known." So had Adrian. But we'd been young and it had been my first love and who thinks of losing your first love so soon after finding him?

"Mmmm…" Lloyd murmured. "So, about that mark you wanted for your lovers…"

I nodded, feeling limp and empty all of a sudden. "Yeah." I rasped. "We need one for Bracken, shedding his heart's blood for all of us." I looked up at Nicky, and saw his expression of complete sympathy for me, with none for himself. Nicky had tried to save Bracken, I remembered, just to save me from pain. He had died to save me from pain. "And one for Nicky, too, who needs to be loved." I finished, and Nicky's look of gratitude almost broke my heart anew.

"Good." Lloyd said happily, turning me back towards the mirror and repeating the little ditty that kept me still. "You came up with the original design—I'll stay true to that. Leave all the rest to me."

GREEN

Ink and Magic

"Where the fuck is she?" Bracken repeated for the millionth time. "She's still sick, you know." Green closed his eyes and counted to two million by tens. He had managed to get Bracken showered and dressed, and for once the Goddess was smiling because there was a basketball game on television, and the other sidhe was occupied raging at the screen and pumping his arms—a ritual Green had never understood. The last two hours had been a combination of two refrains—"Goddammit, the Kings haven't been the same since they traded Christie and Webber." And "Where the fuck is she?" Green couldn't decide which phrase was wearing on his nerves more.

La Mark and Mario had returned shortly after Cory had left. They hadn't found the sylph, but they were pale and shaking, full of a horrific tale of a dumpster full of the stench of death and a pool of what looked like dissolved flesh, and not a living creature, not a mouse nor a rat nor a cockroach anywhere in the alley with it. Green had thanked the two of them, and they had asked, with strained sober voices, if Green could comfort them any way he could. Considering how very straight Mario's orientation and how very hesitant La Mark was about acknowledging his own proclivities, their fear and their disgust and sorrow must have been overwhelming for the two young Avians. But Green was powerful, sensitive to their needs, and all it had taken was a gentle kiss on each forehead, and the two of them had been rolled easily into a dreamless, healing sleep.

"Are you sure they're safe?" Bracken asked again, interrupting Green's thoughts. "I mean, where the fuck did they go?"

One-million-nine-hundred-ninety-nine-thousand-nine-hundred and ninety. Two million. Nope. His nerves were still frayed. "Arturo said another hour at the least when he called, and if you ask me again I'll fry the fucking television."

Bracken looked up at Green from lowered brows, sulky and apologetic at once. Green sighed and looked at the game. The Goddess may have been smiling, but she was still in a bitchy mood about something, because the goddamned Kings were down by three. With a sound of disgust, he threw himself back into the couch next to Bracken and took a chance and rubbed Bracken's back. A year ago…hell, six weeks ago, he could have healed Brack's heart with the animal comfort of flesh and sweetness, but Cory had changed that forever. In becoming Cory's, Bracken had ceased to be Green's, and Green could live with that, but Bracken was hurting and Green couldn't help.

"Sorry." His voice was almost inaudible.

"You want to talk about it?" Please, Goddess, Green prayed, let Bracken want to talk about it.

"That I was mind-wiped and practically raped and then I went and did the same damned thing to my *due'ane?* Yeah. I really want to talk about that."

"You think Cory doesn't understand about violation?" Green asked, honestly surprised. "Have you forgotten the day she vomited power down the sink because she couldn't stand to be touched?"

"No." Bracken murmured. He swallowed, hard. "I haven't forgotten that day."

But the young sidhe's voice wasn't any less bleak, and that air he had of self-loathing wasn't any less grim. They had so much to do and so little time, and if Bracken was still wounded, Cory wouldn't be up for what they needed…Green winced, even from his own rationalization. The truth would help Bracken. That was real. That was truth. But Oh, Goddess, Green didn't want to have to be the one to tell it. Cory's words about being something less than the sun and the moon and the stars were still ringing in his ears, and he told himself she was right. Bracken would still love his leader, and Bracken's heart might heal just a little. Just enough to let Cory do the rest. He stared at the television for a moment. Four minutes left in the game and the teams were down to fouling each other to buy time, so he had maybe a half-an-hour to say what he had to with the comforting buffer of background noise and familiar pastime between them.

He cleared his throat and closed his eyes and took a deep breath, and when he started speaking it still felt like a long plunge into frigid water. "There's a lot that's good about us, Bracken," He said baldly after a moment, "And a lot that we don't talk about that's bad." The other man turned and looked at him, and Green for once was concentrating fiercely on the game as he spoke.

"The downside to being a high elf, and a sidhe, is even though our sexual...fluidity...gives us certain freedoms, it's easy for the worst of us to violate you...us...people in the worst ways and just walk away." He said after a moment, aware the Bracken was shooting him a startled look, and Green took a deep breath and tried again. "They don't see...it has never occurred to them that just because a body isn't yelling and screaming, or chained in a filthy hold, or biting or scratching, that just because you're not begging them to stop...they don't realize that just taking away a choice makes it a violation..." He was doing badly. He was talking in generalities, but, Goddess, just like Adrian, a hundred and fifty years of silence was a fearsome thing to break. And unlike Adrian, Green had told no one before this, not even Cory, who had guessed and accepted, without ever needing the horrible details. Bracken was still looking at him like he was speaking an entirely different language, backwards.

Green stared at Mist like he was speaking an entirely different language, backwards. "I'm sorry," He murmured, "Could you repeat that?"

"You can't leave, my brother." Mist said, reaching up and stroking Green's hair back from his fine, handsome sidhe face. "Oberon wants you. I want you. You're just too valuable to lose, and that's that."

"That's shite." Green had laughed, and swung his small knapsack of treasured things over his shoulder. He'd told Mist that he was leaving. He was a wood-elf; he had been free all his life. "Oberon doesn't care if I stay or go...so I'll go."

Mist's face hardened, was haughty, was proud, was all of the things Green had seen the day before, and had learned to loathe in a remarkably short time. "But I care, little Green, and Oberon cares about me."

"I have many talents as a sidhe." He tried again. "But the thing I'm best at, the thing you all know me for...well, there's really one place that can be used, and it's not a board room or a battlefield, and if it's not getting people property or prestige or protection...well, even elves have their own prejudices against sex, right?"

"No." Bracken said numbly, the game forgotten. "No. That's not what I was taught. That's not what *you* taught me."

"I'm not your whore." He said, looking at Oberon, shocked. "I came here of my free will..."

"And let my child use you of your free will." Oberon said. The great man himself, because Green had pounded so insistently at his shields in an attempt to be free of Oberon's great faerie hill that the King of Faerie had been forced to intervene before

Green shed more of his precious life blood, and weakened Oberon's own powers in his pounding against the walls of a doorless room. "In my home, that binds you."

"I don't wish to be bound." Green responded, knowing his hands were dripping ichor even as he stood, and that he was barely restraining the despair of the trapped bird in his shoulders, and the muscles of his arms, and his heart.

Oberon had grinned then, a flashing, charming grin on his ruddy, handsome face. "Oh, you do have spirit—I'll have to send Titania in to see if you're as good with women as you are with men." His hands went then, to his golden belt of hammered links, and as his black leather pants fell to his ankles Green could taste the bile of despair.

His eyes fixed sightlessly on the screen, Green nodded in response to Bracken's words and pulled himself forcibly out of the past. Sacramento was up by one, Kobe Bryant had fouled out, hurray for the home team. A breath in the present. And then another. And then we don't have to live that awful first moment as the King's favorite courtesan.

"I taught you that way because it's what I came to believe." He said at last, feeling raw. Goddess, Bracken wasn't the only one who wanted Cory at this moment.

Bracken reached towards him, and Green fought the impulse to shrug off that hand and hurt Bracken as Bracken had hurt Cory. He suffered the awkward hand on his shoulder and felt better for it.

"I was a courtesan for a time, in Oberon's court." He continued baldly, knowing that courtesan wasn't even the right word for it, but neither was whore or prostitute, so he stuck with courtesan and ploughed right on. "It was sort of a step up for me, right?" That's what Mist had told him, anyway. He still couldn't leach the irony out of his voice. "Out of the woods, into the court? But no one told me that once I was there, I was trapped."

"Like Cory is now?" More self-pity, more anger turned inward. Green looked at him to snap at him and tell him to pull his head out, but he stopped. Heaven alone knew how confused Bracken must be right now because Green wasn't doing this right, not at all.

"No." Green whispered, having to look away at the last. "Like…like Cory would have been, if Arturo had never walked into the gas station and discovered her power. Or, worse, if he had known, but none of us had ever been able to do anything to help her use it. Can you imagine?"

"She would have died." Bracken said numbly, that hand on Green's shoulder feeling less and less awkward and more and more necessary.

"It may have come to that." Green agreed, but he smiled, and it was both the best and worst a smile has to offer. "But I'd been a wood elf for too long, right? I knew what freedom was, I wanted it back…and the only way to get it back is to get power."

"You get your power from sex…" Bracken said, and Green could see him figuring it out as he said it.

"It seems so simple, doesn't it?" He asked. "But Mist and Morana never got it, and Titania and Oberon were completely clueless. As you have cause to know, I'm *very* good at what I do. The more they kept me trapped in the bedroom like a combination stud-stallion and inflatable doll, the more people came to my bed, people who started to like me, even love me, more than they loved their own leaders. And my power grew. For every sidhe who came to my bed when they might have been somewhere else, I grew a little stronger. And I was a wood-elf, right? Born in the woods, Vernal Green, Lord of Meadows—Goddess how they used to laugh at that. It was so…common, so low, to those in the greatest Faerie Hill in the old country, right? So no one questioned me going off into the woods around the court. Mocked me for it, yes, but none of them questioned me. It's not like I could get past Oberon's orchard walls, and it was obvious that keeping me trapped in my room would kill me, and that would be a waste of a good toy.

"I grew those lime trees in sunlit private and moonlit secret—everyone knows that story. Forty lime trees in a barren new country bought me my Faerie hill. And I stole the power to make those lime trees hale and hearty enough to cross the ocean, and to keep me from withering on the salt water, and for all of us to thrive here, because I could see that they were a thing that would be needed in the new world just like they would be needed on board a ship, and because unlike the rest of the court I knew what sort of business you had to do to survive. So every time Mist or Morana came to me because they liked to…"

Morana stretched, cat-like, as Green came up for air from between her thighs. Mist sat at the head of the bed, stroking her hair as she shivered in orgasm, smiling at Green like a favored pet, who had just performed a service.

"You see, my dear," Mist said, murmuring in urbane tones, as though talking about a pretty painting, "He really is very talented."

"Oh yes," Morana said, propping herself on her elbows and using a fine-boned long-toed foot to rub on Green's bare shoulders like she were petting a cat. "He's wonderful—I'm surprised you didn't share him before now."

Green smiled back, glowing with the power she'd given him in sex, controlling the hammering of his heart with an effort. Neither of them could know, he thought, hiding panic with another carefully placed swipe of his tongue. Neither of them could know that every time they graced him with their needs instead of each other, that he stole the power they gave him just as they had stolen his freedom.

"Because they thought it would hurt me, they really paved the way and paid the hand and turned the key to let me the hell out of there."

Green breathed deeply through is nose and took a sideways look at Bracken, Cory's *due'alle.* "Please don't cry for me, brother." He asked softly from a tight throat, because he could see Bracken blinking against the tears in that way that men have to keep the sobs from breaking loose in their chests. "Please don't cry for me." He wouldn't, *couldn't* cry for himself. He had shed too many bitter tears, trapped in a room done in gold and silver and velvet and silk, without a window and without a hope, and he had sworn that once he'd stepped out of that room for good he'd never shed another tear for it. But Bracken didn't see that, and needed to shed his own tears, and Green had no option but to plough on.

"See...we've all been wounded." Goddess, what an understatement. "We've all been violated. Me, Adrian, Cory, Renny—hell, even Nicky, and now you. It's what happens when you're given great gifts—wonderful, amazing, beautiful gifts. Great buggering git asshole fuckheads always want to steal those gifts for themselves. Being wounded means you held on, that's all. Being wounded means you can heal. If we live long enough with these gifts, and we're not wounded, it means we're probably like Mist and Morana and Sezan and Goshawk and hell, even Titania and Oberon, although I didn't know either of them more than to give them the best fuck available at court, right? If we're not capable of being hurt, then we're not good enough people to deserve the Goddess's gifts in the first place. If you don't know that you have something to lose, then maybe you deserve to lose it, and Blessed Father, Holy Mother, Beloved Son, all of us know what we have to lose, because we've all lost it at one time or another and none of us wants to feel that pain again..."

And then he couldn't speak anymore, because Bracken, who didn't want to be touched, had pulled Green into his arms, and every vow Green had made not to weep anymore for his lost freedom and violated faith fell at his feet with his brother's tears. Both of them held there, still, clenched together so tightly their muscles ached. And they held, and held, and held, until they could breathe freely and look clearly and know that neither of them would be weeping soon again. With an unspoken word, they both pulled back and resumed their human male posture on the couch, face forward, eyes glued to the screen.

"Aw fuck." Bracken said after a moment, his voice almost normal. "The Kings lost by three."

Then there was a pounding across the hall, and the entryway door opened, and both of them ran with relief to greet Cory.

She looked happy, was Green's first thought. Her cheeks were flushed and she'd been talking excitedly through a coughing fit to Renny and Nicky as they entered. Arturo came in behind them, looking amused, like a babysitter surprised to find that babysitting was even more fun than a party on a Saturday night.

"You can't make fun of Arturo." She was saying as she walked in. "The knitting needles are for Grace, and it's harder than it..." Her voice trailed off as Bracken rushed across the landing to her. "Looks." She finished, meeting his eyes cautiously. Her gaze flickered to where Green stood, and an odd smile crossed her face. It wasn't an entirely happy smile; it was as though she were finally recognizing something about him—something about *them*—that she hadn't seen before. Bracken pulled her in to him wordlessly, and she hugged him back for all she was worth, but her eyes stayed fixed on Green's until some bittersweet emotion overwhelmed her and she squeezed them shut.

Suddenly Bracken was swearing and pulling back from her, holding his hands out in front of him, when they had been inside her jacket up against her back. His palms and the front of his fingers were covered in blood.

"Dammit, Cory, what in the hell...!"

She stepped back from him with a little laugh. "Oh...sorry...it's the tattoo..." She murmured.

Green knew his eyebrows must have shot up to his hairline, and a slow grin took over his face. He knew her. He *knew* his beloved. This was going to be something big. But Bracken was not quite so quick, and his exasperation only grew.

"Fuck it all...now I'm going to have to be careful about you until you heal..."

Cory stepped back from him and held her hands out to his bloodied ones as though touching palm to palm, but keeping that distance between them that would keep her blood in her body. She made sure his eyes were glued to hers before she spoke.

"No, *due'alle*, we're going to have to be very careful of each other." Suddenly she grinned at him, to break the seriousness of the moment. "But Lloyd said that if Green kisses my back, it should be enough to heal it completely...so..." She beamed a shining glance at Green. "What about it, *o'ue'hm*—a kiss for everybody, and then we can have the unveiling, right?"

"Everybody?" He asked, surprised and catching the contagious enthusiasm that Cory had wrapped around the group of them.

"We all got one!" Renny spoke up, and she was shining with pride too.

"I didn't want to be left out…" Nicky broke in with a shy smile, and Arturo shrugged, looking sheepish. Green merely raised his eyebrows at him, and Arturo, still trying to maintain that superior calm he was so good at said, "It was, after all, my idea."

"Will it last?" Bracken wanted to know. "I mean…Cory—Jesus, Cory, I can't believe…of all the hare brained…" He shook himself, remembering what he was saying. "I mean, will *everybody's* tattoos stay on? You're all…none of you are human!" He looked up at Arturo, asking for his help, and then remembered that Arturo had one too. "Including you!" He said at last.

Cory was laughing softly at his shock and irritation. She put a quiet hand up near his face and held it there, so everybody watching could almost feel the caress just by watching the nearness. "Ssshhh…. Sh…just see, okay Bracken? They're special. I mean, they're made with sidhe heart's blood, so they're *really* special, but the designs are…" Again, that oblique look at Green, "They're good. They're meaningful. They're real to us…just wait, sweetie, okay? Just wait and see…"

"Well, dammit, Cory," Renny complained good naturedly, "Now you have to go first."

"We have to go wash off the blood and the goop and crap anyway." Cory waved her off. We might as well just let him heal us and go change and the first person dressed can show them when we're done, right?"

It was such a casual decision, Green thought, but equitable and breezy and easily done. In one moment she had resolved a conflict, made everyone feel better, and gave Green a chance to talk to each person who'd returned. She smiled briefly at Green as she moved past Bracken to hang up her coat, and he knew for a fact that she'd done it all on purpose. Whatever had happened since she'd run out of the apartment in blind misery had been not just relieving, but empowering. She was so much his queen now, that the idea that he might never have known her if not for Adrian was enough to make him wonder if the Goddess herself had a hand at getting her a job at the Chevron station.

Arturo waved off the kiss, but allowed Green a brief touch on the skin above his wrist, where the bandage was taped. A tiny green flare and he sauntered off to the shower. Renny's tiny, cat-like face lit up with sly anticipation as she lifted her humongous white T-shirt and gave Green access to the bare spot on her back above her bandaged tattoo. Green took his time then, allowing his lips to linger on her sweet skin. She smelled like cat and eucalyptus trees, and Green wondered if part of the delay had been a change of form and a trip to Golden Gate park for her. She had earned it, these last weeks, caring for them all like Grace's adopted daughter.

As if to answer his unasked question, after the healing had coursed through her she had wriggled and yelped, shivering in a tiny orgasm that he knew must have been a result of her long celibacy since Mitch had died and she'd left his healing bed. "Oh, good…" She murmured. "I can turn kitty cat now, and it won't go away."

"You smell like kitty cat…" Green said back puzzled. Then, thoughtfully, "In fact, you smell like…like Mitch…"

Renny whirled to him, her face lit up from the inside like a shining curtain shielding a modest sun, and blinked her suddenly bright eyes. "Its good magic then…" She said through a suddenly rough throat. "I knew it was strong…I'm so glad…" And with that she pranced off through the hallway to presumably change out of the giant blood and ink stained T-shirt fluttering around her knees, along with Nicky's running shorts.

Green watched her go, puzzled, and still worried. Cory caught his eyes, and gave him one of those tight lipped smiles that halves of a couple give when they're thinking similar thoughts. "She's healing." She said after a moment. "Trust me—today…it will help."

"You need to take her shopping." He said, trying to lighten the moment of worry.

Cory grinned back at him. "I've been telling Bracken that for a week!" She said cheekily, and flashed her still bewildered *due'alle* a smirk and rolled her eyes over her shoulder.

Bracken shook his head. "Well since it's not safe for *me* to go out and walk around the block, I'm sure as shit not taking *you* out anymore." His irritated look became laced with concern. "And you're pale again, and you're still not well."

Suddenly Cory sobered. She looked at Green and Bracken and even Nicky. "Except for the being sick part, Bracken's right." She said quietly. "We can't live like this much longer—not even able to walk down the street without worrying about being attacked. We need to either kick their asses to get rid of them for good, or we need to lick our wounds and go home." For the first time her expression threatened to break, and the struggle to watch her get back under control was painful. She met Green's expression and seemed to pull strength from his empathy. "I'd kind of like to kick some ass." She said hopefully.

"I hear you." Green replied with a tiny, tight-lipped little smile of his own. "And I need to talk to Arturo, but I'm pretty sure we've set a date for said ass kicking, if you can wait a couple of days."

Cory nodded, and some of her earlier exuberance returned. "Solid." She said, with some relief. "I'm looking forward to the details." She smiled then, the same sly, knowing smile that lit Renny's features giving her the beauty she never saw herself. Turning chastely, she pulled her bloodied T-shirt over her head, keeping the front over her breasts and the back around her neck, and Green realized for the first time that she wasn't wearing a bra. A charge ran through him, a bolt of desire so thick that he was surprised it didn't push her forward into Bracken's arms. He hadn't touched her yet. His hands were there, hovering over the bandage which stretched from the waist of her jeans to between her shoulder-blades, and suddenly he was very aware that she was standing, half-dressed and close to healthy, in front of the two men she was bound to for the rest of her life. And in front of him.

Her breath started coming in faster, making the skin between her ribs pull in and push out, and he realized that in that frozen moment she could feel the heat from his hands, the terrible force of his desire, and at the same time, her eyes were locked on Bracken's. Bracken was looking at her with such a dreadful, longing need that Green was surprised she wasn't pulled across the room into his arms with the force of it. And Nicky, who had been standing to Green's left, extended a hand with Green's, as though the temptation to pet that pale, pale skin at her side was too much. There was a heavy, aching, thunderous moment when she was there, skin-bared to the three people who wanted her the most.

The moment was shaped, but not broken, when Nicky cleared his throat delicately, twitching his fingers and pulling his hand back. "Renny will be out of the shower in a minute." He said softly, and Green, Bracken and Cory all shuddered in time. Slowly Green lowered his lips to the spot above her back between her shoulder blades, the highest spot not covered by the bandage. He knew her back by heart now, the dimples and ripples of shoulder and ribs and vertebrae. She had a little trio of freckles just below the base of her neck that he aimed for, his lips warm to her cooling skin, his tongue just grazing her vertebra, and that one touch initiated a shudder of pleasure, of sensation and emotion, through Cory that echoed in Bracken and Nicky and in Green. In a moment of shiver the air around them was static with the tingle of almost-orgasm, and Cory made a little whimper in her throat that almost begged "Bring me."

Green bent his head, kissed that same little spot of skin again, opening his mouth, grazing her with his teeth, and still knew her eyes never left Bracken's. With one hand he reached for Nicky, and brought his hand to the small of her back, right below the tattoo, and as he himself moved a little trail of kisses up to the base of her neck. She shivered under his breath and his lips, and he fought the urge to clench her to him and grind his groin into her back. Instead, with a little turn of his head he sunk his teeth lightly into the join of neck and shoulder, and felt her shudder convulsively, clenching around herself, and finally relax against him in a rush. Next to him Nicky made a little whimper, and Bracken's clenched teeth smothered a grunt, as though they'd all been sucker-punched by desire. Cory fell bonelessly into his arms and he caught her, pulling her up against him and holding her under her arms and around her front, her breasts resting against his forearms. Collectively the four of them gave a long, shuddering sigh, and Cory finished with a giggle.

"That was…well…I don't think there's really a word for that…" she murmured.

"Not one I want to say." Nicky piped up dryly, and Bracken's quirked lips said the same thing.

"I need to shower before everyone else gets out." Cory said after a moment, and Green realized that they were all trapped in an awkward sort of afterglow, because that moment, that heavy hanging moment that had climaxed in Cory's body had been like sex, with only a minimum of touch. A moment of desire, among all of them, bound together in so many tangles of emotion and metaphysics that it would have been like sorting through grandmother's yarn box after a tornado, and with that moment they were suddenly all nicely wound up again, all neat and clean, and waiting to be made into something lovely.

Cory took the hands that Green had clasped around her and pulled them up to her lips to kiss, slowly, so tenderly, and as Green felt her lips move on his skin he wondered if he would embarrass himself and all of them by simply taking her there, stripping her jeans and his in a moment, bending her over on the landing and lunging against her like a beast. But before he could do more than just press his hardness against her back, she moved forward and he let her because he had to, and her bandage popped off like magic was involved, and he stopped thinking about sex and even breathing.

"Goddess." He whispered, looking at the design on her back, still flaky with blood and ointment, but magnificent nonetheless. Beside him Nicky grinned.

"We knew you'd like it." He said smugly. "We all got something like it…it's like our…mark. Well, your mark on our skin. Well…like that Roman tattoo in Gladiator, that says you're our general? Well, sort of…"

"Shut up Nicky." Cory said gently, and realizing the damage had been done she moved forward and dropped her head again. Green gazed at her motionless, and then looked up and met Bracken's eyes, realizing that his own eyes were bright and his throat clogged with an emotion that even he, after nearly two thousand years, could not name.

"Come here, brother." He said after a fraught moment. "Come here. This is for you as well."

Bracken made his way across the room, and then, excruciatingly careful not to touch Cory even at all, he came around behind her and looked at the art that had been rendered on her flesh.

"Goddess…" He murmured, and the T-shirt around her shoulders bunched as she tried a typical Cory shrug without baring her still covered breasts.

"It's us." She said trying not to sound anxious.

"I can see that." Green said, and 'us' was an understatement. Woven vertically up her back was a wreath, one side of lime leaves, with the occasional lime nestled in the thicket of them, and the other side oak leaves—the trademark of the foot-hills, the Sentinal oak—with acorns in counterpoint to the limes. The two wreaths formed a series of three diamonds: the one in the middle was proportionately smaller than the ones on the top and the bottom. In the center of the bottom diamond was a half-bloomed rose. Roses were twined with the wreath of lime and oak leaves on either side, but the half bloomed rose in the center was the focus of the small of her back, and because they had all seen the design that Bracken had pulled out of Mist's flesh, they all knew who the thorn-less rose represented. It was Adrian.

The center diamond was smaller, but showcased inside it was a hawk in flight, a hawk with rust colored wings, tipped in black, like Nicky's hair, and even, on close examination, a sprinkling of cinnamon freckles across a yellow beak.

The hawk and the rose were lovely, and both symbols Green had been half expecting when he realized what she had done. The diamond at the top, though, was a true surprise. The wreath of leaves itself was woven with thorn-less, blood covered roses, for Adrian, because he had loved Bracken too. In the center of the diamond was a sword, a warrior's sword, driven into a granite foundation as though reaching through Cory's tiny body for her heart's blood. There was a red hat—a crumpled, old fashioned cap—engulfing the hilt of the sword. Welling up from the rent in the granite where the sword was plunged, was blood, wet, glossy, falling on the wreath of lime and oak, dripping from the hawk's back, down his talons, down through the crossed wreath again, and bejeweling the rose with crimson. Sidhe magic had wrought the tattoo, and it was no static picture. The blood had motion, the drops traveled, they hugged the contours of the leaves and changed spatter patterns as the drops fell on Nicky's hawk and caressed the rose before dripping, drop by drop, down below the waistband of Cory's jeans. Curious, Green pulled the waistband out, and peered down into the darkness to see where the blood stopped.

"He didn't tattoo lower than the jeans." Cory murmured with some humor in her voice. "He said he had to touch the skin with the needle to make the illusion complete."

"It looks like if I touch it my hand will be wet." Bracken said in wonder.

"But it won't." She reassured gently. "That's you, *due'alle.*" She explained, still anxious. "Spilling your heart's blood to defend us all, right?"

In a rush that had Green and Nicky both stepping back, Bracken grasped her tiny hips with both hands and whirled her to face him. He bent down and hugged her, pulling her up so that her feet dangled above the ground and her T-shirt was mashed between them and she could meet Green's touched, amused, pained gaze with her own over Bracken's shoulder.

"I'm so sorry..." He murmured in her hair. "I would have asked...I swear I would have asked..." And there were tears in his voice that brought tears to Green's, once more.

"I know," she murmured, stroking his ragged, raven-wing hair. "I know you would have asked." Her eyes made contact with Green's, and her next words hurt, because only Green knew she was talking to both of them. "I would have said yes." There was a silence between the four of them, then, a hugging silence for Bracken and Cory, a waiting silence for Nicky, and a silence of pain and contentment for Green. She would have said yes, but he couldn't have asked.

Arturo broke the weighted quiet then when he emerged from the hallway then, his hair still wet from the shower. He saw Bracken holding Cory then, her bare back towards him, and he swore. "I thought we were all supposed to show them together! And why does it smell like sex in here?"

Cory gave a laugh that was half sob into Bracken's shoulder, and Bracken made the same sound. Green passed a hand under his eyes and gave Bracken a shove between the shoulder blades to make him move. "Go get her washed, mate—you can see everybody else's when you get out."

Her legs still dangling above the ground, the two of them made their way down the hall, murmuring quiet things that were truly only for each other's ears. Green blew out a breath, and reached behind him for the railing that separated the kitchen from the conversation pit, and found Nicky's hand instead, so he grasped that. Nicky's hand was thin, but stronger than it looked, and the boy's eyes and smile said plainly that he knew Green had been moved inside, beyond words, beyond tears even. Green stood there, clutching Nicky's hand and struggling with emotions he didn't even know he had.

It was his mark. A mark for him, on her body, proof in some way that she was his in a way that she hadn't belonged to anybody else. He knew—he had known when she'd run out the door—that among every other wound that the sylph's psychic time bomb inflicted, that the idea that she was marked by Bracken and by Nicky and even by Adrian, but not by Green had been one of the worst. But she had fixed it. She had marked herself for him. Their symbols were woven onto her skin inseparably, and it was Green and Cory who embraced Adrian and Nicky and Bracken. She was his. Yes, he had to share her, but willingly, she had made herself his. He was moved, and devastated, and in awe.

"Lloyd does nice work." Arturo said softly.

Green glanced at him, and Arturo took the opportunity to turn his exposed wrist up for Green's view. What he saw made him sit down, dragging Nicky practically into his lap.

"Ouch, Green!" Nicky complained, "You haven't healed mine yet and you just bumped it!"

Green came to himself and apologized profusely, kissing Nicky's shoulder with a sensuousness to make up for the pain. Nicky practically cooed, and leaned back against Green happily.

"I have no words." Green murmured, staring blankly at the artwork on Arturo's arm. Arturo had possessed a hawk's form, when he'd been a god in South America, and that was the centerpiece for the picture—rendered in the bold, flamboyant, brave lines of the Inca, the Aztec and the tribes beyond memory whose art still lived in the pyramids, instead of Nicky's more fluid picture. Clutched in the hawk's claws was a skein of brightly colored yarn, and two knitting needles (wickedly sharp, at that) which were obviously a symbol for Grace. Surrounding the hawk was the wreath of lime and oak that had woven across Cory's back.

"Goddess..." Green tried again. "Arturo...we work in symbols and touch and blood and song...do you have any idea what that symbol will do to you...to us?"

"It means you're my leader." Arturo said simply. "Of course, if I choose to, I could make it go away, but it would take more power than you have, and I'm not that strong anymore." He smiled kindly. "All of that work we just did to keep your part of the country safe and you didn't see this coming?" Arturo shook his head in mock disgust. "We are going to have to teach you to read people better."

Green choked on a laugh that didn't sound like a laugh. He hugged Nicky to him for comfort then, and nuzzled the boy's neck. "Okay, little kestrel, show us your artwork." He murmured, "And then go wash because we have a lot to talk about at dinner."

Nicky's bandage came off—ripping off hair and skin when it did so, which he grumbled through, of course, and Green was not surprised to see the same hawk on Nicky's arm that had been on Cory's back. He too, was surrounded by the woven diamond of lime and oak leaves.

"It's beautiful." He said gently, touching his lips to Nicky's cheek and meaning both the words and gesture. Then he shoved the young man off his lap, slapping his bottom as he went. "Now go wash."

Nicky grinned, and turned around, offering Green a hand up. Green hadn't been prepared for the help, but it would have been rude to refuse. Nicky gave a heave, but Green was really much taller than he was, and suddenly Arturo was there with another hand, and between them, he could have been launched across the room but he wasn't. He met Nicky's shining eyes and then Arturo's bemused, fierce gaze, and answered them with a smile of his own. Both of them had been invaluable—in fact, more than partly responsible—for the party to which he assumed Arturo had successfully invited their enemies. They knew his plan, they knew its execution, and they had both had more than one reason for putting his mark on their bodies.

"I know what you're thinking." He said smugly. "And you're right. We can use this. We can use these marks like the vampires use marks, and we can fuck Mist and fuck Goshawk until they can't stand any goddamned more. We can fuck them for their arrogance and for their pettiness and for all the times they ever tried to fuck with us. We can get them with this. We were looking for a tool, a sign, and you found it."

"Cory found it." Arturo said, but he looked very pleased with himself anyway. "It was her design. The rest of us just sort of…made it our own."

"'You did indeed. I'm…more proud of this than I think words can say…" His throat burned with pride, and with love for the people who had committed themselves to him, and with worry, the ever-present worry. It was the worry that he had first felt over a century ago, when he and Adrian had disembarked from the haunted ship that had been Adrian's home for ten years, and Adrian had turned guileless, autumn-sky eyes to Green and said "What now, Green?" With every faith in the world that Green would know, and make it come to pass. But now Arturo and Nicky and Renny and *Cory* had all marked their bodies for him, and that worry was suddenly so much worse.

Arturo grimaced at him. "Stop it, leader." He said gently. "We'll be safe. You'll keep us safe. We'll help you do it."

"Get out of my head, mate." Green returned wryly. "And you," to Nicky, "You go get showered. Arturo and I will start dinner."

"No, Arturo and *I* will start dinner." Grace said behind him, and Green turned and smiled at their undead den-mother who had apparently just awakened. "And Arturo is going to tell me what in the hell he was thinking, and I'm going to find out if it will work for me."

She came up behind Arturo, five feet, ten inches of lanky, wide-hipped woman vampire, and bent her head gently to kiss the mark on his wrist, the one that had her knitting needles and yarn on it, for her, forever.

"You are some stupid piece of man, do you know that?" She asked, her voice gruff. "I am so much more mortal than you…"

Arturo looked supremely uncomfortable, and Green smiled, enjoying his discomfiture.

"I'll do what I like with my body, woman." He growled, and Grace nodded, moving away and wiping bloody vampire tears from her face with the back of her hand.

"And so will I." She promised, the combination of impudence and love so touchable in her voice that Green and Nicky found themselves moving slowly into the hall to not disturb the two of them. They ran into Renny, who was combing her wild, wild hair into a pony-tale as she padded down the hallway.

"I would imagine from the sounds coming from Cory's bedroom that the whole 'show our tattoos at once' idea fell apart." She said dryly.

"The bandage popped off her back." Nicky explained, and then Green and Nicky looked at her again. She was wearing jeans that, well, would have fit maybe before Mitch had died, but they were close at least, and a buttoned shirt that Green had bought Cory only recently. It was a little big on her, but it wasn't bicycle shorts and a XXL T-shirt, either. It was forest green and fitted to her body, and even shaped like a woman's shirt.

"What?" She asked, uncomfortable. "So, I had to stare at myself for an hour and I realized I looked like a baby orangutan in giant's clothes…I thought I'd try to maybe give a shit about my appearance…" She shrugged. "The last time I dressed like a human was when Andres asked Grace and I out…maybe it's time I took an interest, you know?"

Green nodded, bent down to kiss her chastely on the lips. "You look nice." He told her simply, "Now show us your tattoo."

Renny's tattoo had the same diamond shaped wreath of leaves, with roses twined with them, because she and Mitch had been Adrian's favorite dinner, and a picture of Mitch, in his full were-cat glory, surrounded by a thicket of roses in vases. Green found himself fighting back a smile, and a laugh, because it was Mitch, and they had loved him, and the roses in vases had been his trademark gift for her, and they had meant something, but Mitch looked lazy, and half asleep, and satisfied, and so alive that Green remembered the sleepy eyed, introverted young man they had all loved and not just Renny's grief that he was gone.

"It's perfect." He said, and she turned around to him, beaming.

"You think?"

"It looks just like him." Green told her, and she turned around and launched herself into his arms with a gigantic hug.

"I love you, leader." She murmured. "You kept me alive, you let me remember him, and between you and Cory you made me want to live even without him. Thank you."

Nicky edged his way off to the bathroom in Green's room then, and Green stood there, just stood there, lost in an armful of Renny, happy, nearly healed, and so full of love for him that she made all of the worries worth while.

This was why he was leader, he realized. He couldn't be *due'alle* to Cory, he couldn't claim her as his *Anyaen,* but this, from Renny, from Nicky, from Grace and Arturo, even from the Avians who were almost his truly, from the hundreds of beings who had sealed themselves with touch and blood and song in the last week, and hundreds of beings under those who had given their consent—*this* was what he had chosen. From the moment Adrian had first said "Now what, Green?" And Green had an answer; *this* was the path he'd forged. And it had it's pain, Oh, Goddess, had there been pain, but the child that he loved, these children that he loved, needed him, they marked their bodies, for him and for his beloved and how can you turn down a life that included that, how could that not be worth the sacrifice, and the grief, and the pain? Live after Adrian? Well, he'd been doing it, hadn't he? Share Cory with others? She had magic and love to spare, and she had *chosen* him, without binding or magic but only with her free will and sound judgment. Face down Mist, with his children at his back, shedding their blood to protect the world they'd forged? He couldn't bloody well wait.

He could live with this tribute, he thought warmly, rocking Renny back and forth and enjoying her little purr of comfort. It wasn't perfect, but it would do.

CORY

Rain will fall...

I stared, open mouthed, at the dress in the expensive box with the thick crème colored crepe wrapping. Green and Bracken flanked me, enjoying my reaction I think, but I was too flummoxed to care.

"I'm supposed to *wear* this?" I asked, looking at the contents of the box in absolute horror.

This was it. This was the night of the banquet, the moment of the ass-kicking, the night we took back our lives. Green had outlined the plan two nights ago at dinner, while Marcus, Phillip, and Chet had sat to table looking at me longingly for the leadership I guess that they had not had since Adrian had died. Andres had joined us and his mood had been definitely blood-thirsty. Andres liked the plan. Hell, we *all* liked the plan, or most of it. As far as we could see, it protected the weak, set us up as the strong, got rid of our enemies, and didn't kill anybody—how could we not like the plan? The part where I had to sing on stage could have used some rethinking, but that had been Renny's fault.

"We will need a song." Green had said baldly, after laying out the basic plan for everybody at the table. He'd already told me most of it, but the song was a surprise. It shouldn't have been. "Touch, blood, and song are the basis for all of the Goddess' magic." Green continued. He looked at the collection of vampires and at our own personal red-cap and grinned. "We've got the blood down, and thanks to Bracken and Cory, we've figured out how to touch the assembly with it, but we need a song of binding."

"I don't think you'll find 'Taking Elvish Territory' in the Top 40 count down." Grace said dryly, and we'd laughed.

"You're right there." Green laughed as well. "But it doesn't have to be exact words—it just has to have meaning under the circumstance. A dirge for Adrian, a song of revenge, a song of war…any of these will do."

"How about *Rain Will Fall.*" Bracken chimed in from my side. I looked at him, surprised, and then, even more surprising, I looked at Green and saw him flush. It was like watching a yellow rose turn into a sunset rose slowly, with a flush of peach traveling from his throat to his cheeks, leaving darker peach/red stains at those magnificent high tilted cheekbones, and I watched it, fascinated, because as far as I knew, I had never seen Green embarrassed before.

"I thought that song had died along with Adrian." He said, from an obviously tight throat.

"He taught it to me when I was a kid and driving him ape-shit one rainy night." Bracken told him, an odd smile on his face. Something had happened between Green and Bracken when I'd been off getting all empowered and tat-tooed—something good. Bracken wouldn't tell me, even though I'd spent one whole night in his arms, and Green wouldn't tell me, even though I'd lain with him the night after, but whatever it was, it had healed Bracken of his self-loathing following the incident with the sylph, and it had made Green more open about his past when he'd been a courtesan under the power of Mist and Morana. Men say we're a mystery, but I've got to say the two of them have just baffled me all to hell.

Green shrugged then. "You and I could sing it—we could even make it a show of sorts." He glanced up at Arturo. "You said we should do something dra-matic—between the blood, the song, and the marks on their flesh, I'd say it'd be musical theatre the whole stinking lot of them would never forget." He frowned then, chewing on his lip a little.

"Something is bothering you?" Andres asked. He too had been sitting table with us, and as nice as it had been to see him, a part of me kept reliving the last time Bracken and I had been with him, and that kiss between the three of us in the alleyway, and a part of me I didn't know I had mourned that I would never get to taste Andres the way Bracken had. He knew, I thought, watching him watch me back. He had been there when the vampires and the Avians had been marveling at our tattoos, and Renny had blithely told him the story of the sylph and of Bracken's brush with perfidy, and Andres was looking at me now like he knew I would miss the thought of us, and like he missed it too. I shook my head then. There were real losses in this room, not just the loss of a promise of pleasure. Andres and I would live and be friends, and maybe, if Bracken and I lived long enough and I forgot, just a little more what it meant to be human, we could remember that promise again, but that was a thousand thousand heartbeats in the future.

Green was shrugging in response to Andres' question. "The song is made for a female voice, that's all." He said, and I suppressed a grin. It was an artist's complaint. Green had a fine baritone voice, and Bracken was a low tenor—between the two they'd probably sound glorious—sort of a fifteenth century Simon and Garfunkle or something. But Green had written the song and there are few visions as powerful as those we've created in our own mind. The vision of kissing Andres after Bracken had kissed him was enough to make me weep. Then Renny spoke up, and all of that disappeared.

"Cory's got a great voice." She said blithely, passing a bowl full of mashed potatoes to Mario, who looked at me in surprise. He wasn't the only one.

"He's not talking about singing in the shower, Renny." I bantered through a dry mouth, and she rolled her eyes at me.

"She was in choir when we were in high school. Our teacher kept telling her she had to do something with that voice of hers, but Cory kept saying..." Renny frowned, and wrinkled her forehead, and I prayed she wouldn't remember the rest because I did and it's hard to believe what an ass you can make of yourself as an adolescent until certain friends show up with knowledge you'd forgotten they had. "Oh, yeah." Renny continued nonchalantly, as though the entire table, including my beloveds and Adrian's vampires and Andres' vampires who were complete strangers weren't staring at me with interest, as though suddenly I turned another color or something. "I remember now. You used to say 'my people don't do art.' I never knew what you meant by that." And now she was looking at me expectantly, like she hadn't just bared one of my most painful memories of high school for half of Green's court.

I concentrated fixedly on my steak. Although my energy was up, and I needed maybe one nap a day (lately taken after doing something fairly gymnastic with Green or Bracken) I had yet to gain more than five pounds back. I had the feeling the family had erected a conspiracy to help Cory grow her boobs back, because there were so many high fat, high protein, high carb snacks around the apartment that even Renny was looking a little softer around the edges, which is hard to do with a shape-changer's metabolism. But food was the last thing on my mind right now, and as good a cook as Grace was, I didn't think I could sing with a stomach full of steak. Bracken was sitting next to me, and he spoke into the sudden silence, nudging me a little with his elbow.

"So, what did you mean by that?" He asked.

A lump had formed in my throat. I hadn't seen mom and dad since Thanksgiving, when I'd visited for two days and felt like an alien in my old bedroom (now a converted sewing room for mom) and it was suddenly hitting me that I had almost died—several times, and not only didn't they know that, they had no idea why. I'd called home once or twice, and chatted. You shouldn't be able to sound as normal as I did, sitting in bed because you were too weak to get up and wondering who was going to try to kill you next.

"It's just…" I tried to say past my stupid adolescent pain. This shouldn't hurt so much. I shrugged. Green could tell me about being a courtesan for a hundred years, held against his will by the one talent he really loved about himself. This should be a piece of cake. "Mom and dad didn't…don't place much stock in things like education, or fine arts, or…well, I was catching shit that whole year for taking a class that wouldn't help me drive a truck or be a gas station clerk or something."

The silence gelled around me like rancid gravy. Nicky, surprisingly, was the one who broke it.

"You think that's bad." He said, eyes rolled. "How am I going to tell Ma and Pa Avian Kettle from bumfuck Montana that I'm boinking a man?" I laughed, so surprised that I snarfed milk out my nose, and the rest of the table broke up in relief.

"Good point!" I gasped, when I could. "Wait 'til I tell them I'm boinking three of them!" Nicky and I whooped then until we were almost in tears, and then Renny broke in with, "Well in my family that's better than dating a cop!" And the three of us howled with laughter, until Grace had stood up in disgust and told us in a tone that brooked no argument that if we didn't eat our dinner *right now,* she would feed it to the were-creatures guarding the apartment building outside. We obeyed, of course, because she was Grace and because we loved her like the mother we had mailed ordered at birth but hadn't got, but we knew she'd already cooked extra for the two were-mastiffs across the street in the little park and the were-leopard crouched behind the stairs to the apartment.

After the sylph incident (I kept calling it that, because I didn't want to think of the pain of another creature putting her hands on Bracken, or dying because he hadn't loved her when she had) Green had agreed that A. The enemy had no honor, and would probably try to kill us before, during and after the banquet, and B. Since Orson and the were-creatures felt indebted to us for discovering the enemy in their midst and then dealing with it, we would take up Orson's offer on the honor guard. Personally, I hoped they discovered a spare elf that didn't belong outside of Green's building and tore it into tiny, bite sized pieces too fucking ravaged to be recognized. Green had grinned almost vampirically at the idea and I'd bet a million dollars that he too hoped to find little pieces of Mist-kibble under the brush one day, but so far no such luck.

But later that night, after dinner, Green had cornered me, and made me sing—I'd picked Sarah MacLachlan's *Arms of the Angel* because if I could sing that then I figured I could sing anything, and the stillness and admiration on Green's face when my last note had died pretty much let me know that I'd be on stage in two nights.

A part of me was terrified, but a part of me, the part I'd ground ruthlessly under my Goth-Bitch punk boots my entire high school career, was thrilled. I was going to *sing,* I was going to stand on stage and sing with the two people in the world who loved me best and we were going to blow the place up and *kick some fucking ass.* I could do that, I thought, and I had kept on thinking it, as the whole stinking lot of us filled the now tiny apartment with practice. We practiced magic, we practiced singing, we practiced staging—as much as we could without being in the hotel area—and we practiced what we were going to say when we had the people we wanted to hurt the most gathered in the banquet hall of the place the five of us (we counted Adrian) had created out of love and desperation. We could *do* this, I'd thought, between naps and Bracken's bitching about how my health was still not up to par. We could bloody well *do this.*

"I can't do this." I said now, looking at the slinky little emerald colored satin dress that Andres had bought for me and had sent to the apartment. I pulled it out now and let it spill like water over my hands, and looked at Bracken, who was already dressed in a black silk dress shirt and black wool trousers fitted for the sidhe's unusual frame. The sprites had trimmed Bracken's hair again, and he looked roguish and devastating, even more so because I knew he had a brand new tattooed band of oak leaves, lime leaves and roses around his upper arm twining to his wrist. Our mark. Mine, Adrian's, and Green's, and he was wearing it under his sleeve, for me. He was beautiful, and he was wearing my mark, and between him and Green, I would look like a sparrow in a peacock feather robe, flanked by the real deal.

Green's hair was loose and down to the backs of his knees, after the sprites had combed it and re-combed it until it was a glossy gold waterfall that seemed to move as a though stirred by invisible winds. He was wearing the winter-white counterpoint to Bracken's black outfit, and both of them had big fat emeralds at their cuffs and in their ears, and emerald colored kerchiefs in the pockets of their dress coats. The clothing had all been sent to the apartment—including similar boxes for Renny, Grace, Nicky, the Avians, and the vampires—all courtesy of Andres. I thought the gift had been awesome, until I saw what I was expected to wear.

"I can't do this." I said again, holding the slink-fit backless nightmare up by the off-the shoulder straps. I looked to Green and Bracken for help, but I was standing in my bathrobe, and Bracken was busy picking up the little pieces of stocking and garter and whatever the fuck else went with a get-up like this and holding them cautiously between a thumb and a forefinger, and Green was cloaking an obvious smile with his hand.

"You'll catch a cold in these." Bracken groused, sounding like a mother. "It's bad enough we're taking you outside *again* to spend all your life energy in another fight, but this stuff is just *inviting* pneumonia."

"They're lovely." Green soothed, trying his most grown-up Green voice and taking the lingerie from Bracken's hands with a more practiced touch. The look I sent him must have been panicked because he changed his expression to one of honest concern and looked at my *due'alle* meaningfully. Bracken got the hint, pecked me on the cheek, and shrugged and left muttering "Okay, okay, whatever...he'll be out on business when she's coughing up a lung." But he cast a shrewd look at Green and I, and turned the little lock button on the doorknob as he closed the door behind him.

Green came around behind me, bunching a sheer nylon stocking in his hands and holding it out in front of him. I remember my mother doing a similar thing when she dressed me up to 'send me off to get religion' on the odd Sunday mornings. But Green was warm and strong and definitely **not** my mother. "Here, luv." He murmured in my ear, and I stuck my foot out automatically as he rolled the stocking up my leg.

"I think we have to put the garter belt on first." I said, feeling warm because I was naked under the bathrobe and even between the two of them, my body was not all sexed out yet. In fact, if I'd thought about it, it would seem that I needed to be touched even more now than I had when Green had been my only lover. But then, a little voice in my head murmured, you were dying. Now that I was happy or as close to being happy as I could be with a really odd but really wonderful love life, I understood that before Nicky attacked me, I'd been withering away, root and stock, my heart and my body, turning brown from pain held in. If this last month had felt like an endless refrain of "Adrian is dead" then at least I had purged the grief and the poison of blame and self-recrimination that *not* saying it to myself had built up in my once fragile, wilted little heart. So what? I thought, knowing that if I parted my thighs, even a little, my sex would be open and slick and Green could take me right then. So what if I needed them to touch me? So what if the thought of a night without a strong male body next to mine was like the thought of a night naked on an ice-berg? I was whole. I was healthy. I was powerful. And these men loved me.

"Stop thinking sex thoughts, luv." Green said from behind me, his voice strained, and since I was leaning back against the length of him, I could tell what the smell of my must had done to him. "We're trying to accomplish something here."

"The garter belt." I breathed, and he bent down again, his warm yellow hair falling down over my shoulder, his pale, smooth cheek against mine, and slid the little lace confection up my legs. The contrast between his hand on the silk and flesh of the leg with the stocking on it, and the brushing of his fingers on my bare (shaved!) leg had my knees all shaky all over again. Since he could see me in the full length mirror on the closet door, he could probably see the shiny slickness that had gathered on my upper thigh. When the garter belt was in place, and the little snappy things clicked together over the stocking, his white, long-fingered hand hovered there, over the rust colored fur of my mound, and I swallowed so loud they could probably hear me in the living room, where, I assumed, everybody who had managed to get dressed was gathered and waiting for those of us having some sort of crisis. Gracefully, Green reached his thumb in to the juncture of my slightly spread thighs and rubbed it in the slick little place where I was dripping, and then brought his thumb to his mouth.

"I forgot panties." I remembered with agony in my voice. "We're going to have to start all over again" I met Green's eyes in the mirror, and I knew what he was going to say before he said it, because we had a little time to spare, and because my body needed his and because we loved each other and we felt powerful and revved and we could.

"Do without." He murmured. And in three deft movements he unhooked his belt and trousers, pulled my robe down my body, and bent me over the bed. He was inside me, slick and full and strong before I could even gasp yes, and I was moaning into the quilt on my bed as he thrust. And again, and again, and he brought me, quivering, grunting into the covers, needing more, and again and in a moment he was clutching my sensitive breasts, one in each hand, biting the back of my neck, and pouring himself into me on a groan.

It had been quick and fierce and potent and I tried to suppress a giggle as we lay, face down on the bed, with Green collapsed on top of me. "Oh damn." I murmured. "I have to shower again."

"Don't." He whispered in my ear. "Don't shower. You'll smell like me, like my sex. My power lies in sex, and now it lies in you, yes? I want to know that while we're singing, and pulling Mist's power out from under him, that my come is running down your thighs."

We rarely used sex words, ever. At first it was because they made me feel bad about sex, and not putting a name to the things we were doing became a habit. But now he said 'come' and he was still inside me, still hard, and still moving with our breathing, and his words, whispered harshly in the sensitive hollows of my ear sent me over the long precipice without even knowing it was at my feet.

I was caught unaware, and the reason I don't automatically change the world every time I orgasm is because I can prepare, I can master the magic that my body creates and control it and make it simply about pleasure and not about power. But I hadn't been thinking about power and I was surprised in my pleasure, and our coupling had been powerful to begin with and the burst of power that was surprised out of me was shouted into my Gran's already sparkling quilt, and suddenly the lines of quilting began to twist, changing shape, glowing with green that ran the gamut of turquoise to loden to emerald and the quilting lines, a curling, wreathing pattern to begin with began to spread.

Although it was sudden, the climax itself was a slow, lingering hurtle to oblivion, and I watched, even as my body quivered, as those green lines began to crawl rapidly around the room, adorning the woodwork of the bed, the carpet, the window panes, and even beyond my room. By the time the final shivers had blown through my skin, I heard various exclamations from the collection of people waiting for us in the living room.

This time, it was Green who laughed softly, shakily, because he'd been inside of me as my body clenched, and all he could do was hug me to him and hang on for the ride. "Goddess..." He murmured. "Goddess...I think you've really outdone yourself this time, Cory, luv."

I opened my eyes and saw his arm next to me on the bed, and the sleeve of his ivory shirt was now alive with a subtle glow of that same green floral loop that had run across my Grandmother's quilt, but changed. Changed into the same wreath that ran across my back. I shifted a little, letting him slide out of my body with regret, and saw that his cream-colored trousers (which he was now pulling over his sex-slicked person) were similarly decorated. The pattern, in that rich tumble of greens, had worked it's way up the stocking on my leg, and onto the one on the bed, was worked subtly across the green satin of my dress, and, if the noises from the people in the other room were any indication, Green and I were not the only ones wearing 'Cory's orgasm chic' this evening. Our eyes met, in bemusement, and, in my case, embarrassment, and I have no idea what I would have said because Bracken broke up the moment with a hard knock on the door.

"Green, you had better have her dressed and out of there in five minutes, because if you two pull another deal like that we'll all be wearing ivy loincloths to this thing."

"There's not that much ivy on the fucking planet." I snapped back through the door, and Green's silent laughter shook his body, even as he was tucking in his shirt.

"If you keep fucking around like that, I'm sure you'll make some." Bracken shot, and I could hear his dress shoes (oh, how they hated wearing dress shoes) ringing on the hard wood floors as he stalked back down the hall.

I could barely control myself over the giggles. Green looked at me, that wicked appealing smile on his face, the one that had first drawn me to him in the first place, when I thought Adrian would be my one and only, and raised an eyebrow in question.

I shrugged through my laughter. "I still don't know how to hook the god-damned stocking to the freaking garter belt." I gasped.

Green's laughter turned rueful. "Well, luv." He said after a moment, "Let's see where our self control is now, shall we?"

There were still a few breathless moments, as his hands skimmed the juncture of my thighs, but eventually I was wearing a garter belt and stockings, and Green was slithering my slinky little dress over my head and settling the slits of the skirt along side each knee. He smoothed his palms down my fully exposed back, tracing the line of fabric that would have run about two inches above my granny panties, if I'd been wearing them. The material of my dress was cool and slippery on my bare nipples, and between that and, well, essence of Green tracking it's way down my thighs, I wondered if I'd be in a constant state of arousal throughout this entire evening.

"Call it come." Green murmured to me, clinching that arousal idea, just as my hand reached for the door. "In the silence of your own head, call it come."

"How did you know…"

"Even euphemisms talk on your face." He said obliquely, his voice still low and making me shiver. In a movement, he'd snagged the black velvet and emerald satin cloak that went over my dress and draped it over my bare shoulders, but not before he'd put the warm flat of his hand possessively on his mark on my cool white skin.

I was shocked and titillated and feeling that sultry confidence that sex can give you, and with that power pounding through my blood he opened the door to our assembled friends and allies, and together we stepped into their presence like the King and Queen of love and lust and glory.

Everybody else looked fabulous—and sparkly with our oak and lime wreaths across their clothes.

Mario and La Mark were both wearing winter white, and the subtle, shining green threaded their dress shirts, trousers, and heavy woolen coats, and Phillip, Marcus and Chet had the same look in black. Renny had been given a little backless thing like mine, but in a rich rust color, and the green threaded through it made it look like autumn magic, and her matching cloak as well. Grace's emerald green pantsuit was more subtly decorated, but she sparkled when she walked, as did Arturo, who was dressed in a classic black and white evening suit. The shiny green threads had only possessed Arturo's white shirt—and his now brilliantly emerald colored tie. Nicky was wearing an emerald colored silk shirt, but the design was particularly noticeable on his black trousers and black tie.

Andres was there too—his would be one car in the caravan that we were driving to the hotel—the big five-star Ritz-Carlton that I had created out of sex and desperation and the Ritz-Carlton company would never know existed. He looked at Green and I and then gestured to his now-adorned modishly cut black and green tuxedo, and his rather fabulous emerald-lined black wool opera cape which was a counter-point to mine. All of his clothes were now decorated with that silver/green mark, even as everybody else.

"I had thought the clothes were perfect, little Goddess." He said with some amusement, "And you can't imagine how surprised I am to find that they needed that last, finishing detail."

I flushed. "That's me. The fashion police." I joked lamely, and on that thought, I realized I'd forgotten something. With a quick 'wait here' I dashed precariously back into my bedroom on my heeled satin pumps, where I fetched the little matching evening bag that had come with the dress. It was tiny, but all I needed to put in it was my ID (this was such a human thing to carry, I couldn't actually figure out why I needed it) and my gun. Nicky had brought it down with him since Green couldn't touch it. I guess I figured that if this whole master plan for taking over the universe didn't work, that I was going for my original idea of shooting Mist full of holes and having Bracken bleed him out. Of course, Green's plan had more poetry—and possibly more pain, for someone like Mist—so it was only a back up plan, really, and I said as much when Green asked me about the bag.

"Well, I guess it's better than having no back-up plan at all." He said drolly, and I took that as a compliment.

"Besides," I said grimly, "We still haven't decided what to do about Goshawk." We hadn't. We figured that when Mist and Morana had been overpowered, and we hoped, were crying like little tiny mean spirited babies, that Goshawk would cave, but we hadn't thought of how to mete justice to him. I still wanted my memories back. I could remember my first kiss with Adrian, but not my first sex. I could remember what the Goddess grove looked like, but I couldn't remember making it. I could remember, because we'd had a precious few weeks together, what it felt like to have both my lovers inside me at once, but I couldn't remember the first time, when the shock of sex and power had reformed the world.

"We'll figure it out as it happens, luv." Green said grimly, and he put his hand in the small of my back like a gentleman, and I kept my spine straight like a lady, and we were ready to leave.

We trooped out of the apartment then, and I wondered when I'd see the apartment again. Green had already given the sprites orders to pack and transport our stuff back to the hill that night, as though he were certain of the outcome, and I hadn't argued. I was mostly healthy, I was happy, and my hunger for home at Green's hill was so potent that it nearly choked me. I didn't want to be in this city anymore. I wanted to go home.

Although, the city really was lovely, I thought wistfully as Bracken drove the Suburban down the Embarcadero because I'd asked him to. I'd wanted one last look at the bay in the moonlight.

Grace and Arturo were driving my BMW with La Mark and Mario—one of them would drive it back up the hill tonight—and the hearse and the other Suburban were staying here in at the apartment—the vampires would drive them back tomorrow night, after spending the rest of the night in the city and the day in the apartment darkling. Nicky was sitting next to Bracken in the front seat, and I was in the middle back, sandwiched between Green and Renny. As we were taking this last drive through the city at night I tried to drink in many of the sights I'd been too miserable to indulge in when I'd sort of lived here, and it was sad, because the city was one of the most beautiful places I could imagine in the world, with the exception of Green's hill.

I knew that if I were coming from the East across the Bay Bridge I would see the skyline lit up for the holidays, and here on street level the shops were lit up and busy against the darkness of the bay. It's hard to describe the energy of San Francisco—I mean, you can be walking down North Beach on a street that's full of porn shops and tattoo parlors and liquor stores, and still feel that the little hole in the wall club up the alley will be the perfect place to sit and listen to music that never made it up the hill to South Placer County. Renny, Nicky and I had spent a number of evenings doing just that, and all of us had discovered that there was a whole lot that had never made it to our respective homes, but that was okay, because we could hear it or see it or talk about here in the city.

"Will you miss it?" Green asked in my ear, and I looked up to smile at him.

"I can visit." I replied mildly. I glanced behind me, to the very back seat, where Phillip, Marcus and Chet were packed in, and I knew without looking that the men were waiting for my notice, and dying for my leadership. Adrian, their leader, their *beloved* leader had died, and I wore his power on my neck, and I had ignored that and prayed that it would go away just like my grief. But my grief was a part of me, and my responsibility to Adrian's people was a part of me, and Andres had shown me, in a dozen small ways, that vampires took their character from their person in charge. If Green's vampires were to take their character from Green's people, well, I guess I was the one they would look to.

"I have important things to mind back at home." I said decisively, after smiling at Phillip, Marcus and Chet like it was the most natural thing in the world for me to do.

"Tend to me first, beloved." Green whispered in my ear, with more possessiveness than was characteristic of him. I guess that was to be expected—his come was running down my thighs. His sex and his power were inside me, and I was feeling pretty damned powerful myself.

"Goddesses do it for power." I murmured to myself, having used those words to throw Goshawk's horrific judgments in his face. Tonight, I hoped I was right.

"What do human women do it for?" Green asked in my ear. I turned towards him and whispered, with equal intimacy, "We do it for love, *o'ue'hm*. I do it for love."

And suddenly the car was charged with intimacy and sex and a surge of power so raw that the vampires groaned behind us, and Nicky and Bracken swore a shit storm in front of us.

"I can't drive with a hard-on people!" Bracken bitched. "Try to tone it down until we get there."

But we were already cruising along the bay and under the bridge, so there was almost here, and then Bracken hung a right and suddenly my hotel, which Green claimed had been fully operational for the last three weeks was lit up in fluid green, in the same pattern that was now on our clothes, with Christmas red roses in dotting the front in what first appeared to be those cool tube lights.

"Wow!" I turned to Green smiling. "This is awesome—you didn't tell me you had this done!"

Green's smile was wry. "I didn't." He said shortly. "In fact, I'll bet if you ask the concierge inside, this just happened around an hour ago."

Jesus. I looked closer at the tube lights, and there weren't any. Just intricate, woven lights of crimson and green, springing from, apparently, the slickness dripping from the crowns of my silk stockings. Before I could hang my head in mortification, Bracken pulled up next to the curb and Green hopped out. He was reaching up to help me (so I didn't make a twit of myself by falling out of the damned Suburban) when Bracken turned around and reached back to catch my chin in his hand.

"It's not like every preternatural being in the city doesn't know what made this building in the first place, *due'ane*." He said gently. "Think of it as an incredible show of power, not as your personal life on parade. Then get inside because it is fucking freezing out here."

"Goddesses do it for power." I reiterated, with dignity, I hoped.

"That's right." Green affirmed in front of me, holding his arms out to help me out of the monstrosity of metal that was our transportation. "Now come along, little Goddess." He was smiling, I could see, and kind. Green was always kind, and he loved me, and it was all the impetus I needed to scoot forward and allow him to help me out.

I was just gaining my balance on the damned heels, when Renny kind of screwed that whole dignity thing by shrieking "Max!" and charging out of the SUV fast enough to almost knock me over. I fell into Green's arms instead, but watching Renny scamper in high heels was almost worth the blow to my dignity. Max, who had been standing by the entrance of the carport looking stiff in his formal dress clothes, caught our little were-cat and whirled her in the air, and Renny, for whom self-restraint had never been particularly developed, caught his face in her hands and kissed him so deeply we all watched his knees wobble. He pulled away from the kiss—eventually—and made his way unsteadily towards us, where he stopped with a short, military type bow, although he kept his arm firmly wrapped around Renny's waist.

"Lord Green." He said formally, a warm smile crinkling his eyes. "My Lady." He said to me, wholly serious, and bowed even deeper this time.

"Holy God." I breathed. I hadn't seen Max since the morning I'd woken up from my fever and he'd been collapsed on the couch with Nicky. He'd been awake, on and off, and occasionally I remembered him being in bed with me, when my energy was so sketchy as to need a constant human battery. But that had been in the first days of my recovery before he'd gone back up the hill with

Green, so we hadn't had time to talk to him, and in a million years I couldn't imagine that Officer Max had changed so much as to bow to me.

Green could, I thought, looking at the way he inclined his head. He smiled at me gently, and gave me a little nudge.

"Officer Max." I said, inclining my head just like Green. "It's good to see you." And it was. Max had been here in the beginning, I thought, and Renny had missed him. It was good to have him here towards the end. It was really good to see that nobility that had always been trapped inside him shining out now with the respect he gave my beloved.

Suddenly the seriousness of the moment was broken, and Max grinned. "So—nice place you made here, Cory—what did you do to spruce it up?"

I flushed then, to the roots of my coiffed hair. "Renny, if you answer that, I'll never speak to you again."

"Whatever it was," Max continued, grinning at me evilly, "It spiffed up the old tux here, too—I don't think I'll be able to return it now." And I could see, now that he was closer, that there were green-silver threads woven into his clothes as well.

"Bill me for it, right?" Green told him smugly, and I looked pleadingly at Renny.

"Please, pussy cat?" I asked weakly.

Renny flashed an unrepentant grin from under Max's arm. "Cory, my best friend got fingered by Kenny Albrecht in the sixth grade, and the entire class knew about it by the seventh grade, and she still talked to me. Unless you're going to fry me as I stand, there's not a force on earth that will stop me."

I closed my eyes and breathed "Fuck," under my breath, and Green laughed and propelled me towards the entrance of the lobby. "Now that *that's* out of the way," He said kindly, "We can go inside where it's warm and kick a little ass."

"For this sort of embarrassment, we'd better kick a lot of ass." I answered crankily, and Max stepped forward to open the shining brass and glass door to the lobby, and I couldn't speak at all.

I did nice work, I thought, looking around the lobby with an open mouth. The wood was a light oak, and it covered the floor and a part of the wall where rich green and ivory brocade took over. The couches were rose colored; the throw rugs dark green and decked with wildflower colors of violet and rose and gold, and everything was trimmed with brass and chrome or crystal. It was lovely—amazingly lovely, but it looked a little naked, still.

"It needs artwork." I murmured from a dry throat.

"Our concierge is looking for local artists even now." Green replied. "But it's up and running, and in spite of the fact that it came fully furnished, that's still saying something."

I looked around the spacious lobby and shook my head. Who would come here, I thought. It was beautiful—stunningly lovely, but who would come here?

"We would." Green answered simply.

"I didn't know you were in my head." I told him dryly, but I understood now. The sidhe, the fey—everyone who wanted a five star hotel but who wasn't in the mainstream enough to ask would sleep here. I bet there was even a special menu at the lobby level restaurant. "There's a darkling for the vampires, isn't there." I had created this place, hadn't I? I knew very little about artwork, so there was no art on the walls, but I had been in love with a vampire, so that would have sprouted up with the hotel.

"Absolutely." Green affirmed, still smiling. "Two darkling rooms on all fifteen floors, and a group room for a kiss, down at the basement level."

Bracken came up behind me with Andres and took my arm. I looked up at him sideways, surprised, because this event was supposed to be political, and it would have been appropriate to offer my arm to the Lord Vampire, but Bracken's expression brooked no argument. But that was okay, I thought. It was good that one of my relationships had nothing to do with politics and everything to do with love.

"We're very grateful for the darklings, by the way." Andres said from Bracken's left. "Not every hotelier would be so considerate. And the concierge has been very willing to work with us in terms of hiring…shall we say, a willing and tasty staff."

"Sounds like a great guy—who is he?" I mean, I hadn't hired him, but apparently he was an employee, of sorts. If I didn't have some serious things to do that night, I would have wasted a little time being confused and lost.

"At your service, Lady." And I recognized that tiny, brown-skinned, wizened figure, dressed in a tiny tuxedo, bowing at my feet.

"Master Clorklish." I said warmly, and I returned the bow.

"My people would like to thank you, Lady Cory." He said formally. "When we denied service to the master sidhe of the city, we would have had nowhere to go…nothing to do. This place…" He gestured towards the wide and lovely lobby, and, I assumed, the rest of the unlikely and beautiful space. "This place that you created, it gave us a home, and service. Without service, we lower fey will shrivel up, fade away, and die. With this place, you and Master Green saved our lives."

My cheeks burned. That had certainly not been my intention when the building had sprung up from my power like a big balloon. "I'm certain we would have found someplace for you to serve without it." I said, both moved and embarrassed.

"Undoubtedly." Clorklish responded spryly. "But perhaps not so beautiful."

"Perhaps not." I replied, casting a sideways look at Bracken's proud and achingly beautiful profile. Bracken looked back at me the same way, and I could hear his voice in my head, the night we made this place. *You're beautiful.* I'd said. *I am a sidhe.* He'd replied. There was more to his beauty than that, but he would never see himself through my eyes, so he would never know.

"Would you like to see the ball room, now, my Lady?" Clorklish asked formally, "Your guests are waiting."

"Absolutely." I told him, and my voice was as bloodthirsty as Clorklish's expression.

Our footsteps in the hallway were muffled by a green carpet, trimmed in rose and gold, and again I had the feeling that the walls were a little naked.

"I don't know why it bothers me, but it does!" I said to Green, shaking my head.

Green only smiled in return. "Your power has a way of drawing itself full circle, Cory my luv. Don't worry—I'm sure the next time you visit your hotel it will be decorated to your satisfaction."

"Bloodthirsty enemies are waiting to kill and humiliate us, and you're worried about art?" Bracken grumbled.

"You said it yourself!" I returned, fighting the impulse to pull my hands from Bracken's and Green's and wipe my palms on my nifty dress. "This place is my power—and it's you and me." I tried not to sulk. "I like to think there's art inside the two of us, don't you?" And before Bracken could soothe my ruffled feathers, I added, "And it makes it look like there's a hole in our power, and there's not." This forced Green to answer.

He stopped us just short of the double wide door that led (I assumed) into the formal ballroom. "All it does, beloved, is tell them that we have unfinished business to take care of." He bent down that vast, vast distance from divinely tall sidhe to little human and touched his lips to my ear. "I can smell us...our come, dripping from your soft flesh, Corinne Carol-Anne...I have tasted you, and tasted you and your other lover inside you—and you are powerful. Who does it for power, Corinne Carol-Anne?"

I'd had to lean back to tilt my head and hear him say these insane, erotic, mesmerizing things to me, and only me in the whole world, and his long long yellow hair enfolded us like a third lover, and I was backed up against Bracken who could probably hear Green's words, and smell my musk and the sex of me because he was hard and charged and aroused against my back as I knew Green would be against my stomach. I was breathless and stunned, and Green knew it. "Say it." He whispered. "Who does it for power?"

"Goddesses." I choked through a dry throat.

"Louder." He whispered. "Who fucks their lovers for power?"

More sex words, but it was a strong sex word and it made me feel strong. "Goddesses." And my voice was stronger this time. Bracken shifted at my back, and now his lips were in my other ear, moving, whispering, tantalizing, making me high with desire.

"Who rebuilds the world with sex?" Bracken asked, his hands coming around my waist, fingers touching at my midriff. His palms were warm and smooth against my bare, tattooed back.

"Goddesses." I said again, the whine of arousal in my answer. Both of them had their hands on my body, and although we might never be in the same room naked, I loved them both, and they loved me back and they were whispering heart-pounding skin-naked things and they were *touching* me.

"Who's walking into that room to face the people who killed our beloved?" Green asked, and his cheek pressed against mine, and I felt our pain and our grief and our healing all over again.

"We are."

"And you're our Goddess." Bracken added, and the build-up of arousal and power made my knees weak and my heart strong all at once. Bracken's words were only a small completion and not a total climax, but they made me shudder and fall against the two of them as his words bound us off and allowed us to move into that room with a haze of sex and power and anger and confidence that not even the arrogant Mist and scornful Morana could top.

CORY

And Trees Will Grow...

It's good that I felt that way, because Mist and Morana as well as Goshawk were waiting for us as we walked into the ballroom. Goshawk looked small, was my first thought. He looked small, and out of place, and powerless amid the glitterati of the San Francisco sidhe. Mist and Morana were the only two of them standing, but I could see a group of maybe thirty of the tall and the lovely, shining subtly in their corner of the darkened ballroom. The rest of the room was packed with the lesser fey and Andres' vampires, and they all rose to their feet as we walked in. Green and I drew to a halt, and, ignoring Mist and Morana, who looked both outraged and insulted that we would wait court in their city, Bracken took a step back and the two of us inclined our heads in response to their tribute. There was a lump in my throat. They loved us. They gave us their power and their fealty free of coercion, and we would do anything not to let them down.

After an appropriate pause, the assembly sat down, and Bracken came back up to my elbow, and the three of us made a wheeling turn that somehow didn't feel awkward at all.

"Good evening, Mist, Morana. Thank you for coming." Green said pleasantly. "I trust the food was to your liking?" That was subtle and brilliant of him, I thought. The food would have been excellent—all of the lower fey that used to cook for the high elves were now employed at the hotel. I just bet it had been wonderful, and bitter to the taste.

"We are not here for pleasantries." Morana snapped. "You overstep yourself, Lord Green."

Green pretended to be thoughtful. "No…no…this property was a gift from Lord Andres—and the other fey have stood behind the treaties we signed in good faith. I'm pretty sure if I can arrive on my own property from my own property alive and well, I have every right to sit court here."

"Some court." Morana sneered. "Lesser fey and vampires—don't tell me you base your power on these."

I smiled then. "He bases his power on the love of his people, Morana. Or should I say the love of *your* people. I understand you've had a hard time getting help these days." And it was true—she did look worse for the wear. Andres had purchased our clothes, and they were new and pressed and lovely. The sprites had done our hair, and I knew without looking that it was perfection—although perfection was rare for me, so you can bet I looked at the mass of pins and curls before we left. Morana, on the other hand, appeared…disheveled. Her white blonde hair, which had been flawlessly styled into something long and complex down her back the last time I had seen her was now simply brushed, and unlike Green's hair, which hung smooth and straight and clean, down to the backs of his knees hers showed an alarming reaction to static electricity in the air. I wondered dryly if perhaps the sprites weren't getting a more subtle revenge even than quitting their duties.

"Deserters will be punished." She said darkly, and I merely smiled back. I needed to ask Green what we did to reward sprites, besides send out for pizza.

"I thought we were going to re-forge those treaties, Lord Green." Mist spoke up, and I took a good look at him. Like Morana, he had left his glamour at the door, and he was male, so I assumed he didn't rely as heavily on the mercies of the sprites and nixies for his appearance. He looked okay—sand and fog hair in place, mist-pale features as poignant and symmetrical as the sidhe I adored, but there was still something unsettled about him. His gaze kept darting to me, and then to Bracken and back to Green as though he were trying to figure something out, and he couldn't wrap his brain around it.

"We have yet to dine, Mist." Green replied, still pleasant. He deliberately left out Mist's title, but the other elf didn't even flush. "And then we have entertainment planned for our guests. Whatever you have to say can wait until then." Mist didn't react because he was so preoccupied with studying the three of us, standing there as though we held court with our enemies every day.

"If we have to wait on you to dine, eat already." Goshawk said abruptly, and I figured that he felt he was being ignored.

"No problem." I replied, still sweetly. "I'm going to go eat myself some chicken." Maybe all the manners of the sidhe were rubbing off on me, but we weren't in a battlefield, Green, Bracken and I were the ones who had been wronged, and I wanted some fucking courtesy.

"Not if I eat you first." Goshawk snarled in my face, and I grinned back at him, almost tasting his blood in my teeth.

"Are you sure you can handle a one on one, Goshawk? I don't see any of your people behind you." And I didn't. "In fact, I see more of them behind me than you." And I had the satisfaction of seeing his eyes grow wide and his face whiten as he realized who three of our party were.

"I'll have them all scourged and salted and scourged again." He ground out, and his shoulders strained, as though here were keeping himself from lunging at Nicky, La Mark, and Mario.

"I don't think so." Green answered. "They're ours, now, and you'll have to get through us first."

Goshawk looked at him then, really looked at him, and then at me, and then at the people at our back, and then at the vampires and lower fey that we had invited to this shindig and a look of blank comprehension settled on his features. "You'd die for them." He said, confused.

"Not if they die for him first." I interrupted. Hopefully I was being subtle—I wanted the three of them to know that they weren't just going to fight me and Green and Bracken, if they decided to put up a fight. They were going to have to fight *all* of the beings in that room. Love and unity—such a simple concept. Bad guys so did not get us.

"He should be dead already!" Mist said bitterly, and suddenly I knew what was eating at his brain.

"It didn't work because he loves us." I said baldly, and *now* Mist was making eye contact. "The sylph—you tried to make Bracken kill us, but he loves us. It didn't work."

"I don't understand." He said, and unlike Morana and even Goshawk, there was no arrogance left in him. "It should have worked. We used it to fell the Tuatha de Danaan—they were giants among sidhe, did you know that? Powerful, despotic—they would have eaten me for breakfast, and they were brought low when we used the sylphs as weapons. He was your lover, and Green was home and he *should have wanted you dead!* Why didn't it work?"

"Because Bracken loves me." I told him simply, feeling pity, just a little, for this elf whose most heinous crime seemed to be an inability to see what was in front of his face. "And he loves Green. He would pitch himself off a cliff to save us—not just me, both of us—there's no magic that can undo that sort of self-compulsion. All you did was kill a sylph who had never done you any harm—by the way, did you notice there's a lot of them on our side now?"

Morana might have said something then, something rude, but Mist's look of quiet bleakness was enough to stop her. "I've noticed there is a bounty of all sorts of folk who rose to greet you, Lady Cory." He said.

"Mist!" Morana objected. "How can you give her a title…"

Mist shook his head. "Look at them, my dear." He said softly. "There are over two hundred of their people in this room, and fewer than fifty of ours. This is a trap. And we have no choice but to stay and see how it plays out."

"Ridiculous." Morana snapped, but she suddenly didn't look so arrogant. "They already tried their trap with that nasty crawling stuff that tried to take over our clothes." She sneered at us. "You notice that it didn't work, didn't you? No elf of ours will wear your insignia tonight."

Everyone in our party—and including the vampires, the Avians, and Max there were thirteen of us—looked at her blankly. "Insignia?" Green asked, puzzled.

"That green symbol that tried to take over our garments an hour ago!" Morana spat, but now she was looking more than a little worried. "It's on the outside of the hotel—all of you are wearing it."

Oh Goddess. "That?" My hands made little picking motions at Bracken's black shirt, with its glints of silver-green. "That tried to work its way into your clothes?" Wow—the power of a little nookie to take the edge off.

"Wasn't that your intention?" Morana asked, and I started to laugh. Really laugh, giggle, guffaw, chuckle, belly laugh—all of them at once, and the twelve others who had been in the apartment and thought that what we were wearing had been only a little orgasmic power hiccup all joined in. Laughing, we turned our backs on our enemy and advanced to our high table, because if they thought that was the worst we could do, we were safe.

Well, not really safe, but defensible, because sure enough, as we neared our table there was a storm feeling in the air, a crackle, a build up, the same feeling Renny told me happened when I was about to do something magical and huge. I was standing between my two lovers, with a vampire who had relished of my blood within a yard of me. I was nearly healthy, healing towards happiness, and well fed. Summoning power now was a languid, insouciant thing, compared to the frantic summons I had performed with Bracken making desperate love to me, or standing over his fallen body after an ambush. I turned towards the three enemies we had invited to our table with a nuclear fusion hand and a raised eyebrow, and gestured for Green and Bracken to move to their places before me.

"Nah-ah-ah..." I murmured condescendingly, gesturing with the glow of power in my left hand. "Now don't make me use this—I had plans for a lovely evening. You haven't even seen what we've planned for entertainment."

Morana's temper must have been uncertain, because a gust of power, like a great, frigid wind came towards me, but at its first touch, I cupped my hand like a bell and my power formed a shield between that frigid burst of wind and all those on our side of the ballroom. I stood there and waited for the wind to shriek like a toddler throwing a tantrum, and then subside, while I smiled pleasantly at the blatant disappointment on Morana's face.

When I was sure she had nothing else to throw at me, I held my shield—an awesome thing, glowing over the other two hundred or so bodies in the room—for another heartbeat, and another, just so they would know that the effort cost me nothing (although that was a little bit of bravado on my part—I could feel my strength being tested in those heartbeats) and then I let it drop.

"Are we done playing, Morana?" I asked, trying for that voice my mother always used that made me feel about an inch tall. She looked at me impotently, and Mist's expression was simply sad. Goshawk was confused and angry—he was obviously surprised to find that his new allies were not all that he'd assumed. That was well and good—although I was wondering when he was bringing the Avians in to ambush us. As nice as it might be to believe, nobody was stupid enough to come to a banquet like this with none of his people in tow.

We sat at the head banquet table, where the bride and groom would be if it were a wedding. I surveyed the room from that vantage point, and liked what I saw—more of that light-colored hard wood, more of the dark green and rose appointments, more brocade hangings and crystal and brass I might have liked to have seen some wrought iron in the light fixtures, I thought judiciously, but the fey—all the fey—would not have done well in a room with that much cold iron, and since this was now preternatural central, it had probably been a wise choice for my sub-conscious to make.

"What are you thinking, beloved?" Green asked me from my left. Bracken was seated on my right, and I wasn't sure if this was correct when we'd talked about it, but then Green had pointed out that everybody would be looking to see who was on *his* right and left, and not mine, and I'd felt stupid. No, Corinne Carol-Anne, the world does not revolve around you. But Green had only laughed. *You're the only girl in the middle of men, dearest.* He'd said, amused. *It's only natural to stage you in the middle. But the rest of the world won't be looking at you.* Which had been fine with me then, but after that little show with Morana, you can bet they were looking at me now.

Which was okay, I thought gamely. The last time I had been in a showdown with big bad guys, I had sworn that I would be a player, and not a secret weapon. As it had turned out that time, I had not been such a secret then, either. This should not have been a surprise to us because I'd been killing vampires and assassins right and left on our way to the big battle; but Green, Adrian and I had been totally involved with each other and had assumed, blindly assumed, that no one would care about Adrian's next girlfriend any more than they had about his last one. So we had walked into our last battle, trying to hide what I was, and setting Adrian up to die. This time, we had no secrets, and I was well and fine with that.

Let them look, I thought defiantly, chewing my most excellent steak with gusto. This had been another matter in which I'd been ignorant—I had been going to order the pasta, but Green said that contrary to what his hill had led me to believe, not all of the fey were vegetarians. *We've got a number of kelpies and some downright nasty baen-sidhe on staff. They'd love to cook you a steak. Love to slaughter it and tenderize it for you too.* And that was when I realized how very much my Green was enjoying himself. He should, I thought now, chewing rapturously on a meal obviously prepared with care and zeal. When Adrian had died, it had felt so senseless, so random. Taking this area from leaders who were hurting their people—and who had hurt us beyond measure—was constructive, purposeful—it had *meaning.* Of course Green was enjoying himself. We were going to avenge our beloved. We were going to take back the sense of safety and well being that had been stolen from us.

And revenge for Green's time trapped as a courtesan by Mist and Morana wouldn't hurt him in the least, although he was reluctant to admit it.

"I'm thinking that butterflies in the stomach are not a joke." I said in answer to Green's question. "And I'm thinking that Goshawk's people are lurking behind some corner, waiting to rip us to ribbons. And I'm thinking that if all fifty of those *s*idhe decide to actually stop sneering at us and combine their power, we're fucked."

Green nodded. "Good. Not that you're right—everybody in this room on our side has marked themselves with my power—fifty sidhe are still no contest to two hundred and fifty free preternatural wills. But good—I'm glad you're not arrogant, because this will still take some doing."

"And I have to sing." I reminded him, and then I really turned and looked because his honest smile, the one that had pretty much everybody in the room ready to tumble into his bed with a word, had graced his features, and hence graced everyone at the table.

"I wouldn't miss it for the world." He murmured, and I leaned my head against his shoulder with a sudden yearning for comfort.

"Neither would I."

"Shall we begin, then?" He asked. "Or would you like dessert first?"

I looked down my side of the table. Bracken had hardly touched his food, and his hand hadn't once left my knee during dinner, although he'd made sure my plate was always full and kept rearranging my wrap around my shoulders as though the faint chill in the room would make me break out into fever and plague without it. Renny and Max were picking nervously at their pasta with the hands not interlocked and clenched in Renny's lap; and La Mark and Mario were gazing fixedly at Goshawk with murder in their eyes. Goshawk was staring fixedly back, but I noticed that his face was turning, in sequence, maroon to white to maroon again. I wondered if it was occurring to him that bad things happened when people who were sent on suicide missions didn't actually die.

Turning, I looked down Green's side of the table, and saw that Arturo and Grace were exchanging killing looks with the fifty or so sidhe who were trying to freeze us with their hatred, and Nicky was looking particularly grey-green as he pushed something that looked like raw corned beef hash around on his plate. He, too, was casting stormy looks at Goshawk, and he had a lot to be angry about. The man had taken his faith and abused it, forced Nicky to attack me, whom Nicky loved, then forced Nicky into a position where he would be bound to me forever, when I didn't love him back. Even Nicky's relationship with Green, which Nicky was thoroughly enjoying now, was something he wouldn't have chosen for himself. Nicky, indeed, had a lot to make Goshawk pay for, and I hoped we could do him justice.

So everybody was pissed off and scared, and that was only natural. The only people completely at home were the vampires, who were sampling the wrists of a number of Orson's more attractive guests, but they were just happy because A, it was a free meal, and B, the only thing that kept the sidhe from launching themselves at Arturo and Grace was the fact that those sharp pointy teeth running in blood were so very very close. Part of the kick of being a vampire, Adrian had once told me, was the knowledge that just being you made people wet their pants. I was starting to know why he'd gotten a thrill out of that.

"I think we can do without dessert for right now, beloved." I understated. Our show of bravado had done its job, I hoped, and it was time to kick this pig.

GREEN

And We Will Be Lovers...

Green stood, and surveyed the room with satisfaction. Cory was right—everybody else could eat dessert, but for his people, there would be more satisfaction in a job well done.

"I hope you've all enjoyed your dinner—a hand to our staff for a delightful meal." As applause rippled through the candlelit banquet room, Green smiled ironically at Mist's sidhe, who sat stoically, their eyes flat and expressions fixed.

"But the feast is sold that isn't vouched for, and it's time for me and mine to show you all how pleased we are that you've decided to join us. I know we have business to tend to—but allow us to entertain you for a moment, and the business will pass that much faster, yes?" There was another ripple of applause, and Green bowed and stepped down from the dais, and behind the wooden screens which hid the performers (dubbed the inmates of the Bay Street apartment by Renny) from view, and stripped off his formal jacket.

The girl's dresses came with matching satin scarves, which was either convenience or forethought on Andres' part. Cory and Renny were in the process of wrapping their scarves over the vampire bites on their wrists as Green neared them. Bracken was looking stoic and pale, in the effort not to pull the blood from their bodies, but Cory was hovering the non-bleeding hand over his shoulder, willing him to have the strength to resist the call.

Arturo was offering his wrist to Grace, and she obliged, licking her lips shyly, and sensuously grazing his skin with her lips as she suckled on him, just a little, then left the wound open. She wrapped her own scarf around Arturo' s wrist, and he bowed slightly at the waist, like a knight in shining armor of old, accepting his lady's favor. Grace moved on to Bracken, who looked relieved when his own blood started to flow. Bracken's hunger was the potential hole in the plan, but Green had been reasonably sure that once Bracken's own blood spilled, he'd have more control over his gift, and he grinned at his leader to show that Green had been right.

"All right then," Green said, noting that Max, Nicky, La Mark, and Mario had also been wounded, and had wrapped their wounds for the moment, "Who wants a taste of me?"

"Allow me, leader." Andres offered, stepping up. He grinned then, flashing some fang. "It's not every day I get a taste of the most powerful sidhe in California."

"Are you trying to jinx us, brother?" Green asked, only partly kidding. "Are the rest of your people doing their thing?"

"With some help from your vampires, yes." Andres nodded, indicating the silent vampires, discreetly moving through the crowd and biting as many wrists as they could manage without drawing attention to themselves. "I've got to say, offering a banquet of fey has improved my cachet among my own people considerably. My people are going to be discussing this night for years to come."

"If this works, Andres, we'll have a reprise every year for Christmas...on a smaller scale, of course." Green slid his jacket over his shoulders and unfastened his cuff-links, rolling his sleeve up a few inches for Andres' convenience. Andres, for his part, was gazing at that marble skin with the blue vein pulsing delicately underneath like a mortal man would look at a very beautiful naked woman waiting to feed him steak. Green's lovely skin, his sweet sweet blood, his strong and potent sexuality, and most importantly his power, all of him would satisfy so very many hungers that Green couldn't fault his longtime friend for the little whimper of need that issued from his throat.

Suddenly Cory was at his side, touching his hand. "I like this part." She whispered, and Green was just starting to smile as Andres took his wrist in his small, dry hand and gave it a tentative lick, surprising a laugh out of him.

"That tickles, brother." He said, his voice breathy and a little aroused. After all was said and done he and Adrian and Andres had played together at one time.

"I'm savoring the moment, leader." Andres murmured, meeting Green's eyes above his wrist and flicking out that wicked tongue once more. Everyone behind the flimsy wooden screen could hear in his voice that he was aroused much more than a little. "I'm drinking a great sidhe's blood tonight—licking your skin is like sniffing the cork."

"It's like foreplay, Andres." Cory said dryly—and wetly, if Green's senses were all functioning. "And we sort of need to get out there and get it on." Andres eyed her from above Green's wrist, his expression sly and sweet and sexy. "Little Goddess, I do hope there is a day when you appreciate a little lingering around foreplay."

Cory flushed and looked to the center of the group where Bracken was standing having his wrist loosely bound by Grace. Grace was the only person near him, because nobody living wanted to accidentally touch him and bleed out. He was looking decidedly uncomfortable in his isolation, Green thought, as Brack's unhappy gaze wandered back to Cory. She caught his eyes and smiled and it was the brilliant smile that could make mortal men slack-jawed and stupid. It made Bracken smile back and relax, and say something nice to Grace who laughed in her turn.

"I could have lingered with you for quite a while, Andres." Cory said softly, moving her gaze back to him. "But I have other vintages to tend to."

Andres nodded, still breathing in the pulse at Green's wrist. "Very nicely put, Little Goddess." He murmured, "Just remember, sometimes the best of wines are blended." And with that he closed his eyes and extended his fangs and delicately punctured Green's wrist above the pulse where it would hurt the least, and pulled once, hard, at the sweet ichor that elves bled, his throat working when he swallowed. Green in his turn tilted his head back, savoring the pleasure of the feeding, and whimpered just a little, when all too soon Andres pulled away.

Both men stood then, smiling in each other's half-closed eyes, panting ever so slightly, skin tingling from the short exchange of blood and the solid touch of desire. "Your blood is powerful, leader." Andres said, passing his tongue daintily around his elongated teeth.

"And your bite as pleasurable as always." Green managed. Between the fast, hard sex with Cory and Andres' practiced bite, it would take a Bacchanalian of soft flesh to feed his hunger he thought in delight and agony. Or maybe, it would just take an ejaculation of love and power the likes of which his people had never seen.

"Green," Cory cupped his cheek in her hand, brushing her thumb across his lips, "Beloved, it's time."

Green turned to her and smiled, fierce, feral, and brilliant. She met him with her own power, and he knew that if anyone purely mortal looked directly at them they would be blinded and befuddled for days, rocked in their beliefs of all that was reality.

"Jesus, people, tone it down a little!" Max exclaimed, proving Green right.

"You're making me horny and dizzy and it's a really baaadd combination…"

"I don't know." Renny said from Max's side, "I could enjoy you like that."

Max flushed so hotly that Grace and Andres scented the air for the blood beneath his skin.

"It's time." Green said, full and burgeoning with power and desire and a certainty that he couldn't remember feeling since he'd walked cleanly through the unbroken stone of Oberon's garden walls, levitating forty magically sustained lime trees through those same walls in his glowing wake. With that thought he commanded "Hold hands, people—two vampires on either side of Bracken, but all of us touching." The only non-painful thing Green had learned from the battle that had cost him Adrian was the importance of an enemy making an entrance.

"Now walk." He commanded softly and was rewarded when, hands clasped, he and Cory led all of them, the vampires, the elves, the were-creature, the Avians, and the one befuddled human cleanly through the wooden partition to the bare center of the banquet room.

A collective intake of breath greeted them, and then from those in his camp at least, a thunderous applause. Green inclined his head, accepting their adulation like it was his by right, and was supremely conscious of Cory by his side, beaming at him with a smile that said she had never known differently. Across the room he met Mist's eyes, and saw for the first time real fear and genuine sorrow in his old captor's eyes. I am their leader, Green thought fiercely, and you will have to kill me to harm them, and that will not be easy.

Clorklish stepped forward and Green broke eye contact to look down and smile at his wizened concierge. The little man held an old mandolin in his arms, freshly oiled, newly strung, and not the one Green had been practicing on in the last two days. This instrument, was in fact, one of the few things Green had left behind in Oberon's palace that he had ever truly missed.

"Master Clorklish…" He began, and found he had to clear his throat. "I'm moved…how?"

"I stole it from my previous employer." Clorklish said dryly, with a sideways glance at a narrow-eyed Mist. "Don't hold it against me." He grinned.

"Not in two hundred years." Green grinned back, and the two of them bowed affectionately. He straightened and turned toward the assembly.

"Greetings and Goddess blessings on you all." He said in a voice that would have carried without magic, but was crystalline with it. "We are going to present you with something from our hearts—and hopefully, from yours." There was a laugh then, low and subversive, and Mist's people looked around uneasily. Of course, the glitterati of the fey sat in their own light. It pleased the full blooded sidhe to glow with power and pride; it was one of their strengths and one of their weaknesses, and tonight it meant that they had not seen the other fey inviting the vampires to free their lifeblood from their bodies at Green's command.

"We are going to entertain you with a fiction," He continued, "A faerie tale, a story, something dreamt of dozens of tens of years ago. Imagine my surprise when it turned into…"

"A memory." Cory stepped forward at his right and carried the narrative thread, just as they had rehearsed. "A memorial, a lament, a dirge, a paean…"

"An exultation." Bracken stepped forward carefully avoiding another touch with Cory, but at her other shoulder, "A cleansing, a triumph, a celebration."

"Yes." Green took up his part now. "All of this and more, because this is a love song for our friend,"

"Our lover," Said Cory and Andres.

"Our brother," Said Bracken.

"Our son," Said Arturo and Grace.

"Our leader," Said Renny and the vampires as they stepped forward together in a group.

"Our beloved." They all intoned together, and the echoes of their true love for their lost dear one lingered in the room for more than a few heartbeats.

"We're singing for Adrian." Cory said then, alone, clearly, the heartbreak throbbing in her voice and in her intense, thin face. Her shoulders were bare, and she bore his mark on her back, and it was all Green could do to keep his throat clear for singing. "We will always sing for Adrian," Cory added bravely, "Even though we will live without him."

Green took the mandolin in his arms like a lover he hadn't known he'd missed, and struck the opening chords of an old, old melody that now lay forgotten except in the minds of the fey who had grown up in the old countries and woods of Northern England, Ireland, and Wales. Singing in parts and counterpoint, Green, Bracken and Cory poured their heart into a song he'd written long before he'd left his home, met Adrian, or dreamt of Cory.

Corinna and Allen and Graeme,
Over the hills they ran

A bonny bright girl with a ribbon,
O, two boys as thick as kin.

They toddled under the lime tree,
O, they toddled under the rose
They toddled 'till sun set, behind the
Oak, they toddled from when the sun rose.

Corinna why are you crying, O,
Over a shirt stained red,
Rain will fall and trees will grow
And you will find lovers again.

The little lads grew to tall young men
The little girl grew to their taste
Corinna come kiss us, come touch us, O
We're young; there is no time to waste.

Corinna and Allen were lovers in fall,
Over by yonder rose tree,
Graeme came looking for his beloveds
And wept at what he did see.

Corinna why are you crying O,
Over a shirt stained red,
Rain will fall and trees will grow
And you will find lovers again.

Graeme ran like a man possessed
He ran like he was followed by hell,
He snapped his strong leg in painful two
When into a gully he fell.

So Graeme sat, with bounded leg
When the militia came to town

"Your men have no choice, for if they desert
We aim to hunt them down."

Corinna why are you crying O,
Over a shirt stained red,
Rain will fall and trees will grow
And you will find lovers again.

Allen came calling in darkest night
And begged, "My brother, forgive me.
I fed my love and broke your heart
And we all can no longer be.

But I run away to fight the day
That our young men must wear red.
I leave Corinna to your care, my friend."
And with these words he fled.

Corinna why are you crying O,
Over a shirt stained red,
Rain will fall and trees will grow
And you will find lovers again.

Winter passed, and Corinna wept
That Allen did not write
Graeme steadfast, his promise kept
And prayed for his friend in the fight.

No letter came, no friendly word
Til field and moor turned green
A spent young man came bearing a burden
In which a bloody shirt could be seen.

"Corinna, this is from Allen, know
Your lover now lies dead."

"Oh, Graeme, our friend, my life has ended
I'll never love again."

Summer passed and winter too,
Corinna sat and wept.
Graeme's leg healed, but not his heart
Until his promise then he kept.

"Corinna, come stop your crying, O
We both of us loved him dear.
He wouldn't want your heart full of dying, No.
Not while the Spring is here.

Corinna you must leave your weeping, O
Please, beloved, please come.
My arms are aching to hold you, know
My heart can be your home."

Corinna and Graeme were married, O
As the summer died to fall.
Their hearts still ache for Allen, though
They love each other as all.

And Rain will fall and trees will grow
And you will have lovers again…
Rain will fall and trees will grow
And we will be lovers again.

The end of the song was a repeat of the chorus, broken up and sung in passionate roundels. Cory's voice soared over the chanted refrain of *rain will fall, trees will grow*, aching with the promise of hope and the heartbreak of loss as Green and Bracken called Corinna back to the land of the living. The fey in the audience—Green's fey, at least—caught the chanted refrain and repeated it, and Renny's voice warbled up with Cory's in harmony, intertwining, echoing, repeating the pain and the joy of love lost and found.

The roundel built, and rose, and the emotion in the room crested, a giant wave of anguish, grief, and rebirth, and as their skin prickled with passion, their power—fed by anger and love and sex and emotion—burgeoned, grew, lifted, moved, heaved the pitch of the room to breathlessness, and everyone on stage raised their wounded wrists and released their bindings, and everyone off stage with a similar wound did the same, and Bracken finally, finally, answered the call of all that freely offered blood.

The blood lifted into the air, hundreds of delicate fountains, bearing the bindings aloft with it, and rode the power that Green, Cory, and all those who followed them had raised of their free will and devotion. The blood and silk flew in a whirlwind to the beat of the chanting (*and rain will fall and trees will grow and rain will fall and trees will grow*) and Cory's voice flew over the soaring, plummeting wall of sound (*she will have lovers, you will have lovers, I swear I will love you*) tying it together in a lush climax of beauty and power and pleasure and pain and blood and binding. The whirlwind of blood and power intensified and blew, the power turning the blood white then clear as the cleansing pain freed it of color (*and rain will fall and trees will grow*) and Cory's call ascended the whirlwind of sound and power and glory, until Green and Bracken clasped her hands, and the hands on either side of them until everybody on stage was bound in her soaring, ascending, crescendo of power (*I'll love you forever*)

In the midst of the crescendo there were shrieks, the rent ripping voices of hawks deprived of their prey, as several huge Avians attempted to crash through the wall of power and sound created by Green, by Cory, and by the blood and force of all those who loved them. (*I swear I'll have lovers*) The birds hurled themselves against the field of power, breaking claws and bruising wings and not falling because the field itself bore them aloft until the song rose to its culmination and Cory's voice shredded in crescendo, (*We will be lovers…*)

Again!

At the crash of the finale, of the final wailed word, the whirlwind of blood and binding flew out, transformed, blowing through the entire assembly, Mist's elves, Green's people, like summer wind through a cotton dress, penetrating their skin, their flesh, their bones, their hearts, their souls, and leaving behind a mark, a sweet taint of Green's love, that began to force it's way through their skin.

For those who didn't love Green already, that mark came at an excruciating price. As the cries of pain began to issue from Mist's folk, the Avians, who had been beating themselves against that wall of power ripped through it abruptly, changing shape and falling, naked, bleeding from the tattoos that covered their entire bodies and now rode their flesh instead of feathers. Green was fairly certain these Avians would never change forms again unless he willed it, but they were not his primary concern at the moment.

"Goddess!!!" Mist pleaded, and Morana began to shriek, and Green stood at the forefront of his people and cried "Silence!" In the same great, carrying voice he had used to keep the vampires from killing the were-folk, and he was very greatly rewarded when their voices stopped immediately.

Mist tried to speak, coming from his group of fey, opening his mouth while he watched in horror as Green's mark wound its way up the skin of his arm. He was fighting it—everybody in his group was fighting it, and blood was seeping through his sleeve as the mark rent itself in his skin. But as horrified as he was, his leader had commanded silence, and no noise would come from Mist's mouth as he worked it in futility. Green watched, snarling in joy and anger and triumph, savoring the moment in parts of him that had nothing to do with sex and healing and everything to do with revenge.

"Wondering what's happening to you, are ye, Mist my darling?" He ground out, trying and failing to keep his breathing in check.

Mist nodded, mutely, still not able to fight the compulsion of silence.

"It's my mark, dearest. My mark, which my people put on their bodies willingly. Well, you're mine now. I've just seized your territory and your power and my mark is riding your body, and the bodies of those who followed you." He pitched his voice so the assembly could hear. "If you want it to stop hurting, my people, and to not monopolize your lovely flesh, you simply need to accept me as your leader. Voila—no pain, no blood, no rent flesh, and a much smaller wound—can we understand, yes?"

And with that question, their tongues were loosened, but their voices when they spoke to each other, were subdued. There were suddenly a number of sighs, and for about half of Mist's number the mark worked a simple design on their skin and the pain ceased to be. For others there were howls of pain as the tattoo ripped its way up their bodies, rending their flesh and ripping their blood from their skin.

"Why did you do this?" Mist asked, face taut with pain as he fought the wreaths of leaves and roses battling across his skin.

"Do you see these people?" Green asked, gesturing to the performers behind him, and to the others in the hall who had come there willingly, and his voice shook, and he raised it to reach the assembly of those he now possessed. "Do you see them!"

There were several nods, and Mist met his flaming emerald eyes with eyes the colors of shadows in fog. "Yes, old lover, I see them." He murmured. The flow of blood from his hurts eased a little, as though acknowledging Green's place in his past was enough to ease the struggle inside him.

"These people have shed their blood for me of their own free will." His voice was hammer and razor intense, shaking with emotion. "These beautiful, wonderful, amazing people have **marked themselves** for me, of their own free will. You are older than me, and have been royalty when I've only been your kept concubine, and this one lesson you have never learned. Blood and love given with free will is far more powerful than anything stolen or constrained, ever." He looked over his shoulder, and saw Cory, her eyes shining with freely wept tears and pride for him. Arturo was so fierce looking he resembled one of those fearsome paintings found on Aztec ruins, and Grace, maternal Grace, had her fangs out in triumph. Bracken was covered in sweat, with smears of the blood he had conjured on his face, and it made him look pagan and terrifying, and so did they all.

"They love me." Green finished simply. "And I keep them safe. It's the world's simplest and most profound promise, and you violated it in so many ways…" He gave up the fight against his own tears, and allowed them to fall. "Adrian, Mist. Why send Sezan to kill Adrian, when Adrian was doing you no harm in all the world?"

"He was trash!" Morana shrieked, rushing for Green in a burst of temper. Mist backhanded her with a sudden, shocking brutality.

"So are you." He said quietly. "But you're one of mine, and I've tolerated you. Now be still."

Morana had been knocked to the floor by Mist's blow and with his words she sat back so suddenly in surprise that she almost fell. She looked up at Mist in shock, but Green caught her eye and shook his head, and the order had been made and she would remain speechless.

"I wanted you back." Mist said at last, shaking his head. "It was so simple. My people were prejudiced against the vampires; they had no problems with it. Sezan showed up on our shores, foaming at the mouth for a vampire with white hair and a powerful brother, and a way to kill them both."

"You might have killed them both—Green too!" Cory burst out, unable to stand back and look noble and fierce anymore. "How could you have done that and not known it was a possibility?"

Mist looked at her, his expression so empty and devoid that she stopped short in shock. "I would have rather had him dead, than loving another." He said, his voice bleak.

"Well that's the shittiest decision ever." She replied with deep feeling and Green could have grinned. For all their high talk, their sweet words, it was still music to hear Cory boil it down. "He will survive because we'll die for him. All you did was work the wrecking ball to trash your own building…"

"Mist...Lord Mist..." Another sidhe from Mist's party cried out to him. "It hurts...what shall we do?"

"Concede." Green said compassionately. "Concede and bow. The spell's been sealed—by the touch of my dear ones, by the song for Adrian, by the blood of the entire assembly. Concede and bow to me or..." He looked at Mist, waiting for his old lover, his old tormentor and captor, to finish the inevitable thought.

"Or bleed and die." Mist finished bleakly, before sinking despondently to his knees.

CORY

Again.

Green was as surprised as I was when Mist capitulated. It was probably a good thing he did, because his blood was starting to drip through the sleeves of his dress jacket, turning the front of his shirt crimson and pooling randomly on the pretty wooden floor The pain must have been excruciating but you couldn't tell from the stoic expression on his face. All in all, the whole thing would have been pretty dignified, except, as we were all staring at the rather pitiful figure, kneeling on the floor, Goshawk began to shriek as though he were being eviscerated by his own birds.

"Weak, spineless, groveling coward!" He ranted, coming up to Mist and swinging his foot back to kick him. I was in the best position to stop him so with a silly little hop I ran and swung my own foot, in its ridiculous green satin pump and connected—hard—with his ankle, knocking him off balance so that he nearly fell.

"Back off, assmunch!" I growled. "We protect our people and he's one of ours now."

"You promised me we would fight these heathens! You promised me we would WIN!"

Mist turned defeated eyes to his ally. "Two hundred years ago, I promised Green that he'd be happy. We can see how much my promises mean, can't we now."

"Speaking of promises," I demanded, "Didn't you ever promise to protect your own? Look at them, Goshawk—they're laying there, naked, bleeding, deprived of the gifts the Goddess gave them and all you're worried about is Mist?"

I spared a look for the wounded Avian's, writhing in agony as Green's mark ripped its way up their flesh. They were all men and they were naked, and the twining wreath of oak, lime, and rose that had worked its way along their arms and legs was now heading along strong shoulders, thick thighs and lean hips.

"They are weak!" Goshawk said, but his voice was shaking, and he looked beseechingly at the largest of the men lying at our feet. This would be Osprey, I thought, who had inflicted such pain on Nicky and who did Goshawk's dirty work.

"Goshawk…" Osprey pleaded, "Goddess…Goshawk, make it stop…help me, my master…." The tattoo had made its way across Osprey's wide chest, curling over every ripple of muscle, cleaving his nipples in two, and was currently ripping along his back, along his arms, and up his neck towards his jaw. Every line of the tattoo was dripping blood, and Osprey must have been fighting fiercely because there was more blood than tattoo. "Give me your strength…" He pleaded, and I looked sharply at Goshawk.

"You're not bleeding." Nicky said, materializing at my side. "Why is that, oh great leader. The elves are bleeding. You're people are bleeding…"

Goshawk looked evilly at Nicky, and Nicky kept going, his voice rising with passion and anger.

"How many stolen memories are keeping your skin whole OH MIGHTY FUCKING LEADER!"

"Master!" Osprey called, in so much pain that I almost regretted sealing the spell so finally. But then Goshawk spit at our feet, and bolted out of the room like the fucking coward he was, and I regretted nothing that would cause this bastard pain.

Nicky changed form then, the feathers on his wing iridescent green with his mark, and flew after Goshawk, and I sent a panicked look at Green, who seemed to have the formal part of this dinner well in hand. "Beloved…" I pleaded, and Green frowned at me and made shooing motions that said "dammit go after him" and I shucked my shoes and took off running out the door, then dashed back up to the dais and grabbed my forgotten purse before sprinting back across the stage in front of all of those curious eyes.

I had just turned down the hall that led towards the lobby, when a whirl of rust-colored fur blew by me, trailing an autumn colored piece of silk from her hind foot. Renny stopped for a moment and shook the remains of her dress off her claw, and I could barely spare the thought that she must not have been wearing any underwear either because I was almost collapsing from the effort of sprinting less than a hundred yards. I fell against the hallway wall and panted, coughing from the effort, as my body pointedly reminded me that less than two weeks ago I was laying in a fever, struggling between life and death, and I tried not to weep with the injustice of it. Dammit, Nicky could be dying out there, in that fight with Goshawk...or, worse, he could be killing his old leader. I lived with the death of a hundred enemies on my conscience, I *knew* how that could fuck up a person's soul, and Nicky deserved better than that. Nicky deserved better than a forced marriage with Green and I. Nicky just deserved to be happy.

While I was standing there, panting, two more hawks—humongulous black condors or something close to it—blew past me, with what looked like green bow-ties dangling from their necks. I had time to think, *Shit, like we needed more people involved in this fray* before Grace passed me, flying, looking like some sort of ancient, undead fertility goddess with her green satin pantsuit fluttering in the fierce wind of her passage. I took a deep, coughing breath and prepared to hurry outside to where the action apparently was, when Bracken materialized next to me, sans dress shoes, having blurred down the hallway from the banquet room.

"Good to see we're all recovered, now, and ready for action." He said sweetly.

"Metaphysically I'm a goddess." I told him grumpily. "A little help here?" I gestured helplessly with the purse in my hand.

"Admit you need another week's rest after all this bullshit." He said implacably, and I cast him a killing look and started to pad down the hall.

"Next week is Christmas, and I don't have your gift yet." I panted, and prepared to run.

"Fucking stubborn little..." I didn't hear the rest of Bracken's swear words because he blurred into action, scooping me up in his arms and blowing through the doors which had been a good fifty feet away in almost the same heartbeat.

What met our eyes outside was both comic and terrifying, and I stood and stared into the darkness, wondering how to stop what was going on in it.

Goshawk had turned hawk too, and he must have grown with power, because whatever kind of hawk-shape he took, he was almost prehistorically fucking huge. Even the obviously plastic feathers from what was apparently a magically morphing prosthetic at the end of his wing couldn't mar his grace in flight—or his absolute savagery. He wheeled and dove, shrieking and plunging knife sized talons at the helpless, furious little Kestrel who had harried him, and Nicky would have been a dead duck, except Grace could fly as well as Goshawk, and she was one pissed off mama-vampire up in the air.

But Goshawk was as big as she was, armed with talons and beak, and she had gashes on her body, and one lucky swipe of wing for her and Nicky, and I might be in mourning again. And now two handsome birds—one dark chocolate colored and one the color of caramel frappacino were arrow-ing up to Goshawk, so reckless that Goshawk almost disemboweled the darker one in his first pass. Mario and La Mark were entering the fight, and I just couldn't take it anymore.

I reached for my power first, but we had all just performed huge magic…in fact, I imagined that Green's mark was making its way through more than just the assembly inside the hotel. Green had bound himself in person or by proxy in touch, blood, and song to every fey, vampire, and were-creature from San Jose to Crescent City, and we figured that each and every one of them would be sporting a mark—tailor made to his or her personality, but featuring the wreath of lime, oak and rose—that originated from what we had just done in the hotel. My power was still being tapped to do that. What was usually swimming, just under my skin like a leviathan under water, was now deep, Marianas trench deep, and I couldn't reach it, not now, not in time to save Nicky and Grace and the others from Goshawk.

With a grunt of impatience I pulled the .45 out of my purse. I aimed, but I hadn't fired the damned thing since August, and my arms weren't used to the strain and, bugger-fuck it all, I just wasn't that goddamned strong right now, so my hands shook, and I couldn't get a clear shot. I looked at Bracken in agony, and he cried out, in that magically carrying voice that Green used when things were really tight, "Green's people, **MOVE.**"

And Nicky, Grace, La Mark and Mario stalled like planes to touch on the ground, leaving Goshawk flying alone in the sky. My hands still shook, but I was pretty sure I could manage not to kill him—or anybody else, because the thought of a stray bullet, even one aimed over the bay or into an empty warehouse was enough to make my cold sweat run. I aimed at the middle of an enormous wing, kept my eyes open, said a prayer, and squeezed off a shot. Goshawk plummeted to earth, first as a bird, then as a naked man, landing with a nasty sounding clang/thud on the roof of the empty dot.com building across from us.

"Fuck." I muttered, staring helplessly at the roof. I couldn't even see his body because of the flat angle of the warehouse, but I didn't hear any aluminum crinkling so I figured the odds of him just flying away were thin.

I looked around—La Mark, Mario and Nicky had changed back to human now, and were looking at me in surprise and shock. Grace was licking a gash on her arm and eyeing the roof-top with a look of supreme annoyance.

I shrugged at them. "He doesn't get to hurt anybody else." I said sharply. Then, a little abashed, "Uhm…so, very carefully, could somebody go get him down?"

Grace sighed, and took another swipe at a wound with her tongue, trying, I assumed, to stop the slow bleeding. "That's me, I guess." Since she was the only one who could fly in human form, the other option would have been to have one of the boys fly up there and throw Goshawk's body over the side. Judging by the fierce expressions on their faces, I wasn't so sure if he'd be alive when he hit ground. With a lanky bound, Grace was airborne, oddly elegant once she was in the air, heading for the top of the warehouse.

I turned towards our embattled Avians and safetied the gun; then, in an effort to calm them down, said. "Uhm…guys…" They looked at me, seeming to snap out of their battle fog as they did so. "When she gets back, she's going to need to feed—any volunteers?"

La Mark nodded then, reluctantly, and I thought that was fair. Of the three Avians, La Mark probably had the least grievance against Goshawk, although Grace fed quickly, and there would be enough revenge to go around.

I heard the roof give a little, then Grace sprung in the air, Goshawk, seemingly smaller as a human than he had been as a bird, struggling in her arms. His movements were fierce, and he kept trying to reopen her wounds, and she was about midway to the ground when she swore, "Mother *FUCKER!*" before dropping him at our feet. She landed next to him and kicked him—hard—in the ribs. Before Grace had even moved back, Renny was on top of him, her teeth buried in his neck, her paws on either arm. I noticed she buried her claws in his shredded bicep with unnecessary force. I could hear her growling over Goshawks' shrieking, even as he tried feebly to change from hawk to man and back again, finally settling on human, or something like it. Later, I thought inanely, I would ask Nicky why Goshawk had been clothed at the banquet, but was naked now.

I stalked up to the prone, defeated figure, not paying attention to my bare feet or my shredded hose. This fucker had **hurt** us, dammit. He'd tricked Nicky into attacking me. He'd forced Mario and La Mark to risk their lives against Green. He'd attacked me, lying vulnerable and asleep in the arms of my lover. And he'd stolen from me things which shouldn't be stolen. Adrian. Ah, God, Adrian—I had relived his death again and again and again in this last month—only his death, never his life. Oh, Goddess, I wanted to remember the first time we made love. I wanted to remember Adrian and Green and I, touching together for the first time, and the shock and the wonder and amazement that must have been. His ending was so much worse without his beginnings in my memory.

Renny was still on top of Goshawk when I knelt down next to them. His eyes were rolling wildly around his head, his face was bloody against the horrible gravel, and still we could hear him screaming, epithets, curse words, who the fuck cared what he was screaming, this was over now. My feet were sliced, diced and bleeding on the gravel and broken glass of the parking lot, and now my knees too, and I didn't give a shit. I took the .45 and pressed it against the base of Goshawk's skull and released the safety. There is something in that little metallic click that makes everything go silent. Goshawk stopped squawking, Renny stopped growling, and even Grace stopped gulping from La Mark's neck at that click, and all attention was focused on me, my gun, and Goshawk's skull.

"I want my memories back mother fucker." I said clearly into the silence. "And if you don't give them back willingly, we'll see if they come back to my heart to rest when your brains are outside your head."

He mumbled a little, and I gestured to Renny who pulled her head up so his head bent back at the neck. "If you kill me, they die with me." He spat, losing blood and gravel with his speech. "And you don't know how to get them back. So it appears we're at an impasse, whore-bitch. How does it feel to have no power, no power at all?"

I'd thought about this—I had an answer. "I wouldn't know." I said simply. "How about you? How does it feel to have no friends? No friends at all."

That hurt—even his posturing couldn't hide the fact that leaving Osprey, writhing on the floor, covered in Green's symbols, crying out his name had been a bigger act of cowardice and desertion than even Goshawk could bear. "My friends are not worthy of me." He whined, his voice near tears.

"Now see, there's where we differ." I looked up at Nicky and nodded him towards me. "My friends are more than I've ever asked for. I give thanks to both God and Goddess every day for my friends. And in spite of the fact that we started off with betrayal, I'll never regret the day Nicky became a part of my life." I looked up at Nicky and smiled, my face cold and angry but not at Nicky, and he knew that. "You remember, Nick? Remember when our relationship *really* started to change?"

Nicky nodded, and I was pretty sure he knew where I was going with this. "I remember." He said grimly. "It was the night I tried to kiss you. Do you remember Goshawk?"

"It was the night you failed." Goshawk said, trying to sound stern, but Mario and La Mark had picked up on what I had planned, and they knelt by us too.

"It was the night that saved our lives, Goshawk." Mario said gently. "My only regret was that it was my life that was saved and not Beth's. She would have loved this, you know. She would have kicked your skull into pulp—she was protective that way."

"She was a woman." Goshawk muttered. "She wasn't worth your skills, my child, you're better off without her."

I held out my hand, because Mario was tensing up like he would be the one to kick Goshawk's skull into pulp, and I kind of needed his brains where they were. "No one who has truly loved could really think that." I said quietly. "Your beloved, all those years ago, was better off with the Goddess than she ever would have been with you. And God doesn't admit you exist, so even your misogynistic worship is self-defeating. No. I bless the day Nicky came into my life, and in a moment you will too, won't he guys?"

"How far back do you want us to go?" Nicky asked, eyes flat. He looked like such a school boy I thought sadly, with his preppy, spiky rust colored hair and his yellow-green eyes. How sad that he should know exactly what I was thinking, even in the midst of my bloodlust.

"Back to the beginning." I said with certainty. "He thought his love would be better off without life—let's see how he is without memories of her. He's a six-hundred year old virgin—it's like he cut himself off before he even began. Let's see if he learns something this time around."

"Should we leave him some modern references?" La Mark asked, dabbing at his neck with the collar of his shirt. He needn't have bothered—Grace is a very neat eater—but I was surprised by the question.

"You can do that?" I almost whispered. I mean, I'd been all bad-assed and serious before, like I knew what I was talking about. I didn't want to announce to all of them that really I'd been making this up as I went along.

"We can release the ones that aren't his, too." Mario said quietly. "They'll go back to where they belong."

My heart felt like it had sprung from a cage. "Mine too?" I whispered for real. "My memories too?"

Nicky, crouched right next to me, put his hand on my cheek, leaned forward and kissed me, gently on the lips. It didn't feel like Adrian, or Bracken, or Green, but it didn't feel like a brother's kiss either. It was a start. "I guarantee it, sweetie."

"Yes." I said with shining eyes to all of them. "Leave him some modern references, so he doesn't go mad. Release the stolen memories back into the world—

for better or worse, they belong to other people." I bit my lip then. "But does that mean you'll be stuck with..." I wrinkled my nose. "Eww..." They all looked at me in surprise. "Won't you have...that..." I made a shooing motion with my hand, "Crawling around in your brains? Ick!" I could tell by their horrified expressions that they hadn't thought about keeping Goshawk's memories for their own.

"We could give them to Osprey." Bracken said grimly, coming up behind me and resting his large, warm hands on my shoulders. The contrast to the night air reminded me that it was fucking cold out here, and I was wearing a backless evening gown and shredded thigh highs. For the first time in a half an hour I also remembered that I was going without underwear, and blessed that I'd rather shred my new dress than crouch on my feet because no one got a crotch shot—including Goshawk.

But Bracken's suggestion cheered the Avians quite a lot. "Osprey..." Nicky said dreamily. "That son of a bitch deserves his contempt..."

"He's had a hard-on for Goshawk for years..." Mario said darkly.

"And Goshawk let him kiss his ass and sneered at him behind his back..." La Mark chimed in. "And Osprey did his most sadistic crap to...Seth. And everybody like him." The three of them nodded, in perfect agreement. Osprey, it seemed, was about to get his comeuppance.

"Perfect." Nicky said in a voice dark with evil. "We'll do it."

"You can't." Goshawk had heard our conversation without a word, as it should be with the cold nose of a .45 pressed into your skull, but I'd relaxed my grip and clicked the safety back on as the boys were talking, and now he started thrashing about in panic. "Please...Goddess..." He begged me, and I wondered if he was calling me Goddess, or finally reverting to the true faith of Her children and I didn't give a shit. I unclicked the safety and he shut up again.

"They'll do it or I'll kill you, you sniveling coward." I said evenly, possessing in that moment the pure joy of knowing that I had killed before and that I would do it now again. "If you think I'm lying, ask Bracken."

"She's killed vampires by the dozens." He said casually, heavy hand still on my shoulder. "You're like a fly on a window."

"You won't be able to." He whined. "I have too many memories. Too much power."

Nicky guffawed. "And I have Green's entire collective to back me up. Let's see who wins okay?"

The three young men prepared to put their hands on Goshawk, and as I remembered from Nicky's treacherous kiss, that's all it took. The touch of a friend, the blood rushing in your ears, and a song of betrayal. Or vengeance. I went to put my hand on Nicky's shoulder, wobbled, coughed and was suddenly in Bracken's arms. I was not surprised enough to drop my gun however and I clicked the safety and held it out rather awkwardly to Grace, who took it before it could harm Bracken.

"Nicky needs me..." I said.

"So much of your power is in the air right now it could light up San Fran, Oakland, and half the peninsula." Bracken said darkly, after stepping away from Grace and the gun. "As is my power as well, so don't worry about bleeding out through your feet and knees because I can smell the blood on you. But you're shivering uncontrollably, and the Avian's have dark business here that is best done on their own. It's time to get you inside."

"I'm not afraid of dark business!" I complained. "I want to see this through..." My voice trailed off in a cough that took my whole body and I wanted to stamp my foot. Didn't I deserve to see this through? Then the boys made contact with Goshawk's body, and the marital link between Nicky and I snapped into place and it felt like I was pumping blood from my body, the energy drain was that quick. Even mighty Bracken's knees wobbled, and Goshawk screamed and fought and cried, and just when I thought my vision would go black the screaming stopped, and the boys made a sound, a collective gasp, a groan, the orgasmic sound of stolen memories I guess, and Goshawk stopped screaming entirely. I peered down, and saw that his eyes had gone blank and his face was slack and sightless, and Mario, La Mark, and Nicky just kept touching him, their faces changing so quickly with the memories passing through that I almost couldn't tell what emotion was which. I was so mesmerized by their expressions that I didn't notice Master Clorklish until he pulled on Bracken's sleeve.

"Lady Cory," He cried, obviously upset, "Come quickly, Green needs you..."

I looked up at Grace, who was recovering from her wounds at preternatural speed. "Go, sweetie." She said, shooing at me. She looked down to where the men crouched, Renny still holding the wounded Goshawk down with her whole one-hundred pounds of were-kitty. "We'll be fine."

And then Bracken was blurring again, back to the hotel, back through the hall, back to the banquet room, and I was afraid, truly afraid of what could await us.

It was better and worse than I'd imagined. Morana lay sprawled on her back, bleeding from her mouth, her neck apparently broken, and Arturo was standing over her looking fierce and brutal and very unapologetic at her demise. He must have hit her with some serious power, to keep her neck from healing—or maybe she just hadn't been that powerful to begin with. Mist was collapsed in a heap on the ground, blood running from his mouth, and Green was kneeling next to him, looking frustrated and sad.

Max saw us stop and came next to us. "There was some sort of power surge— the lights went dim, and Morana tried to throw something at Green. Arturo stopped her—just one red-glowing backhanded slap and...well...you can see that part, but Mist..." Max faltered, looked sad. "He...it was like Hercules, breaking out of his chains...but he was trying to throw off Green's mark...and then the lights went bright again and Mist clutched his chest...and..."

And burst his heart against the bonds placed on it. And had chosen death rather than live with his one-time concubine as his altruistic master. Even I could read the rest.

"Put me down." I murmured, and Bracken did without comment, even though I left bloody footprints on the ground as I walked.

I came up behind Green, resting my hands on his back, and heard the darkness and sadness in his voice as he spoke to an obviously dying Mist.

"I would have called you friend, Lord Mist." He was saying quietly. "I might even have called you brother."

Mist's pale eyes had been resting on Green, but they darted to me, and his face settled into hard lines. "But never..." He stopped, because his words were burbling through blood. It pooled from his ears, from his eyes, and clogged his throat as he tried to speak. "But never...beloved." He choked. And then his eyes lost their focus and his body its life. Green turned his face into my soft stomach, and I held his head as he tried to master the potent, thick emotions roaring through his soul. He took a deep, shuddering breath and stood suddenly, gracefully looming above me as the leader he had to be as he met my eyes.

"Until Adrian," He said hoarsely, "All he would have had to do to have me back was to ask for my forgiveness."

"You can't force someone to love you by making them a slave." I said, hoping I didn't sound as young as I felt.

He took my hand, still reeking of the gunpowder, and kissed it. "Your free will alone makes me strong." He murmured, then he dropped our joined hands to his side and turned towards the amassed assembly that sat, stone quiet, as only the Goddess' children could.

"I've had enough banquet." He said in his most carrying, politic voice, and his listeners rustled dryly, like silk leaves, in response. He smiled back at them and continued. "Most of you here have marked yourselves with your free will, and I cherish that. Everybody else has been marked because I can not afford an enemy at my back, and I refuse to kill without cause. If anyone feels like Mist, that they cannot live with my mark in their flesh, they may petition me for freedom on Imbolc."

"January 28th." Bracken whispered to me from my other side, because I realized that I was squinting at Green in confusion. "It's a sabbat of the Goddess—a time of new beginnings."

"In the meantime," Green continued, his eyes crinkling at the corners, one of the few expressions he had that made him look older than Bracken, "Be our guests here, stay, be merry, celebrate the Child's birth, the Goddesses Blessing, and our good fortune at living another year and being, for now at peace."

The roar of applause at his announcement was deafening and sincere, and I found myself beaming up at him in my shredded gown and my tattered, marked flesh, pleased and proud and feeling as though—for the first time since summer—I could be comfortable in my own skin.

The wave of released memories crashed into me at that exact shining moment and would have knocked me off my feet, if Green hadn't caught me.

Adrian. The pale, moonlight hair, the autumn sky eyes—having them above me, for the first time, flesh to flesh, knowing he was mine. Adrian. Kissing me, smiling at me, moving inside of me, licking the blood off my thigh, glowing like the moon. Adrian. A pale twin to Green, suckling at my breast, skating cool fingers down the skin of my stomach, biting my neck in orgasm as the three of us moved together in desire, in power, in love. I could feel his teeth in my skin, his body inside of mine, the energy of the three of us building in my solar plexus and building and building until it erupted and my head tilted back against him…Oh my love, my beloved, my moon and my stars, oh my Goddess, *Adrian…*how could I have ever forgotten you when you were here, you were right here in my heart all along?

Arturo told me later that young women all over the city erupted into sudden laughter or tears that night, and found that their hearts were lightened of a burden they didn't know they had. Nicky told me that Goshawk was given scut work to do in the kitchen of the hotel, where he sits, devoid of his memories, of his corruption, of his meanness, peeling potatoes in penance, simple as a child. La Mark and Mario told me that the memories of Goshawk that they gave Osprey made him mad; he now wanders the lower floor of the hotel cursing Goshawk's name, but not recognizing the simple man his beloved, his tormenter has become. Neither of them will be able to fly unless Green wills it so, and that is a gift Green will never give. Bracken told me that the bloody footprints that I left as I walked to comfort Green glowed golden, and sank into the hardwood of the banquet room floor, and I've seen them since in the hotel, looking like a promise of spring.

Green told me that he healed my wounds with a kiss that I was too distracted to notice, and that I promptly fell asleep afterwards when they bathed and changed me in one of the hotel rooms getting me ready for the trip home. All of this was good to know, because the last thing I remember from that moment at the hotel was sobbing against Green's chest, weeping, truly weeping with happiness, for the first and best blessed time in my entire life.

Oh, Adrian. I remember you. Adrian, my beloved, I loved you I loved you I loved you I would have *died* for you, and I forgive you for leaving me first. Oh, Adrian, I remember our firsts as well as our last, and the time in between is no longer tainted with anger or recrimination. I remember you, my lover, my friend, Green's partner, my first. I'll never let you out of my heart again.

GREEN

Peace on Green's Hill

She would be asleep when they got home, which was only a little disappointing to him. He had wanted her to see the hill all lit up, spectacular and lovely, as they first came up the drive, but on top of her euphoria from her returned memories, the blazing faerie hill would not have made the impression he was hoping for.

But it was okay, he mused, as she snuggled closer into him in the back of the car. It was all okay. Grace was driving, and Arturo was in the passenger seat, driving her crazy because she'd been hurt in the exchange with Goshawk. Grace was giving back her two cents, because Arturo had stepped in front of Green to catch Morana's final vindictive throw of lightning, and Green was pretty sure the two would be in each other's pants before they'd unloaded the Suburban. The three Avians had been in the middle seat, chattering in low, excited, voices for the first part of the trip. Around Carquinas, Green told them that they could change forms and fly wherever they wanted, as soon as they got home, if only they'd settle down for now. Within minutes they were asleep, La Mark snuggling his head into Nicky's chest in a way that would have appalled them both if they'd been awake. He wondered if it was their independence or their act of vengeance that had kept them brilliant and buzzing with power, but he was so bone deep weary that he didn't care. Bracken had been glued to Cory's side as soon as her feet were healed, and was leaning against her now, dozing. His head had slid off her shoulder and into her lap, and Green rested his hand in his brother's hair, stroking it sometimes in automatic comfort.

They had done it. They had seized control of the fey holdings of San Francisco, and every creature north of Fresno, west of Nevada and south of Oregon owed his liege to Green. Green could hardly fathom the amount of power—or of responsibility—that this new power would entail. Bracken's presence in Cory's life may well be their salvation, Green thought sadly, as Cory burrowed even closer to his chest. She was brave, and whole, but the truth remained that the amount of sheer magic that she would be called on to wield would need her to remain whole, and happy, and loved. And he wouldn't be there to do it.

"Stop worrying, beloved." She murmured, as they slowed down through Rocklin. (Even the fey knew about the cops in Rocklin.) "You're keeping me awake with your worrying."

"Is that why you drooled all over my chest?" He asked, smiling. "Because I was keeping you awake?"

Her hand came up to her mouth to check automatically, she chuckled lowly when she realized he was kidding. "Tell me what's wrong, and I can go back to sleep." She commanded sleepily, putting her head back on his chest. Bracken murmured, and threw a long heavy arm across both their laps. His gifts had been key in their little adventure—he was almost as exhausted as Cory.

"I'll be gone a lot, *Anyaen.*" He said honestly. "It's an awful and frightening responsibility, and I will have to leave you in order to fulfill it."

She frowned, which in sleep was a pretty expression. "I can come with?" She asked.

"When you're not in school, yes." He told her gently. "Sometimes. But you're second in the power flow, luv. The spell we wove tonight—touch, blood, song—Arturo's only bound with free will. If something happens to me, it will flow to you, and from you to Bracken, and possibly to Nicky, and if you share blood with the vampires then it will go to them. We'll need you on the hill."

"I'll have to share blood, won't I, if I'm going to lead them." She stated more than asked. Then she sighed. "Maybe I should just quit school...I mean..." She smiled wryly up at him. "Love bravely. Loving bravely means planning for a life with you, and not worrying about what the human world expects my education to be."

Green shook his head. "No." He said unequivocally. "The degree is something you wanted—you're not allowed to give it up for me."

"Well not *for* you..."

"It doesn't matter anyway." He finished firmly. "I learned much of what I know about human laws and human business by trial and error—I'm the only one in the compound who can run our little collective. You had it exactly right when you signed up—with the exception of that mad amount of units, that is. You need business, and politics, and human history. We need you to have those things, if we're going to keep our people safe."

"Okay, okay…" She murmured, and he felt bad. Here she was trying to sleep and he was taking the pleasure out of a quiet ride home. "I get it. I go to Sac State for my degree in Queen-ship, you'll be out of town, which means that maybe there's a reason I've been collecting lovers like puppies, and when you come home…" She smiled up at him, half-closed eyes lazy and sexy with desire, "Well, we'll just make up for lost time."

He bent his head and kissed her, a sweet, long, sleepy kiss and tasted her hope, her healing, her wellness. She hadn't coughed once, since he'd healed her feet, he realized. "It won't be that easy for me to be away from you." He confessed softly, and could have kicked himself when he saw the sheen of tears in her eyes.

"Do you think it will be easy for me?" She asked, her voice rough. "Do you think I don't know what we've traded, you and I, for the safety of everyone we love?" He felt her hand against his cheek, chilled, from wiping hidden tears from her cheeks, and placed his on top of it. "Let's be happy for now."

"I am happy for now." He said into her hair. "You are well, and we are whole…"

"And we will be lovers again…" She sang, before falling back asleep for the last thirty minutes of the trip.

The Avians popped out of the car like they'd been charged with double-espressos, and had their luggage unloaded and delivered to various rooms almost before Green could wake up Cory and Bracken.

Bracken stumbled a little, as he pulled himself out of the back of the SUV and Arturo and Nicky were there, helping him to through the garage to the stairs.

"Put him in Cory's room." Green called. "She's with me tonight."

"Make sure she sleeps in." Bracken grumbled.

Cory chuckled against Green's chest. "I can't." She murmured for his ears alone. "I don't have his Christmas gift yet…"

"You can order on-line." He said, not firmly enough.

"Nope." She was waking up now, even though he had her firmly in his arms. "You're taking me shopping."

"Haven't you been?" He knew she'd been shopping. He'd given her a generous allowance when she went to the city for school, and between she and Renny, it had barely been touched until the week Andres had escorted Cory and Bracken out. It would figure that the only time she felt comfortable spending his money was on gifts for him and his people.

"Not for Bracken or Nicky or Renny." She said plaintively. "And I want to go with you."

Her expression was stubborn, almost mutinous like a child's, and he could suddenly see that she wanted a day, a worry free, fear free, illness free day, with him. With him alone.

"Do you think we could escape the house before Bracken wakes up to complain?" He mock whispered in her ear as they swung up out of the stairway from the garage.

"I heard that." He called. He was flanked by Nicky and Arturo, a few feet ahead of them in the hall.

"We'll make sure you don't hear us leave, then." Cory said sweetly.

"Like I could miss that..." Bracken grumbled. "She moves like a hundred pound wrecking ball in the morning." Arturo and Nicky swung him off into Cory's room, which was across the hall and a few feet before Green's, even as Nicky was asking if he could bunk with Brack after he was done night-flying.

"Sure, brother, as long as you don't snore."

"Nicky snores like a buzz-saw." Green whispered in Cory's ear. "The last night we spent together I kept dreaming of a model train that ran right by my ear at regular intervals."

Cory giggled, and Bracken called out, "I heard that too!" And then the door closed behind him.

At that moment, Max and Renny, who had returned in Max's mustang, came up the stairs.

"Can I bunk on the couch, Green?" Max asked after catching sight of the two of them.

"You'll bunk with me." Renny yawned behind him. She'd spent a good half-an-hour pinning Goshawk's body down that night, and another twenty minutes running around in nothing but Max's dress coat before the fey at the hotel could rustle her up a pair of sweats like the ones they'd dressed Cory in. "Gees, Max, like I'm going to actually jump you *tonight...*"

Before Max could protest, Green intervened. "You can sleep wherever you wish, Max—but the living room fills up at six a.m. and Renny's bed is big enough to swim in." And he shut the door behind him, pretty sure that Renny would have her way.

"I smell potential disaster in that direction." Cory murmured as Green sat her on the bed. He pulled off her shoes and started to undress her like a child, but when he pulled her sweatshirt over her head, she leaned into his touch, making sure his hands skimmed her bare, pointed breasts before they pulled her shirt over her head.

"So do I." Green admitted. Her hair had been washed free of gel, and he ran his hands through the short, curly strands now that it was smooth and soft again. "But one crisis at a time, shall we?"

Cory raised her hands to his waistband, unhooking his slacks and dropping them to the floor before giving his half-erect member a delicate lap. He gasped in surprise, and in a moment he was no longer only half-erect, and she smiled in that fully adult way she had developed since she'd come to Adrian's bed. "You still taste like me, beloved." She said, her eyes meeting him over the long length of his body. "And you are wearing too many clothes."

They made graceful, slow, sleepy love that left them sated and exhausted and full of each other. As they drifted off, Cory murmured to him, half intelligible musings, until he murmured "Good night, *o'ue'eir,* " In her ear to hush her up.

"Good night, *o'ue'hm.* " She returned, and then, so softly, he wondered if he were imagining it, "Good night, Adrian."

He was asleep before he could ask her why she said that, and had forgotten it in the morning.

CORY

Good will towards man, woman, elf, vampire, were-creature, sorceress, and family members who don't understand.

Green was more fun to shop with than he was to shop for. The week before I had been forced to special order something from Grace, who set the nymphs and sprites who work in her shop right on the task with rolled eyes for the late date, but good humor because it was unusual and difficult, and apparently faerie crafts-people don't get enough of that these days. But a framed wall hanging embroidered with the mark that rode my back couldn't be found in Pottery World, and so Grace's people got to ply their craftsmanship with justly earned pride.

But that was Green—he owned his entire faerie hill, over a hundred businesses, both small (like Grace's shop) and large (like Chevron franchise stores), and a fleet of cars, but lived in a room with plain oiled boards and clean, aesthetic lines and no decorations or tchotchkes to speak of. Even his clothes—what wasn't white T-Shirts and jeans was tailored white silk, wool, and linen. I wondered that he could bear to be around me with my clutter and my noise and my chatter, but even I couldn't question all that was our love. If I was going to give him a gift, it had better be damn fine and thoughtful, and as proud as I was of the scarf I'd made and it's painstakingly even borders, I felt too much like a child giving mom & dad a clay ashtray although no one in the house smoked, and hence the special order. So Green (with Grace's help) was covered.

Grace got yarn—there were some really nifty yarn and fabric stores in San Francisco, and I'd made Andres take me there and ordered a truckload of whatever caught my fancy—it was going to be delivered to her shop on Christmas Eve, and I could hardly wait. Andres got a case of differently colored satin kerchiefs, embroidered with the lower diamond on my back—the one with Adrian's rose in the center. Grace's people had to do this too, but since Grace, Arturo and I all went in on the gift together, I didn't get nearly as much crap about the late order. Arturo got wine—good stuff, not rotgut—because he was the only one on the hill I saw who drank it at regular intervals. I'd had to have Andres buy this for me too, because I'm not twenty-one yet, which I can't hardly believe, since I feel a thousand thousand years old sometimes, but not today. Not Christmas shopping with Green.

First we went to the Galleria in Roseville, much to Green's disgust, and bought out Wet Seal and Hot Topic for Renny—now that she was finally dressing like a human, she didn't have anything to wear. I told Green we would have to come back in the summer, and he pulled out his pda and did something funky and said it wouldn't be necessary, his personal shopper would deal with it. I rolled my eyes that he even had one, (a personal shopper—the mini-computer was very Green) and he grinned and said he'd put more than one nymph and sylph through fashion design and business college, and I should be grateful to see that I wasn't just a charity case. I'd kissed him breathless then, in front of the Build-a-Bear store and in the middle of the frenzied Christmas crowd, earning a lot of dirty looks from the people who had to wade around us, especially because I had to straddle him like a tree and climb his body to actually touch my face to his. Then we moved on to Bracken.

Bracken got sports gear from top to bottom, sweats, jerseys, T-shirts (because I'd commandeered a lot of his old ones) and I looked at the pile of clothes and it didn't feel like enough for my big brother, my new beloved, my *due'alle*. I didn't think his scarf would be finished by Christmas day.

"Too bad we couldn't get his shirts signed." I mourned as the cashier rung it up, "Because a lot of it has players names on it, and I know Peja and Bibby are favorites." and Green pulled out his pda again, and grinned smugly.

"A friend of Arturo's walks dogs with the Maloufs." He murmured, and he got kissed again. At that point I went to grab the handled bags with the sports gear and Renny's clothes, and realized that all of our bags had disappeared.

"Sprites." He murmured, and all I could do was laugh, giggling helplessly until he maneuvered me through the crowds to the food court, where we both agreed we'd rather go hungry until we got back home and then he ordered me to eat something anyway.

"They'll grow back eventually." I told him cheekily through a mouthful of orange peel chicken, and his face, which had been relaxed and casual and happy for the entire morning grew so stern that people around us shivered. The sun, which had been shining through the glass canopy over the court seemed to dim and several people, overheated by the crowds and the activity, pulled their hats out of their pockets and jammed them on their heads.

"I could give a flying fuck about the size of your breasts, Corinne Carol-Anne." He said with feeling. "It's your body, your fragile mortal body, that I want to feel whole, substantial, and living, beneath me."

Oh, Goddess…what wounds we inflicted…Bracken had felt this way—why had I thought Green wouldn't? I put my hand on his, and smiled, a shaky, fighting tears smile.

"Love bravely, Green." I said quietly. "That's all I can tell you. Love me bravely and I'll do my best not to die on you before my time, okay?"

"Right." He murmured. "Love bravely…easier said than done."

"Tell me about it." I murmured dryly. I had three lovers to care for, and I didn't want to lose a single goddamned one, never again. Which brought me to…

"When are you and Nicky going to…consummate…our little binding?" Green asked suddenly.

"Stop reading my mind." I ordered, only half-heartedly.

"Your thoughts are so clear, they run across your face. I don't hardly need to read your mind." He replied with arrogance, but I knew that he did. "And it's important." Green murmured, seriously. "Nicky…he'll grow ill, if he doesn't bond with us in the span of the moon…I know you didn't ask for this, luv, but…"

"Don't worry, beloved." I told him, seizing his hand and kissing it. "I already have a date planned. I was thinking the twenty-seventh—you know, the twenty-sixth is all about Christmas hangover and let-down, and there's really nothing to do on the twenty-seventh…you know…it could be, like, something to get excited about. I figured we'd go out on a date and have dinner and see a movie and everything."

Green nodded. "Good thinking." He agreed. "It will make Nicky feel special, and it will make the act itself…"

"Seem like love." I finished quietly, and now Green kissed *my* hand in understanding, and in quiet sorrow of what the two of us would never say, never put into words between us, because we had both come to love Nicky as a friend.

"So what are you getting him for Christmas?" He asked on a more cheerful note.

I grinned. "You're going to need to help me out with this one…and we're going to have to go to another mall." The auto-mall.

Nicky got a motorcycle—a new, shiny, powerful Honda, with lots of fiber-glass and pin-striping and power, with matching leathers. He'd been so depressed when I mentioned Adrian, driving in on a glass-pack Harley like a heavy metal knight on a shiny chrome charger, that I thought that maybe the motorcycle would give him the mystique he felt like he didn't have. It was set to be delivered on Christmas Eve too, and soon we were driving home, Green at the wheel because I had driven down and he seemed to feel that I was too mortal to be allowed to helm my own automobile. I reminded him that he'd been the one to buy the big BMW in the first place, and his reply was that he should have known better—I was almost too short to reach the pedals. My voice was lost in outrage, and when I'd stopped spitting with laughter and indignation we lapsed into a quiet companionship that I shattered when we passed the Horseshoe Bar exit, which I'd take if I were going to my mom and dad's house.

"Shit." I moaned. "I need to tell my parents I'm home." I had called them earlier in the week—I always seemed to do most of my visiting right before I thought I might die—but it was hard to talk to them. They knew I had dated a boy in the summer—they thought we had broken up. They knew I had moved in with a friend's family—they thought it was Renny's parents. They assumed I had been working and going to school—they didn't know Green paid my way because Green would rather slit his own wrist than let his lovers do without. I had given them a prettily wrapped gift certificate to Grace's store, because I knew they would enjoy the handicrafts, but I was afraid, so afraid, of what they would say when they saw me, the thinner, paler, happier version of me than the punk-Goth-bitch they had gotten used to before I'd met Adrian and faded out of their lives.

"They know." Green said, slanting a glance at me for my reaction and interrupting my neurotic panic spiral. "I called them this morning when you were in the shower and invited them to Christmas dinner."

I swallowed, hard, felt nausea roll over in my stomach. Took several deep breaths, closed my eyes, and when I opened them, spots were still dancing there.

"Pull over at Penryn." I said, trying to keep my breathing regular. "I'm going to blow chunks."

"Don't you dare." He ordered. "You'll throw up in your own seat if you don't tell me why you've been avoiding them for six months."

I looked at him, miserable, obviously nauseous with pain, and struggled to put it into words. "I didn't tell them about Adrian." I murmured, remembering when Bracken had been forced to scrape me off the floor when I'd tried and had come up with that lame 'we broke up' excuse. "It's like, if I tell them that Adrian died, it will be admitting that the little girl they loved is…is dead…is gone…and that I'm not her anymore."

Green took the exit in spite of his ultimatum, and he pulled off now in front of what used to be the Ground Cow, and was now one of those restaurant/gas station strip malls. He turned towards me, undoing my seatbelt and scooping me into his arms where he cradled me like the child I'd just said I wasn't.

"Of course you're her." He murmured. "What…you think if you tell them that the sun and the moon and the stars aren't where they set them last, that they won't love you anymore?"

For a minute, we both thought the pain would take over and I'd lose it, because I saw his hand going for the door, but then my lip quivered, and before I knew it I was sniffling like a baby. I used to be much tougher than this, I could swear I was.

"Yesssss…" I wailed, falling into little pieces of Cory, old and new on his nice white wool coat.

He put me back together again, of course. But he brooked no arguments—Mom and Dad would be there, at the full court banquet that celebrated the birth of the Son, the living proof that for a moment, anyway, God and Goddess reconciled, loved each other, and lived in peace. And, he said, while I was still gulping for air on his stained coat, I was going to sing.

I tried to put up a fight, but it was no use. I had a voice like an angel, he said implacably, and it was tradition in his hall that those who could, stood up and entertained.

"I bet Arturo doesn't sing." I shot back, a little panicked.

"No—but he has thrown knives in the past." Green said with a smile. "He hasn't had time to practice this year."

And we had practiced this song until it shifted the fabric of our reality. He hadn't needed to add that part, because it was true.

Which is how, on Christmas Eve, after dinner and before presents, I came to be standing between Bracken and Green in a white wool dress with Christmas-green tinsel trim, about to sing *Rain Will Fall* in front of my parents and the vampires and Green's entire Foresthill enclave.

Mom was a stringy, hardworking woman who had waited tables for most of her life, and Dad was a truck-driver, wiry, wizened, almost shorter than Mom. But they dressed in their best clothes for Christmas, and (Arturo reported) had been pleasant and shy when Arturo had picked them up. They greeted me, in my tinsel-decked dress with hugs and kisses and happiness, and I felt a quiet shame that I would have missed Christmas with Mom and Dad because I had worried that they'd do anything else.

My parents were awed by Green's hill, especially Green's banquet room, which was the hollowed out bottom part of both a hill and a mountain, and paneled in wood that had been hewed with Green's own hands, and varnished in his sweat, blood and tears. Tonight it was lit up with faerie lights (which looked just like Christmas lights if you weren't looking close) and hung with tinsel of real silver and real gold, and strewn with crystals that reflected the purest of blue, green and scarlet rainbows, and the beauty itself almost left them speechless.

They were pleased to see Renny, who had been with me during the semester when I'd come to visit, and pleased to meet Max again, who had forced a lunch invitation last summer, and a little disappointed I think to see the two of them together, holding hands shyly. They didn't know what to make of Nicky, I think, who was not above flirtatious banter and touched my hand casually, because we'd been on that level before the attack and I was happy to be back at least there now. I knew Bracken's tall, gruff presence both threatened them and aroused their curiosity. His possession of me was unmistakable—he sat at my left at Green's table like a stark centurion, hand at my back, attention fixed on me constantly, ready to defend my honor or feed me more meat, if need be. Green, of course, sat at my right, and was ever the genial host, and they responded to his kindness gratefully, with pleasant conversation about work, and the best Christmas lights of the season, and whose child had been in the church nativity play that year.

In fact, they met all of the denizens of Green's hill pleasantly, which is to say that the combination of glamour, Grace's eggnog, and my parents' own lack of whimsical willingness to believe in anything supernatural meant that all they saw was a really big group of people who seemed to live in this nifty apartment building that they'd never seen before. Green and I had done nothing to disabuse them of that notion, and if they were confused by my relationship with the three men, then they were too happy to spend the holidays with me to care. We had a couple of uneasy moments when Mom told me that I looked good now that I lost my baby fat, and over dinner commented that if I didn't stop eating, I'd gain it all back again, and I thought Bracken would come through the table at her, but both times I passed my *due'alle* a pleading look, and he'd subsided without a word.

But now I stood in front of everybody, and Green nudged me, and I knew I was expected to say something profound. He raised an eyebrow, like he would make the speech instead, but I felt like a coward then, and, besides, I'd actually written something down and I had it in my head.

"Everybody here knows who this song is for." I started quietly, but my voice became stronger with conviction. "We miss him. I missed having Christmas with him. You all miss his leadership. He meant more to us than songs or tears or words can say, so I won't try. But know this. Rain will fall. Trees will grow. And we will miss Adrian forever, but we will learn to be happy again."

And then the three of us launched into the song. The fey at the tables joined in for the chorus, but when we were done, there was a thunderous silence before the place erupted with teary, heartfelt applause.

We held shaking, sweating hands, and bowed, and then the band—made mostly of the lower fey who looked like homeless people in their glamour—started up something lively and lovely, and the whole assembly stood up to dance. My parents joined in, looking like they wanted to make their way to me, and I sent Green a panicked look. Not now, not when I was shaking with emotion, when my throat was clogging with tears I hadn't shed during the song. Not when Bracken looked like he wanted to sob into my shoulder and Green needed to hold us both. So it was in that tumult afterwards that, Green led us, Bracken and I, quietly out of the crowded banquet hall and up the stairs to the crown of Green's hill.

"Where are we going?" I asked softly, grateful to be out of the celebrating crush of bodies—grateful to be anywhere, frankly, where I wouldn't have to answer questions right at that moment.

"To see your Christmas present." He said, suppressed excitement in his voice.

"Mine?" I asked, surprised. He had a tree, of course, a great tree, coaxed out of the ground and standing on pampered roots in the living room, covered with a carpet of grass and earth and giving shelter to more presents, wrapped by the delighted sprites, nymphs, naiads, dyads, elves, pixies, fairies and general lower fey who, according to Green, lived for holidays of any kind. I knew (because several sprites, buzzing with excitement, had pointed out to me) that there was a Queen's ransom of presents underneath the tree with my name on them—many from Green, Bracken, Grace, Arturo, Renny and Nicky, but an embarrassing number from the lower fey themselves, who seemed to feel that I deserved them for being their Queen. I wasn't sure if I could unwrap all those presents myself, and one more seemed to be gilding the lily a bit.

"All of ours." Green said quietly, turning towards me and kissing me softly, which was awkward from one stair and a foot and a half of extra height, but it felt really good anyway. He turned again, and we continued up to what was now called the Goddess grove.

Tonight, it was all that fairie-land was cracked up to be. It was lit by lights, like sun-glowing jewels among the trees. Lights clothed the female form of the oak, cloaked the male forms of the lime and rose, and turned the erotic grove into a dance—a seductive one, for sure, but sometimes, when sex is cloaked by subtlety, it becomes more beautiful as an act. The grove, tonight, was more beautiful than anything I'd ever seen. And, at the crown of the hill, above the trees, more lights were strewn, in various colors of crimson, red, and scarlet, to make up Adrian's rose, big as a house, bedecked with lighted dewdrops and hovering above us like his blessing. It was almost enough to make me cry.

And then Green led me to the bench.

It was carved from a massive piece of granite—which is sort of the kudzu of the lower foothills—and thus the cushions of woven grass and rose-petals that hung over it. On the side was a sculpture, a likeness of Adrian that was only achieved in my dreams. Next to the picture, one word: **BELOVED.**

And now I did cry, burying my face into Green's stomach, Bracken behind me, both of us shedding quiet tears of clean grief for Adrian.

"It's beautiful," I murmured after a moment. "Thank you, beloved."

"Thank you, brother." Bracken echoed, and we all took a deep cleansing breath together.

And that was when mom and dad popped out of the trap door to the grove and my knees almost gave. "Green…" I whispered frantically, "They can't see…they can't know…" that the female form in the Goddess grove was me. No one wants to know that much about their little girl, I thought, panicked.

"Sshh…" He soothed. "They won't. You trust me, right?"

I nodded then, and tried to wipe some of my grief off my face, and turned, flanked by my bright sunshine lover and my dark, granite lover and greeted my parents.

Mom took my hands in hers. "You sang beautifully." She murmured. "We had no idea…" She trailed off, probably because my eyes had narrowed, and she remembered the fights we'd had when I was in high school. She looked around then, exclaimed over how lovely the grove was, how beautiful when it was all lit up like this. Then Dad stepped forward.

"What happened to Adrian?" He asked gruffly. "Why didn't you tell us that he'd died…why give us that bullshit story that you 'broke-up'."

I pulled them, slowly towards the bench, and showed them his memorial. "I didn't tell you," I said after they had looked at it quietly for a moment, "Because it's taken me this long to believe it myself." My voice broke, I looked over my shoulder at Green and Bracken, and they moved closer to me, close enough to touch, if I only leaned back. "I thought that if I told someone who wasn't there…at the…accident, when he died…"

"It would make it real?" My Mom asked, and then I was in her arms, and she and Daddy were holding me, and the little girl in me who still believed in faerie tales and happily-ever-afters thought, "It will be all right. We'll be all right." Even as they wept in my arms.

Later, after they left, I lay with my head against Bracken's chest, and my bottom on Green's lap. Bracken was dozing on Green's shoulder, and Green was touching both of us, and we were at peace. It *was* peaceful here, I thought. Adrian and I had come up at night, after we'd made this place, and spent a giddy hour giggling over what the three of us, Adrian, Green, and I, had been doing when the trees had chosen to mimic us in our lovemaking.

My eyes were half closed, and I could almost see his sharp-planed face looking out from the rose tree next to the bench.

"I can see you here, beloved." I said softly to him.

"You can see a lot of me here." He replied, grinning wickedly. His autumn-sky eyes sparkled—the one part of him that was not translucent.

I grinned back, or tried to—I was so close to sleep, and peace, that I wasn't sure if he could see.

"You can't believe how much we all miss you." I told him, wanting him to know.

"I can't believe what an asshole I was to leave you all." He said, and a diaphanous hand reached out to touch me on the nose. It was cool, and smooth, and real.

"We forgave you." I almost laughed. "But it took some doing."

"Bracken taking good care of you, then?" He sat down on the grass in front of me, and I tried to move, to get a better look at him, but Green's hand was resting on my hip, and Bracken's chest was so, so comfortable.

"He's learning." I smiled, nuzzling closer to inhale Bracken's strength, and his scent like clean rocks in the sun. "I think he'd like to compare notes on how big a pain in the ass I am."

"Not so bad." Adrian replied, flashing a little fang. He moved again, into my line of sight, and I smiled dreamily, glad to see him again. The grove was sheltered by Green's magic, but a stray breeze came through. Adrian's hair ruffled, and I shivered, and Bracken's arms tightened around my shoulders. "There seem to be people who want to keep you around."

I almost laughed, but my eyes were closing, and I couldn't help it and I wanted so bad to stay and talk to him some more. Bracken stirred, moved his hands around me like he was going to take me to bed.

"Don't go." I begged, my voice barely there. "Please, Adrian, don't go."

His kiss on my cheek was cool, a whisper of wind, bare breath upon my skin, but it was real. "I'll always be here, Cory." He murmured. "Believe that, okay?"

"I'll come looking for you, beloved." I told him, willing him to keep that promise.

"I'll stay waiting for you, beloved. Tell Green hi for me…he worries too much." Adrian touched me again, and his hand brushed Bracken's warm, solid bicep through his dress shirt. Bracken shivered and woke up for real, and shifted me in his arms again, this time in earnest, and I could only follow Adrian with my half lidded eyes as my world shifted and I was carried towards the trap door.

"No…" I whispered, "Adrian's…"

"Shhh…*due'ane.*" Bracken whispered in my hair. Lovely Bracken, who would die for me, who would carry the weight of loving his brother's lover with as much grace as he was carrying me out of Adrian's garden.

"'Love you, Adrian." I murmured, and Bracken was looking at me with sorrow, and frowning, and I would have to fix that frown in just a moment.

"'Love you too, Corinne Carol-Anne." Adrian called after me, his voice a thin echo of a breeze in the cool Christmas moonlight. Then Bracken was taking me down to my room, and Green was following after.

978-0-595-37914-9
0-595-37914-1